When the doors pa.ₙ₋ ₋ looking at her crunched form on the floor. Deirdre's eyes burned from mascara and tears. She scrambled to her feet, about to say something to excuse her gross crackhead-like appearance, but he spoke before she could.

"Ever been to the roof of this joint?" he asked and took a pack of cigarettes out of his shirt pocket.

"No," Deirdre said, wiping her eyes with a shirt sleeve.

"First time for everything." He stared up at the lighted numbers.

When they reached the top floor, Deirdre followed him toward a dark, narrow staircase that ascended to a level only accessible by foot.

"How do you know the way out from up here?" Dee asked.

He turned to her, his eyes a sly leer.

"Ah yes, that's right, it's because you're a fireman."

Through a vault-like door, the two stood on a flat roof. Halfway across the expanse was a helipad with small red lights twinkling on the surface. Rob lit a cigarette and flipped the metal Zippo closed.

"You gonna offer me one or not?"

"Oh, my bad." Rob reached into his pocket for another. "I didn't know you partook in this sort of thing." He handed over the tobacco and the lighter.

They puffed in silence for a few minutes, the wind swatting at their white-clouded exhalations as the faint echo of impatient taxis blared in the distance.

Praise for Dawn Turzio

"The quality of Dawn's writing is indeed a standout."
~*Alexandra Owens, former Executive Director,*
American Society of Journalists and Authors

F.D.N. Wives

by

Dawn Turzio

This is a work of fiction. Names, characters, places, and incidents are either the product of the author's imagination or are used fictitiously, and any resemblance to actual persons living or dead, business establishments, events, or locales, is entirely coincidental.

F.D.N. Wives

COPYRIGHT © 2022 by Dawn Turzio

Cover Art by *Jennifer Greeff*

The Wild Rose Press, Inc.
PO Box 708
Adams Basin, NY 14410-0708
Visit us at www.thewildrosepress.com

Publishing History
First Edition, 2022
Trade Paperback ISBN 978-1-5092-4517-8
Digital ISBN 978-1-5092-4518-5

Published in the United States of America

Dedication

To the fireman who made me his fire wife. I loved you before, I love you during, I'll love you for after and always.
And to my fire children, who allow their daddy to go out into the dangerous world to save people. Even on Christmas. XoXo

Chapter One

Megan breathed in the crisp Brooklyn air, second-guessing her senses. The atmosphere was thicker than usual, with an ash-like quality she could almost taste, but since the new medication, everything was off. Still, the smokiness remained pungent.

Meg glanced back at the boys, then turned to Rob. "Hey, babe, do you smell that?"

Rob was already scanning the perimeter over the steering wheel. "Yep. Something's burning. And it's coming from there."

Megan's gaze followed his pointing finger.

"Mama, are we there yet?" Five-year-old Trevor asked in a slow sing-song voice.

"Almost home, buddy," she said, but all focus was locked beyond the windshield.

As they reached the stop sign at the corner, a lady wearing curlers and a smock ran up to them, arms flailing like one of those tall gas station balloons. "Children live there! Do something!"

Megan eyed where the woman gestured. A bank of blackened clouds billowed from a single-family Tudor directly across the bustling two-way. "I see it."

"Me too." Rob pulled the car over to the curb, a safe enough distance from the blaze, and threw it in park. "Call 9-1-1, Meg."

Megan was about to say something when he leaped

out and bolted toward the house, where flames pushed violently from the first- and second-floor casements.

Trevor stretched up from his booster seat. "Mommy, what's Daddy doing?"

She went for the cell in the center console and began dialing, trying to feign an air of coolness. "Daddy's making sure people are safe, sweetie." With each number pushed, her mind raced. *Oh my God, oh my God, dear God, why now?*

The 9-1-1 emergency operator answered.

"There's a house on fire. My husband is trying to help. He's a fireman, but off-duty and by himself," Megan started, watching as Rob darted to the door and began pounding on it. When no one opened it, a faint weakness washed over her. *He's going to force himself inside.* Her mouth fell open, but nothing came out to remind him that his entire family was in the car, that he had no gear—*no equipment*! Rob then picked up something from the stoop and began using it to break the lock. When the door buckled, he disappeared into the thick gray.

"Ma'am, what's your location?" the operator repeated, voice elevated.

"Yes, location. Sorry. We're on Remsen Avenue, but I can't see the address, hold on." Megan rolled down the window and inched further out the side of the car to read the cursive numbers. "It's two-two-seven-four Remsen Avenue."

Suddenly, Rob dashed from the house and went around to the rear. "Where's he going?" Her attention drifted from the call. Then he reappeared carrying a skinny garden hose barely spewing water. "He needs backup. *Now!*"

Trevor started crying. "Mommy, I'm scared! Why is Daddy still over there?"

"Ssh." Megan listened while the technician's typing clicked through the line. "Don't worry, sweetheart." She reached behind with a free hand and stroked his leg while the baby, who was fast asleep in his car seat beside Trevor, had a drop of drool seeping from his mouth. *Sweet heaven, that cherub could sleep through anything.*

Beads of sweat formed at Meg's temples despite the briskness of the September morning. She rubbed her head, still aching, *always aching*, then adjusted the wool cancer cap that preserved whatever hair follicles were left. "Where's the fire department? Are they on their way?"

"Yes, ma'am. An engine's been dispatched. They're on their way. Remain on the line in case you need to relay anything about the situation."

She gripped the phone, eyeing the front door like a hawk for any signs of Rob or anyone. *If kids live there, I hope they're at school by now.*

Blaring sirens riddled the air, followed by the bass-like grumble of a horn. "They're here!" Megan announced, the cell firm to her ear.

Rob came storming out covered in soot. He leaned over the railing and puked on the lawn.

"Get the man some O2," one of the firemen commanded and then stormed into the building.

Megan sat frozen in the seat as a paramedic fixed an oxygen mask over Rob's face. It wasn't the first time he was being treated for smoke inhalation, and surely it wouldn't be the last. *I can't die. None of us are ready.*

****

Megan massaged her forehead, careful not to pull

out the Bluetooth. "I have no clue how he's going to do it."

Usually, to friends and, more specifically, to Rob, she'd pretend that having cancer was a part of life and being victimized by it was out of the question. But now things were different; the doctor's latest plan to get rid of the invasive ductal carcinoma in her breasts required a double mastectomy.

"What do you mean, Meg?" Erin asked.

"Ugh, where to begin?" Megan paused and got up from the bed; talking about the disease was seldom. It was flat-out annoying harping on the unknown when there were well-known, more important things to be done. Like nighttime routines. She'd gotten those accomplished in a certain way, and right now it was way past dinner for the boys, already pushing seven o'clock, which currently infringed on their scheduled bathes. They'd previously arranged for Rob to handle everything the night before surgery. However, neither the jangling of pans nor the rush of water from the tub were in earshot. She tried to ignore it and instead closed the bedroom blinds, but the sun's descending rays were a reminder of what happened that morning.

Megan began to pace, resisting the urge to "micromanage," as Rob called the new thing she did (which was technically "active avoidance" of the situation as per the therapist), and tried to focus on the friend patiently waiting on the other end of the line.

"What I mean is, well, our guys are firemen. We knew this was dangerous before marrying them and yet,"—anxiety manifested in her chest alongside the blighted cells—"and yet lately, I've been wondering how Rob's going to continue doing it when I'm gone. You know, just today I was reminded of the severity of what our guys actually do. Er, there was this raging house fire. No one was hurt, thank God." Megan paused and shook off the image of Rob vomiting on the grass. "What I mean is, *we* are their significant others. *We* are their insurance policies. It's us who are first-due at home with the kids while they respond fulltime to the neighborhood. It's always been like this unwritten rule, you know?"

"I never thought of it that way."

"You never had to. But now, we do. Well, mainly me." Megan sighed, fearing victimization bubbling beneath the surface. Images of Erin and Gail sipping tea, discussing her condition, began to play.

Erin: Poor thing. A thirty-four-year-old mother of two not only battling cancer, but she's also showing signs of obsessive compulsion.

Gail: God, have mercy on that poor soul.

"Meg," Erin started. "Are you afraid Rob won't be able to keep it together?"

Megan shook off the pretend conversation and reentered the current one. "Am I afraid for Rob? Well, heck yeah. There's no guarantee of full remission after my surgery. And men suck at keeping it together. With his job being as risky as it is, how is he going to juggle firefighting *and* parenthood? Who's going to help him?" Megan bit her bottom lip and began patrolling the room again. "Rob's parents do stuff only on a have-to basis, which irks the ever-living shit out of me. And, and, how could I ask my father to help when Mom is also struggling with a life-threatening diagnosis? A person with dementia isn't able to care for small children."

"Meg, stop it. You know that whether you're here or not, Jay-Jay and I will always be there for Rob and the boys. And Gail, well, she'll be their third grandmother spoiling them with pizza and ice cream for days."

"They'd all be in Heaven," Megan said, chuckling, then halted. "No pun intended."

"Really, you need to end this unnecessary stress. You're not going anywhere anytime soon."

Megan could hear the popping of a cork on the other end of the phone. "Red or white?"

"Merlot," Erin replied.

"Ooh. A good red is like a warm hug for your insides."

"I'll have an extra glass in your honor."

"Yes, please do." Megan stood straight and faced the mirror. Her cheeks were slightly sunken in, but not in that killer cheekbone kind of way. And the rosy complexion she'd loved had grown dusty since the fight to stay healthy began. The muscles in her throat began to constrict. "Go enjoy. I have to pack. See you tomorrow?"

"Of course. Love you."

"Love you, too."

Meg pulled out the Bluetooth and tossed it onto the bureau. The lip of the top drawer was slightly ajar, exposing a favorite satin bra. She pulled it from the pile and held it up, the deep scarlet hue shimmering in the light. In college, it was never really a bother if the straps poked out of a shirt.

"It adds color to my ensemble," she had quipped when Erin noticed it.

"It makes you look cheap," Erin said and tucked the elastic bands back under her top.

Megan grinned at the isolated memory, yet so fresh.

"Hey, Meg, do you know where my keys are?" Rob said, entering the room.

She threw the undergarment into the drawer and slammed it closed before spinning around. "No, I don't."

"What are you doing, sweetheart?" He glanced behind her. Half of the bra was dangling out the side of the furniture. His face softened. "Come here, honey."

Megan wrapped each arm around Rob's broad shoulders and took in the soapy cleanness of his naturally tanned body. Her eyes wandered from him to the space above their bed where their wedding picture hung and studied the image of herself like a distant locale on some ancient map.

Rob's fingers crawled up the back of her neck. "Tell me what you're thinking."

She pulled out of thought and away from him to scratch an itch on a bald spot. "It's just a lot to process."

Rob looked on. "What is?"

"This." She tightened the knot of the headscarf. "And you running into burning buildings, and the possibility that our kids could be orphans, and…"

"Stop." He took her hands in his. "Yes, you are sick. Yeah, I'm a firefighter. And, yep, we're parents. But, Meg, we've got this."

"We?"

Rob squeezed their palms together. "Yes, *we*. In sickness and in health, remember?"

"So, you understand that my illness could totally change our lifestyle?"

Rob's face twisted into a look of confusion. "Why would it? They found the cancer, and now it's being eradicated."

"I know. It's all, just, so scary."

Rob kissed her fingers, then let go and moved in for another embrace. Megan nestled into his shirt and allowed herself to stay there for longer than a few seconds this time. "Thank you for being by my side every step of this crazy way."

"I should be thanking you," he said. "Especially after this morning."

His head leaned forward and rested on top of hers. She admired his ability to use physical and emotional strength to help others, the brawny six-foot-three stature that made him more than capable, and he was smart. Not book smart, rather he was savvy. He could talk sports with the ringers and politics with the elderly without batting a lash.

Her gaze trailed down and examined the way the diamond necklace, last year's Christmas gift from him and the boys, hung between both bosoms. She touched the jewelry, then held it up. "Maybe we should make this into a bracelet."

"Why? They're not removing your neck."

He was also a jokester.

A soft knock sounded on the door. "Mommy?"

Rob looked to Megan, who gave an affirmed nod. "Come in, buddy," he said and turned the latch.

Trevor walked in clutching his space robot and climbed onto the bed. "Mommy, are you going to be away for long this time for your operation?"

Megan sat beside him and stroked his arm. "Why do you ask, sweet pea?"

The boy held up the doll. "Because if you are, then I want you to have Zip, you know, to keep you safe."

Megan peered at Rob, then looked again at their son. "You'll really let me have him?"

He bobbed his head.

"Wow, thank you. I know how much he means to

8

you."

Trevor placed the toy on Megan's lap and hopped off the bed. At the door, he stopped and turned his head. "Zip and I already prayed for you, so you can just hug him when you talk to God tonight. Zip knows what he has to do. Me and God told him."

Megan motioned him back and gave him a strong hug. "Do you know how much I love you?"

"This much." Trevor stretched his arms wide and stood on his tippy-toes.

She took hold of his fingertips and pulled them gently. "To above and beyond the biggest of stars!" she said in a space robot voice.

"That's not it, silly," Trevor said and tucked his hands under his armpits.

"Come on, big guy. Your brother's in bed, and now it's your turn." Rob lifted him.

Trevor's fists shot out ahead of them as he pretended to fly. "Up, up, and away!" he called as they exited the room.

Zip slipped off Megan and onto the floor. Through blurred vision, she got to her knees and clutched the toy.

Rob reentered the room and closed the door. "He is one brave little dude."

"Yes, he is."

Rob knelt on the carpet. "Just like his mother." He took her into his arms and then stood.

"No, not me," Meg replied as he eased them onto the bed again. "I always considered you the brave one."

"Eh, it's just part of the job. I don't do anything more than I was trained to do. But you, on the other hand." He shook his head. "You keep on truckin'. No manual. No advisers. You're learning about this disease as you go and taking it all in stride with each passing day."

She glared down. "We'll see how strong I am after my breasts are cut off."

"Oh, stop. Boobs are overrated." Rob leaned in for a kiss. "Besides, you have the best oncologist on the East Coast."

"Erin and Gail say the same thing," she said and began tracing the outline of his mouth with one finger.

"See? Listen to your friends." He inched off the mattress and grabbed the empty duffel bag from the carpet. "Now, what to bring? Time is tickin' away, and you need a good night's sleep."

Chapter Two

Blood squirted across the pink material of Deirdre's scrubs, yet she didn't flinch. Salvatore, a sixty-five-year-old patient suffering from a rare form of breast cancer in men, glanced at the spatter-soaked fabric and then up at her. "What a way to start the morning. I'm sorry about that. My veins have been stubborn my whole life."

"No apologies needed, Sal. Some people's veins ooze stubbornness."

Salvatore's laugh was as weak as the inside of his arm. He lifted his free hand and motioned for a high-five as the bandage was being sealed to his skin. Deirdre acknowledged it with an elbow, then ripped off the dirty plastic gloves and launched them into the garbage before sitting on the chair by the bed. "What part of Sicily are you from?"

"How'd you know I was from Sicily?"

"Wild guess," she said and winked. "Your name and olive complexion gave it away."

The man looked down at himself.

"Your birthplace is noted on the chart." Deirdre smiled warmly and held up a clean palm.

"Palermo," Sal said, slapping her hand before curling his fingers around it. "I came here for the American Dream in May 2001. But everyone is still home except me."

"Really? How come?"

"September eleventh. I came to open a restaurant, The Evangeline. Found beautiful property downtown—Battery City. No one believed I could do it except my twin. That's who the restaurant was named after."

"Wow, what an honor. Your sister must have been elated that you did that."

"Evie died in a car accident when we were nineteen. Hit-and-run. We planned on coming here together until that happened. So, I came by myself to keep our wish alive. Business was just starting when boom, airplanes into buildings—and so, here I am. No sister. No business. How do you say…" He scratched his temple. "Loner?"

"Ah, you're a loner." Deirdre rested a hand on the bedrail. "Me too."

The creases on Sal's forehead deepened. "You? Loner? I don't believe you."

"Put it this way, I have a small family. No parents. No siblings. I missed that privilege. Having a sister must've been fun."

Salvatore watched as Deirdre stood and fluffed a new pillow for him, double-checked his arm and the speed of the IV drip, then wheeled the tray over with his breakfast on it. She removed the cover and peeled the plastic wrapper off the utensils, setting them beside the plate of food.

"Your patients are your family," Sal said as a napkin was tucked into the collar of his hospital gown.

She stopped and gazed at him. "How do you figure?"

He smiled. "Wild guess."

Deirdre didn't say anything else. Instead, she moved to the foot of the bed and fumbled with an empty bedpan, not wanting to admit he was right. She did consider these people family, nurturing them like any family member would. The companionship was a personal need of hers that was kept hidden, even from herself, often chalking it up to the business of nursing.

Salvatore picked up his fork and helped himself to some of the egg on the dish. Knowing he had trouble swallowing dinner last night, Deirdre lingered near the sink and washed her hands a bit longer than necessary just to make sure he didn't choke.

"Tasty?" she said, working both fists under the steady current.

Sal gave a thumbs-up, his long chin moving up and down as he chewed. When he swallowed and then sipped his coffee with ease, she trusted that he was okay to eat on his own and left the room.

"Deirdre Henricksen, dial one-one-three-one. Deirdre Henricksen, one-one-three-one," a voice announced.

"Right here," Deirdre said, advancing to reception.

"Kelleher was looking for you. Mentioned something about a scheduled surgery he has this morning," the clerk replied.

"Thanks, Betty. Did he say anything else?"

The woman spied Deirdre from behind a computer screen and smirked.

"I know, I know. Stupid question." Deirdre fiddled with the ball and chain attached to the pen on the counter when an alert sounded.

"That's coming from Salvatore's room," Betty said, eyeing the monitor. "Go, I'll page Kelleher."

Deirdre raced through the corridor to the last room on the right where Sal was lying limp, his heart machine displaying a flat green line. She hurried to his bed and threw aside the breakfast tray, then checked his mouth and throat, but they were clear of food. She spun around and grabbed the paddles from the wall.

"I'm here," Dr. Kelleher said, rushing in.

He went for the defibrillator, but Deirdre didn't budge. Instead, she rubbed the electrical pads together and pressed them to Sal's chest, counted softly, then released another surge that zapped at his heart.

The doctor grabbed the old man's wrist after his torso juddered in a lifeless flop. There was a moment of silence as Deirdre waited for a response from either Kelleher or Salvatore. Dr. Kelleher shook his head.

Deirdre tried again and again without success. "Shit," she whispered and reluctantly backed away from the body.

"Time of death: zero-nine-thirty," Dr. Kelleher said, then walked out.

In that short interlude of stillness, a thought of Sal and his twin Evie entered her mind. As a child, Deirdre yearned for a sister, always wanting to share special secrets siblings kept. Alas, hearing Salvatore talk of Evie made her feel somewhat closer to him—to them, which was the danger of getting to know patients.

"You can rest peacefully with your twin now," Deirdre whispered and pulled the sheet over Sal.

At the nurses' station, Deirdre read the clock above the coffeemaker and, out of sheer auto-pilot mode, prepared a fresh pot.

The doctor scribbled his notes and dropped Sal's file onto the stack. "Good job in there. Your patient dedication and bedside manner are nothing short of stellar."

"Thanks," Deirdre replied, sounding grim, and offered him a cup of coffee.

Kelleher took it. "As a matter of fact, it's been brought to my attention that you've been requested."

Deirdre looked up. "Me? For what?"

"I have a double mastectomy in an hour. Someone in the woman's family apparently knew you—or *of* you—and they asked that you tend pre-and post-op."

"Really? I've heard of people requesting doctors, but I didn't know they could ask for specific nurses."

"You'd be surprised what people with power and money can do." Kelleher did a quarter turn, then paused. "Oh, and tell Tammy to cover your rounds for the rest of the morning."

"Okay, thanks, doctor."

Deirdre stayed behind as he marched down the hall. Kelleher was someone to be admired but often came across as insensitive, a classic "one case to another" type of medic with hardened flesh, skin that toughened with the job—*at* the job—and Deirdre feared hers would someday do the same. Once he was out of sight, she slumped in the nearest chair and toyed with the skinny red stirrer in the foam cup. *How could he just move on like that? It's like his brain is a radio whose signal can easily pick up another station.* She sipped the hot drink, then stood.

On the way to find Tammy, the door to Salvatore's room was ajar. She imagined saying, "How's my favorite Sicilian doing?" to which he'd reply, "Molto bene," but instead, a transporter was situating a mobile bed to take him to the morgue. A tear escaped. *Pull it together, Deirdre. Change your station.* She wiped her face, hoping the room would remain empty for a while. Possibly forever.

Chapter Three

Erin parked the U-Haul in the driveway and stared at the cookie-cutter townhouse in suburban Prospect Heights, Brooklyn, where she'd grown up. It was the last place anyone would want to return to.

"We'll be closer to Megan and Rob and everyone at the firehouse," Jelani had said, which was true, but still.

Erin sighed and depressed the seat belt button. Until yesterday, she and Jay-Jay (the name she usually called Jelani unless they were arguing) had spent the first couple years of their thirties living together in a chic part of Manhattan. It didn't matter that their studio was the size of a closet, and they were totally cramped—it was theirs, which, to her, made all the difference.

"But just think, Er, an *entire house* will be ours. For free!" Jay-Jay refuted when they learned of Erin's inheritance. He was so amped at the idea of them as homeowners that he went ahead and made the arrangements for the closing, which coincided with the day of Megan's surgery.

Erin swallowed hard, nervous for Megan and, honestly, for herself. She gazed at the overgrown weeds flapping against the same rusted gate, then considered the rest of the landscape.

For the last seventeen years, while her parents were still married—and about that long it took to accept their divorce—Erin believed the closets of the house contained paradoxes—things known and not known of their nuptials: of why Dad was so sad that he drank, only to become angry with everyone when he did, especially to Mother, who took the brunt of his emotions until *she* became sad and abandoned not only her husband but the role as Mom, too.

"My childhood—their endless fighting—it's what I'm afraid I'll see every time I enter a room there," Erin admitted the night the new "asset" came to light.

"Just because your parents weren't happy there doesn't mean we can't be," Jay-Jay had said as he cradled Erin in his lap. She plucked at the sponge-like fibers of their otherwise soft twin mattress while he continued. "Their issues were far deeper than a house, Erin. There was domestic violence. Violence clearly not capable from drywall or caulkalone but from fisted hands and beating hearts. *We* are not *them*. *We* can make it work."

Jay-Jay's determination echoed deep into the drums of each ear. Since the house was indeed a gift, a total surprise from her estranged father who, after the separation, traveled to a far-flung state—*maybe Wyoming?*—and became a recluse until his death. Also, because of the unmistakable optimism Jay-Jay had for it, Erin couldn't say no; a small part thought maybe, just *maybe*, he would see the enormity of the sacrifice she was making and therefore would be more willing to try another round of in vitro fertilization.

Her reminiscing broke when Jay-Jay pulled alongside Erin in his pickup and turned off the ignition. "Hey, sexy," he said, beaming.

Good Goddamn! Erin's insides did that fluttery thing it always did when his caramel mouth framed them porcelain teeth.

Jay hopped out and walked around the flatbed, slapping a hand against the side. "We made it," he said, coming up to the cab and glimpsing inside.

"Oh, yay! We're here!" Erin tried smiling like him but failed miserably as she glanced again at the dirty gray building.

"Come on"—Jay-Jay motioned—"let's check out the interior for a better sense of the layout."

Erin bit back, deciding not to remind him she knew the lay of the land all too well and stepped out of the car. She picked up a box from the passenger seat and followed him to the front door, also resolved to sneak out to visit Megan at the hospital after the move was underway.

"Keys?" He shifted the crate and extended his free arm.

Erin handed him Father's only set, the one with a worn-out *#1 Dad* keychain on it, a gift she'd given him in the second grade.

"I couldn't bring myself to sell the house, yet I couldn't live in it either," Dad wrote in a letter attached to his will. "I heard you've married. Congrats, kiddo. Consider this a belated wedding present. And listen, don't be fooled by the past, Erin. That brownstone is prime real estate. It'll need some TLC, but it's ideal for you and your growing family."

Growing family. She wanted so desperately to believe that could actually happen but thought such a miracle might require an exorcism on an otherwise faulty reproductive system.

Jay-Jay inserted the key into the lock. As he twisted the knob, Erin's arms began to shake.

"You okay?" he said and turned back.

"Yeah." Erin's breath caught for a second. "Well, no." She gestured at the entrance once deemed the gateway to a personal hell. "That, and the fact that Megan's surgery is today, Jelani."

"Let's go inside and put these things down. There's something I have to tell you."

Erin's almond eyes grew round. "Tell me what?"

"No, no. It's all good. Trust me," he said and entered the house.

As they climbed the stairs to the landing, a weird sense of home flushed over her. She set the box on the floor and seized the railing secretly hoping the feeling would last.

"I have to check the water heater in the basement real quick but"—the corner of Jay-Jay's mouth perked up—"I'll be right back."

"Um, okay." Erin watched as he disappeared down the rear steps, then walked toward the bedroom that was hers as a kid. Entering, she switched on the light. *The mint green is gone.* She spun around, studying the beige walls. *And the rainbow border.*

Erin sat on the carpet, the only thing unchanged in all those years, and fiddled with the wiry threads, recalling the first time Megan came over freshman year, during rush. They were so tired from the sorority's hazing that they went directly to the bedroom and crashed for fifteen hours straight. She chuckled, glancing at the now empty space where the daybed once was.

Jay-Jay peeked in. "What's doing?"

"Oh, nothing, just reminiscing." She crossed both legs, patting the carpet. "Come."

He slid inside and sat on the rug.

"Jay, I'm worried. *I've* always been Megan's 9-1-1, but this, this cancer is so unpredictable."

"I know." Jay-Jay took hold of Erin's hands. "That's why I'm glad you're going to see her."

"What?" Her nose wrinkled up. *There's no way he knew I was going to sneak away!*

"So…I went to Gail when I realized I screwed up the dates of the closing and the surgery. I wanted to make it right—*had* to make it right. Anyway, she secured a Family Transport van from the fire department's volunteer unit."

"But those vans are only for *firefighters* with cancer, not spouses."

"We're talking about Gail O'Neil, remember?"

Erin remembered. After the divorce, when all the neighbors pecked at her family situation, clucking like hens at the bus stop or the grocer, the only person who appeared unlike the Pollyannas was a siren named Gail, the firefighter's wife down the street who often hung up brand name duds to do real chores including gutters and leaders and changing the oil in the family's cars instead of waiting for a man to do it or hiring help. She'd rung Erin's bell one unusually quiet Friday night, pizza in hand.

"Hungry?" the lady had inquired and held up the box.

At first, Erin hesitated, not sure of this stranger's intentions, but when Gail didn't step foot inside without permission and continued to extend the offering without questions or heckling, Erin was certain this person didn't have ulterior motives and was right, basking in Gail's company, of how gutsy yet nurturing she was. "You *must* meet my friend Megan. You'll love her." Erin was correct yet again.

The three became inseparable: Erin and Megan blossoming into womanhood and prospering, in part, from Gail, who thrived on their companionship despite the almost two-decade difference. They all agreed that what they had was something special.

Erin sat up, nose-to-nose with Jay-Jay. "And? Did you get a van?"

"And," Jay replied, his voice calm. "While Gail called Family Transport, I reached out to the guys at the station and asked them to move our things into the house while we drove Megan to the hospital for surgery. Everyone should be here any minute."

"So, we got a van?"

"And some movers."

Erin grabbed his face and kissed his mouth so aggressively they fell over.

"I love you," she said, finally letting go, and weaved her fingers between his again, exploring the topography of their intermingling skin tones. *Like the smooth blend of vanilla and chocolate soft-serve: something truly Americana.*

The loud rumble of a truck rattled the bones of the old house. Erin jumped. "Is that them?"

"That's them," Jay-Jay said and stood. "Let's rock."

The bile in Erin's stomach churned as footsteps from several of Jay-Jay's fire buddies echoed up the stairs. *This is it. Getting Megan cancer-free. Transitioning this house into a home. Let that be it, Lord, let that be it.* She suppressed the knot and raced out the door toward the red, white, and yellow fire department van that pulled into the driveway.

The tinted glass on the driver's side descended,

revealing Gail's face. "Hop in, sister." The vehicle's doors unlatching punctuated the command.

"You're driving?" Erin got on tippy-toes and peeked inside. Rob was sitting in the passenger seat in his uniform. He gave a small wave. Erin smiled at him, then looked to Gail again. "Wow, you're good."

"Only as good as our precious cargo." Gail pointed a manicured thumb behind her. "Now get in."

"I'm here, I'm here," Jay-Jay huffed, the opening of his FDNY uniform shirt flapping as he ran.

Erin stepped aside as he reached for the door handle. "Thank you for doing this," she whispered when he eased by.

"Thank Gail," he replied. "She's the mastermind of it all."

Chapter Four

Gail turned into the parking garage of the New York Cancer Specialists (NYCS) building and eased up to the attendant. "Good morning. How much?"

"Emergency vehicles can park over there." The man pointed to a vacant spot in the corner. "Free of charge."

Gail squinted at the chap, her lawyer instincts deepening the crow's feet. "Is that so?"

"Yes, ma'am." He signaled again to the space across the lot. "Stay as long as you need."

"Well, then." Gail retrieved one of the crisp fifties from a leather wallet and leaned out the side. "This is for you." She stuffed the money into the gentleman's hand and pressed his fingers around it. "Thank you."

"My pleasure, miss. Have a nice day."

The days aren't ever nice *at a cancer hospital.* Gail saluted him as the window rolled up to separate them once again and tapped on the gas.

"Go slow," Megan said. "There's no rush to get me upstairs and on the operating table just yet."

Gail released the pedal so the van slowed to a crawl and stretched an arm around the seat to stroke Meg's leg. "You're going to be in the best hands," she said in the rearview, then eyed Erin, Jay-Jay, and Rob. Their muted mouths immediately morphed into confirmatory grins.

"Oh, absolutely. No doubt about it. The best of the best," they chanted while Gail steered into the spot and silenced the van's ignition.

Rain started to slam against the window panes of NYCS, the sound echoing into an otherwise quiet lobby. At Gail's command, Erin and Jay-Jay hung a few feet behind but were still in earshot as Rob and Megan signed in.

"They'll be so nervous their hearts'll be pumping louder than the receptionist's directives, so your job will be to listen in and make sure they understand," Gail instructed via text on the way up, then threw the phone back in the Louis Vuitton Crossbody. She put her hands on Megan's shoulders and massaged out the tension, recollecting the time Harry was here for his initial surgery.

"Man, I wish it were my goddamn gall bladder like the doctors originally thought," he had said, cutting off the secretary mid-spiel.

When he went to wipe his brow, Gail not only noticed his drenched forehead but that his hand was wobbling vigorously. "Why don't you go sit down," she'd said and took the pen from him. "I can fill out the measly paperwork, right, sugar?" Gail didn't wait for the clerk to actually answer because a lawyer never asked questions they didn't already have the answers to.

While Megan, Rob, Erin, and Jay-Jay were busy at check-in, Gail ducked into a single-person bathroom next to the elevators and pulled out the cell phone.

"Kelleher speaking."

"Hey, Doc, it's me, Gail O'Neil."

"Mrs. O'Neil, yes, how are you?"

Just peachy. "All's well if our arrangement's in place for Megan Dunham."

"Megan Dunham," Dr. Kelleher repeated, his voice

25

trailing. "Ah, yes! The team has approved your request."

It better be with all the litigating I've done for this place. "Excellent. Thanks, Doc."

Gail ended the call and returned the phone to the bag. "She'll be fine, we'll all be fine," she told the mirror, then flipped on the faucet and splashed water on both cheeks to wash away the budding tears before walking out.

"Where's Megan?" Gail asked and approached the gang in the lounge.

"They took Meg up. Room 604. They didn't seem too welcoming to us," Erin said, motioning to Jelani.

"It's typical pre-surgery protocol to have anyone who's not family remain in the waiting area. I wouldn't take it personally." Gail scanned the sign on the wall beyond Erin's shoulder in search of the nearest elevator. "But you and I are her *sisters*," Gail continued coolly, "so let's go up and make sure everything's in order. Jay-Jay, you stay here. Hang tight."

They maneuvered around him and headed for the elevator bay.

When Gail and Erin reached the room, a nurse in pink scrubs burst by them and entered.

"There she is!" Gail wanted to touch the woman's hand, to say hello and give the biggest of hugs but decided to save it for later.

"There's who?" Erin craned around.

"Ssh." Gail pulled Erin to the side. They leaned quietly against the doorjamb.

"Hello, Mrs. Dunham," the lady in pink said, walking in a brisk trot toward the bed. "My name is Deirdre Henricksen. I'll be your pre- and post-op nurse."

Megan startled. "Wait a minute. Deirdre

Henricksen? From NYU? Class of '08?"

"Holy shit," Erin muttered and nudged Gail.

Deirdre stopped mid-stride in front of Megan. "Yes. That's me." Her eyes narrowed. "Megan…"

"O'Leary—my married name is Dunham."

"Megan O'Leary! If there's a keg, there's Meg—ha! How could I forget the most fun person in college?"

Megan laughed, then looked down. "Was. I *was* the most fun person."

Gail and Erin watched Deirdre saunter to Megan's side. "I'm sure that's a crock," Deirdre said.

"A total crock," Rob chimed.

Gail laughed as the two women exchanged smiles.

"Deirdre Henricksen, dial four-two-two-zero. Deirdre, four-two-two-zero," a voice boomed from a mounted speaker.

"Excuse me one moment." Deirdre stepped away from Megan.

Gail shoved Erin into the hall before anyone saw them.

When Deirdre left the room, Gail heard Rob say, "Wow, small world, huh?"

"Not that small," Gail interjected and reentered the room with Erin.

Rob gaped at them.

"What do you mean?" Megan said, wearing an equally puzzled expression.

"One night during Harry's stay here, he was having a bad episode, and the terror of it paralyzed me in the chair—*me!*—could you imagine?" Gail paused. "Anyway, this nurse swooped in and took charge. When I finally came to, I realized she looked awfully familiar. And that's when it hit me: this woman was the girl you and Erin palled around with some years ago. That pretty Spanish-looking gal I'd chatted with at the kitchen table about things teenagers normally didn't care about while you 'n' Erin sat in front of the TV painting your nails and gossiping about boys was all grown. And an oncology nurse, to boot. Like, holy shit, right?"

She glanced at Erin and chuckled, then pulled out the keys to the van. "Anyway, the minute I found out about your latest diagnosis, I cashed in on a few favors, just some things I'd done in my law-practicing days for the hospital's director, and got Deirdre assigned to you. Easy-peasy." Gail smiled and held up the keyring. "Now, I'd better get going. Jay-Jay is downstairs. We were all going to come up together, but they wouldn't allow it. I'll take him back to the house, Er, so you can stay. I'll be back tonight."

Gail went to Megan.

"You, you did all this? For me?" Megan's eyes glistened with tears.

Gail knelt and cupped Meg's head in both hands. "It's not that surprising. We've been emergency responders to one another for years now, you know that as well as I do." She pressed her lips against Megan's temple, then rose again and went to Rob. "See you later."

After dropping Jay-Jay off, Gail steered the Family Transport vehicle onto the parking pad of her son's sprawling Brighton Beach residence; another squall of driving rain bombarded the neighborhood. Under the seat, Gail found an umbrella and then made a run for it.

"Gramma!" Logan banged on the glass of the storm door at the top of the steps as Gail wrestled the brolly closed.

In the house, she slipped off the wet coat and hung

it on the hook. "Come here, peanut," she said, scooping him up. "I see someone was eating Oreos." Gail laughed and took a tissue from the pocket of perfectly starched slacks. "Where's Daddy?"

Logan pointed to the kitchen as Gail cleaned his chocolate-covered mouth. "You look so much like your grandfather."

She put him down before the sadness (and cookie goop) settled on her. The baby darted toward his dad.

"Hi, Mom. Coffee's fresh. Grab some while it's still hot," Jeffrey called when Gail entered the room.

"Are the Oreos fresh too?" She kissed the side of Jeffrey's head and reached around him for one off the counter.

"What time do you want me home? I know you have to see Megan."

Gail's ears perked upon hearing him say Megan's name; they rarely spoke of their friends or social lives, which, according to Jeffrey, should be separate and apart from family matters. He had a habit of keeping everything in life pure business.

"Come home at the usual time," Gail said, mouth half full of cookie. "I can't visit until she's out of recovery, so I won't be going back until tonight."

Jeff looped his tie and tucked the end into his trousers. Unlike his firefighter father, he had chosen the corporate world, managing a hedge fund on Wall Street. "As bland and boring as a stark white shirt," Harry used to say. Gail was secretly happy with Jeffrey's conservative choice.

"Have a great day," Gail said and walked him to the door.

Jeff hugged his mother and son, then kissed the

29

picture of his dad on the server before he stepped out.

Gail twisted the lock and grabbed the frame from the table. Focused on Harry's eyes, the whites always pearlesque no matter the circumstances, she recalled with cinematic-like clarity the day they met: a fire was raging in the college cafeteria; firemen helping everyone get out of the building without being trampled. Gail, a late twenty-something law student, was one of those people. When both eyes met the firefighter's, he grinned and slipped his gloved hand between her fingers. Instantly comfortable with this stranger, Gail allowed him to escort her to safety. And later, dinner.

"Pop-pop," Logan squealed, patting the photo.

"Yes, Pop-pop." Gail kissed the picture, a closeup of Harry in a faded navy FDNY T-shirt, his full head of salt-and-pepper hair as sexy and casual a-la George Clooney as he proudly showed the camera a sizable catfish at the end of his line. "Give kissies!"

Chapter Five

Megan's eyelids felt glued shut. It took some time to pry them open without using fingers since both hands and arms also felt as if they were weighted down with some sort of adhesive.

"Hello?" Or at least that's what she thought was said, but with her dry, tight throat, a barely audible croak came out. There was no answer, which wasn't really a surprise because the room felt empty. Megan wiggled a few fingers, the only other parts that could move, maybe because they didn't ache like everything else. *I'm a prisoner in my own body.*

Footsteps in the corridor echoed closer. Meg strained for a look, but things were still blurry. At that moment, she wished the mattress would suck her body up whole.

Deirdre emerged at the entrance. "Meg, are you awake? It's time to take your meds."

Megan blinked in the direction of the door. The nurse entered, holding a Dixie cup. "These'll make you feel a little relief." Deirdre adjusted the bed upward, then tucked the remote under Megan's hand. "Okay, open your mouth and say, *ah.*"

The pills were cool on Meg's tongue but not as refreshing as the water that followed. "You're probably wondering where everyone is," Deirdre said, refilling the cup and setting it on the nightstand next to the pitcher.

"Erin ran to the bathroom real quick, and Rob went to the cafeteria to make some calls. He said something about checking in with the in-laws and, I think, Gail." She plopped into the nearby chair and ripped off the name badge. "I'm hungry."

"Starving," Megan said, finally. "What are they serving?"

"Not sure." Deirdre retrieved a cell from her scrubs. "But, come to think of it, there are better eats in the neighborhood where we can order from. It's time for something edible for the both of us."

Megan scanned the controller and pushed the button to sit up a bit more. Plastic tubes poked out from under the bedding. "That's incredibly kind of you, but you don't have to spend your spare time in here. I'm probably the worst company right now."

"Nonsense. What are you in the mood for? There's a decent Italian place down the street, but you should actually go light—say, there's a wonderful soup and salad café—all organic—"

"Say no more," Megan interrupted. "I love soup, especially this time of year."

"Oh, me too. A good lentil or split pea," Erin said, rejoining them.

"Mmm, yes. Or homemade chicken noodle." Megan raised a brow. "Think they have that?"

"Yes, and the broth will be good for you," Deirdre said and got up. "Let me get the other girls' food orders at the station. I'll be back in a jiffy."

After Deirdre walked out, Megan realized no money was given; rekindled friendships were one thing, but not the paying kind. "Wait!" She glanced at the end table drawer where the wallet was when the oversized gown slipped off a shoulder, exposing the bandages.

"I got this," Erin said and snagged her purse off the radiator. "I'll go pay Deirdre and give you some privacy."

"Thanks." Megan swallowed hard. "Can you close the door behind you?"

"Of course." Erin blew a kiss, then walked out.

When the door clicked shut, Megan lifted a hand, grazed the textured covering, and carefully touched one of the drains. Surprisingly, it didn't hurt. She poked the top of the dressing. A red four-inch horizontal incision was held together by surgical glue. She then pulled the dressing on the other side and saw the same on the left as on the right. "Great. I'm fucking Frankenstein."

She let go of the gauze, her arm flopping down like a fish. Water welled in each eye, but she turned on the television anyway and waited for Erin and Deirdre to return.

"Chow's on," Deirdre announced, walking in with Erin; both carried a shopping bag.

"That was quick."

"This is Manhattan, babe," Erin added.

Megan watched as the women, particularly Deirdre, took Styrofoam tubs from the carriers and put them on the round table near the bed. *Deirdre has a strong work ethic.* Megan continued to look on as Deirdre took care of every detail like Meg would do in the classroom: making sure each child was comfortable and prepared, even if it meant dipping into one's own pockets to ensure this. "I admire your spirit. It's something I once had."

"You still have it. It's just taking on a different form right now." Deirdre slid the portable tray table across the bed. "For you, my lady."

"Mmm. It looks so good." Megan stared at the hearty soup and then, very slowly, raised her arms. "Please, ladies. I want to give thanks."

Megan gripped their hands and recited a prayer of grace. When done, she focused again on the food.

Erin shifted up each sleeve, grabbed the tiny bag of oyster crackers, and peeled it open. "Meg, don't forget these."

"Or this." Deirdre placed a spoon in Megan's other hand.

Megan closed her fingers around each item, every movement a small calculation. The crackers dropped onto the soup then, with the utensil, Meg pushed them deep into the broth and finally took a bite. "Mm," she said, mid-chew. "I couldn't taste a damn thing since the start of this ordeal, but now I kinda can. This is friggin' delicious."

The girls giggled as they ate.

"I haven't had this much company at mealtime since my boyfriend went off to Randall's Island," Deirdre confessed.

Megan sipped from the bowl and wiped with the back of a wobbly hand. "Randall's Island? Is your beau a fireman?"

"Yeah. Cliff Baxter. He's assigned to a firehouse in Brooklyn but is a drill instructor at The Academy right now."

"Wait. You're *still* with Cliff Baxter?" Meg looked at Deirdre, all thoughts trailing off to the annual summer barbeque Gail and Harry would host in their enormous yard for the entire firehouse. The loud music, the crispy thin crust pizza cooking in the outdoor stone oven, but mostly the banter between friends and the firemen. They would stay in Gail and Harry's pool the whole time, drinking and playing water volleyball. "Geez, you guys have been together for-like-ever."

"Seriously," Erin added. "But, why haven't we seen you at the company picnics or the dinner dances? I mean, no offense, I think that's great and all, but wouldn't we have run into you by now?"

Deirdre sat upright. "Well, Cliff and I have been dating on and off for a while. I was supposed to go to the dance last year, but I had a scheduled surgery and couldn't." She dropped the spoon into the empty bowl. "Hey, who knows, maybe we'll all boogie together this year. But enough about that. What do you do for a living, Meg? Domestic goddess, career woman, what?"

Megan snickered. "Domestic goddess? That's a good one. Actually, no. When I'm not in the hospital fending off cancer, or home fending off chores, I'm in a classroom defending today's youth." She made a fist and shot it out in front like a superhero, then looked at Deirdre with a sly eye. "You'll get a kick out of this one: your man's mama is my boss."

"Ha!" Deirdre smacked her lap and stood. "Then you're definitely one tough cookie. Inside and out."

Megan's bed started to descend. "Eh. I miss them— my students, my principal, my life before all this. You probably think I'm loco missing Mrs. Baxter too, but when you're in a position like mine, you miss anything and everything B.C."

"B.C?"

"Before cancer."

Deirdre gave Megan a solemn look.

"I haven't seen my class in weeks. Think they miss me?" Meg toyed with the rosary dangling from her neck.

"Of course they do," Erin chirped. "Maybe you could Skype with them or something?"

Megan stroked the headscarf. "I'm not ready for them to see me like this."

"Then maybe you can make them a card or poster or something," Deirdre said, assessing the scattered food containers. "They'll see you the way you were again in no time."

"Oh, I know. I can have Rob go up to school and give them a talk on fire safety."

Erin approached Megan's bedside. "That's a good idea. He could bring them coloring books."

"And let them play with his helmet and gear—it'll be a real treat even if I'm not there. Wow, thanks for helping me figure this out, you guys. I almost forgot about that."

Deirdre motioned in the air. "It was all you two."

Erin's cell phone rang. "Excuse me, ladies, this is probably Jay-Jay calling with an update on the move." She left the room.

"So," Megan turned to Deirdre, who was busy cleaning. Meg touched the string of rainbow-like pearls attached to a cross that dangled between the surgical drains where breasts once were. "Do you believe in God?" she asked, glancing up.

Deirdre, who was slouched over a wastebasket throwing out the scraps, looked up and sighed. "I don't think you want my opinion on that."

"Yes, I do. I'm not one of those Jesus freaks who spews biblical quotes to get you on board."

"Okay then. Once upon a time, I believed there was a man in the clouds who made the world he saw down below a better place for all who believed in him, but then terrorists hijacked planes and attacked the World Trade Center in the name of 'God.' And now,"—she paused, eyes trailing to the window—"Now I equate the whole concept of God with Santa Claus—a man that parents want their young children to believe in for the sake of having a belief, only to find out later that you were being lied to the entire time and he isn't real."

"Technically, the legend of Santa Claus stemmed from a man named Nicholas, who was very real," Megan said.

Deirdre laughed. "That may be, but for me, it's more complicated than that."

Megan held up the religious insignia she'd always worn. They twinkled even under dull institutional lighting. "I don't know if this works, but I want to believe it does. Childish or not, faith is all I've got." She tucked it beneath the collar of the hospital gown and patted it like a protective shield over the wounds.

Chapter Six

Gail slowed at the main entrance of the fire station, the sight of it a consolation. Sometimes, it appeared as if nothing changed, and Harry was still in there, working a long twenty-four-hour shift.

"First, it was Erin's stop. Now yours." Gail turned to Rob and noticed his glassy pupils. "You okay?"

He inhaled briskly, the noise an outright sniffle.

Gail sighed. "You must be so overwhelmed." She put the van in park and rested on the steering wheel. "Listen, you stay strong for that beautiful wife of yours."

Rob chuckled and teared up simultaneously. "She wants me to do a fire safety lesson for her class."

"Wonderful. You're going to do it, right?"

"I don't know if I can." Rob stared ahead. She noticed his right leg's disquiet, seesawing up and down. "Her absence will be like this giant elephant in the room."

Gail's spine straightened. "You have to do it. You can't possibly say no."

Rob went for the door handle, then stopped. "Why do you care so much? I, I know you're friends and all, but you've really gone above and beyond this time."

"How is what I do any different from what you boys do for each other in the firehouse?"

Rob ran a hand through his dampened hair. "I mean, we barely hear from our family and here you are getting this department vehicle that *I* couldn't even get. Then you go and personally select a nurse!"

Gail looked to the station and the parking lot adjacent to it. Everything was still in that moment. "Do you have a minute?" She gestured to the lot.

Rob nodded. "Sure."

She veered into a spot that faced the firehouse and shut the ignition. "I don't quite know what Megan shares and doesn't share with you about us—about me—but…" Gail stared out the windshield at the bright red garage. "That big ole door always reminds me of Christmas."

Her voice carried the story as it replayed: a piercing bell suddenly ringing, followed by the intercom, "Santa Claus is on the roof! Attention all—Santa is on the firehouse roof!"

Roaring cheers from the children echoed throughout the apparatus floor. Gail stood around as families filed outside. Megan checked the clock, then took Gail's hand. "Follow me."

They joined the herd, spilling onto the street where firefighters had the road blocked off. Red lights swirled as everyone gathered in front of the rigs.

"Ho, ho, ho!" laughed Santa from above.

Gail looked up, then turned to Megan. "Where are Trevor and Kenny?"

"Up front. Rob always makes sure they have the best spot," Meg said and raised her cell phone for pictures.

Jay-Jay, dressed in his bunker gear and a holiday elf hat, maneuvered the long neck of a tower ladder by the controls in the bucket. As the machine inched upward, another alarm sounded, this time indicating a 9-1-1 emergency.

"Oh no, not now," Gail muttered.

Megan gasped. "What the hell?"

After Santa was lowered and hauled inside the truck, he got on the engine's loudspeaker while the other firefighters fumbled into it. "Be back in a few, kids. Ho, ho, ho and hang tight."

Gail surveyed the crowd, then locked eyes with Megan. "Now what?"

"I have an idea," Meg said and smiled. "It's showtime!"

Gail felt sudden heat in both cheeks. "I don't know where the—"

Megan raised a palm. "Erin knows." She whistled the distinct two-fingers-in-mouth Brooklyn whistle.

Erin's head jerked in their direction and promptly headed across the street. "What's up?"

"Where's the Mrs. Claus outfit?"

Erin's grin widened. "It's up in the locker next to Jay-Jay's. Number 54. He put it there so it would be easy to find."

"Nuh-uh, no way. I told you that gig's long gone for me." Gail jammed her hands into each coat pocket.

"Nonsense." Megan turned on a heel. "Tame the masses, Er, we'll be back in a jiff."

Megan gripped Gail's arm and escorted her back into the firehouse. "Man, this is going to be epic."

"For who?" Gail said, lagging.

She sensed Megan's disregard moving ahead to the line of metal lockers, reading the numbers on them until she stopped and flung one open. "Got it!"

Gail hesitated. "Why don't I dress you? I'm nothing but a defeated old hag, but you—you're still optimistic and young."

Megan hunted through the garments and rushed over

with a mound of tulle-like material. "Nice try."

Gail flashed Meg the stink-eye and then undressed. "Fine. Just go easy."

Together, they transformed Gail through the bulk and fluff. They stood beside a mirror when Gail caught her own reflection; the thrill of dressing up as she did with Harry to surprise the children flooded back. "Bonnet?"

"Bonnet."

Gail secured the strings. "I'm ready."

"See? You're not as defeated as you think." Megan took Gail's hand and led the way to the main entrance, then poked out the door of the station. "Attention, everybody. I just got wind that someone else from the North Pole is here."

Erin pushed a button, and the red garage door opened. "It's Mrs. Claus!" Erin shouted as Gail stepped into view.

"Mrs. Claus is here, Mrs. Claus is here!" Several kids cheeredand darted toward Gail. She exchanged warm smiles with Erin and turned to Megan. "Thank you," Gail whispered, then disappeared into the crowd.

Rob unfastened his seatbelt. "So basically, Megan is helping you rediscover your purpose since Harry died."

"Well," Gail squeezed the steering wheel of the Family Transport at the reality of what was about to be lurched from her throat. "Yes."

Chapter Seven

"I never thought it would be this hard." Leonard
took a swig from his beer and fiddled with the cardboard
coaster on the bar. "I worked my whole life, twenty-five
years in that firehouse, and now…" He paused and slung
his head. "It's like my attendance isn't required
anywhere."

"Dude, it's okay. You're not the only one."

Leonard felt Rusty's grasp on his shoulder. He
looked out the window where the ocean rumbled in and
retracted with one fluid motion. He regulated his
breathing so that it was in sync with the tide's movement.
The seaside landscape of Long Beach, Long Island,
always had a soothing effect on Leonard and so he and
his late wife, Nell, had settled there for the calm, laid-
back lifestyle it offered its inhabitants.

"It's like we're on a permanent vacation here," Nell
had said one summer evening as they rocked together on
their porch swing.

Leonard missed Nell as much as their children—one
daughter and a son—who were both away at college. His
eyes met Rusty's. "I just thought retirement would be
different," he said and kicked back the rest of his drink.

Rusty, not yet retired from the fire department,
looked at his friend, wearing a shit-eatin' grin.

"What are you so happy about?" Leonard said and
elbowed the man's side.

"Why don't you come to the firehouse once a week, say every Sunday, and cook with the guys? You know they'd love to have your fine culinary ass whip up something, anything, instead of the slop they try to make."

Leonard let out a boisterous laugh. "No way, brother. I hate cooking at the firehouse—too many chiefs and not enough Indians."

"Ah, come on," Rusty said.

Leonard hesitated, staring down the barrel of his beer.

"What else do you have going on?" Rusty looked at him and waited.

Leonard's fixated stare lingered on Rusty, knowing he was right.

"That's right. Nothing. I expect to see you in the kitchen on Sunday at the change of tours. We'll take the rig to the store for the ingredients." He finished his scotch and tossed a twenty on the bar. "See you Sunday."

Leonard watched his friend exit the pub and then ordered another round.

"So, what are you gonna make?" the bartender said, resting an elbow on the counter.

Leonard picked up his new beverage. "I'm not sure yet."

Shortly after Nell died, Leonard's family signed him up for a cooking competition hosted by the local television station. Being a longtime lover of food—and also a graduate from a top culinary school—Leonard rolled up his shirtsleeves and prepared "the most delicious lamb chops in the tristate area," according to the panel of judges. His win jump-started a second career as a quasi-celebrity chef alongside his full-time employment as a firefighter with the FDNY.

"Maybe salmon," he said as he stared blankly at the television across the room. "Grilled salmon with an herb and lemon compound butter."

The barkeep looked at him in wonderment. "It's fascinating how quickly you can think up a recipe." She snapped two fingers. "Just like that."

"This recipe actually isn't that complex, but, you see, firefighters have to make their food fast—keep it simple."

She shrugged. "It's still impressive. My idea of simple is something microwavable."

"What pairing is good with grilled salmon?" Leonard said, his eyes still focused on the flat-screen.

"Pinot Noir."

He cracked a smile. "See? It's all about what you're into."

Her dimples deepened as she swiped the wooden surface with a wet rag. "Touché."

Chapter Eight

The timer on the oven sounded as Erin struggled to open a can of corn with an old handheld. "Come on, you little pest!"

Jay-Jay walked in and went to the sink. "What's the matter, sugarplum?"

"I can't get to any of our stuff." Erin held up the metal contraption. "So, I have to use this thing I found in one of the drawers. It's probably my mom's from 1993."

"Give yourself a break. We're just getting settled here. Don't go crazy with a fancy dinner when most of our kitchen is still in boxes."

She ignored him and secured a potholder from one of the crates on the floor, then whisked open the oven and pulled the roasted vegetables from the heat. Everything was burnt. "Shit. Shit, shit, shit!" The oven door slammed. "I wanted our first real meal to be nice. Is that too much to ask?" She threw the oven mitt and hunched over the charred medley, the smell of overdone food triggering a memory of Mother. The woman hated to cook but did it diligently in this very space, day in and day out, for years. Occasionally, Mom was proud of herself; however, when Dad's temper flared, full plates were thrown.

Erin stopped and glimpsed at the wall that hamburger meat once slid down, then glanced at the doorway where Mama had fled. She focused again on

Jelani; there was no way her parents' messed-up relationship was going to cloud what they had worked so hard at establishing.

"Pizza?" Erin said, forging optimism.

Jay-Jay slid his thumbs into the belt loops of her jeans. "Perfect."

His touch sent a tingle up her spine.

He pressed gently against the counter. "I see you fighting your past to be here. It's challenging, I get it. But, you're doing a wonderful job. Don't lose sight of that." He planted kisses on her nose, mouth, then chin. "I love you, Erin Harper."

Erin combed through Jay-Jay's high-skin fade, concentrating on the milky texture of his fresh cut, and reflected on how they ended up here—literally and figuratively—in the first place. Between the house that she'd always considered anything but a dream and their multiple efforts at conceiving, which required numerous medical interventions that failed, the term "best-laid plans" was a never-ending kerfuffle.

She closed her eyes and recounted when they were free-spirited college kids, thinking of how simple life had been when the only worries were finals or ten-page papers. It's that period in their lives that she wished could've been bottled and kept forever.

"I love you too," Erin said, nerves aflutter, as she focused on Jay-Jay and took in the treasured details of his remarkably straight nose, smooth skin, the overall masculine quality of thedeepened lines between his large hazel eyes.

Two birds began to sing in the reddening Norway Maple outside the kitchen window. Erin craned around, watching as they pecked and danced along a limb.

"And we can most certainly make time for you to birdwatch," Jay-Jay said. "You know, revisit the more positive times of your youth."

A keen interest in birds emerged one summer as a child. Mother had enrolled her in a nature class at the bird sanctuary across the street from the house. Erin fell in love with observing the different species and became an avid birdwatcher, journaling every find, which later led to a career in teaching ornithology.

"Geez, I haven't done that in this place in years." She turned back to Jelani and knuckled his shoulder. "That's an excellent idea. I'm going to look for my old notebooks and, on my next day off, I'm going on an outing."

"You got it, boss." He gave a mock salute and then left the kitchen.

Erin grabbed the phone and ordered a pizza with extra cheese. When the call ended, the birds began tweeting loudly. "Hello. I used to watch your parents and grandparents. Maybe even your great-grandparents. I can't wait to find out." She poked the glass, then spun around.

Adamant on making their start there a fresh one, Erin went to one of the boxes across the room where their wedding china was and unpacked a few pieces for the dining room table; the finishing touches were their personalized flutes. She then dashed into the kitchen toward the fridge, hoping there was some alcohol inside to fill their glasses. On the inner shelf of the otherwise barren refrigerator was the unopened bottle of Moet from their wedding night. "First, birding. Now, champagne and pizza? It's like that man and I share the same brain sometimes," Erin said and reached for it. "Hey, maybe we'll even have sex later."

****

Erin and Megan always joked that after they became wives, the bedroom was never feast, rather all famine.

Not tonight, Erin thought as Jay-Jay rolled off the bed and slipped on his Calvins. She lay still, feeling sexed yet hoping fornication was more than just an orgasm. Even with cystic ovaries and a uterus lined with fibroids, there was hope.

"Tired?" Jay-Jay asked, crawling back to Erin's side.

"Kind of. It's been quite a day."

"Don't worry about this house. Like I said, we'll make it a home. *Our* home."

In addition to being a fireman, Jay-Jay owned a contracting business, Interior Attack Inc., a real bonus for acquiring the place since it was bigger than anything they could have ever afforded, particularly in this part of town. With no mortgage, having all their friends nearby, and in the event they did have children—now residing in a top-rated school district—Erin knew Jay-Jay was determined to change up the property by ridding it of old ghosts through renovations. Although no one was sure Jay or anyone could do it, she had to let him at least try.

Erin nuzzled his neck and inhaled deeply, taking in his scent. "I'm not worried. We're working on our growing family. That's all that matters."

"Hey, if it happens, it happens."

"Unless." Erin circled a finger around his chest hair.

"Easy, kiddo. Those two tries with IVF really set us back. Not to mention how they treated us like science projects with calendars, kits, thermometers, apps, and whatever the hell else we did before that. I'm pretty sure

God was trying to tell us something."

"Pretty please? I really think it'll take this time. I can feel it."

"Focus on your career. It's thriving. And now that you're back to living across from the bird sanctuary, it's like a win-win."

"Why can't I do both?"

Jay-Jay smacked his forehead. "Because it's another fifteengrand. We already spent over thirty thousand—*thirty*!"

Erin's body jerked up. "Yeah, and?"

"Newsflash…we're middle-class, Erin. We don't make that kind of money." Jay-Jay pulled away and inched upward. "Didn't we say we were going to use whatever was left of our nest egg to fix the house?"

"You mean the house I got us for *free*?" She turned and went to switch off the lamp.

"That's not fair," Jay said, reaching over and taking her hand off the light.

"What's not fair is that I can't get pregnant like every other woman." Pouting, a heavy, exasperated sigh escaped her lips.

"You're right. That part is absolutely unfair. But, you have to understand that there's no guarantee IVF will work now or, or *ever*! And what if you're sick again like the last time—"

"Don't talk to me about the last time. I miscarried after only a few days. It doesn't count. I deserve a do-over."

"That was the do-over!"

Erin snatched the covers and flipped onto her belly, this time shutting the light. She was strong-willed but also as fragile as blown glass when it came to babies.

Chapter Nine

"The children will be delighted to see you," said Mrs. Baxter, Megan's principal. "I'd say call me Shelly, but..." She glanced over a shoulder and batted her lashes.

"No, no. Mrs. Baxter it is." Rob contained his firefighting equipment as he carried it up the steep, narrow hundred-year-old steps of the elementary school. The metal clamps clipped to his bunker coat clanked while the bulky duffel bag, fire extinguisher, and other tools to show the kids dangled from him.

"We're almost there," Mrs. Baxter said, voice airy and an octave lower.

"No problem." Rob transferred the bag's strap to his other shoulder without skipping a beat.

Through the corridor and around a bend, they entered Megan's classroom. It was the only one sporting white curtains with embroidered apples on them, window treatments different from the brown plastic shades that covered the other classroom casements. There were colorful tablecloths atop circular work tables and bright bean bag chairs instead of regular ones, artwork on equally cheery bulletin boards, Clorox-cleaned desks, and an organized library where the spines of the books lined the shelves like soldiers. The real topper was the string of twinkling white lights around the chalkboard.

"The children will be here in a minute. They're on their way back from the gymnasium," Mrs. Baxter said. "But feel free to set up wherever you like. The substitute will help you with whatever you need."

"My wife has quite the eye for interior design," Rob said, gesturing at the workspace. "And everyone's friendly. I can see why one would want to return. Coming here never gets old."

"I appreciate that, Mr. Dunham. And please know that we adore Megan and wish her a speedy recovery."

The sudden quiver of the principal's words caused Rob to look her way. He'd always overheard from the other wives how difficult she was, but that was something he was yet to witness.

Mrs. Baxter yanked a tissue from a nearby box and blew hard into it. "Pardon me. I do that a lot these days. It's so embarrassing."

"What? Clean your nose?"

They both laughed, which caused the principal to cry some more.

"It's okay. I find myself doing it in unexpected places too," Rob said.

Mrs. Baxter snagged another Kleenex from the holder and held it out.

"Thanks." Rob took it and tucked it into his shirt pocket. "I'll put it in here for safekeeping."

"Ah, well." Mrs. Baxter glanced at the clock. "Enjoy your visit, Mr. Dunham. I had better get back to the main office. I've got a meeting in five."

Once he was alone, Rob put his duffel on the area rug under the windows and walked to Megan's desk. Neatly arranged along the edge of the workstation were four pictures: their wedding photo, one of their two boys playing soccer, the class on picture day, and one of Megan and Erin squished on Gail's lap last Christmas.

Rob picked up the holiday photograph and inspected each woman's facial expression; how wide open their mouths were while their eyelids were clenched. He imagined the pre-snapshot jousting and the hardy laughter that ensued and choked back his tears with a chortle.

He returned the frame to its place and walked over to his things. As he counted out twenty-four coloring books, his cell phone rang.

"Hey, honey." His heart flickered at the sight of Megan's face on video chat.

"How'd it go?" Megan asked, smile meek.

"I haven't started yet. The kids are in the gym, but they should be here any minute. I'm all ready for them."

He pointed the phone at the activity books and his gear. "Oh, and you really outdid yourself this year. This classroom belongs in a glossy magazine." He was about to add that Mrs. Baxter had broken into tears but decided it wouldn't do anyone any good sharing the sentiment.

"Thanks. Listen, babe, I just got word that I'm checking out of here tomorrow. Tell my students I'll be back soon, okay?" Meg's voice was audibly hoarse.

"Okay, will do. Get some rest. I love you." Rob hung up just as high-pitched voices resounded by the classroom door.

"Now, now, boys and girls. Let's settle down so that our special guest can see just how grown-up we are," said a proper-sounding lady in the entranceway.

Rob made eye contact and headed over.

"I'm Susan Rabinowitz," she said and placed a hand on his shoulder before directing attention to the class again. "I'd like everyone to say good morning to Firefighter Dunham."

"That's Mrs. Dunham's husband!" a boy at the front of the line said to the person behind him.

"Like, no-duh," the kid said and jabbed him.

The line leader elbowed the boy's mid-section and resumed his position in front of the adults.

Rob stood erect and clasped his hands together. "Ladies and gentle germs, my name is Rob Dunham— yes, Mrs. Dunham's husband." Rob looked down at the boys and gave a nod. "But you can call me Firefighter Rob."

"Does anyone know why Firefighter Rob's visit is so important?" Ms. Rabinowitz asked.

"Because Mrs. Dunham is sick," a child said.

Rob felt a pang in his heart. He shoved his hands in his pants pockets and waited with bated breath for the teacher to respond so he didn't have to.

"Well, not exactly." Mrs. Rabinowitz motioned to Rob's outfit. "But I'll give you a hint. It has to do with fighting fires."

"Oh, I know!" a girl said, hand shooting up.

"Yes, Becky."

Both Mrs. Rabinowitz and Rob stood quiet.

"It's because October is fire safety month."

Rob released a burst of air. "Correct-o'-mondo! Now, if you'd all sit on the carpet, one at a time, then I can show you some really cool stuff."

Chapter Ten

The motor of the brand-new Harley, a Street Bob with a Hard Candy Custom paint job in Apple Red Flake, grumbled. Deirdre squeezed the handlebars just above the gas tank where the New York City Fire Department's Maltese cross symbol and the digits 343, the number of firefighters who died in the line of duty on September 11, 2001, were engraved in the middle.

Deirdre remembered how fascinated, as a young girl, she was with firefighting. The black bunker gear and gleaming red trucks were alluring, but it was more about the brotherhood, the true camaraderie among the men that made it appealing. Her obsession with motorcycles boiled down to a single word, which, technically, was the same verbiage that came to mind along with firefighters: badassery.

She secured the buckle of a red speckled helmet and pressed each shiny black leather boot firm to the ground to steady the seven-hundred-pound machine she'd dubbed Fiona (after alternative rock badass, Fiona Apple) to an upright position. Deirdre knew Fiona owned her, not the other way around, having witnessed one too many accident victims succumb to their wounds during rotations in the ER. She swung a heel back, hiked up the kickstand, and shifted into gear, ready to leave the neighborhood.

This. Deirdre pumped the gas. The freedom of the

open road consumed her mind, body, and lungs, as well as the long, brown hair that flapped like an American flag in the wind. She continued to Randall's Island to join Cliff for Family Day, an event for his recruits at the fire academy. It was the first time he ever invited anyone. She was initially going to accept the overtime at work, knowing better than to expect much of his invitation, but decided to go last minute because, hey, why not?

She pulled into a parking space and locked up the bike as light rain started to shower down. "Ugh. Is New York the new Seattle?"

She weaseled through the crowd toward the rows of seats. Cliff's mom was somewhere in the masses, but Deirdre didn't bother looking.

"Please rise," a man in a flashy navy-blue uniform said.

Everyone silenced as they scrambled to stand. Deirdre scurried to an empty chair and joined in the reciting of the Pledge of Allegiance. Goosebumps sprouted on both forearms; the anticipation of what was to come consumed her.

She sat again and crossed one long leather-clad leg over the other and watched intensely as various politicians spoke about different things. From behind the small makeshift stage, a loud voice blared over a bullhorn, signaling the audience's attention to the tall building adjacent to them. A man sporting fire gear from head to toe started repelling from the structure. Deirdre quickly raised a hand to her perfectly arched brow, cupping it to block the hazy sun that poked through the breaking clouds, and read the last name written in yellow at the bottom of the man's bunker coat: BAXTER.

"That's him!" Deirdre squeaked, her sensitive green

eyes fixated on Cliff.

Several yards of rope constructed into a bowline harnessed Cliff Baxter's lean body as he worked his way downward. Deirdre stared at his butt while he did this. All the women did. And who could blame them? The rope he was perched on framed his undercarriage just so.

Cliff's students started down the building, cheered by the onlookers. Deirdre clapped along, feeling lucky in this moment that she was the one dating the lead showstopper, a brave New York City fireman.

Other new firefighters began operating a tower ladder, dousing a fire that roared out of the upper floor windows. There was glass, smoke, sirens.

When the demonstration ended, the audience dissipated, and Deirdre saw Cliff standing with his mother. She walked to them with a smile but was greeted with eye rolls from Mrs. Baxter. Deirdre bit the inside of her cheek and looked away. *Wretched woman.*

Cliff's school principal mom never liked that Deirdre was a biker, but it was more than that. She was certain Deirdre was to blame for Cliff's decision to drop out of med school to run into burning buildings for a living. The woman also believed Deirdre, too, settled by becoming a nurse instead of a surgeon. The real clincher, though, was the deep disdain about Deirdre being adopted; she'd once said in a heated argument that still makes Deirdre cringe: "You don't *really* know your roots now, do you?"

"Hey, sexy," Cliff said, his lips tickling Deirdre's ear. He handed her his cell phone. "Can you take a pic of us?"

Cliff draped his arms around his mother. Shelly wore a wintry smile, so Deirdre snapped the photo, purposely leaving his mother out, and handed the phone to Cliff.

He returned it to his jacket pocket without looking at the image. "Thank you so much for coming," he said and turned to his mother. "Deirdre has work in a little while, so we're heading home." He kissed his mom on the nose.

The penciled eyebrows on the old woman formed a set of McDonald's arches. "You're not riding on that death trap she calls transportation, are you?"

Cliff petted her head. "Mother, please. I'm a big boy." He laughed and looked to Deirdre. "Ready?"

"More than ever." Deirdre slipped a hand in his, acknowledged Shelly Baxter in jest, and did an about-face on a boot heel.

****

Deirdre walked the floor with Megan's discharge papers in search of Dr. Kelleher. When she turned the corner, he was standing alongside Megan, who was wobbling toward a wheelchair.

"What are we doing?" Deirdre asked, rushing to them. "Her energy is stagnant. She's not bouncing back like the others."

He settled Megan and pulled Deirdre to the side. "We need the bed. It's been almost a week, well over the allotted recoup time. Vitals are stable. She just needs to increase food intake, which she'll be doing *at home*."

Deirdre glanced at Megan, who was adjusting the droop in her blouse, wanting nothing more than for Meg to go home, but was grossly aware of the harm in it. She clutched the paperwork and went over. "You sure you're okay to leave, my friend?"

Megan shot up a thumb. "I'm fine. A-okay."

Her response was more buoyant than Deirdre had expected, which caused unease. *Maybe she really is fine.* Deirdre knelt anyway and scribbled on Megan's copy of the papers. "If you need anything, call me. Please?"

Megan squeezed the notes. "I will. No one understands my medical needs like you do."

Rob approached the women and hovered over them. "What's doing, ladies?"

"Oh, and I gave this fine gentleman here specific instructions from dispensingmeds to pillow fluffing. I've even included a recipe for homemade buttermilk biscuits. Doctor's orders." Deirdre winked up at Rob and tapped Megan's knee.

"God reunited us for a reason," Megan said and removed the rosary. "I know you're not one for religion, but you sure are one for friendship. I want you to have this."

Deirdre was about to decline the offering as it seemed the only material possession of personal value to Megan during the hospital stay but then refrained. It was polite to accept a gift so intimate.

Deirdre bowed. Megan maneuvered the beads and tucked them under the collar of Deirdre's scrubs. "Nobody needs to know they're there. Just you."

Rob grabbed the handles of Megan's chair and released the brake. "Ready?"

"Ready," Megan declared.

Deirdre stood and stared as they wheeled down the hall toward the elevator.

****

On dinner break, Deirdre stowed her uniform inside a locker and fled the grounds. The traffic downtown was light, and a parking space in front of the Jesus store freed

58

up. She steered Fiona into the lone spot. Statues and bibles decorated the shop's windows. *Shit. I don't know about this.* Someone appeared in the glass and nodded. "Well, now I have no choice."

Deirdre locked up the bike, even though she doubted anyone would steal anything in front of a religious business. But then again, this was New York. She made it to the door and tried to enter quietly until the bell dangling above wailed, alerting the shopkeeper and every customer inside the place. Deirdre gave a sheepish wave to the patrons and walked straight to a case where various relics were on display.

"Can I help you?" an elderly man asked, shuffling over.

"Uh, yeah. I mean, yes. Yes." She freed Megan's rosary from beneath the heavy leather jacket. "I need a replica of this."

The man pulled his reading glasses from the top of his salt-and-pepper hair and touched the beads around Deirdre's neck gingerly. "Mother-of-pearl," he said. "Follow me."

Deirdre followed him down an aisle filled with beautiful white candles of varying sizes, making a mental note to come back to this area to buy several for the fireplace that no longer worked in the apartment.

In the far corner of the store were several swiveling racks of rosaries. The man found a mother-of-pearl similar to the one Megan gave her. Deirdre examined it, a surge of connection pulsating at the sudden thought of her former patient Salvatore and his sister Evie.

"Would you be interested in a keepsake box?"

Deirdre startled back to the present. "Sure."

He led the way to a shelf of trinket boxes. Deirdre

picked a little silver heart-shaped container.

"I can engrave it for you if you'd like," the man said.

She pondered it for a moment. "Yes. Please write, 'Friendship is our religion.'"

Chapter Eleven

Megan eyed Rob, amused as he rigorously fluffed a pillow and placed it beside his, swatting it and making it plump. He then set a glass of water on the nightstand and took out four colorful pills from their cases, lining them up neatly, and then put a snack—a chocolate chip granola bar—next to them. As he reread Deirdre's instructions and reviewed the placement of things, Megan eased herself away from the doorframe, carefully placing the cane on the carpeted runner so that he couldn't hear her.

In the living room, Megan hobbled to the coffee table where her mug was and picked it up. The television was on, but the boys were busy playing with their Matchbox cars. "You guys sure are best friends," she said, beaming down at them.

"Mommy, can you play with us?" Trevor's oversized lashes flapped like silky outstretched wings.

The puppy-dog cuteness of his stare motivated her. "Sure, buddy. Anything for you."

She sipped the Chai, successfully returned it to the table with minimal splashing, then gripped the arm of the couch and got to the floor.

Kenny passed over a fire engine. "Mama, truck."

She kissed his forehead. "Yes, firetruck. Woo, woo!"

The boys laughed and made siren sounds with her.

"Look at you," Rob announced, walking over. He knelt and gave Megan's earlobe a nibble.

"That tickles." She tucked her chin, then lifted a weak finger to his cheek. "I'm glad I'm home."

"Me too," he said and turned to their sons. "All right, you guys. It's time for bed. More playtime with Mom tomorrow." He gathered the toys and walked them to their room.

When the recitation of prayers came from down the hall, Megan reached for the cane and mustered to a standing position. With hard concentration, she inched forward, one hand clutching the handle while the other held the empty cup. Step by step, Meg heaved to the kitchen sink, but the walking stick caught her ankle. Suddenly, there was a burst of white from behind each eyelid, followed by a sting to the nose. A warm, wet sensation trickled out.

"Meg?" Rob said in a loud whisper.

"O-over here." Megan's sandpaper-like garble barely scraped the linoleum.

He ran to the kitchen. "What the?"

She looked up at him, both nostrils throbbing and already swollen. "Don't. I don't need a lecture right now. I'm thirty-four. I should be able to put my own dirty goddamn teacup in its goddamn place."

"You have to stop this." He took Megan into his arms. "Yes, you're thirty-four, but you have cancer. The battle will never be won if you don't give yourself a fighting chance to heal." He pushed back the lengthy pieces of the headscarf. "You're a modern-day Wonder Woman. *My* Wonder Woman. Stop feeling like there's something to prove. Anyone who's ever known you knows you're a marvel."

He helped Meg balance to a standing position and yanked at the paper towel roll. In one swift motion, he flipped on the faucet with his elbow and saturated the napkins. He gently placed them under her nose and together they eased to the bedroom.

"You went through all this trouble for me," Megan said, eyes fixed on the nightstand, remembering the care he took setting it up.

Rob tugged at his hair. "Yeah. Is it all right?"

"It's perfect." Meg took the pills and chased them down with water. "All I need is a set of rosary beads, and this arrangement is complete."

"Wait. Where's yours?" Rob yanked open the end table drawer.

"I need to buy a new one." She pulled out the cell phone from her robe pocket. There was a voicemail from Erin, but before returning that call, Deirdre popped into mind.

"Sooo, how's your first night home?" Deirdre said over the receiver.

"I have to say, my firefighter has truly come to my rescue." Megan looked longingly at Rob, who was changing out of his clothes; a longing to be breathless, longing to be naked, longing to be held tight in a fit of ecstasy. But, physically, it was not possible. Meg dabbed at each watering eye with the bloodstained tissues.

"Oh, so good to hear!" Deirdre said.

Megan overheard the scratchy sound of Scotch tape and the crinkling of wrapping paper. "What are you doing?"

"Listen, if it isn't too much trouble, I'd like to stop by your house tomorrow. I have something for you, and it's my only day off this week."

Megan's face suddenly brightened; the giddiness of having a new best friend was the equivalent of having a new boyfriend. "Gosh, yes. I'd love to see you."

"I can be there by one. That okay?"

"Perfect." Megan ended the call and anxiously turned to Rob. "Deirdre is coming for a visit tomorrow. Do you mind?"

He crawled into bed, smiling. "Nope, not at all."

****

After a busy morning, Megan retreated to the bedroom to get dressed. Outfits these days consisted of sweaters and leggings, clothes that were easy to put on and take off without snaps, buttons, or zippers.

In the bathroom mirror, Meg examined the nose area, but it wasn't bruised. She set out some cosmetics and, ignoring the tremors of her fingers, began applying makeup. The mascara wand wavered at the lash line, immediately causing black smudges all over the eyelid; the other one didn't come out any better.

Rob wedged his head in. "Need help?"

Megan turned to him, mortified. "Get out!"

Rob jerked away and shut the door.

Megan looked in the mirror. "My face is the only pretty thing left. Why can't He at least give me that?" She threw the mascara wand and pushed everything else into the wastebasket beside the counter.

"Can I please come in?" Rob said from behind the door.

"Leave me alone."

"You don't mean that." Rob entered and flipped up the lock.

"Look at me! I'm a goddamn nightmare. The walking *zombie* dead."

64

"No. You're very much alive," he said, sitting on the tiled floor and pulling Meg onto his lap. "And you're very much my Megan. My gorgeous, beautiful wife."

"Stop the nonsense. I'm a horror, a freak show."

"Well, I'll be honest," he said and swiped a thumb under the smudging. "I can't ignore this creepy black goop."

They laughed at the mess.

"Come on. Let's wash it off and start again," Rob said.

They helped each other up.

"Forget mascara. Can you do just my lips instead?" Megan said and situated herself on the closed toilet seat.

"Uh, sure." He retrieved the makeup from the garbage pail and arranged the cosmetics on the counter again. "This one?" He picked up the only tube of lipstick and waved it.

Megan nodded as he flicked off the cover and fiddled with the mechanism that made it move up and down.

"Stop, you'll break it!"

"All right, all right, calm your hormones." He raised it just a little and leaned into her.

Megan started giggling. "Firefighter Dunham's putting out my makeup emergency."

"Ha, ha. Now, sit still," he said, steadying his hand.

Megan puckered and tried not to move. The cold, smooth stick touched the bottom of her lip. Rob's tongue poked from the corner of his mouth as he focused, which caused Meg to belt out another laugh.

"Stay still!"

"Okay, okay." She sat upright again and got quiet.

When he finished, he secured the headscarf, an eye-catching red sequin number. "This one is nice," he said, tying a knot.

They both faced the mirror, and Megan smiled. "I thought so too."

The sleek black turtleneck camouflaged a non-existent bust, and the matching leggings hung daintily on her frame. She grinned at Rob and then slid into a pair of red Tory Burch flats. "It's all in how you accessorize."

"I'll make a note of it," he said, shaking his head, and exited the bathroom.

****

The rumble of a motorcycle shook the windows of the Dunham residence.

"Deirdre's here," Megan announced and got up from the kitchen table.

Trevor whizzed by to the front door yelling, "Awesome! Motorcycles are so cool!" as little Kenny ran behind, cheering.

"Where's your mommy, kiddos?" Deirdre said, shutting down the bike and leaning over.

"Right there." Trevor aimed a thumb over his shoulder. "Can I sit with you?"

Deirdre tapped the gas tank and then picked him up.

"Me too. Me too!" Kenny tugged on a pant leg.

"One at a time, boys," Megan said, walking slowly toward them.

Deirdre looked up and smiled. "It's okay. It's cooler than a pony. I get it."

Trevor wriggled his head into the sparkly helmet as Kenny pushed the different buttons and gears on the handlebars.

"Beautiful wheels," Rob said, joining them at the curb and helping Deirdre settle the children back on the

66

ground.

"You ride?" Deirdre asked, dismounting.

"Used to. Sold the bike after having these two." He lightly hip-checked Trevor.

"I wish he never gave it up," Megan chimed.

Deirdre and Rob looked at her.

"What? I love motorcycles. Firefighting wasn't the only thing that attracted me to you," Megan said and nudged him with the walking stick.

Rob's face turned crimson. "You two ladies have fun. See you later." He waved the boys inside.

"Now it's my turn," Megan said, hobbling to the twinkling apple-colored machine.

"Um."

"Just kidding, silly. But, I definitely want a ride on the back of this bitch when I'm better." Meg chucked a set of car keys at Deirdre and pointed to a blue Volvo station wagon parked near some trees across the street. "Think you can take us to the diner? I'd love to buy you lunch, but I can't drive my loser cruiser yet."

Deirdre laughed. "Yeah, sure. Come on."

Megan got in the car and flipped down the visor for a peek in the mirror. "Bless Rob's soul. He applied my makeup this morning."

Deirdre steered out of Megan's neighborhood, and they headed for the mall. Meg gazed out the window, admiring the color of the sky when something dropped onto her lap.

Megan eyed the tiny box. "What's this? Did I miss something?"

Deirdre made a left into the mall parking lot. "Just open it."

With unsteady hands, Meg tore at the decorated

paper. "Oh, my God, Dee!" She held up the silver heart-shaped trinket box and read the inscription aloud: "Friendship is our religion."

Megan lifted the lid, eyes widening as the beads came out of the box. "I love everything about this."

"It's like our own version of friendship charms," Deirdre said and retrieved the rosary from under her jacket.

Megan started to cry. "You have no idea how much this means to me. I'm so incredibly happy to have you in my life again."

Deirdre shut the car as Meg worked the necklace over the sequined scarf.

"Let's order beers with our burgers," Deirdre suggested and helped Megan out of the passenger seat. "There's something I've been wanting to ask you."

"What's that?" Megan said as they strolled toward the eatery.

"Well, uh, if you don't mind my asking, who gave it to you? You know, the rosary you gave to me?"

The women entered the diner and were escorted to a secluded booth at the rear. "Two tall boys, please," Deirdre said to the waitress as they sat. "Sorry, Meg, go ahead."

Megan scooted onto the seat. "So, to answer your question, my maternal grandmother gave it to me right before I received the sacrament of Holy Communion in the second grade. G-Ma was a real nurturer. Just like you. Don't think I didn't notice that the minute you saw me, you began nurturing me. You're the only other person who has ever done that besides her."

The server put two large glasses of beer on the table. Megan picked one up and continued. "You see, I never met my birth mother."

Deirdre's mouth fell open. "I didn't know this about you in college."

"No, you didn't. We were too busy being kids in those days. And now, well...anyway"—Megan took a breath—"I was given up for adoption right after my mom had me because of her addiction to the fast life: drugs, money, and men—lots of men. My grandmother didn't even know I existed until my adoptive parents reached out to her. They wanted to make sure I knew someone from my biological family, yet they wanted to keep me safe at the same time. So, instead of seeking out my mother, they chose G-Ma. I'll forever be thankful to them for doing that. Best decision they ever made."

Deirdre finally picked up the beer. "My mother passed away on the birthing table."

Megan blinked hard. "What?"

"She was an older woman who never married but always wanted a child. I was to be that child, the 'little phenomenon' through artificial insemination, according to her sister. Anyway, my mom died from excessive bleeding due to complications and the hospital's inability to secure the amount of blood needed, given the rare type she had, type O negative. My mother was a universal donor but not a receiver; O negative people can only receive their own type. Anyway, there was a shortage." Deirdre stopped and took a giant swig from the yellow fizz. "I don't know much else about what took place in the delivery room. All I know is that my birthday is a tragic reminder of my mom's death, not the celebration of my entrance into this world. I went from 'little phenomenon' to enfant terrible in a matter of minutes."

"Geez. No wonder you have a disdain for God. I

think I would too." Megan eyed the burger that was put in front of her, then picked it up and took a bite as Deirdre continued.

"I was supposed to become a doctor at first. That was my aspiration when I was old enough to understand all the stories my mother's sister told me about my mom. It was as if she told them to me so that I'd pursue a career in medicine. I don't know for sure if that was the true intention, but that's the message I got. Anyway, somewhere along the med school line though, I felt compelled to experience more in life than biochemistry, anatomy, and books. I knew medicine was a field I needed to be in, but I didn't want to void myself of a life altogether, so I volunteered in a hospital to learn more about various employment opportunities around the place and finally settled on a position that suited my needs. I discovered being a nurse was satisfying. It's a role that's incredibly important that still provides the autonomy I felt I needed."

Megan swallowed and put down the food. "How'd you meet your mother's sister?"

Deirdre felt Megan's gaze on her. "Aunt Jenny adopted me right after my mother was pronounced dead and raised me with my Uncle Greg."

"And how did you end up in Oncology?"

"Cancer tripped and fell on my aunt. Seeing her body wilt was horrifying, but watching it heal was nothing short of miraculous. It's because of applied science and medicinal therapies that there was a successful second chance. Aunt Jenny overcame the disease and is a survivor. Like you," Deirdre said and smiled. "And here I am, a nurse in Oncology, and here you are—living proof that what my team and I do is worthwhile."

Megan plucked at the mound of fries beside the hamburger, the new rosary glistening prominently above them. "Well, I wouldn't say I'm a survivor just yet, but I'll heed that optimism of yours."

Chapter Twelve

Erin craned around to find Jay-Jay still fast asleep; his arms and legs splayed out as his belly raised and descended like a small movable mountain. She twisted the other way to check the time. *8:02? Huh. That's weird.* Jay had a habit of getting them up at the ungodly hour of five, whether he had work or not.

Erin unfurled from a fetal position and crept out of bed as he let out a light snore. She tiptoed to the window to see which feathery friends were perched in the trees throughout the yard; the fall season most exciting for an ornithologist, but then closed the curtain and went to what was, at least for the moment, their spare room. The laptop was dead in one of the many boxes strewn about, but she took it anyway and settled near an outlet so it could charge while in use.

"All fertility options for getting and staying pregnant," Erin typed into the search engine and jabbed the return key.

The last time Erin tried to get a handle on her reproductive system with counsel, the doctor prescribed Clomid, an oral medication that was supposed to help conceive but didn't. Following that were multiple rounds of fertility treatments: injectables called Lupron that were inserted into the upper thigh, coupled with a cocktail of Follistim and Menopur, which was manually injected into the stomach. These meds not only took over the cabinet and fridge, but they also consumed her life. Then it finally happened.

"Congratulations, Erin, you're pregnant," the specialist said, holding up the test results.

"Oh, my God. Babe! I could really get pregnant!" Erin boasted to Jay-Jay, who stood cautious beside the examining table while wax paper crinkled from her fit of joy.

Like a freight train barreling full-steam ahead, there were baby registries and nursery planning, but, after a few short weeks, and what Erin later explained to Megan and Gail as "a sudden urgency to 'go' with cramping similar to the worst period imaginable," she miscarried.

At first, when talks of trying again began, Jay-Jay thought her verbiage was a form of grievance, that she was still in shock over the death of their fetus. His assumption wasn't entirely accurate. Soon after the whole in vitro experience, the grief mutated from utterly unbearable to mildly unbearable, and then to a constantly dwelling on the capability of *getting* pregnant, which birthed a belief in science and all its greatness, even if conception was short-lived and from a petri dish. This left Jay-Jay to mourn on his own, occasionally talking to the guys in the firehouse but ultimately coping with things solo. When he realized Erin was serious about another go at it, he reluctantly went through the motions of their next (very unsexy) attempt. Five days after the second procedure was performed, there was another miscarriage. That was the last straw for him.

"Yes, you're getting pregnant, but you're not *staying* that way," he said.

Erin detested his sentiment and was determined to find something—anything—that was more effective for enduring a full-term pregnancy.

"Assisted hatching?" Erin muttered, leaning into the computer screen. "What in the world is that?"

Her eyes moved to and fro like a pendulum over an article from *Scientific American*. The research was wordy, but the words "assisted hatching" were something they hadn't yet encountered in their fertility journey. Erin gripped the sides of the laptop, waves of excitement flooding her gut. There was no mention of cost, but as far as finances were concerned, there'd be a way. *I think this is it!*

She raised both arms in the air and let out a squeal, ignoring the giant box that toppled over from a fist crashing into it, then scanned the room in a dreamy haze, imagining a nursery. *Maybe we'll paint it a pale yellow.* An old office chair suddenly snagged her attention. *That was Dad's.* This room had been his workspace. Immediately, Erin was eight again and watching Dad yell at Mom. From near the doorway, her younger self observed Mother's attempt to push by Father, which led to a hard slap. The sound of his hand on Mom's cheek had jolted Erin; she'd never known why they were fighting.

Erin gasped, snapping out of the memory. "No, not here. I can't have a baby sleep in here." The computer slid to the floor as she went to the front door, where the car keys dangled on a hook.

****

Gail's obscenely loud doorbell startled the morning crickets. Still, Erin remained on the porch expectantly.

"Ugh. Okay, okay," Erin heard from behind the scarlet barrier. There was a thud followed by the crank of metal releasing.

"You all right?" Gail asked, tying bathrobe strings together.

The dewy late-September air swirled between them, sending a chill through Erin's body. "Yeah, yeah, I'm fine. I'm just trying to get used to that house," she said, rubbing both arms to avert the cold. "Can we go for coffee?"

Gail looked down at herself. "Um, yeah. Once I get changed."

Erin looked down at her own garb of oversized sweats and laughed. "Eh, changing's overrated."

"Not for me. Come in." Gail spun on a slipper and started up the stairs.

"I hear there's a new Internet café that just opened on Seventh. Have you been to it yet?" Erin called from the foyer.

"No." Gail's voice echoed from the second floor. "Let's try it out. I'll drive."

****

In the coffee shop, Erin led the way to the digital billboard-sized menu. "Have any idea what you want?"

"What about holy water?"

Erin eyed Gail like she was nuts.

"For your house," Gail continued. "You know, to bless it. Get those bad spirits out."

Erin blinked and turned back to the menu.

"Okay, then. A large decaf hazelnut, per favore."

"Holy water, huh?" Erin said. "That's actually doable."

"It's worth a shot." Gail trailed off to a vacant computer. She gave the mouse a little jiggle, changing the screen from black to a bright blue welcome, and signed into an email account.

"Anything good?" Erin settled the hot drinks and eased into the adjacent seat.

Gail reached for the coffee. "I wish."

"Why? Waiting for something in particular?"

Gail pulled off the lid and watched the steam escape. "Wouldn't it be nice to get a message from a long-lost friend or a lover from eons ago? You know, something to spice life up a bit?"

Erin's eyes widened. "Is that what you want?"

Gail slouched in the chair. "Maybe meeting someone will help me stop dwelling on Harry. I don't know. Does that even make sense?"

"Of course it does. You're only sixty. What if you live 'til you're a hundred? What are you supposed to do—be alone for the next forty years?"

"I'm sixty-two," Gail said and tasted the drink. "Seriously, though. Being a widow is quite boring. So much quiet and definitely too much downtime."

"Right now, with the craziness of moving, I crave any alone time, but I can totally relate. When everything around me is finally still, I get jittery within minutes." Erin lapped the froth of her beverage.

Gail glanced into the cup. "I'm so over the lonely. My wine fridge needs a Budweiser, know what I mean?"

Latte squirted out of Erin's mouth. "Oh. My. God. That is the funniest thing I've ever heard you say!"

Since Harry's passing, wine had been the only remedy for sleepless nights. Gail purchased a tiny refrigerator for her bedroom for convenience...and maybe as a bit of a luxury since the kitchen was downstairs on the main floor, a place too far to venture to at night.

Gail perked up. "Actually, a Bud Light. Someone

toned. Healthy. Someone masculine, like Harry was."

Erin shook her head, still cackling and hacking, as she dabbed her sweatpants with a mound of napkins.

"What? You don't think this fine wine deserves that?" Gail said.

Erin licked her fingertip and touched Gail's leg, retracting as if it were on fire. "You're sizzlin' girlfriend! Of course you deserve it."

They laughed and continued with Gail's emails, reading up on some of the latest shoe sales and online coupons sent to her.

"Hey, listen, before we head home, I need to stop at the pharmacy," Erin said and stood.

"What for?"

"Since my doctor isn't in yet, I wanted to ask the pharmacist about a different procedure. It's like IVF, but not."

Gail raised a brow. "Again?"

"Well, yeah." The corners of Erin's mouth turned up. "*This* is what'll make me happy, not some stupid jinxed house."

Gail pulled on her coat and took out her keys. "What did Jay-Jay say?"

"It doesn't matter what Jay-Jay said. I got him a house for free." Erin huffed and abruptly exited the café.

Gail clicked the car's key fob from behind, and Erin got in. Neither of them uttered a word the entire way to the drugstore.

In the parking lot, Gail turned off the ignition and began examining her cuticles. "I'll wait here."

"Suit yourself."

Erin flung open the door, leaped out, and marched away. In the store, she weaved through the aisles to get to the pharmacy at the rear. "Why wouldn't it be packed?" she muttered and stood at the back of a lengthy line.

The small, frail woman in front of her turned and went to say something when suddenly she dropped to the ground.

"Ma'am?" Erin got down on her knees. "Ma'am, are you okay?" The lady didn't flinch when Erin touched her. "She's not okay." Erin looked up at the people who began to gather. "She's not okay! I need help!"

A teenager whipped out a smartphone and aimed it down at her.

"You better be dialing 9-1-1," Erin hissed, eyes darting to the kid's mother. "Either you or your little asshole spawn better get the pharmacist."

When the mother and child didn't budge, Erin jumped to her feet and fled the store. She ran to the car and swung open the door, practically ripping it off the hinges. "Come on, I need you," she said, breathless. "An elderly lady just passed out in line right in front of me. You know CPR."

Gail hopped out and raced across the lot with Erin. "What the hell happened? And, what about the pharmacy personnel? They should know CPR!"

"None of them were paying attention. Too busy counting pills and answering calls, I guess."

They entered the store and rushed to where the commotion was. "I'm not a nurse, but I know CPR," Gail said and knelt beside the sales clerk who was searching for a pulse. "Anything?"

The young man shook his head.

Gail rested an ear on the lady's chest. "Nothing."

Erin bent down and put a finger under the woman's

nose. "She's definitely not breathing."

Gail parted the woman's lips and pinched her nostrils closed. She took in some hard air before pressing her mouth to the stranger's.

Erin looked on as Gail alternated between breaths and chest compressions. The lady's body lay flat, helpless. Erin took the woman's hand in hers. "Come on, breathe," she said, stroking the warm, wrinkled hand.

"Make way, make way," someone shouted.

The onlookers parted from the circle, and two emergency medical technicians stepped in with a bag of equipment.

"She's not responding," Gail said, lifting her head.

"Thank you, miss, we'll take it from here." The EMT pressed the stethoscope to the woman's chest and checked different areas.

The other medic faced Erin. "Is this your grandmother?"

Erin unraveled her fingers from the lady's and retracted. "No, no. I don't know who she is. But she was alone when she fell."

The man's eyes drifted down to Erin's silver FDNY pendant. "That was very nice of you to keep her company like that. I'm sure the family will appreciate it." He took the purse that was lying on the ground. "Is this yours?"

"I believe it's hers."

As the paramedic unzipped it and retrieved a wallet, Erin and Gail helped each other up.

"I'm so glad I have you," Erin whispered.

"Me too, Er, me too."

They kept their eyes locked on one another for a moment, then linked arms and walked out.

"Shit, what a morning," Gail said on the drive home.

"You can say that again." Erin kept her eyes focused on the passing trees. "Guess we all could use some holy water."

Gail steered the vehicle up to the side of Erin's truck and hit the brake. "Whatcha doing for the rest of the day?"

"I desperately have to do my lesson plans." Erin sighed. "I'll call you later."

She got out and tossed her bag on the hood of the pickup as Gail turned off the road and into the garage. Erin peered inside for the keys. *Don't even.* With the flick of a wrist, she dumped out the contents of the pocketbook. No keys. She ran to the driver's side and jerked the door handle. "And you're locked. Great." She cupped her hands around her eyes and pressed against the car window. There was no sign of the keychain in the center console, on the dashboard, or on the seats. She moved to the rear window and investigated further. *You've got to be kidding me.*

Erin hurried up the walk and banged on Gail's front door. After what felt like forever, she went around to the garage and did the code on the keypad. The motorized door jerked upward, its pulleys cranking loud as they revealed Gail's white Audi parked alongside a slew of Harry's toolboxes that lined the walls. A few drawers were open, and the workshop was a bit messy as if Harry himself had been tinkering in there just a few hours ago; Gail liked having certain rooms that way.

She wriggled past Gail's Sportster, heat still emanating from the undercarriage from its recent use, and entered the house.

"Gail, it's me," Erin called as she walked by the

scanner. It was transmitting information on a fourth alarm somewhere in the Bronx at rapid-fire speed, but she didn't stop to listen as she normally would have and instead went to the kitchen. "Gail, it's me. I'm locked outta my car." Erin went to the overhead cabinet that was open and saw one of Harry's old whiskey tumblers was missing. She twisted around and went into the dining room. Sure enough, the liquor cabinet was open, a bottle of Jack Daniel's on the table next to it. Erin picked it up and looked inside. "You don't even like this stuff," she muttered, then put the mouth of it to hers and stole a sip. "But I do."

She traipsed to the radio and rested against the server. "Gail, are you in the bathroom?" She strained to hear an answer as a male dispatch relayed messages about a 10-75 to responding firefighters. It was a frantic game of verbal tennis. Erin was familiar with the lingo, understood that a 10-75 was code for active fire and that the fire personnel arriving on-scene were calling in a 10-42 Code 2, which meant that wires were down. Live electrical wires. The operator ordered a 10-47 for traffic assistance.

"If you remove yourself from the emotional part of it, listening to a scanner is similar to watching a soap opera. It's addictive," Gail once explained when Erin asked why a civilian would own the thing.

She eyed the radio and suddenly realized where Gail could be. She hightailed it to the basement, where Gail was sitting in front of the desktop with a beverage.

"There you are!" Erin exclaimed.

Gail jumped in her seat. "Of course, 'here I am!' The question is, what the fuck are you doing here scaring the shit out of me?"

"I'm so sorry," Erin said and approached her. "My car keys are missing so, technically, I never left." She peered at the computer monitor, the opening page for OurTime.com on the screen. "I am a woman seeking," she read from over Gail's shoulder.

"Never mind!" Gail jabbed the power button; a framed photo of Harry toppled off the desk. "Jesus Christ, I'm such a fool." She grabbed the picture and clutched it to her chest. "Harry, I'm so sorry. So, so sorry."

"No. Don't do this. I won't let you." Erin sat on her knees near Gail's chair to face her. "Listen, maybe you're just not ready to date yet." She reached up and swiped at Gail's silvery strands. "But one day you will be. And when you are, your conscience will be in harmony with your heart."

Gail glanced lovingly at Harry's image. "I'll never find someone like him. He knew everything, sometimes without my ever saying a word. What I was feeling, if I had a shitty day, what I was craving for dinner that night. How could someone ever fill those shoes?"

"See, that's the thing. You're not looking for a replacement because you know no one could take Harry's place. What you're seeking is companionship. There's a difference." Erin eased the frame from her and put it back on the tabletop. "We know that you're having a hard time grieving, that's why we're constantly in your face trying to keep you busy. We *must* plan a night out, like, pronto. Between my move and Megan's surgery, it's been rough, but I'll set up something."

"Wait," Gail interrupted. "We never found out about the other IVF thing."

"I grabbed some literature before everything

happened, but that was it." Erin crossed her legs and sighed. "I hate to say it, but what's another day, right?"

Gail placed a hand on top of Erin's. "Take your own advice: everything will happen in due time."

"Yeah, I guess." They sat quietly for a moment when Erin's cell phone rang. Erin took it from her belt. "It's Megan. Should I tell her to come over?"

"That's up to you. Didn't you have lesson plans to do?"

"Lessons-shmessons." Erin tapped the screen and answered. "Welcome home, bitch. Now get over here. It's girl o'clock somewhere!"

Chapter Thirteen

Deirdre steered Megan's station wagon down a beautiful tree-lined street peppered with old Victorian homes. It was a section of Brooklyn that had aged gracefully along with its occupants, who seemed to be reveling in the majestic weather of an Indian summer.

"That guy is seriously enjoying himself," Deirdre said and pointed to a mature man who was smiling while he plucked weeds. She continued people-watching as the car crawled along.

"You know, you're going about fifteen miles under the speed limit," Megan said, also looking out at the locals. "It's still Brooklyn. These people might think we're about to do a drive-by."

Deirdre pressed the gas pedal and accelerated to the house at the end of the block. "This it?" she asked, now pumping the brake.

"Yeah, pull into the driveway."

Deirdre did as she was told, then shifted the gear into park and sized up Gail's house, with its expansive wraparound porch and multi-car garage. "I've never been here before," she said, shutting down the ignition. "Nor did I know she was rich." She handed Meg the keys and exited the car.

"Gail comes from money," Megan said, planting the cane on the blacktop and hoisting herself out of the passenger seat. "But you'd never know it. If you recall, her husband, Harry, was a fireman, born and bred. They lived in that townhouse on Erin's block for most of their marriage. Being with him made her more blue-collar than us." Megan laughed and started toward the porch. "But, after their son grew up and moved out, they sold that place and bought this one."

"That's right, Harry was a firefighter," Deirdre muttered, following Meg inside.

The main foyer, with its tall cathedral ceiling and minimal furniture, was inviting. Regardless, Deirdre thought that in a place like this, one would be greeted by a lady dripping in diamonds and oversized gold pieces, yet Gail welcomed them with subtle sophistication. Deirdre took note, however, of something odd going on in the background of the space. It sounded like a walkie-talkie, but everyone was ignoring it, so she tried to do the same.

"Meg, I'm so glad you brought Deirdre along," Gail said and hurried to where Deirdre was standing.

Deirdre felt Gail's fingers slide between hers, all thoughts of being included a bit overwhelming.

"What would you like? Something fancy and fruity, or are you a beer gal?" Gail asked, leading the way to the kitchen.

"I like it all." Deirdre laughed and took a seat on one of the barstools at the center island.

While Gail grabbed a bunch of ingredients from the refrigerator, Deirdre spied Erin as she entered the room and took a seat on the opposite side of the breakfast nook. She didn't know what to make of Erin now that they were full-fledged adults. She thought her granola-meets-J. Crew style could go either way—harmless or pompous.

Erin's eyes finally met Deirdre's. She didn't reciprocate Deirdre's smile. *Maybe she's got something on her mind. Or, she's just a bitch.* Deirdre reverted her attention to Gail, who was making a fuss with the blender.

Megan walked to the women and steadied herself against the counter. "Deirdre is dating Cliff Baxter," she said to Gail over the slowing rumble of the mixer.

"Oh yeah? He's so pretty in a girly-man kind of way," Gail said. "But that mother, ugh." She poured a pink substance into a row of martini glasses.

"His mother's the worst," Deirdre said. She pinched her nose. "My Cliff is in Rescue, you know. He's oh-so-important. No one is as good a person 'cause he came out of my golden vagina—blah, blah, blah."

Gail laughed so hard she snorted. Megan tried to resist but ended up chuckling into her hand. Erin didn't react at all, seemingly unaware of the joke as she searched around in her satchel. "Deirdre, can I ask you a question?" Erin pulled out the pamphlet about assisted hatching and set it down in front of her. "What would you do if this were the only way you could have a child? I've already done IVF twice. Think this is worth a shot?"

Everyone's laughter ceased. Deirdre stared at the glossy booklet and avoided looking up. Instead, she cleared her throat awkwardly. "Uh, I'm the wrong person to ask."

"Why's that? You're a nurse."

"Yes, you're right, but I work in oncology. Fertility is not my area of expertise," Deirdre said, shifting on the seat. "'Cause, to be honest, the only thing I know about child-rearing is that I'm on the pill, and my boyfriend still wears condoms."

Erin kept her sights on Deirdre. "So, you probably think it's a waste of money. Maybe you're right. I'm thirty-five now—a used tire."

"Don't say that!" Megan said. "Don't give up. God will give you a fetus when He's ready."

"That's easy for you to say. You already have two kids. And you didn't need *His* assistance."

Ouch. Deirdre hurried the cocktail to her lips.

Erin snatched the literature and headed for the door.

"What the hell has gotten into her?" Megan said, head shaking in disapproval.

Deirdre put down the cup. "I'm sorry. I shouldn't have said anything."

"No. She asked you for your opinion, and you gave it to her. No one can hold you liable for that."

"Maybe I shouldn't have been so, you know, truthful."

Gail swooped in and refilled Deirdre's goblet. "No, no. We had a rough morning. She's just looking for advice."

Megan positioned the walking stick in front of her and began to hobble away. "If that's what Erin needs, then she's obviously not leaving. We can't let her."

"Erin, come back here," Gail shouted from over a shoulder, then faced Deirdre again. "If you don't already know, Erin's a bit sensitive," she whispered, "but with good reason. For one, she had a hard time with her parents' divorce. I think being an only child made it exceptionally difficult, but that's not fact, it's simply my opinion. What's fact is that it made her hell-bent on having a big, thriving family once she got married. But— and this is the biggest *but* of them all—she has uterine fibroids and polycystic ovary syndrome, which has caused such trouble with getting pregnant: irregular periods, poor egg quality, you name it. The doctors say she still has a chance at having a baby, though they're just speculating."

"Uterine fibroids are more common than you may think, but PCOS can be problematic." Deirdre looked down the hall at Erin. "Wow, that must be tough."

Gail craned her head. "Yeah, I'd say. But she's become obsessed with the entire fertility thing. It hasn't even been four months since the second IVF procedure, which, by the way, cost her and Jay-Jay a small fortune, and she's already talking of more. She found something online called assisted hatching or something like that, and she's clinging to it for dear life. She's afraid that the older she gets, the more likely her biological clock will conk out any minute. It's like a personal quest against time."

They hushed and focused on the women talking at the far end of the house.

"Why are you leaving?" Megan asked, approaching Erin.

"You already know why." Erin went for the doorknob, but Megan intercepted with the cane. "Being a wife, being a mother, none of it is easy. Not for me, not for you—no one." Meg lowered her voice, but Deirdre could still hear it. "We're all going through setbacks. The trick is to believe that you're okay and have some confidence."

Erin slung her head. "I hate that I have no control over this, Megan. None whatsoever."

"I know what you mean." Megan settled the walking stick in front of her. "Come on. We belong with them."

Gail put a hand on Deirdre's shoulder and swiveled

around. Deirdre winked and slurped more of the drink as Megan and Erin returned to the kitchen.

Erin plunked her satchel on the empty stool and sat beside Deirdre. "I'm sorry it's been a little too much information from someone you haven't seen in, like, forever."

Deirdre shrugged. "Don't sweat it."

Erin's smile weakened. "Man, life was so much easier when it was just a career. I miss those days sometimes—when it's just you. You must love being a free spirit. Nothing's permanent. There's so much freedom in that."

Deirdre felt Erin's stare burn into her. "Eh," Deirdre replied, altering herself on the seat. "The grass here is just a different shade of brown."

"Ha! You got that right," Gail said, strolling to them. "Listen. Whatever you need, Erin, we're here."

Deirdre straightened. "Hey, actually, I do have a few suggestions, if you don't mind my sharing."

Erin brightened a bit. "Yes, please. I'm all ears."

"There's this foundation, Pay It Forward Fertility, that assists in helping couples with the expenses of these procedures. Do you have health coverage?"

"I do."

"Hmm, then never mind. It's for those without it. But there's another option—different, but, in my opinion, could be gratifying."

Erin became taut, her glance never wavering from Deirdre. "What? What is it?"

"I think you'd be a perfect volunteer in the PEDS unit over at the local hospital. You know, hold the babies and help the neo-nurses."

"They'd let me do that?"

"Well, sure. They have a program called Cuddlers Who Care, where people offer up their time to assist the neonatal staff with babies. I hear great things from the unit. They've got a pretty stringent screening process, but my friend Trudy is the Director of Neonatal Services. I'll ask her how we'd go about getting you in on a recommendation," Deirdre said.

"That's a spectacular idea," Megan said, beaming at Deirdre. "Erin would be a fabulous cuddler!"

"I would, wouldn't I?"

Deirdre could practically see the excitement emit from Erin like sunshine through fine white linen. "As I said earlier, I'm a nurse, not a reproductive guru, but I do know that some of these parents are so overwhelmed with work or the sight of their three-pound baby that they have a hard time touching them. You'd be a real asset, I know it."

"My gosh, you are exactly what Megan says you are: a true blessing." Erin pulled Deirdre in and squeezed.

"See? Deirdre gets it. It's like she's the missing link we've needed to complete this circle. You know, a friendship foursome, like Carrie, Sam, Miranda, and Charlotte," Gail said.

Erin rolled her eyes. "Yeah, yeah, like *your favorite TV series, we know*."

"Why them?" Megan said. "We could be our own crew." Meg held up a hand as if reading a marquee. "The F.D.N. Wives: four smart women coupled with courageous firefighters from the city…who also have a lot of shit on their plates."

"Bahaha! F.D.N. *Wives*." Gail raised her martini glass. "I love it."

"Abso-fucking-lutely." Erin lifted her cup, then paused. "Our first secret," she said, lowering to a whisper. "Don't tell a soul 'bout us. They don't need to know, and we don't need to 'splain."

Deirdre murmured, "That's so awesome," and crossed her heart with an index finger.

Chapter Fourteen

"Well, look who it is," Rusty said to Leonard as he walked across the apparatus floor of the Brooklyn firehouse. "I wasn't sure if you were gonna show up or tell us you got stuck in church."

Leonard pressed a shopping bag to the guy's chest. "I never break promises. Here. Go zest some lemons."

Rusty snatched the bag and hauled it to the kitchen at the back of the station. "I thought I said we were getting the ingredients with the rig."

"We are. You don't think I bought fifty salmon filets on my own dime, do you?" Leonard released a hearty laugh and slapped Rusty's back. "I love you guys, but not that much."

Leonard grabbed a bowl and a paring knife from the chopping block as Rusty set out the fruit. "As you work on those, I'll start on the garlic and herbs, the essentials for the butter sauce."

"10-4," Rusty said and gripped the handle of a sharp blade.

Leonard took a clove of garlic from the dozen on the counter beside bushels of fresh herbs. Other firefighters started trickling into the kitchen, weaseling between them.

"What are you making, pixie dust?" one man said, pointing at the yellow flecks mounding in Rusty's bowl and cackling at his joke.

"It's called zesting," Rusty said.

"Hey, jackass, get out of my kitchen," Leonard snapped. "If you want to eat real food tonight, stay out."

"What, you don't like my Sunday night pizzas on speed-dial?" The guy smacked Leonard's back. "It's good to see you, Len."

"Thanks, my brother." Leonard wiped his sweaty brow with the crook of his arm. "It's good to be back. Now don't let the door hit you in the ass on the way out."

He and Rusty prepped the butter in a vat-like container; everything made for consumption at the firehouse was made in epic proportions. As the number of people in the room multiplied, Leonard felt himself getting angry. "I can't fucking do this," he said and tossed the knife in the sink. "I hate cooking with a bunch of pains-in-the-asses breathing down my neck."

He went to rip off the apron, but Rusty stopped him. "Relax. They're leaving." He started herding guys toward the exit. "Everybody out!"

"What are we making?" someone shouted over Rusty's shoulder.

"Salmon," Leonard snarled, his hands moving swiftly as he resumed mincing the garlic.

"I don't see no fuckin' fish!"

"That's because you haven't paid for it yet, numbnuts." Leonard grabbed a nearby dish towel and threw it at the guy.

"All right, all right. I'm out, I'm out," the fireman said, backing away, and flung the rag onto the counter.

Leonard placed the knife down and scooped up all the cut pieces of the raw ingredients, scattering them into the butter mixture. He did this until nothing remained on the cutting board and then cleaned his hands. "Okay,

Rusty. Let's go get the rest of this meal."

"How much?" the lieutenant asked, entering the kitchen.

"Fifteen a man."

He whistled and forked over some money from his wallet.

"You can't put a price on quality," Leonard said, collecting the bills.

"This is true." The lieutenant sauntered toward the exit. "I'll tell the others. We'll be on the rig."

The fire truck exited the garage and headed to the local fish market. Leonard hopped out with Rusty while the rest of the gang leaned against the bumper of the apparatus, some lighting cigarettes.

The butcher, a personal friend of Leonard's, hand-selected the filets and individually wrapped them in wax paper. More than halfway through the order, static sounded from Rusty's walkie-talkie, along with a few emergency transmissions for Brooklyn. One of them was for a fire in a multiple dwelling not too far away on McDougal Street.

"That's us," Rusty said and rushed for the door.

As Leonard finished the purchase, the engine started rumbling outside, the red lights flickering.

"Keep the change," he said to the clerk, grabbed the packages, and sprinted out.

On the truck, he stowed the fish in a cooler under the bench and crammed into a seat. The other men had buckled in already; two looked tense, the others carefree, with all eyes staring out of the little square panes on either side, watching the houses fly in and out of view.

The driver whizzed down a quaint, tree-lined street and slowed to a stop in front of a big Victorian mansion.

The firefighters hopped out and grabbed their gear as the chauffeur stretched the line of hose to a nearby hydrant. Leonard jumped onto the curb and followed behind. From the front, the building didn't appear to be in trouble, but the smell of smoke was distinct in the air. As the men circled to the back, charcoal-colored clouds shot out of a window.

"We've got heavy black smoke pushing from exposure three," the lieutenant said into his walkie-talkie.

Two firemen barged into the house through the rear door and realized it was a grease fire—flames shooting up from a frying pan. One of the men aimed a fire extinguisher at the stove and doused the blaze. The other half of the crew broke away to check the rest of the house to ensure there wasn't fire anywhere else.

Leonard caught sight of an elderly woman coming out of a nearby bathroom. "Are you hurt?"

She looked at him, a wet towel wrapped around her hand. "I burned myself on the stove trying to put out the fire," she said and revealed the wound to him. The skin on her palm was red and already blistering.

"Do you want to go to the emergency room?"

"No, it's okay. I'll be fine. I just need some ointment."

"Follow me." Leonard exited the house and headed to the truck for the first-aid kit.

The woman trailed behind him to the rig, looking a bit distressed. "How am I ever going to cook for my guests?" She held out the hand so he could further examine it.

"Guests?" he asked, applying a liberal amount of medicated cream on the injury and wrapping it with fresh gauze.

"This is a bed-and-breakfast. I cook every morning and sometimes at dinnertime too. Tonight, I was supposed to serve eight incoming guests."

Rusty walked over and put his arm around Leonard. "Lady, you're in luck."

Her face changed to a look of confusion.

"You happen to be standing in front of a food connoisseur. One who takes great pleasure in cooking alone."

Leonard grinned. "Do your guests eat fish?" He reached into the truck and pulled out the cooler.

"Salmon, particularly," Rusty said.

She looked at Leonard and then at Rusty, her mouth forming a smile. "Yes."

Chapter Fifteen

Megan limped to the storage closet and took out a stack of new sketch pads. "Since you all aced your long division quiz on my first day back, I've got something special planned for the afternoon. Please clear your work surfaces and take out a pencil."

She walked cautiously up and down the rows dispersing the books, then went back to the closet. "These will be for later," Meg said, waving a bunch of Crayola boxes filled with multicolored pencils. A girl in the middle aisle raised a hand. "Yes, Addison?"

"Are these supplies for us to keep?"

"Yep, to keep." Megan's dark eyes twinkled. "You know how in science we've been studying the habitats of North American birds?" Megan didn't wait for an answer. "Well, we are going to learn how to draw birds in nature!"

There was a collective gasp from the kids, followed by a few small yesses.

"Does this mean we're going outside?" Addison sat straighter in the seat, her face brightening with a smile.

"Uh-huh."

The little girl's pigtails wagged as she danced and clapped in the chair.

"Mrs. Dunham, I suck at drawing," said a boy at the back of the class.

Megan tried not to scold the otherwise sweet child.

"No, you don't *stink*, James. Besides, I'm going to show you different ways to do it, which leads us right to the first artist that I want you to meet." Megan, who personified education, moved along in her long flowy dress to the SMART Board and turned it on. "Meet Roger Tory Peterson, a birder and artist." She clicked the remote and presented the first slide. "As you can see, his specialty is drawing silhouettes of birds." She waited as her students observed the dark images of winged creatures, then flicked to a second website. "And here is another artist's work. His name is John Muir Laws. Take a look at his sketches. What is the difference between Roger's drawings and John's?"

"Um, that guy's birds are like shadows, and the other guy's look like the real thing?"

"Very observant, Chauncey—"

"Mrs. Dunham?"

"Yes, Chauncey?"

"I don't think I'll ever be as good as that man." Chauncey's chubby brown cheeks glistened pink as he pointed to the latter artist's work.

Megan let out a boisterous laugh this time. "Me neither! But you know what? That man's awesome drawings weren't always that awesome. He started out drawing leaves and twigs and worked his way up to harder things as he improved. His process is called Nature Journaling, and we're going to try it on our future nature walks."

Billy's hand shot up. "Can we go for a walk now? We were really good at lunch today. Please, please, *please*?"

"Um," Megan hesitated, then read her watch.

"Aw, come on, we deserve it!"

"Okay, okay, you talked me into it," Megan said. "But first, let me tell you why keeping a nature journal is so important." She went to face the SMART Board once more when she lost balance and stumbled into Addison's desk. Meg blinked hard, trying to shake off the twinkling silver specs floating by her eyes, but it was no use.

"Mrs. Dunham, are you okay?" Addison asked and touched her arm.

Megan maintained a soft voice. "I, I'm not sure. Can you go to the office and get Mrs. Baxter for me?" Though the little glittery stars were fading, her impaired vision remained.

The students started muttering to each other and getting fidgety when Mrs. Baxter entered the room and hurried to Megan. "The secretary is calling in a substitute. Take the rest of the day."

"No, no. I can do this. I think it's just the meds," Meg whispered. "It sometimes makes me dizzy on an empty stomach. I'll be good when it's lunchtime."

Megan sucked in a breath and attempted to stand, but Mrs. Baxter insisted. "Really, it's best that your body heals in the privacy of your own home." The principal didn't say it's also best for the welfare of the children, yet her body language told Megan she meant that too. "Now, let's call your husband."

"He's at the firehouse."

"So, who can we call to come for you?"

Just as Megan's lips parted, the school nurse walked in with a wheelchair and the substitute teacher.

"Here," Megan said, handing over her cell. "Call any of the women listed under Fire Wives; they're my emergency contacts." Meg then clutched the arm of the mobile chair and smiled at the nurse. "Barb, can I rest in your office while I wait?"

"You most certainly can," Barb said and helped Meg sit comfortably.

They mazed through the hallways and into Barb's little slice of the school real estate. The flat-screen mounted on the wall was the first thing that attracted Megan. "Wow, Barb, I didn't know you had one of these."

"It's for security. Could you believe it?"

"What do you mean? For, like, school shootings?"

The nurse's face took on a morose expression. "Welcome to the twenty-firstcentury."

Megan settled on the leather examining table, reclining as far as the backboard would allow, and watched the live footage displayed in small squares across the larger screen. There was subtle movement in some wings, but overall, it was quiet. Until someone stormed through the oversized twin-door entrance of the school. Megan squinted hard at the television. "Is that?" An image of a woman resembling Gail rushed past the school safety agent. "It is." Megan leaned in for a better view. "Hey, Barb, does this thing have sound?"

Barb walked to the screen, aiming a remote at it. "That square, right?"

"Mm, hm."

She zoomed in on it, then the volume bar stretched across the monitor.

"Ma'am, wait. You need to sign in," the officer shouted. He came around fast from behind his desk, but Gail was faster.

"No offense, buddy, but I don't have the time to sign your little logbook," Gail barked and marched toward the main office. "Where's Megan?"

Megan felt the heat brewing in both cheeks. "Can you switch to that one?"

Barb enlarged the square of the reception area where a woman was rising from behind a computer. "Excuse me? Who are you?"

Gail pushed back her hair and retrieved a wallet. "I'm Gail O'Neil, here to pick up your staff member, Megan Dunham. Ever heard of her?"

The safety agent snatched Gail's driver's license and studied it. "You'll have to follow me and provide a signature. Dolly, you can call up to Megan and let her know that"—the guy glared at Gail—"her ride is here."

Megan inched forward. "Barb, that's my friend. Can you help me down?"

"Sure. I have a direct connection into the office through this door. Your friend is right on the other side of this wall." Barb unlatched the heavy lock, then put Megan in the wheelchair.

"No need to call upstairs," Megan said as Barb pushed her through the doorway. "I'm sorry for all the fuss. It's been a trying time for everyone."

Gail's eyes lit up when she saw Megan. "Baby girl, let's get you out of here and in the throes of some quality sushi. Takeout, of course." She went to hug Megan, but Meg retracted.

"Gail, this is Officer Floyd," Megan said, nodding in the guard's direction. "And this is Miss Nancy." Megan leaned on the half-wall that separated the secretarial staff from the public and pulled herself up from the chair. "I'd appreciate it if you acknowledged their efforts in keeping our children safe."

Gail guffawed. "Oh, sweetie, I'm here for you; you

know I'm no threat."

"Yes, but they don't know that."

Gail turned, looked at the eyes blinking at her, and straightened. "Right," she said. "I'm…" An intense rumble erupted from her throat, followed by, "I'm sorry."

Megan wormed her fingers through Gail's. "Thank you, as usual, for saving the day. Now let's get you signed in. And out!"

They laughed their way to the podium while Gail autographed the ledger and chuckled some more to the car. "Sorry I came across bitchy back there. You know how stressed all this gets me," Gail said.

Megan squinted. "You don't have to tell me twice. Cancer's a real inconvenience."

"Yeah, I'd say it's more unpredictable than anything."

Chapter Sixteen

A coolness ran up Erin's spine in the NICU, unsure if it was from the whitewashed walls that were more industrial than people-friendly or from frayed nerves.

"Because we have up to five, sometimes six newborns at a time, we can't give every baby the attention they want the moment they cry," the director said, scanning over Erin's application as they walked. "Don't get me wrong. We don't enjoy hearing them upset, nor are we ignoring them. It's just that we don't have enough hands-on-deck for their urgency. So, your work here will be crucial and is much needed."

Erin imparted an appreciative grin.

"I have your medical clearances and spoke with your reference—you come highly recommended." Trudy glanced up from the paperwork.

Erin gulped. *No pressure there.*

The supervisor closed Erin's portfolio and tucked it under an arm. "Let's get this tour underway, shall we?"

"Sure." Erin cupped both hands behind the small of her back and followed.

"Here is little Imani," Trudy said, stopping in front of a plastic bassinet. "She's fifty-nine days old now but was born three months early. She's currently our oldest patient. Her mom was diagnosed with a brain tumor, so she had to deliver early and has been in our neurology unit undergoing treatment while Imani stays with us."

Erin studied Imani's chocolate skin, which was reminiscent of the silky brown texture of a song sparrow.

"Even though she's our eldest, 'gestationally speaking,' Imani has a lot of catching up to do. But preemies are fighters. They develop in the vast expanse, not unlike their full-term counterparts."

"I'll hold her whenever you need."

"Well, she's sleeping right now," Trudy said and chuckled.

Erin's cheeks grew hot. "You know what I mean."

"Oh yes, I was kidding. I'm sure you'll have the chance to cuddle Imani at some point during your time here." Trudy moved ahead to another crib and reached into it. "Now here's somebody who's awake." The woman folded an arm so that the baby could lie comfortably in the crook to look around. She held out a finger, which the infant curled his own little digits around, and she wriggled it in Erin's direction. "Say hello, Tobias."

Tobias was a pale baby with colorless peach fuzz for hair. Erin's mind rewound to the time when a tiny white kiwi clawed at her thumb. "Hey there, T-bird," Erin said, trying to sound casual, and tapped the top of the child's hand; babies were obviously very different from fowl.

"Why don't you have a seat in the rocker, and I'll set you up with him," Trudy said and flicked her chin at a chair a few feet away.

"Um, yeah, okay, great." Erin sat flush in the seat as Trudy grabbed a few cloths from a neatly folded pile.

She handed them to Erin. "Situate these on your shoulder. Tobias has reflux and can spit up at any time."

Erin arranged two over her shirt and set the rest on her lap. "Okay, I'm ready."

She received Tobias carefully. The baby looked up at her, his tongue poking out of the O-shape his mouth made. "Hi, buddy. You're so cute."

Erin's flimsy limbs worked hard to keep steady beneath him. Tobias sat content until his chest started jerking up when he breathed. Erin's heart froze at the gesticulation. "Um, Trudy." She nervously manipulated the boy. "Trudy, something strange is going on. I need you." The baby's upper body kept convulsing outward. "Holy shit, this kid is having a heart attack."

"No, no. Nothing to be alarmed about," Trudy said, scrambling across the room and taking Tobias from her. "He just has the hiccups."

Like a deflating balloon, Erin sank in the chair as Trudy patted Tobias' back, bouncing him as she went. *So much for remembering the stuff on the training video.*

"Would you like to try again?"

Erin shook her head no.

"It's okay if you're not quite comfortable yet. It can take some time to get used to. Would you like to shadow Allen, our senior volunteer? He comes in on Thursdays."

"That's a good idea," Erin said and stood. "I think watching someone who's been doing it a while will help me see the ins and outs from a volunteer's standpoint."

Trudy returned Tobias to the bassinet and faced Erin. "Great. Pick any Thursday you like and just show up. Allen never misses a week."

On the ride home, Erin tried to think of something quick for dinner, but her mind kept returning to the NICU. She really wanted to hold Tobias again, but what if something else happened? She turned the corner and spotted Jay-Jay's pickup parked in the driveway. *Great, now I have to talk about it.*

The sound of drilling echoed from down in the family room, forcing Erin to cover her ears. After descending the stairs, she flickered the lights to let him know she was there.

Jay-Jay looked up and lifted his goggles. "Hey. How'd it go?"

The thought of telling him pummeled her ego. Her pocketbook slipped from her shoulder and crashed on the floor. "Not as easy as I'd expected."

Jay-Jay set the drill down and swatted the sawdust away. "Sit."

Erin crouched beside him, for once not caring about getting her pants dirty. "I was holding a baby, a really cute little boy, when he developed hiccups. But I didn't know they were hiccups. All I saw was his chest convulsing. So, I panicked and called the nurse over. I may have dropped an F-bomb or two as it was happening. I don't remember."

Jay-Jay rubbed Erin's back. "Getting nervous on your first day is normal. Spewing F-bombs in a nursery with infants, however…"

"I know, I know. But the woman knew I was scared. She suggested I shadow the senior volunteer on Thursday."

"Did you take her up on it?"

Erin started plucking dirt particles off her black clothing. "Yes, but I think the responsibility of holding someone else's baby may be too big a risk than if it were, let's say, my own."

"Nah, you can't think of it that way. I'd never be able to enter a building that's on fire if I stopped and analyzed it like that."

Erin glanced at him. "How do you do it? How do

you shut off your mind like that?"

"It's the same way you do it when I leave for the firehouse. How do *you* do it?"

"Well"—Erin focused again on the ground—"I try not to harp on what you actually do. And when I think too much about it—and believe me, there are times that I do—I remind myself that *you* are 9-1-1, the person with the answers to help people, and then I'm better."

"Exactly. I just disconnect myself from feelings and get the job done. Like, I know there's someone in danger, and I must rescue them, so that's what I focus on, the rescuing. If I go any deeper than that, like think of the person as someone's spouse, mother, father, child, whatever, then my head gets away from the real reason I'm there, which is to save them."

"Aha. So, with the babies, I should just focus on cuddling them so they can develop faster and ultimately go home to their parents because that's the job."

"Bingo. I mean, you don't have to be a robot, but go in there knowing the mission and your purpose, and everything will come naturally."

Jay-Jay adjusted the goggles over his eyes and picked up the power drill. "Not to be rude, babe, but I've got to finish this before I head to work in a few. I've got an overnighter, and I'm up for the twelve-by."

"Ugh, that damn twelve-by. I don't know how you guys stay up all night manning the firehouse while having to respond to everything. They should have separate security for that like they do for schools."

****

Erin slurped up the rest of the chocolatey milk and put the empty bowl in the sink.

"Cereal for dinner? Jay-Jay must be at the station,"

Megan said, giggling.

"I love cereal for dinner. And the entire bed to myself." Erin stretched, then switched the phone to the other ear as she began toward the room. "We've both had trying days. You at work and me, well, you know. I'm pretty much done with today."

"Same," Megan said mid-yawn.

"Okay, then. 'Til tomorrow." Erin pressed her lips close to the phone and smacked an audible kiss before ending the call.

Erin dropped onto the mattress face-first. She nuzzled into the supple pillow's fabric, a small sense of calm enveloping like a blanket. It took a few minutes to steady her mind with her breath, but once established, the effects were like a salve. Cozy. Settling, even. *Finally, some quiet.*

Until all thoughts drifted to the agenda. Always the agenda. Erin flipped onto her back and stared at the ceiling, scared that the next conversation with Jay-Jay about trying to conceive once more would be a bust. She knew the likelihood of him being on board with assisted hatching was pretty much the same as asking for a Ferrari on Christmas.

Her mind filled with rapid-firing images of cuddling infants in the hospital and how to remain emotionally disconnected. But that's just it. She *wanted* a connection, that deep, solid bond between mother and child. Her fingers curled around the comforter, rumpling it. *We've got to try again. He has no idea what it's like. The want, the need. I can't live without exhausting all options.*

She sank deeper into the memory foam as the sun dipped behind the horizon. She scanned the blackened room, her esophageal muscles constricting as her brain mulled over how unfair it was that men could enjoy the uncomplicated parts of child-rearing. *Being an infertile woman is just like this: a dark freakin' abyss.* She closed her eyes, but they still felt open. *Maybe he's right. Maybe if I stop trying, we'll all be better off.* A guilt-ridden sensation sprung from her gut. *Fuck my life.*

She concentrated on the annoying hiss of the radiator to drown out the noise in her head.

"Maaa!"

The sound rocked Erin's core. She sucked in a large amount of air, her nostrils pinching closed from the force, and listened, hoping the wail was a one-shot deal. A subsequent cry pierced the space somewhere beyond the room; the blanket now feeling like sandpaper with each increased decibel.

"What the hell *is* that?" Erin tossed the covers and leaped from the bed. Scurrying to the door, she stumbled over one of the moving crates. She bit hard on her bottom lip to conceal a scream identical to the one that was coming from somewhere across the house, which was getting louder. Warm tears welled as the sting pulsated in an unrelenting rhythm. "Okay, okay, mercy."

Erin limped down the hall to the window. Nothing was there. She hobbled down the steps and jiggled the lock of the entrance open. At the foot of the staircase was a dark, furry creature. Erin poked her head out and squinted for a better look.

"Meow."

Erin shrieked at the alley cat looking up at her. "Shoo, you bird eater! You're nothing but a filthy hairball!"

She slammed the door and wobbled back to the bedroom. "God, please. Please, don't tell me *that* is your way of saying I'll never have children." She collapsed onto the bed and tried to laugh, but all that came out was a sob.

Chapter Seventeen

Jay-Jay's body swayed on the vinyl seat of the fire truck as it blasted down a city street with its lights and sirens on.

"We have a confirmed pin," the dispatcher said, his voice loud and stern through the static.

Jay-Jay clipped the radio to his bunker coat.

"No sleep tonight," hollered the lieutenant and let out an obnoxious yawn.

"Sleep? What's sleep?" Jay-Jay shook his head and glared out the window.

The rig pulled up to the car accident. Two vehicles were involved; a sedan was on its side between an SUV and a telephone pole. Jay-Jay and the crew hopped out. Some firefighters were already on-scene herding bystanders away from an electrical cord sparking and bouncing on the wet ground.

"There's a live wire, Frank," the truck officer said, hurrying to Jay-Jay's boss as he stepped off the truck.

The lieutenant considered the distance where the shadowy line danced about, then turned to his men. "Rick, stay here and monitor that wire. Steve, go get the cable clamp, and, Jay-Jay, check that vehicle for any victims." Frank pointed the antenna of his walkie-talkie to the car on its side, then swiveled on his heel and raised the walkie to his lips. "Dispatch, put in a call to the electrical company. We need them here ASAP."

Jay-Jay approached the car and climbed carefully onto it. Inside, he saw a man trapped behind the steering wheel, his head slumped and bleeding. "Shit." He pressed his palms on the edging of the semi-opened window and gave a hard push, but the entire car teetered. He gripped the glass and balanced himself. "Hey, guys, over here," he said, jerking his head. "I've got the pin in here. Bring me a backboard and the Jaws."

Two firefighters below him were busy securing ropes and chocks to the car's front and rear fenders to stabilize it, but two others went to get the equipment.

"Okay, now," someone yelled.

Jay-Jay waited, sweat dripping off his nose. When the guys returned, he grabbed the Jaws of Life and began cutting the driver's door open. A team of paramedics rushed to him with a gurney and supply bag.

"I need a collar," Jay-Jay shouted from above the twisted metal.

A medic tossed him a plastic neck brace. Jay secured it under the man's chin and then situated the backboard behind him. Another firefighter climbed up and helped ease the guy out of the wreckage. Together, they lowered the man to the ground.

The other paramedic quickly took the victim's wrist and checked for a pulse while her partner worked the straps of an oxygen mask around his head.

"Oh, my God! Is he dead? Did I just *kill* somebody?"

Jay-Jay heard the commotion and peered over his shoulder. By the ambulance was a bloodied woman crying, both arms heavy with a child. Her face wore a look of horror as an EMT tried to check her eyes with a lighted pen. She dodged the beam to see what was going on, squealing as uncontrollable and loud as the toddler's.

Jay automatically thought of his wife at home, desperate to have a baby. He shook Erin out of his mind and turned back to the paramedics. "Well?"

"His heart is barely beating. We've got to get him in *now*," one said.

They hopped to their feet and raced to the ambulance, clutching the gurney.

"You're all going to the hospital to get a good check-up," Jay-Jay said, walking to the woman as the man was lifted into the truck.

Jay-Jay looked down at the little boy and up again. "They checked him out, I assume."

"Yes, he's fine."

"Good. And you? Are you feeling any pain?"

She shook her head.

"Let me help you, anyway. Your son can stay with you." He assisted her onto a stretcher, her fingers remaining locked with his until the paramedic secured oxygen over her airways and signaled he was ready to put them on the bus.

"Thank you," the woman said, finally releasing her grip.

"It's okay." Jay-Jay reached up and grabbed the handles of the truck. "You'll both be okay."

"Fireman!" the little boy blurted and patted Jay-Jay's bunker coat.

"Hey, champ, protect your mommy," Jay said, ruffling the boy's hair before closing the backdoors. For a split second, his heart fluttered, and he felt the urge to call Erin and tell her to move forward with the third round of IVF, but he quickly dispelled the idea at the thought of a different turnout at this crash.

"All clear," he shouted and tapped hard on the

truck's end.

The ambulance jolted to life and pulled away from the crash site. Jay-Jay watched for a moment, then ran to help his colleagues who were containing the live wire in the street.

****

Jay-Jay watched as a sliver of sun seeped into the bedroom and illuminated Erin's face.

"Honey?" he whispered, going to her. "You up?"

Erin's eyes opened. "Hi, babe," she mumbled.

Jay crawled onto the comforter. He weaved his arms around and pulled her close from behind. Erin quietly wriggled into the crook he made. "I love you," he breathed and planted feathery kisses on her neck.

"Mm, me too."

For a minute, there were no more words, and her muscles relaxed against him. *Yes.* He tightened himself around her like a firm cocoon, his eyelids drifting closed. *This.*

"Honey?" Erin suddenly sounded wide awake.

"Mm-hm?"

"I found a different procedure that may help us stay pregnant."

Jay-Jay's eyes sprung open. His mouth was about to open too, when Erin broke away from his grasp and flipped onto her belly. "It's called assisted hatching. It was designed for people like me—people with poor egg quality and failed IVF attempts."

"Er, you already know where I stand. Why do you keep insisting to do this again?" He buried his head in both hands.

"Because it's not only what I want, it's what *we* want. You said being a father was a dream of yours and you very well know being a mother is mine, so why not give this entirely new method a chance? They say the success rate is extremely high."

Jay dragged his fingers slowly over his face, his skin stretching like putty. "Can we please discuss this later? I've had a long night, and I really don't have the energy right now."

"I'm sorry," she said and inched closer to him. "I didn't ask you how your shift was."

"Busy."

"Any fires?"

"Nope. No fires."

Erin jerked up to a seated position. "Then, what did you do? Oh, I know. Cook a delicious meal with the guys, probably talking and joking while you were at it, and, let me guess, *sleep* in the bunkroom. Well, you know what *I* did? I wracked my brain all night—*all night*—alone and depressed, worrying about babies in hospitals and a baby in my belly, and this, this stupid house, and what the hell our future holds!"

Jay-Jay glared at her. "So, pick up more classes at work if you need more things to do."

"You know I'd love to, but the university is cutting back on course offerings. And anyway, it's not as easy as you think. Teaching is way different than picking up overtime and hanging at a firehouse."

"Back up a minute. So, you think that's what I do at work? You think I 'hang out' just because I didn't respond to a fire?"

Erin rolled her eyes. "Come on. We both know you have plenty of downtime there."

"Is that so?" Jay-Jay scooted up and rested his weight on both elbows. "If that's what you think, then

I'd love to prove you wrong. Tell you what. Tonight, we're going to pretend we're at the firehouse."

"I don't understand."

"I'm going to simulate mock calls like the ones we get from the 9-1-1-call system."

Jay-Jay sat up fully this time and slapped his hands together. "Every time there's an emergency, we have to get dressed in our snow pants and boots and run outside to the car. Yep, that's exactly what we're going to do."

"Yeah, okay." Erin's voice dripped with sarcasm. She threw the covers aside and stood.

Jay-Jay leaped to his feet. "Why not? This'll show you what our shifts are like at the station." He stuck out his hand. "So, you in?"

"Of course not. I don't have time for this."

"Oh, really? What else do you have going on? You already marked your midterms. I saw the stack on the desk."

"Look around this place." Her arms waved around the room. "It's a major shithole!"

"You can take a break from your work in this so-called shithole for a night."

Jay-Jay extended his palm out further.

"Fine." Erin pressed her hand to his. "My snowsuit is buried somewhere in the winter boxes. Good luck finding it."

****

In the bedroom, Jay-Jay splayed out their attire, two pairs of boots arranged on the floor at the foot of the bed. He couldn't help but chuckle when Erin walked in. "You ready? Time to cook our meal."

"More than ever." Erin's tone was snarky as she did an about-face and stomped out.

They met at the kitchen counter and together they began breading chicken cutlets and putting them in the pan. That's when an alarm sounded. Erin startled and looked at Jay-Jay.

"Shut the flame. Let's go," he instructed and pushed the pan to the back of the stove.

Erin did as told, then Jay-Jay disappeared into the hall and ran to the bedroom; she followed. He got dressed in one quick motion as she wrestled to get the outerwear over her thighs. "We don't have time. Let's go! Let's go," he said and took her hand. Erin stumbled out of the room, trying to zip the suit.

When they got outside, Jay-Jay leaned against the car and glanced at his watch, but mainly at Erin, who was breathless and disheveled.

"It's a gas leak. These take a good twenty minutes or so."

"Now what?"

He went and lifted her onto the trunk. "A quick lesson." He took out his cell phone and rested his arm on her knee. On the screen was a video clip from social media of a house exploding due to copious amounts of unwelcomed gas inside. Shingles flew into the air and, like wavering moths, fluttered to the ground. Fire trucks arrived on-scene as the highest one touched down.

"Were there people inside? How could you guys run to something potentially gory?" Erin looked up at their house and shuddered. "I mean, I think it's awesome that you had that drive to become a firefighter, but personally, I never had the balls."

Jay-Jay shrugged. "I like helping people. It's something I've always wanted to do." He knew his reply didn't surprise her; she'd heard it a dozen times. "And besides, you don't need a penis to do what I do, you know." He put his hands around her waist. "Ready? It's time to make those cutlets."

Erin smiled. "Yep."

He lifted her and set her on the curb. "Don't get too cozy in there," he said, motioning to the house. "We have a busy night ahead."

Once in the kitchen, Erin discovered their two breaded pieces of chicken had drowned in the pan's pool of oil. Jay-Jay examined them over her shoulder and plucked them out. "No worries. There's more. Happens all the time." He tossed the meat into the trash and started again.

"Huh. What a shame," Erin said, reigniting the flame on the stove. "A lot of food must be wasted at the firehouse."

During dinner, Jay-Jay galloped his fork from plate to mouth in a steady motion.

"Sweet Jesus, slow the hell down. You're gonna choke," Erin said, staring at him.

"You have to eat fast or you won't get to finish," he replied between bites.

"Why?"

"Because we could get a run any minute."

Erin pushed out of the chair. "Excuse me, nature's calling."

Perfect. Jay-Jay kept his ears tuned in to Erin's actions: the light switch snapping on, the whirring of the bathroom fan commencing. When the porcelain lid of the toilet clanked against the tank, he made his move.

"Just got a call. Let's go. Let's go!" Jay-Jay announced, barging into the bathroom.

"But I'm mid-stream! And we haven't finished

eating yet!"

"Hurry it up," he said and smacked the jamb. "It's a car accident involving a woman and her child."

She shot him a sharp look. "Don't play like that."

"I'm serious. Get up. Let's go!"

Erin cleaned and raced to redress, then headed out to the car again. She leaned on their vehicle, heaving yet waiting for the report.

"Two vehicles are involved; a sedan is on its side between an SUV and a telephone pole. Some firefighters are already on-scene. They're keeping bystanders back from an electrical cord that's sparking and bouncing on the wet street just a few feet away."

Jay-Jay tapped the trunk of the car. This time, Erin hopped up without assistance. "Was this a real job you responded to?"

"Last night."

Erin's eyes widened. "What happened to the lady? Was she really a mother?"

"Yes." Jay-Jay hoisted himself onto the backend. "She and the boy were fine. They had a few minor scrapes and some bruising, but otherwise okay."

Erin bit her upper lip and glimpsed at the azure sky. "What if this is it? What if we never have kids? What's left to look forward to?"

Jay-Jay jumped off the car and faced her. "There are a million things we could do. We could travel—see the world! Just think, we'll have the freedom to do anything we want."

Erin's nose scrunched. "Won't that get old?" She gasped. "Oh, my God. When we get old, we'll *really* be all alone. Who's gonna wipe our asses when we can't?"

"Let me get this straight. You want kids so that

you'll have your butt cleaned when you're old?" Jay-Jay busted out laughing. "Kids these days put their parents in nursing homes before it's even their time."

"You schmuck." Erin shoved his shoulder. "That's not what I'm saying at all."

"I know. What you're really saying here is that having a husband isn't good enough. Why? Why isn't being married and accepting our fate good enough for you?"

"Because I want to be a mother too. Why is that such a bad thing?"

"It's not. But you have to realize that it's not going to happen the way we want it to. If you want a child so badly, then let's adopt. At least we'll be spending a shitload of money on an actual person instead of a bunch of doctors trying to concoct one for us."

"Wow, that is so incredibly insensitive. Those doctors got me pregnant. *Me!* The person who thought I'd never conceive because of my shitty reproductive system, but it happened. *Twice!* Now, all it has to do is stick and we can have our *own* child, not someone else's genetic makeup." She stormed up the path and into the house.

Jay-Jay took the keys from his pocket and unlocked the truck. He hopped in without skipping a beat and reversed out of the driveway.

****

The tavern was empty. Jay went to his favorite stool at the far end of the bar, right by the jukebox.

"Long time no see," Lucinda said, sauntering over. "The usual?"

Jay-Jay nodded.

The bartender flipped a coaster onto the counter and

then dipped an arm into the refrigerator under it.

Jay's thoughts were still centered at home. *It's crazy how we can almost have a moment, a real understanding of each other, and then she returns to this baby shit.*

The pop of a Corona cap brought his attention back to the pub. He watched absentmindedly as Lucinda propped a lemon wedge on top and pushed the beer to him.

"You know what? Give me a shot of tequila too," he said.

Lucinda chuckled. "Is it for better or worse?"

"Eh, neither." Jay-Jay took a small joint from his chest pocket and put it between his teeth. "Being married isn't necessarily the best thing that's happened to me, but it's definitely better than dating. That shit's the pits."

Lucinda grinned as the liquor poured into a little glass. "Dating isn't so bad."

Erin had been confident and fun while they were dating. Now, that felt like such a long time ago. Jay-Jay removed the unlit cigarillo from his mouth and rolled it between his fingers. "Yeah, well, those days are long gone for me."

Lucinda leaned against the back of the bar and pulled an e-cigarette from the waistband of her jeans. "What a shame." She took a toke and blew a stream of smoke in his direction. "You should just light yours, relieve that stress you've been carrying around."

"Nope, it's bad for your health."

"Ha! So are infernos."

Jay-Jay looked at Lucinda for the first time since entering the place. Her auburn hair, normally twisted up like a straggly mop, was as smooth as a long, silk curtain; she'd also lost some weight.

He hopped off the stool and walked around the bar. "Is this what you want?" he said and lifted Lucinda onto it. He pulled her to him by the belt loops so that they were nose-to-nose.

"You know it is," she purred.

He traced the length of her nose with the tip of his, then pulled away. "What kills me is that you know I'm married, yet you don't care."

"Says the man who put me on a countertop." She batted her lashes, then gripped the collar of his T-shirt and wrangled him in.

Jay cupped Lucinda's face, gently at first, until their mouths touched, and the softness of her lips raised the spirit in his jeans with all its pent-up testosterone. His hands lowered to the line of buttons on her blouse and gave a good yank, releasing the most perfectly sculpted rack he'd ever seen. And, with no hesitation, dove right in.

****

With frayed nerves, he drove out of the pub's lot and headed for home. He'd never so much as laid eyes on another woman and now just had sex with one. His grip tightened around the leather steering wheel, and he cocked his head side-to-side, allowing the tension in his neck to loosen. *You done fucked up, Jelani Harper. There's no way around this one.*

Once back home, he tiptoed into the bedroom. He was almost at the bed when Erin flipped on the light. He froze, not uttering a word.

"Really? You reek of booze," she said, voice seething.

"Yep, I drank." He moved toward the light switch.

"That's it? That's all you can say?" Erin swatted him

with a pillow. "Fuck you."

"What do you want from me?" He got on the bed and sat. "I love you. I love that we're here. And I love the life we already have. But I'm not sure what *you* love? What do you love, Erin, because I'm pretty damn sure it's not me." The skin on his knuckles tightened as his fingers curled and settled beside each leg. What he did in the bar was wrong, *very wrong*, but it didn't negate or justify Erin's behavior in *their* bedroom.

"I love you! And all those things," Erin started. "Well, except for this house. And how we can't get pregnant—but give me a break! You can't blame me for that."

He saw the muscles in her throat dip; his own unconsciously did the same.

"You know what I love? I love the lifestyle so many firefighter wives have," she continued. "The one where they pack up their kids and whisk them to their husband's firehouse picnics and camping trips and Christmas parties. That's ordinary, Jay-Jay. For them, that's completely ordinary. But not for us. Why is it so damn extraordinary—so damn *hard*—for us?"

Jay said nothing. He knew the question was a rhetorical one. Instead, he stayed on his side of the bed, hunched over the bottom half of himself, marinating in the undeniable distance wedged between their individual wants and needs.

"Anyway," Erin said, no longer hysterical, "I called Dr. Ansaldi earlier for an appointment, and he fit me in at the end of the month, a Thursday. Could you believe he had an opening so soon? He's always booked solid."

Jay-Jay jumped up. "Of course, he had an opening! He sees dollar signs when he hears your voice." Erin glared at him, but he continued. "And, whoa, whoa, wait a minute! Didn't you have an arrangement at the hospital to work with that lead volunteer guy on Thursdays in the NICU?"

"Yeah, so? I can change it to any day I want. It's *my* time, not theirs."

Jay-Jay shook his head. "You are such a good-hearted person. You give so much of yourself to the university, to your friends, but what about me? *Us*? I thought volunteering would be a good idea, but when it comes to this fertility stuff, you transform into someone else entirely. I can't explain it."

"Whatever. Then don't come with me to the doctor," Erin said, tugging at the sheets.

He reached over and turned off the lamp. "I wasn't planning on it."

Chapter Eighteen

Deirdre's key jammedin the lock to her apartment. She wiggled it furiously and thrust a hip into the aluminum barrier when something crashing sounded from inside.

"Hello?" Deirdre called out, entering the foyer. There was some scurrying in the back bedroom. At first, she thought it was the cat, but then there was a soft furry nudge on her ankle.

Another thud. Heart pumping fast, Deirdre rushed into the kitchenette and grabbed the biggest knife from the cutlery set. She squeezed the handle and crept down the hall. "Hello?"

A shadowy figure zoomed out of the bathroom, straight into the bedroom. "Shit!" a man whispered.

Deirdre held up the weapon and kicked the bedroom door completely off the hinges. The cat darted by as she entered the room where a stark-naked Cliff was wrestling with his underwear. He toppled to the floor as he turned in her direction.

"Are you fucking serious?" Deirdre lowered the knife. "What the hell is going on here?" She watched him worm into his briefs, then looked to the left and then the right. "Where is she?"

Deirdre walked to the closet and swung open the door. A Spanish man no older than twenty was cowering in the corner. He peered up and flinched.

"Julio?" she said, eyes widening.

"I'm, I'm sorry," he said and braced himself like he expected to be hit.

Deirdre stared down at him, her mouth dry. "Get. Out."

The guy scampered out of the room on all fours like a scared puppy, his pants scrunched around his ankles. He kept tumbling, trying to right himself. When he was gone, she turned back to Cliff. His bottom lip quivered, despair written all over his face. "Please, let me explain."

"Julio, the super's son." Deirdre's head got woozy. "The super's son? What the hell were you thinking?" She suddenly let out a wicked laugh. "Oh, let me guess. The pipes in the bathroom backed up again, but when he came to fix it, you got your pipes cleaned instead, you motherfucker." The silver edge of the knife twinkled in the moonlight. She aimed it in the door's direction. "Now, it's your turn. Get out."

"Can we talk?"

Deirdre stood firm. "Absolutely not."

Cliff looked down and closed his jeans, the sound of the zipper slicing through the space between them.

"Leave," she said, teeth gritting, and pointed to the hall with the tip of the blade.

Cliff obliged. On the way out, he stopped to say something, but Deirdre closed her eyes and directed a finger at the front door, which was still partially open. "The one thing, the *only* thing I've asked you not to do in this relationship is the exact thing you just did." She shook in disgust. "Man, woman, dog, cat, whatever. You cheated. In *my* bed! I need to process this. Alone."

With his head lowered, eyes averting hers, he handed over the spare key.

After he left, Deirdre rushed to the sink and threw up. Mr. Sultenfuss encircled her feet, rubbing against them. Her hand jerked the handle of the faucet to clean the mess. When she came to, she turned and rested against the counter.

Across the room was a stack of mail on the table, some of it his. Deidre charged at the pile. "You bastard!" Envelopes flew, some plopping to the floor while others fluttered down slowly like stray feathers. She lowered onto a chair and cradled her head, Salvatore's Sicilian accent echoing. *How do you say—I came alone?*

"Loner," Dee said aloud, looking up. The room was still, except for the drippy faucet. She glanced at it and the overstuffed drying rack beside it.

Nerves stretched tight, she marched to the dishes. "I don't think so." With one quick motion, she grabbed Cliff's favorite cereal bowl and fired it into the trash. She scoffed, her verdant eyes twinkling through caked mascara. She then grabbed his mug, the red one shaped like a fire hydrant, and threw that away too. This continued, working around the galley, then the living room, and into the bathroom, purging everything he kept there. When she got to the bedroom, she stopped at the dark shadowy rectangle where the door used to be. Images of sex flashed through her mind. Of Cliff. Of Julio. Of Cliff's surprised look. She took a step back and picked up the cat. "Come on, buddy. We're not sleeping in there."

She set Mr. Sultenfuss on the couch. Rearranging a few pillows and some blankets to make it as comfortable as possible, she crawled onto it, fluffing the shams, fixing the covers, but still couldn't get in a position that felt like home. The tick from the clock on the wall seemed to get louder.

"I can't stay here!" Deirdre yelled, then went for the helmet and keys on the entertainment center before dashing out.

Chapter Nineteen

Wine splashed into Gail's glass when the doorbell rang. *Who on earth is it at this hour?* She put down the bottle and secured her robe.

"Coming!" Gail's voice echoed as she took hold of the drink and descended the stairs.

Behind the front door was Deirdre. And behind her was a motorcycle.

"Hi," Gail said, a bit confused. "You ride?"

Deirdre held up the helmet.

"That's officially the coolest thing about you." Gail unlocked the screen barrier. "Everything okay?"

A small stream trickled down an otherwise stone-cold face. "Was that invitation a few weeks ago, you know, the one into the foursome—the F.D.N. Wives—something legitimate? 'Cause I could really use it."

Gail's heart did a two-step. "Of course," she said, opening the door wider. "Come on in."

Deirdre quietly stepped into the house.

Gail gripped the cup in one palm and took Deirdre's hand with the other. "Man troubles?"

"You could call it that," Deirdre said and sighed.

Gail led the way to the bedroom and patted the mattress. "Have a seat." She then headed for the mini-fridge. "What a day. My grandson was hyper all morning. Then, after watching him, I brought soup to Megan's—she's better, by the way. Those dizzy spells subsided, and then I visited Harry at the cemetery." Gail retrieved the last bottle of wine from the shelf and undid the cork. "Here you go," she said after stealing a sip and handed over the entire thing.

"Thanks." Deirdre took it and gulped.

"You don't have to talk about it if you don't want to," Gail said, reaching for the television remote. "And don't think for a second that we don't value your friendship. What you've done for Megan—my goodness, no one could ever put words to it. And, not to mention, your sage advice to Erin also." She clicked the virtual menu and searched through the digital TVguide. "Like *Gals, Sex, and the Country*?"

"Love it. But I haven't seen it in a while."

Gail chose an episode. "I think you'll appreciate this one."

As the infamous instrumental theme song began to play, the two women reclined on the massive heap of cushions against Gail's headboard and sipped their drinks.

"I forgot how much of a jerk this guy was to the main female character. I can't believe she chose him over Bruce," Deirdre said and surveyed the thin neck of the wine bottle. "I thought I had myself a Bruce: caring, hardworking, sensitive, considerate." She had another swig and put it on top of the fridge, then took out her phone and thumbed through the photos. "I mean, look at him." Deirdre aimed the screen in Gail's direction.

"Cliff was always charming and soft-spoken when I saw him in the firehouse. He even has soulful eyes," Gail said, then glanced up from the photo. "But he's a hero to many and a stranger to one, huh?"

"Yep. He cheated on me today. In my own bed."

"Sounds like he's a jerk in Bruce's clothing."

"Funny thing is, the guy he slept with is my super's son."

"Hold on. I'm not following. The *guy*?" Gail paused, staring.

Deirdre bowed her head.

Gail snagged another look at the pic. "Wait a minute."

Deirdre joined in and stared at the image. "What?"

"Shelly Baxter's son is gay."

Deirdre clutched the cell and popped to a seated position. "Oh my God, I totally forgot about Shelly."

Gail stretched an arm to turn off the television, then rested a cheek in her hand. "Don't panic. I think she's an overly dramatic asshole. And, no offense, but this explains a lot."

Deirdre broke into a fit of laughter mixed with some tears.

"Seriously. Every time I saw that Baxter woman at the firehouse, she'd always have some cockamamie complaint about something," Gail said. "She was never happy with anything, especially when it came to Cliff." She paused, remembering all too vividly how Shelly had carried on at the Christmas party about her son's biker girlfriend and put two-and-two together. "So, did you, you know, *suspect* any of this?" Gail said.

Deirdre frowned. "*Suspect?* How do you 'suspect' your lover is gay? I suppose if you're talking about my 'gaydar' then I'd have to say that either I don't have one or it's suffering a major malfunction."

Gail's face reddened. "Yeah, that was a stupid question. I don't know what I was thinking. Forget it."

"It's not stupid. I should have known." Deirdre

threw herself onto an airy pillow. "But with scrawny little Julio? Why him?"

Gail stirred on the bed. "Who's Julio?"

"Ugh, this pipsqueak of a man. My super's son. He does maintenance around the building for his dad, and the toilet in my apartment has been acting up. Cliff probably called him to fix it again while I was at work and, I guess, well, you know what happens next." Deirdre fiddled with the rosary beads. "The more that I think about it, I'm repulsed. Cliff is such a good-looking man; I'd imagine he'd have picked someone muscular, manlier, not this twerp."

Gail stroked Deirdre's forehead with her thumb. "You don't need people like that in your life, sweetie. Take it from me. I've been through it too before I met my husband."

"I'm sure." Deirdre rolled onto her backside and studied the swirly patterns of paint on the ceiling. "You know what the worst part is? The worst part is that I have no idea how long this has been going on for. And what's even more bizarre is that I'm wondering what he's going to do about his mother."

"Hopefully, he'll tell her."

Deirdre snapped out of the trance. "Um, I'm not so sure about that. Not when it comes to straight-laced Principal Baxter. I'm actually kind of scared for him."

"As ignorant as Shelly is, she deserves to know. But what about his dad? I've never heard about him. Ever. And none of the wives has dared to ask."

Deirdre shrugged. "You know, I always just assumed he wasn't in the picture. He was always a non-event, so I went along with it. Maybe he secretly has daddy issues?"

"Eh, maybe. Maybe not. It's pretty irrelevant, come to think of it." Gail sat up and crossed her legs. "But imagine how much easier everyone's lives would be if Cliff came out? Then he can be the person he really is."

"That's easy for you to say because you're one of those chill moms." Deirdre shimmied upright. "But not Shelly. Are you kidding?" Dee laughed, then stopped and plucked some lint off a pillowcase. "Seriously, though, you're right. Because then I would've never been in this mess. Hey, you think maybe I'm the reason he's gay?"

"No, you ass." Gail nudged her arm. "If anything, it's because of *Shelly*." She roared with laughter. "Really, the reality is that no one is to blame. Come on. Let's get some shut-eye."

"Sleep? I can't sleep after this."

Gail forked over the remote. "Well, then it's you and the boob-tube. At my age, I'm lucky I can stay up past ten."

Gail turned over, drifting in and out of sleep, as Deirdre stared wide-eyed at the rest of the episode of *Gals, Sex, and the Country.* She awakened fully, however, when Deirdre wept loudly at one point during the show but pretended to still be asleep not to embarrass her. Dee then began cursing at one of the series' characters. "Don't you do that! She likes you, you idiot. Deep down, she wants to be with you, but you're gay. You don't see her the way she sees you!"

There was rustling in the bed. Gail finally got up and flicked on the light.

"I'm sorry. I think I just pulled a muscle in my neck," Deirdre said, rubbing it. "That's where I usually hold stress."

"I have a solution." Gail grabbed the empty bottle of booze from the nightstand and raised it. "More alcohol."

The women erupted into hysterics until Deirdre winced in pain. Gail propped up and started massaging the area. "One of the muscles on the right side of your throat is tight."

"I feel that." Deirdre tried to turn her head in either direction. "Ugh, this sucks."

"Have work later?"

Deirdre inhaled deeply and, on the exhale, let out an exaggerated yes.

After a few minutes of trying to unkink the knot, Deirdre pulled away and stood. "Nature's calling," she said, then walked to the bathroom.

Gail got up and fixed the bed, envisioning Deirdre walking right into the heartbreak. She stopped rearranging the spread and tiptoed to the bathroom. With an ear pressed against the closed door, she asked, "You okay in there?"

"Yeah."

There was a whimper followed by the whoosh of the faucet. Gail slowly backed away and resumed fixing the bed.

"Thanks for letting me stay." Deirdre reentered the room, drying her hands. "That apartment is the last place I want to be." She reached for the motorcycle helmet and jacket off the chair.

Gail watched, feeling disappointed and hurt for her friend. "But it's the middle of the night. Why don't you stay until morning?"

"Nah, I'll just keep you up and that won't be good when you have your grandson."

"Actually, I'm taking Erin to a doctor's appointment

tomorrow. Are you sure you can drive with your neck?"

"I have no choice. Whether I go now or in a few hours, I'm sure it'll still be stiff."

"Well, at least take some Ibuprofen." Gail grabbed a container off the dresser and popped two pills into Deirdre's palm.

Without moving too much, Deirdre took the medicine and put on the headgear. "Later, gator."

Chapter Twenty

Gail held the door for Erin as they entered the office of Ansaldi and Ansaldi, a husband and wife gynecological practice that focused on obstetrics and reproductive endocrinology. Erin, who saw both specialists interchangeably over the years, was quickly met by several expecting women and *happy* soon-to-be fathers sitting in the waiting area.

"Well, isn't this awesome?" she mumbled. Jelani hadn't so much as uttered a word to her since their blowout. And neither had she.

Erin hugged her purse to her flat tummy and rushed to reception. Scribbling her name on the clipboard, she hurried back to Gail, who had a seat ready for her.

Erin picked up the parenting magazine from the table and thumbed through to avoid making eye contact with the others.

"Mrs. Harper?" the receptionist called from behind the glass. "Is your insurance the same?"

Erin nodded.

"And are you here for the follow-up to the last IVF treatment?"

Erin's face flamed. As much as their inclusive environment was a nice touch, she cringed at the lack of professionalism from the front desk. She stood and felt the other patients staring. Gail went to get up.

"No, I got this." Erin went to the secretary and stuck

her head into the opening of the plastic partition. "I'd appreciate it if you didn't shout my information for the entire room to hear. There's something called the HIPAA law, in case you've forgotten?"

"Oh, sorry." The lady fanned Erin's folder and continued studying its contents.

"Yes, I'm here to talk with Dr. Ansaldi in Endo about previous IVF procedures and the possibility of assisted hatching," Erin said in a loud whisper.

"Okay, he'll be with you shortly."

"Actually, I can see her now," the endocrinologist said, entering and retrieving Erin's chart. "Come in, Mrs. Harper."

Erin glanced back at Gail, who winked and shooed a hand as if to say, "It's okay, I'll be right here."

"Shall we?" Dr. Ansaldi opened the door.

Erin nodded and followed him to one of the examining rooms. Her chest tightened with angst. "Thank you for taking me on sudden notice." Erin removed her jacket. "It's just that I'm ready, you know, *really* ready, and I'm not getting any younger."

"Time waits for no one." The specialist handed Erin the paper dressing. "I'll be back in a few minutes."

She undressed, slipping each bare arm through the tissue-thin sleeves, and jumped onto the disposable waxy paper covering the examination table.

"Knock, knock," Dr. Ansaldi said and reentered the room. "So, Erin, I overheard you mention assisted hatching to my secretary. In your previous treatments, the eggs were fertilized but failed to attach to the uterine wall. For a pregnancy to be successful, we want that implantation to be firm so the embryo doesn't expel from your uterus. There's no way of predicting how many tries of IVF it would take to establish this strong attachment, but recent studies do indicate that assisted hatching has more favorable results."

"Yes, I've read the research. Problem is, you and all your predecessors said the same about intrauterine insemination, but that didn't happen."

"In your case, we found that IUI was like putting a Band-Aid on a stab wound."

The doctor went to the wall of literature and retrieved a photocopy of an article from Harvard. "AH, as assisted hatching is known in the medical field, consists of varying techniques that manipulate the zona pellucida—that's the strong membrane that forms around the ovum as it develops in the ovary. At any rate, in order to fertilize an egg, a sperm must penetrate the thinning zona pellucida. If fertilization takes place, the zona pellucida disappears entirely to permit implantation in the uterus, the possible solution to your problem. Depending on the individual, AH is done bylaser, mechanical, or chemical means to facilitate embryo implantation."

Erin already knew she wanted to do it but had to fake the funk, play devil's advocate, in order to answer Jay-Jay's questions later.

"Sounds invasive," she said, eyeing the newspaper clipping.

Dr. Ansaldi pointed to the article. "An emerging body of evidence suggests that AH has improved clinical pregnancy rates, particularly in poor prognosis patients."

Erin looked at the doctor. "Listen, I'm all for giving it as many shots as it takes. It's my husband who needs the convincing. He thinks we're just wasting money." She waved the paper. "Maybe this'll help."

"There are lots of reasons people stop trying, money being the main issue, especially if insurance has a set limit on IVF or doesn't cover the AH procedure. Then"—Dr. Ansaldi paused, unbeknownst of its effect—"there's also the physical and emotional toll it takes on the couple involved, which you are already aware of." He turned to the sonogram machine and worked his hands into a pair of rubber gloves. "But enough about that. Let's have a look, shall we?"

Erin lay on the table and stared down at the concave portion of her stomach. The gynecologist hovered over it, emptying a tube of jelly onto it. Erin flinched. "Oh man, that's cold."

"Sorry. The warmer broke yesterday," he said and pressed the wand to her pelvic region.

Erin watched Dr. Ansaldi squint and move closer to the computer screen, the wand moving frantically across her abdomen. "What's the matter?"

"Just a second," he whispered.

She watched him examine the bubbly images of the sonogram, pressing hard on her torso.

"Ouch." Erin tried to wiggle away from the pressure.

"That's quite big."

Erin halted. "What is?"

The doctor pushed a few buttons on the keyboard, and a printer started spitting out black-and-white pictures identical to those on the computer. "From the looks of it, a rather large cyst has developed on your uterine wall." He leaned in and pointed to a circular mass in one of the photographs. "I'm going to have to do a transvaginal."

"Do whatever you have to, just please tell me that it won't affect my last chance at having a child."

Dr. Ansaldi handed over the images. "Erin, look, I'll recheck everything: your uterus, the uterine wall, fallopian tubes, ovaries, but remember that these parts haven't been functioning properly, causing your irregular periods and giving you trouble since you were a teenager."

Erin took the photos and stared at them. "Then it's obvious I'm the ideal candidate for AH."

The doctor ignored the sarcasm and continued prepping the machine. "Okay, lay back."

He picked up a wand that resembled a lightsaber and began the second exam. "Tell me, have you missed a period or two?"

"The total opposite. Lately, it's been a bloody Niagara Falls down there," Erin said. "I mean, to the point I need to change pads every hour. But I thought because most of my life they've been so mild—trickles of blood for a day or two—that my body was making up for lost time. Or it was just stress-related." Erin paused and looked at him. "This is a bad thing, isn't it?" When the doctor didn't answer, Erin started to weep. "My life, it's just, like, a series of infertile events." Her hand whizzed through the air like a comet.

The endocrinologist cleaned the wand and replaced it in the holder. "We'll need to do a biopsy."

"So, is another procedure even possible?" Erin said and reached over for a Kleenex from the computer cart. "Or is it completely out of the question?"

He shrugged. "No, we won't rule anything out just yet. But we are going to have to perform a reevaluation of your reproductive organs, including a *non*invasive surgery called a laparoscopy, to see what's going on. The worst-case scenario is a myomectomy, which is the surgical removal of just the fibroid, with reconstruction and repair of your uterus. We'll also check blood work and make sure there aren't any issues concerning your thyroid."

"Thyroid? Again?" Erin blew her nose loudly into the tissue.

"Yes, your thyroid. As you know, it's underactive and, if not properly treated, can affect your fertility."

"But I'm already taking pills to control it."

"Your body may be trying to tell us something. We might have to up the dosage or change the medication entirely."

"It's always something." Erin wiped the gel off her stomach with the smock and slid off the crinkly paper. "So, when's my next appointment?"

"I'll see you in two weeks," he said and closed the file. "But you'll have a few lab appointments before the surgery is set, with a follow-up with my other half. I'll be in touch sooner with any test results and, if we can push the time up for the surgery, we'll do just that."

Erin redressed and followed him out of the room, trying to remain composed as she thought of how—or *if*—she should share the news with Jelani.

****

"Jay-dawg! You got a guest!"

A visitor. You have a visitor. Jay-Jay shook his head and took the steps two at a time. He wasn't expecting Erin because of her doctor's appointment. *Maybe it's Ma.* He skipped the last few stairs, landing with a thud on the apparatus floor, and walked toward a tall redhead pacing the entranceway of the garage. *Lucinda?*

As if she heard him, she spun around. Jay immediately noticed her eyes were swollen from crying,

141

something he'd never seen at the tavern. "What's up? Are you okay?"

Lucinda rubbed a hand over her torso. "I-I." Her pupils darted back and forth, then focused again on him. "Can we talk somewhere private?"

"Uh, sure." Jay-Jay scratched his chin, hesitant to invite her into the firehouse. "Let's go over there."

He started to the lot with the bartender in tow. "So, how'd you know where I worked?"

Lucinda let out a snort. "Every hat, jacket, and T-shirt I've ever seen you in has your company logo on it. You're like a walking advertisement."

A deep heat penetrated Jay's cheeks. "Ya got me there."

Jay stopped behind an old rig and tapped the bumper for her to sit.

"So, um…" Lucinda's voice cut out, forcing an extremely unattractive throat-clearing.

"Too many cigarettes, huh?" Jelani chuckled, but she straightened, lips pursed.

"I'm pregnant."

"Um, congratulations?"

"It's yours."

Jay jumped off the truck. "How could you be so sure?"

"What's that supposed to mean?" Lucinda crossed her arms and squinted at him.

"You tend bar. We had a one-night stand. And I'm absolutely certain I wasn't your first."

Lucinda stood tall. "You say that like I'm some sort of hooker!"

"Ssh!" Jay-Jay swatted his arms, looking nervously around. "Quiet it down, okay? I didn't mean it like that."

She stared at him expectantly.

"Are you kidding me, Lucinda? You show up at my job and tell me you're having a baby—*my* baby, no less." He held up a finger. "No offense, but, one, we hardly know each other. Two, I'm married, and three, I'm pretty sure it's not mine."

"Well, then let's get a paternity test if you don't believe me."

Her tone was so stern, Jay suddenly felt lightheaded. He sat again. "You're serious."

"As serious as a heart attack, my friend."

Jelani eyed her. "We aren't *friends*. We hardly know each other, and now we're procreating together. This is total marriage suicide."

Lucinda sighed. "You don't have to leave your wife. I don't want to be with you. But what I *will* need is child support."

"Please. Just stop talking." Jay clutched his hair. "Fuck. Fuck, fuck, fuck. My life is over. Completely ruined. I can't *fucking* believe this."

Lucinda pulled out a ripped piece of paper from her jeans pocket and shoved it into his chest. "This is my number. When you're ready to man up and claim your child, give me a shout." She turned around and took a few steps but then paused and glared back. "Or if you want to move forward with a paternity test. Either is fine by me."

Nausea washed over Jay, his future crushing like the pebbles beneath her boots.

Chapter Twenty-One

Megan squirmed into an orange sweater.

"Which one?" Rob held up two different wigs.

Meg poked through the opening of the shirt and studied the hairdos. "That one."

Rob tossed the burgundy hairpiece on the bureau and helped situate the sleek brunette one onto Megan's scalp. "I like this the most," he said, pushing some hair away from her eyes. "It looks the closest to the real thing."

She finger-combed the strands, careful to separate the tangles.

"Mommy, Mommy, is it time to go? I'm ready." Trevor ran into the room.

Megan turned to her son, whose Halloween shirt was on backward. "Come here, champ." She pulled him in close and fixed it. "Now we're ready."

She gripped the cane in one hand and held Trevor's tiny fingers with the other. "To your class pumpkin patch, we go."

Trevor helped her get up. "I want the biggest pumpkin in the entire school." He yanked his hand from hers to show just how big.

Megan mushed his short spiky hair. "It's going to be so fun, I can't wait."

"I'm so happy you can come, Mom." He took her palm and squeezed it all the way to the car, warming her

144

heart.

Rob parked in front of the elementary school and helped Megan out of the passenger seat. "If you need me, call," he whispered and then opened the back door to unfasten Trevor from his booster. "And you"—he lifted him—"pick the fattest pumpkin you can find." He held up his hand, and Trevor slapped it with all his might.

"Let's go, kiddo," Megan said.

Rob settled him on the ground and stayed behind as they strolled to the school entrance.

Inside the building, Megan was mindful of the kids that whizzed by, walking slower. For a small fleeting moment, she daydreamed of her own class and how they were faring lately. She looked at Trevor. "What's your favorite subject?"

"Recess," he said and did a little jumpy dance alongside her.

"You're just like your father." Meg chuckled as they entered the classroom.

"Hey, Trev!" Miss Beel, his teacher, said.

Trevor let go of his mom and gave Miss Beel a big hug, then ran to a group of children eating sweet treats and dancing to *Monster Mash* playing over the Smartboard speakers. He bounced along until a bowl of candy on a nearby bookshelf stole his attention.

Miss Beel turned to Megan. "Welcome, Mrs. Dunham. It's so nice to see you. The other moms are right over here." She escorted her to a small table where four women were sitting around an untouched tray of orange and black cupcakes.

"Megan, how are you? I heard the news of your cancer at last month's PTO meeting," one of them said as Meg settled in a chair.

Megan smiled, studying the lady's face, hoping a name would somehow appear on her forehead as the other women gawked in a sort of collective wonderment.

"Uh, I'm okay, thank you." Megan reached over and took a cupcake from the batch. She held up the dessert, peeled away at the paper cup, and took a bite. "Mm, it's like being a kid again," she said, savoring it.

A lady sitting directly across the table eyeballed the surrounding parents in horror. Another picked up a cupcake and started pulling off the wrapper. As it was brought to her mouth, a third woman followed.

"Wow, this is the first time the moms are eating here," Miss Beel said, doing a little clap. "Aren't they delicious? I baked them myself."

Orange icing colored Megan's lips. Her tongue reached out and licked the evidence clear. "Life is too short to skip dessert. My advice—eat more cake."

Miss Beel washed down a treat with some apple juice, then lowered the radio. "Okay, everyone. It's time to go pick some pumpkins!"

The boys and girls cheered and hopped about as the moms cleaned up after them.

Megan held Trevor's hand as they walked at the back of the line to the schoolyard, where stacks of hay, pumpkins, and scarecrows were strewn about like a real farm atmosphere.

"Whoa, this is great," Trevor said, admiring the transformation of the inner-city playground. "Come on, Ma. I think I see a giant one."

Megan trailed behind as he ran to a plump orange fruit. He tried to pick it up by its stem. "Wait," she called out. "You don't want to break that off."

Miss Beel went over to Trevor. "Golly," she said,

pretending it was too heavy. "Someone's going to need a wheelbarrow for this one."

Trevor pumped his fists in the air as Miss Beel brought his prize over to where Megan was sitting on a square mound of straw. "When we get home, we can carve it, and pluck the seeds, and roast them, and make a pie, and—"

"Hold on there, kiddo." Megan rested her hands on his tiny shoulders. "First, let's see if Daddy's working tonight."

"He's not. I know he's not. He told me when we were brushing our teeth. He said me, him, and Kenny would carve the pumpkin when we got home."

Megan stared into her son's big almond-shaped eyes, marveling at his exhilaration. "Okay, okay, you gave me an idea," she said and giggled.

"I did? What? What? Tell me; tell me."

"We'll invite Auntie Erin to the house and Aunt Gee-Gee and Logan." Megan retrieved the wallet from her purse and handed Trevor more money. "Go tell Miss Beel we're buying a few more pumpkins."

****

Megan played the song *Thriller* as Rob answered the door with two anxious children underfoot.

Erin carried a shopping bag filled with Halloween candy into the house. When the boys noticed, they began tugging on her legs. "Is that for us? Is it, is it?"

Erin laughed. "It most certainly is." She quickly set down the sack so they could ferret out the goods. "Oh, my gosh. Think they're excited?"

"Just a wee bit," Megan said, walking toward them.

Rob accepted Erin's jacket and led the boys back into the dining room.

Erin did a side shuffle to Megan with her arms extended like claws. "'Cause this is thrill-a!"

"Thrill-a night!" Megan sang, shimmying.

The doorbell chimed again.

"Logan!" Trevor and Kenny shouted in unison, scrambling to the front of the house again.

Arm-in-arm, Erin strolled with Megan to the dining room table.

"So, what's the latest in *Harperville*?" Megan asked.

Erin rolled her eyes. "It's so hard pretending that it's not always something."

"You're not kidding." Megan yanked out a chair and slid into it. "What's happening now?"

Gail entered the room carrying a bottle of wine. "Hey, ladies. What'd I miss?"

"Oh, I'll need some of that, Aunt Gee-Gee," Erin said, pointing.

"I'm on it." Gail made a sharp left into the kitchen.

Megan looked around. On the opposite side of the room, Rob was occupied with the little ones and their pumpkins, Gail was in the kitchen pouring wine, and Erin, although in minor distress, was right by her side. A warm feeling washed over her. "I love a full house." A smile spread across Meg's face. "Don't you?"

"I love the idea of one…just not sure about it anymore," Erin confessed.

Megan kissed Erin's temple and then took a glass from Gail as she set them on the table.

"That's not for you. Your head'll end up in the toilet," Gail said, taking it back.

"I know, I know. It was only a sip." Meg pulled out a chair beside her for Gail and turned back to Erin. "So, what's your news? You've had me on edge since this morning."

"Dr. Ansaldi found another cyst." Erin's focus remained on her leg that bounced wildly. "It's taking up a large part of my uterus. It looks pretty scary."

Megan's eyebrows furrowed. "He can remove it, can't he?"

Erin bit her trembling lip. "Mm, hm. Surgically. I've gone for the biopsy to see if it's benign." She took out the original sonogram and slid it onto the tabletop.

"I say let them poke and prod. It'll get you answers," Gail said. "True honest-to-God answers!"

"But what if I can't handle the answers?" Erin's voice elevated over the music, causing Rob and the boys to look over. "Sorry, sorry." Erin sank back into the chair.

Gail and Megan gathered closer to the picture.

"It's not that big," Megan said, probing the image. "After they take it out, you'll be back to normal."

Erin reached for her drink.

Megan patted Erin's knee. "Are you okay?"

"Of course I'm not *okay*. We all know I'm never going to have a baby."

"You don't know that for sure. Wait for the test results to come in and let the doctor do his job, which is to get you pregnant, *which* we already know he could do," Meg said.

Erin's mouth formed an uneasy smile. "You're right. It's just…this whole thing is driving me crazy."

Gail looked up from the photo. "Why's that?"

"Because this is yet another roadblock, you know? And Jay-Jay, he's not on board with another procedure, even if this tumor thing is benign. It's like nothing's working—the house, my fertility, volunteering, my *marriage.* Everything sucks."

Megan picked up a water bottle and brought it toward her lips but stopped. "As the talented author Anne Lamott—though not an ornithologist—said, *take it bird by bird.*"

Erin looked at Megan and then at Gail. Her expression lightened, but she didn't respond.

"Megan's got a point," Gail said. "Start with Jay-Jay. Go on a date and *be* a couple. No baby talk yet, then move on from there. As a matter of fact, why don't you take my Groupon for a ballroom dance class? Both of you need a night out. You can add him on as your partner for an extra ten bucks, and you'll be set. Maybe go for tapas and drinks first to loosen up, then let your hair down and go dancing!"

Erin's face recoiled. "Yeah, right. I have two left feet, and he'll never go for something so formal like ballroom dancing."

"What! Why? That's the best part. It's what makes for a fun night, especially if you have a few cocktails beforehand. Then you can laugh when you step all over each other's toes. To me, it sounds like the perfect recipe for some memory-making," Megan said and winked at her.

Erin looked from one to the other, pondering their suggestion.

Gail stood and retrieved a printout of the deal from her purse. "The only stipulation is that it expires next weekend, but otherwise, you're good to go." She creased the paper and tucked it into Erin's satchel that hung from the chair.

Megan got up and went to the family's Big Band CD collection in the entertainment center. All of a sudden, a boisterous instrumental composition started blaring over the speakers.

"Yes," Gail yelled and grabbed Erin's hand, heaving her up off the seat.

The two women stood nose-to-nose. "Like this," Gail instructed, taking Erin's other hand. She guided Er through some slow moves, then picked up the pace. When Erin fell into a rhythm, Gail let go and started dancing by herself.

The children turned away from their pumpkins to watch. Everyone else, including Erin, stopped to look on as Gail let loose. She appeared mesmerized by the song, shuffling feet and contorting legs in ways she'd never done in front of them. In her trance, her movements were fluid transitions from one part of the melody to the next, like an invisible partner was guiding her. At the end of the tune, Gail curtsied and dropped onto the couch behind her. The room stilled.

"Um, holy shit?" Rob said, brow raised.

"Oh, honey, that's not even half of it," Gail snorted.

"It's as if you were dancing enough for two," Erin said, seating herself by Gail's ankles.

"It's just a natural part of me. But, if Harry were here, he'd not think twice of keeping up."

Erin looked to Gail anticipatively. "It's a longshot, but maybe there's hope for the Harpers."

Gail reached out and lifted Erin's chin. "Now there's that positive attitude rearing through."

Megan beamed at them and advanced the water bottle over the table covered with candy corn and pumpkin guts. "Here's to more dancing and many Halloweens together."

****

"Holy guacamole, what is that?"

Megan's eyes sprung open. The bedroom was darker than midnight, and she couldn't see a thing but was certain the fiery hot sensation in her vagina needed immediate medical attention. She tried to sit up, tried to see what time it was, but her legs wouldn't move, like they weren't a part of her anymore. "Rob, wake up," she said, pulling off the covers.

"What's the matter, honey?" he mumbled as he rolled onto his back.

"I think I forgot to pee today," Megan said, rubbing her abdomen.

"Please tell me you're kidding." He hopped to his feet and switched on the lamp.

Megan started to sweat profusely, the walls suddenly closing in. "I don't know. I guess I didn't have to go." She gasped, then fainted.

Chapter Twenty-Two

Deirdre was relieved that the main lobby was relatively quiet for twoa.m. when reentering from her dinner break. She headed for the elevator bay, contemplating all the ways of telling Megan what had happened with Cliff the other night.

She looked down and stepped into the lift, bumping right into Dr. Kelleher.

"Oh, hi, Doc. Sorry." She scooted aside to let him out.

"Deirdre," he said and grabbed her shoulders. "I was just about to call you."

"Call *me*?" She was confused. *Did I miss a meeting?* "For what?"

"It's about our patient, Megan Dunham. She's back…was rushed in with paralysis to her lower extremities, suffering a severe urinary tract infection. We have to perform emergency surgery. Get prepped and meet me in OR. 7 in ten minutes."

Deirdre's heart squeezed. She pulled away, the rosary thumping against her chest with every strained intake of breath. "I, I can't do it. Ask Sondra."

"But you're the best I've got. Why would I ask Sondra?"

Deirdre couldn't look the doctor in the eye.

Dr. Kelleher adjusted the brim of his glasses. "Deirdre, are you all right?"

"I'll, um…I'm fine. See you in ten." She pushed past him and poked frantically at the panel of buttons, the doctor staring as the elevator closed. After it jerked upward, Deirdre slid down the wall.

"This can't be happening," she said, clenching globs of hair.

When the doors parted again, Rob stood there, looking at her crunched form on the floor. Deirdre's eyes burned from mascara and tears. She scrambled to her feet, about to say something to excuse her gross crackhead-like appearance, but he spoke before she could.

"Ever been to the roof of this joint?" he asked and took a pack of cigarettes out of his shirt pocket.

"No," Deirdre said, wiping her eyes with a shirt sleeve.

"First time for everything." He stared up at the lighted numbers.

When they reached the top floor, Deirdre followed him toward a dark, narrow staircase that ascended to a level only accessible by foot.

"How do you know the way out from up here?" Dee asked.

He turned to her, his eyes a sly leer.

"Ah yes, that's right, it's because you're a fireman."

Through a vault-like door, the two stood on a flat roof. Halfway across the expanse was a helipad with small red lights twinkling on the surface. Rob lit a cigarette and flipped the metal Zippo closed.

"You gonna offer me one or not?"

"Oh, my bad." Rob reached into his pocket for another. "I didn't know you partook in this sort of thing." He handed over the tobacco and the lighter.

They puffed in silence for a few minutes, the wind swatting at their white-clouded exhalations as the faint echo of impatient taxis blared in the distance.

"What kind of bike did you ride?" Deirdre sat on the black tarmac and crossed her legs.

"A Triumph." He sucked on the cigarette and squatted next to her. "A 1994 Thunderbird 900. Black."

"Nice."

Rob flicked off the ashes of his stogie, then scratched his head. "Listen. You have to take care of Megan when she's under, I mean extra good, *really* good care—"

Deirdre raised a finger to his lips. "Nothing but the best."

He took her arm and pulled her to him. She let him cry into her shirt, rocking him as he let himself go. "Fuck, man. I don't know how to be a father without her."

Tears snuck away from Deirdre. She launched the cigarette across the roof, then stroked his hair. "When are you back in the firehouse?"

"Tomorrow. Why?"

"Have you considered talking to the Counseling Unit?"

He pulled away from her. "I've been thinking about it."

"The least they could do is give you emergency leave, if nothing else."

Rob stood and reached for her hand.

"Wait, before we go," she said, getting up and walking to the roof's ledge. She looked out at the city with its unrelenting aliveness, then glared up at the night sky and pointed both middle fingers high in the air.

"FUCK YOU!" She kept them there for several seconds, then turned to Rob. "Okay. I'm ready now."

****

Deirdre walked out of the OR and went to the waiting room. Dawn had already passed; another day was in full swing out the city window.

Rob was slouched over, asleep in a chair, when Deirdre entered the room. She knelt beside him when he slowly opened his eyes. They were bloodshot from the intensity of the night.

"How is she?" His voice sounded dry, exhausted.

Deirdre glanced at her hands. An hour earlier, they were covered in Megan's blood. "She's in recovery."

Rob blew out a hard breath and took Deirdre's face in his grasp. "Thank you, thank you, thank you."

Her stomach dropped knowing certain things but wasn't authorized to say. "Don't thank me."

"She's still alive, isn't she?"

"Yes," Deirdre whispered.

"Then it's another day we have with her." He planted a firm kiss on Deirdre's forehead and met her gaze again. "Can you take me in?"

"Sure."

They helped each other up; Rob walked ahead to open the door for Deirdre. She quietly led the way to where Megan lay, still heavily sedated.

Once inside, he went straight to the bed. He slipped his arms around her and cradled her. "It'll be okay. We'll get through this," he muttered.

"Get through what?" Meg croaked.

His eyes darted in Deirdre's direction. "She doesn't know yet?"

"No," Deirdre mouthed.

Rob let out a loud sniffle when Megan's heart monitor started emanating a series of rapid alerts.

Dee slid between them and took hold of Rob. "Go get some water. She's getting anxious, so the machine detected it."

Dr. Kelleher stepped in and walked directly to Megan. Deirdre spun around and kept her sights on the doctor.

"Mrs. Dunham?" He shined a lighted pen in her eyes. "Mrs. Dunham, can you hear me?"

Megan's voice and movements were slow to respond. "I, I can hear you."

"Good, good," Dr. Kelleher replied. "There are some things I have to tell you. First, you're in the Critical Care Unit."

Megan's head shifted left to right on the pillow, seemingly looking around, and then she squinted at him. "Critical Care? Why?"

Deirdre squeezed Rob's arms as Kelleher stuffed the little flashlight into the breast pocket of his lab coat. "You have a severe urinary tract infection."

Meg's mouth formed an O, but nothing came out.

"The UTI was caught in time. It was spreading to the surrounding organs in the lower half of your body, which was causing them to shut down. Mrs. Dunham, please tell me, have you been experiencing vaginal pain at all since your return home?"

Megan rubbed her lower region. "No."

"Are you sure?"

She hesitated. "Well, it hurt when I urinated a few times and, and I forgot to urinate another time. But I thought everything was off from having the catheter in from the surgery."

The doctor retrieved a piece of crumpled linen from his coat and dabbed his forehead. "I have some news."

Megan let out a low groan as her eyes opened wide.

"Mrs. Dun—Megan, after you were admitted, my team and I immediately began checking you through the insertion of a small scope. The micro-camera displayed suspicious inflammation in your ovaries, which resembled cancer-like cells, so, with your husband's permission, we performed emergency surgery to eradicate it."

Megan winced. "And?"

"And the results were not good."

Tears immediately crawled down Megan's cheeks.

"Wait!" Deirdre pulled Rob back to the bedside. She connected Megan's hand with his and gripped the other, then nodded at the doctor.

There was a slight rumble in Kelleher's throat before he went on. "Megan, you have stage four ovarian cancer. When we attempted to remove the portions, we found an overabundance of cancerous cells. We took out as much as we could, but the truth is, there was more there than anyone would have expected to find."

Chapter Twenty-Three

Erin plowed past security toward the elevator with a disheveled Gail in tow.

"Ladies, where are you going?" a burly officer asked, his voice hot on their trail.

Gail remained incredibly silent as she clung to Erin's arm.

"I don't fucking know," Erin barked and punched the elevator button with the side of a fist. "Do you people have specific cancer wings in this place? I mean, it's all cancer here, so how would one know where to go?"

The man shook his head. "What exactly is the person you want to visit suffering from?"

"I don't know! They originally diagnosed Megan with breast cancer, but now it may be worse. She arrived here a few hours ago. They said it was an emergency."

"Well, you're never going to find 'Megan' unless we look her up. Come to my desk, and we'll take a look."

They started toward his podium when a loud commotion erupted in the vestibule.

"It's a bird!" someone yelled.

The guard rushed to the noise. The women had no choice but to traipse behind.

A displaced pigeon was flapping wildly, repeatedly crashing into the glass of the revolving doors and falling to the floor.

"Go help them," Gail said finally. "I'll meet you up

there."

Erin's eyes danced between Gail and the chaos ensuing a few feet away. "Okay." She let go and ran to the officer. "Mister, go get me some rubber gloves."

The guard looked at her like she was nuts.

"I'm an ornithologist. I work with birds," Erin said, then faced the crowd. "Calm down, everyone. The more excitement we stir, the more flying it'll do."

"Here you are," the security man said, returning with disposables.

"Good. I'll handle this while you locate my friend." Erin put on the gloves and kneeled a few feet from where the pigeon was walking. "Coo, coo," she said, her tongue rolling slowly on the oos.

There were a few laughs from onlookers, but Erin ignored them and kept her lips rounded. "Coo, coo."

The bird jerked its head in her direction.

"I have bread from my sandwich," a little girl said. "Want it?"

Erin waved the kid over and patted the ground. The girl's mother nodded and sent her to Erin.

"What's your name?" Erin whispered.

"Olivia," said the child, holding out the bread.

"Olivia, why don't you break it apart and put it around us. When he's nice and close, I'll scoop him up."

"Okay." Olivia began making crumbs and spread them about. She even threw a piece at the pigeon. "So he gets the scent," she added.

Erin gave a thumbs-up. "You're like a mini first responder."

The two worked as a team: Olivia luring the fowl with food while Erin tried to grab him. After a few near misses, the crowd's anticipation was thick.

Erin squatted lower and continued to coo softly. The pigeon, pecking frantically at the bread, seemed to pay no one any mind. That's when she curled her fingers and moved in a bit more aggressively.

"Gotcha," Erin proclaimed as both hands closed around the bird's body. She cooed some more as the pigeon attempted to escape while Erin got up. She held it close to her but invited Olivia to pet it while the bystanders clapped. "Aren't they fascinating?"

"My dad calls them rats with wings, but I don't think they are," Olivia said.

"Thatta girl. Even rats are interesting if you give them a chance." Erin motioned to the exit. "Want to come outside with me and set it free?"

Olivia jumped up. "You bet!"

****

Once near Megan's room, Erin saw Rob walking the hallway in her direction. "Rob!" She rushed forward and hugged him, holding on to him longer than she'd expected to, but she couldn't help it; her endorphins were as high as the pigeon's flight. Letting go, she slipped a palm into his and pulled him into the room to find Gail curled into herself on a chair as Deirdre rubbed her shoulders and Megan in a fetal position, not facing anyone.

"Meg?" Erin said, tiptoeing around the bed. "You up?"

Megan's eyes stayed closed. Erin stroked her head and touched her hand.

"There's nothing that any friend or family member could possibly say right now that would make things better," Megan said.

Erin stared down and pulled away. "Why are you

saying this?"

"I'm Stage Four, Erin!"

The incessant hum of a fluorescent light bulb overhead interrupted the silence in the room.

"That's the only truth I can focus on right now. I'm not mad at you or anyone, I'm just pissed at life, at the shortcomings of it. If I only knew it would be so incredibly short, I would have lived." Megan raised her arms. "Undoubtedly *lived*. Just like that. In a big, bold capital letter kind of way."

Erin tried to control the welling of tears building.

"Deirdre, I want a ride on the back of your motorcycle," Megan proclaimed.

Everyone turned to stare at Deirdre, faces painted with alarm.

"Um, okay," Deirdre said and flashed a nervous smile. "As soon as Dr. Kelleher gives us the approval, you're on."

"Screw Kelleher. And screw his approval. The minute I can stand up and walk out of here, have those keys ready."

"You got it, boss." Deirdre motioned a stout salute.

"And Rob, book that Disney cruise for us. The kids need a vacation just as much as we do from all this cancer-schmancer crap."

Erin watched as Megan blurted outrageous orders, wagging a weakened finger. On impulse, she grabbed Meg's hand and placed it on her ever-so-slightly bloated belly. Megan finally stopped talking.

"I'm not well either," Erin said, "but remember what you told me about faith? It's all we've got. And, if all goes well—with your treatments and with mine—we can put all this bad shit behind us for a little while longer.

Hey, maybe you'll even experience the movements of a new godchild."

"Are you serious? You'd want *me*? As a *god*mother?"

Erin nodded. "Absolutely. You're my sista' from another mista'."

Megan gently massaged Erin's tummy. "It'll happen. And when it does, I'll be even more honored than I am now, if that's humanly possible. But first, go dancing. Please."

****

"Jay, I have a Groupon," Erin said, fumbling with the dish rack. "Thought maybe a date night was in order."

Jay-Jay looked up from his cell phone. "You want to go out with me?"

Erin laughed yet was secretly dying inside from his reaction. Had she been that bad a wife? "You are my husband, aren't you?"

Jay-Jay chuckled. "Well, I sure hope so. What's this Groupon thing you're talking about?"

Erin went to her purse. "It's an entire website that offers discounts on cool stuff." She unfolded the printout and showed him. "Like, for example, this one is for a dance class, but they have others for wine tasting, skydiving, you name it."

"You want to take a dance class? With me?"

Why is everyone so shocked by my decisions lately? Erin's face grew warm. "I thought it would be fun, you know, because it's different. And an escape from all the hospital and sickness surrounding us lately."

Jay-Jay took the Groupon and studied the picture of the man and woman poised in the advertisement. "Okay.

When?"

"Did you just say *okay*?" Erin's voice practically squealed with surprise. "For real?"

"Yes, I'll do it."

Erin did an impromptu happy two-step.

"When do you want to go? By the looks of it, I'm guessing we'll need a lesson STAT."

"Ha, ha." Erin jabbed at Jay-Jay's shoulder. "It expires this weekend, so check your firehouse calendar and let me know when you're free."

"I already know I'm off Friday night, so book it."

"10-4," Erin said, giving a faux tip of the hat, and retrieved her cell.

Chapter Twenty-Four

Gail arrived at the gift shop as the metal gates went up.

"Morning," she said and walked in behind the clerk. She turned down an aisle and scrutinized the selection of trinkets. As usual, everything screamed sympathy. Gail remembered Harry's hospital room and how it wreaked of the doom and gloom undertones of "Get Well Soon" balloons, cards, and stuffed animals. She'd always examine the items decorating his surroundings and think, "Stage four cancer patients really don't 'get well.' They die. Couldn't you give a token that speaks of life—especially to one well-lived?"

She continued around the small store, trying not to lose hope, probing the shelves until something halfway decent was found. "I guess this'll do." She snatched a recordable teddy bear from a pile and headed to the register.

Back at the elevator bay, a crowd stood waiting, so she headed to the closest staircase and went up to Megan.

Entering the room, she spied Deirdre and Meg in an embrace. "Oh, I'm sorry to interrupt."

"Don't be silly." Deirdre hopped to a standing position. "Come and join us."

Gail approached but stopped at the edge of the bed. Megan bore what she'd always thought was the look of death: grayish-green skin over protruding bones. An image of Harry in this moribund state flashed through her mind.

"You okay, Gail?" Megan said and gave a little wave.

Gail snapped to and forced a grin. "I'm sorry, sweetie, here."

"Thank you," Meg said, trying to sound cheerful as she received the gift. "It's adorable." She read the tag on the blue plush teddy and pushed its stomach to hear the recorded message: "The little golden ticket in the bear's hand will grant you support and serenity. Use it, my friend. You won't be sorry."

"Is this like Willy Wonka or something?" Megan chuckled, glancing at Gail, and pulled off the note.

As Megan read it, she frowned.

Gail clutched her pocketbook, her breath hitched for a moment, and sat on the vinyl chair despite the urge to leave. "You could call Cindy Clyde the Willy Wonka of the cancer support circuit. Right, Dee?" Gail eyed Deirdre nervously, who was checking an IV attached to Megan's wrist.

"Oh, absolutely. Cindy Clyde was built for this line of work," Deidre replied.

Gail focused on Megan. "I know you're not a fan of shrinks, but Cindy is a social worker who chose to dedicate herself to helping cancer patients and their families because she knows firsthand about this horrific disease."

"Okay, thanks." Megan hesitated, then tucked the paper into the drawer of the end table.

Gail drew in a breath and looked to Deirdre, the desire to flee stronger than ever. Deirdre shook her head, wearing an expression that Gail interpreted as "no harm, no foul," though she wasn't entirely sure.

"This is going to sound childish," Megan said, piercing the awkward gap of silence, and held up the stuffed animal. "But, I love teddy bears. I haven't had one in years…for obvious reasons."

Gail let out a little laugh, which was more of a sigh of relief. "I can't stay long, but I can take you to the chapel real quick if you want."

Megan smiled. "Sure, let's go."

Gail jumped up and helped Deirdre situate Megan in a wheelchair.

"I'm going to stick around here and continue my rounds," Deirdre said. "I'll see you two soon."

On the way out of the room, Gail spotted a poster of a palm tree hanging randomly on the wall. *It's time to plan something away from all this.* She continued wheeling Megan down the hall, thinking it had been quite a few years, probably before Harry's diagnosis, that she'd been on a vacation.

"Oh shoot," Megan said, touching her collarbone. "I forgot my rosary."

Gail stopped pushing the chair. "No problem." She turned the wheelchair and headed back to the room. When they reentered, Deirdre stood by the opened nightstand drawer with the note from Gail in her hand.

"Unless you magically sprouted cancer and now need guidance on developing your exit strategy, I can't imagine why you'd want that number," Megan said.

Deirdre's head jerked around. "Cindy is here every so often. I was going to call her and ask when she was coming in so I wouldn't miss the visit. I'm so sorry, I should've checked the schedule."

"I'm still not understanding," Megan said, arms

crossed.

Deirdre straightened. "She has a great network of therapists at the ready, and I'm thinking of talking to somebody about my newly failed relationship. I was going to tell you, I just didn't know how."

Megan shrank in her seat. "Newly failed relationship?"

Deirdre looked to Gail, then at Megan, and put the note down. "Cliff is gay," she said, eyes glassy, and started toward the door. "I'm sorry I went into your things, Megan. I should have asked." She stopped at Gail. "Can you fill her in? I gotta go."

"I shouldn't have been so mean," Megan said once Deirdre had left and cried into the bear's fur.

Gail wheeled Meg to the bed. "Don't beat yourself up. I'm glad to see she's interested in counseling. It's a good thing. Really."

Chapter Twenty-Five

Rob opened the fire station's garage door as Deirdre's motorcycle pulled up.

"Thanks for letting me stop by on short notice," Dee said, wiggling out of the helmet.

"No problem. Come in. Chow's on."

Deirdre shut down the bike and hopped off.

Rob made his way across the apparatus floor, Deirdre strolling beside him.

"Something Italian, huh?" she joked, referencing the thick smell of garlic.

Rob grinned and pushed through the flimsy swing door to the kitchen.

"Guys, this is Deirdre, Megan's nurse," he said to those sitting at a long conference-like table.

Deirdre gave a sheepish wave to the rest of the men as Rob grabbed one of the oversized porcelain bowls stacked in the center. He took hold of the ladle and scooped up a mound of steaming spaghetti.

"Whoa, whoa. I can only manage about half of that," Deirdre said.

"Man up 'n eat up," he teased, handing her the massive portion.

"Oh, so it's like that, huh?" She swiped a fork from the pile of utensils. "Challenge accepted."

A couple of guys whistled. "Aw shit, Dunham."

He shooed their comments and trailed off to the

lounge.

"Welcome to the TV room," he called from over his shoulder. "No one will come in here, so you can talk freely." He snatched the remote and lowered the volume of a football recap.

Deirdre set the food on the coffee table and pulled out a piece of paper from her pants pocket. "I lied to your wife—kind of—so your lips need to stay zipped."

He sat slowly and listened.

"Gail gave Megan the contact information of a social worker, Cindy Clyde, but she was put off by the gesture. The thing is, I know this lady from working with my patients, and I believe you guys would benefit from seeing her. Cindy specializes in working with cancer patients who have small children."

Rob felt his Adam's apple do a weird dip as he swallowed.

Deirdre pushed Cindy Clyde's contact info across the table. He glared at it and again at Deirdre.

"Meg used to talk to someone. Dr. Stanton, I think her name was, and they had a falling out. Since then, Megan hasn't believed in third-party interference. Not even from priests, and you know how religious she is."

Deirdre took the paper.

"But," he continued, "if you could somehow get this woman to pop into the hospital room unannounced, Meg will have no choice but to meet her."

"Well, what do *you* think about therapy?"

"Hmm." Rob's forehead scrunched as he put down his bowl. His mouth opened partway to answer when a loud ringing blared throughout the firehouse, and a rapid-speaking man started spewing information. *Saved by the bell.* Rob jumped to his feet. "Gottago."

****

Rob's eyelids pinched closed as the speed of the engine jogged his anxiety. *What's Megan doing right now? The boys? Maybe Deirdre's right about therapy.*

The tires screeched to a halt and the doors flung open. Fire was shooting from the windows of an apartment complex.

"Let's rock," one of them said as he grabbed an ax and hopped out.

Rob jumped off the truck but stood frozen at the curb as the other fireman disappeared into the building. Like his brothers, running toward danger satisfied him. In his mind's eye, he was like a superhero, dousing ravenous flames. But now, with Megan gravely ill, it was becoming different, less heroic.

Thick black trails of smoke rushed out of several casements, a red inferno dancing beneath it. Residents came scrambling out, some in pajamas, one wearing nothing but a blanket. They crossed to the other side of the street, necks rotating for another glimpse.

Rob's mind raced as he scanned the area. His glance darted left, then right, but his feet remained stationary. Lines of hose were stretched while other fire trucks arrived on the scene. Firefighters holding extinguishers dashed by as several ran to the back of the complex. A ladder was cranked to the window where the blaze was, and a fireman climbed up it.

The radio on Rob's chest rambled codes, all language he understood. "10-45! Repeat: I have a 10-45!"

A first responder bumped into Rob, causing him to stumble forward.

"What the—? Why aren't you in there?" the guy

yelled, yanking at Rob's arm.

"I'm, I'm…"

Rob was now in the building's lobby.

"Put your hood on properly," the firefighter said and grabbed at Rob's helmet. "More dip shits on the job, yeah, just what we need." Rob fixed the protective material so that it covered his ears and neck, and the man slapped the hardhat down on his head. "Now c'mon. Take the line." He pulled Rob close as he took the hose's nozzle into his grasp.

The fireman led them up the stairs, where they were met by smoke. Rob swallowed hard and tried to compose himself.

"*Mi hijo! Mi hijo!*" A heavyset Spanish man jumped in front of them and waved to an apartment door at the far end of the hall.

"Okay, we got it. You need to leave." The firefighter pointed to the staircase.

"*No puedo*," said the Spaniard. "*Soy elsuperintendente.*"

"*Fuera!* Get out! Tell the *bomberos!*"

"*Si, si.*" The super shook his head madly and headed for the steps.

The fireman continued down the hall with Rob to the apartment, where the door was emblazoned with soot. A plume of smoke escaped as he pushed it open. Flames roared at the back of the place, but it was hard to tell which room it was coming from because there was junk piled everywhere. They stepped further inside, even though it was difficult to see where they were going. The only thing Rob could make out was the shadowy backside of the pissed-off firefighter. He finally thought to scan the last name on the guy's bunker coat: Marshall.

It's Chase Marshall! Thank the good Lord. At least when he realizes it's me, he won't be too much of a douche.

Chase Marshall was dedicated to the job but was also jaded by it. At midcareer, who wasn't with all the antics the city tried pulling on a regular basis?

Rob pressed his shoulder against the nearest wall and continued in. The deeper they went, the blacker things were. Between the heavy gear, anxiousness, and then the heat from the blaze, sweat poured down the sides of his head. So did the tears. Rob didn't dare move until he felt a tug on the hose.

"Here we go!" Marshall shouted and gave the knob on the nozzle a firm twist.

The rush of water was immediate, jerking them backward. Rob's arm sprained behind him as he tried to break his fall, but when he landed, he didn't hit the floor. He hit a body. "Holy fuck, there's a person here! There's a person!"

Marshall continued manning the line, apparently unable to hear him.

Rob glanced all around as the fire raged in front of them. The pain was excruciating as he stretched his arm, but he ignored it and ripped off his glove to check the person's pulse. He felt a bunch of bangle bracelets when he grabbed the victim's wrist. *It's a woman.* He pushed up the jewelry and felt around, but nothing. He reached for his radio. "I have a 10-37, code 3. I repeat: 10-37, code 3."

With all his might, he got up on his knees and pulled the body to him. As he lifted the upper portion of the lady, he saw her pregnant belly. *Are you fucking kidding me right now?* He propped her arm around his neck and wrestled to stand, a limp hand whacking his cheek.

That's when he saw one of the bangles was an identification bracelet. *Lucinda Wellet High Blood Pressure Do Not Resuscitate.*

"Jesus Christ," Rob said, grinding his jaw as he pushed on, fighting his way through the mix of heat and hurt.

Parts of the ceiling started to fall all around. Rob stumbled forward onto Lucinda, the sleeve of her shirt igniting. "Fuck!" He smacked it out with his glove when an adjacent wall suddenly collapsed on them.

Chapter Twenty-Six

The vacant road led Deirdre to the apartment she'd been avoiding ever since the breakup. Luckily, none of the neighbors were out, but she hurried up the walk anyway.

The hinges creaked as the door opened. Everything was dark. Mr. Sultenfuss let out a weak meow and circled Deirdre's legs, snuggling up against them when she entered. Dee flicked on the living room light and took him into her arms, then checked the place for unpermitted entry while gone. So far, nothing appeared to be disturbed.

In the kitchen, she set Mr. Sultenfuss down and started refilling his automatic food and water dispensers when there was a knock on the door. She startled, grabbed the feline, and held him close as if he were a shield as she tiptoed to the entrance and eyed the peephole.

Sunglasses were on Gail's face, which was unusual at eight o'clock at night in mid-fall.

"Hey, what's up?" Deirdre said, exhaling loudly, and let Gail in. "Everything okay?"

Gail stepped into the apartment and removed the shades. "Megan's husband was just hurt in a fire."

"What?" Deirdre dropped the cat. The animal landed on all fours and scurried away. "I was just there."

"Just where?"

"At the firehouse. I was talking to him about the counselor and was trying to push him to talk with her." Dee paused. "Then the bells rang, and he had to go."

Gail sighed and reached for Deirdre's hand. "We need a plan. We can't tell Megan. God knows she doesn't need the added stress, but we have to think of something. We have to help the best we can."

They went to the couch a few feet away.

"I was just *there*," Deirdre repeated and sank onto the cushions. "How did this happen?"

"When I got home, I heard melee over the scanner. It involved Rob and Jay-Jay's company, so I called Erin, but no answer." Gail stood and took out the phone. "I'll call Erin again. Maybe Jay-Jay knows more by now."

The ceiling fan whirred lazily above them as Erin's cell rang over Gail's speaker.

Deirdre studied Gail as they listened to the ring, and then voicemail picked up.

Gail ended the call and tossed the mobile back onto the ottoman.

"How am I supposed to remain quiet with this?" Deirdre's voice was as deep as her concern. "We have to tell Megan."

Gail stayed silent.

Deirdre glared at her. "What? You don't agree? She's our friend, and that's her *husband*, for Christ's sake."

Gail sighed and returned the sunglasses to her face. "This is a tough one." She squeezed Deirdre's hand and bent down to pet Mr. S. "Make sure your mommy gets some rest."

Mr. Sultenfuss's throat radiated with content as he pressed his body against Gail's shins and then shimmied between Deirdre's.

Deirdre picked him up and walked Gail to the door. "I'll try my best to stay out of it," Dee said, undoing the top lock. "But I can't promise anything."

Gail nodded and descended the stairs. "You have to do what you have to do, but you didn't hear that from me."

Deirdre closed the door. "Good grief. If it were my husband, I'd want to know." She held up the cat. "Right, buddy?" He wormed away, landing with a thud, and sprinted down the hall.

Chapter Twenty-Seven

Erin's cell phone sounded as she and Jay-Jay entered the dance studio.

"It's date night. Let's turn these off," Erin said and clicked the button instead of checking the call.

"Agreed." Jay-Jay powered down his and positioned himself on the dance floor, watching as Erin sucked in a deep breath, slimming her long body like an egret. The depths of her pupils were little portals to a soul he loved. He admired Er's strong will, that ambition to accomplish everything she set out to do, and he was happy that, for the first time in quite a bit, their time wasn't being spent disputing their reproductive future. Then Lucinda's face appeared in his mind. His eyes squeezed shut, but the image wouldn't go away.

"Take zee lady's hand in jours," said Francois, the dance instructor. Francois's French accent was more cutting than canny. "Do not look at jour toes, just leesen to my eenstructions and move like-a so."

Jay-Jay's train of thought immediately returned to the studio. Erin's bottom lip was tucked under her two front teeth, biting back a laugh. He forced a smile and glanced at his shoes.

"Ah, ah," the man's voice echoed from the far end of the room. "Eyes up!"

Jay-Jay's head lurched upward as Francois pushed a button on the radio. From his peripheral, he noticed that, despite the teacher's abrupt, drill sergeant-like manner, his sudden cha-cha had flair, his hips possessing a smooth, melodious sway.

Francois danced back to them and clicked his heels. "Jou ready?"

"Yes," Erin beamed.

Jay-Jay nodded and fixed his gaze on his wife's smiling mouth, wanting to savor every part of her perfectly lined teeth that glowed behind the outline of such succulent lips. He knew once it was time to confess after he'd mustered up the courage to make, and attend, the appointment for paternity testing, that Erin's upturned pout would never be directed at him again.

"We start wiz zee foxtrot," Francois said as he took the pair's arms and straightened them into ninety-degree angles. "Now curl jour fingers like-a so. Jou keep jour hands like-a zis as jou dance and move jour feet like-a zis: slow, slow, queek, queek. Slow, slow, queek, queek." Francois did a small demonstration with an imaginary partner.

"Do I lead?" Jay-Jay asked when the instructor stopped.

"Oui, Monsieur. I weel guide jou." Francois pressed his hand over Jay-Jay's and Erin's weaved fingers and counted to three.

At once, Jay-Jay felt Erin tug him back as they tried to step in sync with the music, which caused him to trip forward.

"Ah, ah," Francois said to Erin, wagging his index finger.

"Sorry, I'm a teacher too. I guess I'm used to being in charge of things."

Jay-Jay regained composure, and they started again.

"Very good," Francois said, clapping out the rhythm of their steps as they proceeded without error. "Is about conveection."

"Conviction," Erin repeated to Jay-Jay.

There was a smidge of flirtation in Erin's stare, a look he hadn't seen in well over a year, but now, he felt like a fraud. He gave a smile back; her prowess was the glue that had always bound them together. Right then, he decided to hold on a bit tighter before she'd let go for good.

As they glided about the room, occasionally taking turns tripping over one another, Jay felt her need to lead subside and became more fluid with him. *Why did we wait so long to do something like this?* He lifted and twirled her around.

"I love you," Erin mouthed, the tip of her nose grazing his.

"God, I love you too," he said and brought her in for a kiss.

"Zat's zee spirit!" Francois squealed and continued following them along.

Chapter Twenty-Eight

Megan's eyes gradually lifted while Deirdre puttered with the machines by the headboard.

"Where is everybody?" Meg said, rubbing her eyelids and letting out a vigorous yawn. "It's Friday night. Where are my boys?"

Deirdre quietly untangled a few wires.

Megan picked up her cell phone and began typing a text message with two frail thumbs but stopped mid-sentence. "Do you think he's done with me?"

Deirdre whirled to stare at Meg incredulously. "What? Of course not! Why do you say that?"

"Look at me. I've aged about twenty years. I'm bald, have discolored skin, weigh about eighty pounds soaking wet. Nothing's attractive about me anymore."

Deirdre walked to the bed and sat. "Megan, I have to tell you something, but swear to me you won't go crazy."

"Crazy is all I am of late." Megan focused on her friend. "Okay, I promise. I think." She noticed Deirdre's hesitation. *Not good.*

"Rob had an accident at work today. He's okay, but he, too, is in a hospital. All of his wounds are curable, and he's in a stable condition."

Megan turned to the IV connections. "Help me," she said and began detaching herself from the tubes. "Take me to him."

Dee jumped up and shut down the heart monitor so the alarm didn't set off.

When Megan was wireless, Deirdre took out a set of keys. "Stay here for a minute." She unclipped the name badge and rushed out of the room.

"Here, put these on," Deirdre said, reentering and tossing a sweater and pants onto the bed.

Megan, who spied the motorcycle helmet, joyfully dropped the hospital gown and got herself dressed. After she did, Deirdre wheeled over a chair and put Meg in the seat, plopped the gear on her lap, then covered it with a blanket.

Megan tried not to jostle in the chair as Deirdre sprinted them toward an open elevator.

"Huh, that's rare," Deirdre said, panting as they entered. "Great timing."

Megan gazed up at her. "Thank you for this."

Dee winked and secured the helmet to Megan's head.

When the elevator reopened, they rushed out and across the lobby, straight into the parking lot. She helped Megan climb the motorcycle, then reached into the rear saddlebag and pulled out a belt.

Megan looked confused. "What's that for?"

"It's normally for pants, but not tonight." Deirdre straddled the bike, then fastened the leather band around them. "Like a seatbelt. But I still want you to hold on to me tight," she said, kicking up the stand.

"10-4." Megan gripped Deirdre's waist.

Deirdre revved the engine, causing the rosary beads to vibrate and tickle Megan's chest. She then straightened the handlebars and drove away.

The motorcycle accelerated onto the highway.

Megan held on as they sped forward, enjoying the wind brushing past her.

"This is freedom," Meg yelled and pressed her eyes shut. "Sweet Jesus, it's like the cancer is flying right off my body. Go faster!"

As Deirdre gunned it, Megan imagined the diseased particles scattering on the deserted road in their wake.

When they arrived at the other hospital, Deirdre reattached the identification badge and grabbed a wheelchair from the ER. As Megan shifted into the vinyl seat, her grip tightened around Deirdre and pulled her close. "I don't know how we ever lost touch."

"We graduated," Deirdre said, chuckling. "No, seriously, I went off to med school and, unfortunately, didn't keep in touch with anybody."

"Well, you complete me. You're the one that feeds my soul the adventure, spontaneity, and security it needs right now."

Dee grinned. "What about Rob?"

"He's the one that nurtures my desire for intimacy, fantasy, and family."

Deirdre lifted Megan's chin so that they were eye-to-eye. "You live life poetically. I've always admired that quality in you."

Megan blushed and closed her eyes. Suddenly, there were light kisses on each lid.

"Come on, my love, let's go find that man of yours."

****

White bandages covered Rob's head, neck, and shoulders. His face brandished a red hue, but he appeared unharmed, just asleep.

Megan wheeled herself closer to the bed and extended an arm. She touched his fingers poking out from underneath the covers.

Rob slowly opened his eyes and, with his free hand, pulled back the blanket partially off his body. "I won't be able to change diapers for a little while, sorry, hon," he said.

Meg looked at his other arm wrapped in a hardened cast. "We'll figure it out. I'm just so glad you're alive."

"Me too." He ran his fingers over her bare scalp when footsteps clamored from the hallway.

Erin and Jay-Jay bolted in.

"Oh my God, what happened?" Erin said, rushing to Rob's bed, still clutching Jay-Jay's hand. "We're sorry we missed all the calls. We were on our date night."

"There was a fire in the Prospect Apartments," Rob said, then turned his gaze to Jay. "I grabbed a 10-45. Pregnant."

Erin gasped.

An eerie silence drifted through the room as all eyes turned toward her. "I'm sorry, go on," Erin said, shooing away the attention.

"She was brought here," Rob continued. "Jay, can you check her status?"

"Uh, sure." He released his hand from Erin's and started out.

Erin turned to follow. "I'll come with you."

"No!" Jay snapped. "I got this."

"Let him go by himself, Er," Rob said, rubbing his forehead. "They'll more than likely give a firefighter information if he's alone."

Megan waved. "You gonna say hello to me or what?" She laughed as Erin blinked a couple of times.

"Holy shit, Meg. *Meg!* How the hell did you get here?"

Megan held up a wobbly hand. "Long story, girlfriend. Long story."

"Okay, people, my turn," Deirdre interrupted and moved to the bed. "Listen, you guys. You're both going to need a lot of help. I mean, *a lot*. Meg, your parents can't do it alone, so I'm going to do what I can for Rob and the boys when I'm not at work."

Megan glanced at Rob and then at Deirdre. "We didn't even think that far ahead," Meg said. "Thank you so much."

Dee smiled. "That's what friends are for." She stretched her arms around them, and they formed a group huddle.

"And Jay-Jay and I can help whenever Deirdre's at the hospital," Erin added, walking over.

Jay reentered the room, and everyone's head popped up.

"What's the matter, Jelani? You look like you just saw a ghost," Erin said.

All eyes remained on him.

"Nothing. It's nothing. The 10-45 is fine," he replied and swatted at the air.

Megan looked to Erin, who was busy watching Jay-Jay linger in the doorway. *Something's definitely up with him.* Meg eyed Rob, but his rising shoulders indicated he had no clue what was triggering Jay's nerves.

Chapter Twenty-Nine

"Erin, I have to tell you something."

Erin pulled herself away from an email and peered over the computer screen. "What's up?"

"It's good news and bad—well, it's not really *bad* news because it's an opportunity that I, I mean *we*, can't refuse."

Erin remained expressionless. "Is it with contracting or the FDNY?"

"Neither."

Erin sized him up. She'd been down this road with Jay before. FEMA, the Federal Emergency Management Agency, always called him for rescue missions. They had deployed him to various hurricane sites around the country. Mudslides and wildfires in California. He'd even flown to Haiti after the massive earthquake. He'd been sent to so many catastrophes to participate in life-saving efforts because of his specialty training with the fire department that she knew he was referring to this. But communication was normally sparse, and the deployments were unpredictably lengthy, which often left her sitting on pins for weeks-on-end wondering when—or even *if*—he'd return. Still, the last time he worked in disaster relief, he had brought home close to forty-grand. It was money they used for both rounds of IVF. So, in a way, saying no was not in the cards.

"Where to this time?" Erin asked, trying to sound

even-keeled.

"Nowhere," Jay whispered. "There's a tragedy right here."

Erin shut the laptop. "I'm listening."

Jay raised his hands to his head and paced the floor. "I fucked up, Er. I fucked up bad, and I'm really sorry."

Erin jerked back in the office chair. "I'm not following. You said you had good news. How does you fucking up equate to good news?"

Jay stopped in his tracks. "Because maybe—just maybe—there could be some light to my mistake. My"—he paused and blew out a breath—"my massive mistake."

"Will you spit it out already?" She leaned forward fast, and the chair swiveled. One foot banged hard on the floor, putting an end to the chair's movement.

"I slept with Lucinda, the bartender at the tavern. It was only one time."

"What?" Erin halted in the seat. "When?"

Jay-Jay turned and faced the wall, his forehead thumping against it. "Months ago. The night I had you play firefighter, but then we got into that fight."

"I remember that night." Erin sucked her teeth and slammed a fist on the desk. "Face me and talk to me like a real man!"

Jay stood up straight and faced her. "It was only one time."

"You say that like it matters!" She pointed a finger at the wall. "Actually, turn the fuck around and stay in the corner. You don't deserve to look at me."

He did an about-face. "You don't have to worry about her," he whispered to the wall.

"What the hell does that mean?" Erin sat again, but

the chair was anything but comfortable.

"She's in the hospital on life support."

"Wait a minute. Was *Lucinda* Rob's 10-45?"

Jay looked down at his shoes.

"Answer me!"

He flinched. "Yes."

"But Rob said the woman was pregnant." The room suddenly became fuzzy.

"She, she is." He cleared his throat. "The hospital is keeping her body alive until it's time to deliver. I'm the baby's father."

Erin placed both elbows on the desk and rested her head in her hands. It felt like someone just stole their golden ticket for happiness. Feeling woozy, she said sternly, "I need you to leave."

The office door opened, then closed without a single sound of a footstep. Erin fell back in the chair, gasping and sweating. *Dear Mother of God, what did I do to deserve this?*

She endeavored to ease the pain growing inside by concentrating on her air intake, but a wave of nausea consumed her. She grabbed the wastebasket by the desk and threw up violently into it.

When the dizziness finally passed, Erin set the pail on the floor. Never had she *ever* wanted her mother until now. She rolled herself back to the laptop and double-tapped the Facetime app on the home screen. When her own image appeared, all breathing ceased. Her face was paler than paste, the bags prominent under each eye. *And I thought* he'd *seen a ghost.*

Instead of calling, Erin text messaged.

—Gail, please tell me you're free tomorrow...—

—Sorry, chick, I'm working on getting out of here

for the weekend. Why, what's tomorrow?—

—Dr. Ansaldi's. Damn it, damn it, damn it.—

Okay, don't panic, you got this. She linked all ten fingers together and pushed up into a stretch. *If the tumor is benign, Assisted Hatching it is. And now I don't need douchebag's approval.* Her knuckles cracked in unison.

A subsequent message popped onto the screen from Gail.

—Megan's obviously not available but, depending on what it is, maybe Deirdre can help?—

Erin's arms dropped into her lap. Did she really want someone she felt she hardly knew coming to a personal appointment? And at a time like this?

—I'll see. TTYL.—Erin typed and left the computer to pour herself a glass of white.

On the way to the kitchen, Erin caught sight of Jay packing a duffel bag. She stopped a little past the doorway and then backed up. "Did you honestly think I'd accept your lovechild as my own?"

His cheeks puffed as he exhaled. "That's—"

"*That's* what, Jelani?" She folded then unfolded her arms. "The only thing *that* is, is fucking absurd. You really are a moron."

Erin stampedoff, got the wine, and returned to the computer. She didn't want to talk about any of this but felt she'd implode without some sort of human distraction. She jabbed at the face-to-face button and called Gail.

"You're going on a legit vacation?" Erin asked when Gail appeared.

"Don't know yet," Gail said, flipping through a brochure. "Harry and I collected a few of these over the years, but the thought of taking a plane alone has me queasy."

"Alone sounds dreamy," Erin retorted.

Gail laughed. "Easy for you to say when you have someone to come home to."

Erin tried to remain indifferent but gave in, knowing the uncontrollable nostril flare would be a dead giveaway. "Yeah, no. That's not happening anymore."

"Oh, honey." Gail's laugh faded. "Did you two have another argument?"

Erin squeezed a fist. The thought of saying what Jay did aloud caused a thickness in her throat that suffocated her voice box.

"Like I've said, you two need to work on each other. And I mean more than just one date," Gail said.

Erin looked as Gail grabbed a couple of the brightly colored pamphlets from a pile on the table and fanned them in front of the screen. "Maybe take one of these."

"The dancing was great," Erin croaked. She shifted upright in the chair and drank the wine to soothe the tension. "But, actually, we're on the path to divorce court, not an airport."

"Don't say that. All relationships have their ups and downs. You're both just going through a rough patch."

"I wouldn't call cheating a rough patch," Erin replied.

"What? That prick!" Gail scowled at the glossy leaflets and, with a quick swoop, heaved the spread into the trash can.

"What? The pictures of buoyant couples lounging poolside sipping fruity umbrella drinks didn't do it for ya?" Erin said, her words soaked in sarcasm. She stole another taste of Pinot Grigio, glad the conversation was diverting organically back to travel. "What about a bed-

and-breakfast?"

Gail crossed each leg atop the big buttery leather high-back. "I-I don't know. I've never been to one. I mean, I want solitude, but I don't want to be completely alone."

"Well," Erin began, "there's this quaint Victorian B and B not too far from where we live. Sounds perfect for the solace you want. The owner is a World War II survivor, her husband a Vietnam Vet, and the clientele there happens to be both active and retired service members. They usually go there to clear their heads— you know—read books, drink tea, commiserate with one another, eat a home-cooked meal they otherwise wouldn't have because they are widowed."

Gail's face filled the entire screen. "How do you know about this place?"

Erin shrugged. "I read about it on social media."

"Ew." Gail sank back again.

"Oh, stop. This B and B was meant for you. Shit, I'd go if I were in your shoes. Pack some vino, and you're set."

One corner of Gail's mouth perked up. "Come with me!"

"I can't. I have Ansaldi's appointment, remember?"

"Grr, okay." Gail sank into the buttery leatherback chair. "So, you're saying there's a possibility of a local place where I can escape? A spot for people like me— folks with dead partners?"

Erin whipped out her smartphone. "I'll search it right here and prove it to you."

Gail held up two sets of crossed fingers as Erin typed on the keypad.

"Got it," Erin said and aimed the device in Gail's direction. "Grab a pen."

Chapter Thirty

Deirdre picked up Mr. Sultenfuss after reentering the apartment and marched directly to the bedroom; her leg accidentally grazed the sheets of the mattress. She shuddered. *Ew. Those are the first to go.* Dee put the cat on the dresser and retrieved a pair of rubber gloves from the first aid kit in the top drawer.

The protective wear snapped onto her wrists, and she got to work, ripping off the bedding.

"I really can't believe I didn't see this coming. I bet you did, though, huh, Mr. S?"

The cat's head tilted slightly.

Deirdre headed for the closet. On the floor was a folder with the fire department logo on it. She studied it, wondering if all the excitement about Cliff's budding firefighting career masked what was really going on. In the past, this penchant for men in uniform had blinded her from the liars and narcissists, but now, she'd know a cheater when she saw one. Dee turned and threw the folder in the trash.

Mr. Sultenfuss brushed his body against her boot.

"I'm sorry, pal, but I can't stay. I'll be back for you real soon, though. I promise." She went to double-check the cat's food, water, and litter box.

Before leaving, she gathered clothes in a fresh garbage bag, then bent down and petted his soft back. "I'll figure things out. Get us a nice place away from here."

With the bag slung over a shoulder, she seized the handle of the front door and exited the apartment.

****

"What are you doing back here so soon?" Megan asked as Deirdre strolled in with her things.

"This is going to be my new residence for a little while." Dee hurled the trash bag onto the vinyl chair.

"You can't stay at your home, huh?"

"No way."

"I don't blame you. I wouldn't be able to either." Megan patted the bed.

"We'll be roommates," Deirdre said, hopping onto the mattress.

"Don't be silly. You're not really going to try living here."

"All I do is work, anyway. Besides, where the hell am I gonna go? And with what money?"

"My house."

Deirdre's head perked up but dropped again. "What about my cat? Are your boys allergic? What about Rob?" She nibbled at an already haggard fingernail.

"You have a cat?"

Deirdre stopped biting her cuticle. "Yeah."

Megan stared without batting an eye.

"Oh no, please tell me you don't hate cats," Dee began. "I thought you were perfect, and now you're going to screw it all up."

"I think it's amazing that you're into felines. It's just that you strike me as more of a dog aficionado—like being the proud owner of a Mastiff or some other tremendous hound."

Deirdre laughed. "I love dogs. *Under*dogs. That's

what cats are, and they're my favorite."

Megan pushed away hair that blanketed Deirdre's face. "My children love cats too. Welcome to the Dunham household."

Deirdre rested a cheek on Megan's shoulder, then kissed it. "Thank you."

They lowered themselves onto the pillows and listened to the blips of the machines play a sort of lullaby. Deirdre's eyes followed the dancing lines until they got so heavy they closed.

At dawn, a glint of sun slipped through the curtains. Deirdre carefully stretched and peeked over at Megan, but she was still asleep. Dee snuck out of the bed, prancing barefoot into the bathroom to prepare for a twelve-hour shift.

After attaching the nametag to her garb, she slipped into her Crocs, stowed the trash bag under Megan's bed, and tiptoed out.

Throughout the morning, Deirdre popped in and out of the room. At lunchtime, she was about to ask Megan where to order food from when she spotted Erin sitting beside Meg on the bed, a bunch of colorful balloons swaying above them. Deirdre pushed lightly on the sanitizer dispenser on the wall, debating whether to enter.

"She's coming to live with you?" Erin asked.

"Yes. She needs a place to stay. She can't sleep in the very spot where Cliff had sex with another person," Megan said.

"I wish Jelani would've cheated in our bed. It'd give me a reason to burn that place down." Erin sucked in a heavy breath.

Jay-Jay cheated? Deirdre massaged the disinfectant

into her hands and rested quietly against the wall.

"You're way better than that Lucinda whore," Megan said.

They fell silent, and Megan shifted on the mattress.

"Hey, you think Deirdre would come to my doctor's appointment later at Ansaldi's?" Erin asked.

"Don't know. Ask her."

Deirdre pushed off the wall and cleared her throat loudly to make herself known. "Ask me what?"

She walked toward them as if she hadn't been in the room and shoved both hands into the pockets of her scrubs.

Erin patted the top of the bed. "You and I have a lot in common, *man*-wise, and I could really use someone who gets it—who gets *me* at this point," she said. "The short version of my saga is that I've got an appointment tonight at seven with the fertility specialist, and I could use the emotional support. I'll tell you specifics about what happened on the ride. Our miseries can enjoy each other's company."

Deirdre glanced at the clock. "My shift ends at four. I've got to jet back to the apartment for the furniture pick-up at five, but that shouldn't take long; it's all getting donated, then I'm heading to Megan's to get my cat situated." She looked at Erin. "But, yeah, I can go. Meet me at Meg's at six-thirty."

"Oh, thank God," Megan chirped and pressed her hands into a prayer pose. "Please call me after, you guys, and, Dee, I'll give you the entry code to my garage. Rob already knows to expect you."

****

The driver from Goodwill slammed the rear door of the truck and handed Deirdre a clipboard. She signed off on a piece of paper and gave the man a tip.

"Thanks," he said and turned on his heel.

Deirdre watched as he returned to the vehicle and pulled away, her past wheeling down the road with him.

"And just like that, everything's gone," Deirdre said, the cell phone now pressed tight to her ear.

"Consider the upside of this," Megan said. "When I'm discharged, we'll be roommates! I'm way more fun, promise. Now, get the hell out of there. The garage code is five-five-one-three."

"Okay." Deirdre unintentionally sniffled into the phone when hanging up.

She kneeled by Mr. Sultenfuss, who was unhappy being in his carrier. He let out a loud, drawn-out growl. "I know, I know," Dee muttered and stuck her fingers in the crate. She stroked him until a car stopped a few feet away. "Okay, Mr. S, that's our ride."

The drive to Megan's was surprisingly quick. When the cab pulled up to the house, Rob was walking out of the garage and down the driveway.

"How are you feeling?" Deirdre asked, eyeing his cast as she stepped out of the vehicle.

"As good as one could be like this." He laughed and took hold of her bag with his other hand. "They discharged me a few hours ago, but I have a follow-up with my primary in the morning."

Deirdre nodded and followed him into the house. The cat released a set of rambunctious cries when the carrier was placed on the floor.

"What's its name?" Rob asked and sat on his heels for a better look.

"Mr. Sultenfuss."

Rob's laugh sounded more like a bark. "What the

hell kind of name is that?"

"From the movie, *My Girl*. You know, Dan Aykroyd's character. Come on, that's the best Macaulay Culkin flick from our youth."

"Don't know it," he said and attempted to stand.

Deirdre helped him up. "Figures you wouldn't."

Trevor and Kenny ran to the travel container and knelt beside it. The cat's paw poked out and swatted at their fingers as they tried to touch him through the small grates.

"Easy, guys, he's a bit scared," Deirdre said and pushed his furry nub back inside the box. "But don't worry, he doesn't have any nails. He was declawed when I got him."

Trevor's curious eyes focused on Deirdre's. "What's declawed mean?"

"It just means they cut his nails very short," Rob interjected. He put his uninjured hand on his son's head and gave it a friendly scratch. "Trevor loves animals. He wants to be a veterinarian when he grows up. Right, buddy?"

Trevor studied his own fingernails, then looked at the cat again. "When can I pet him?"

Deirdre unhinged the lock on the cage and carefully opened the door, but Mr. S darted between her legs toward the couch. She tried to catch him, failing miserably.

"Psst. Come here, Mr. Sultenfuss," Deirdre said, getting to the floor and crawling toward the sofa.

Trevor and Kenny crouched on all fours and followed, giggling as they moved.

Rob went to the kitchen and returned with a bowl of tuna fish. "Here, try this." He gave it to Deirdre.

"Guaranteed it'll work."

She set it down in front of the animal; the room suddenly quiet. Mr. Sultenfuss's little pink nose appeared from behind the couch, followed by his yellow marble eyes, which glistened at his audience. After about a minute, he dashed to the food and buried his head in the bowl.

"Wow, he totally likes that stuff," Deirdre said, listening to him chew.

"They all do." Rob picked up the garbage bag that was lying in the middle of the floor. "Let me guess. Louis Vuitton?" His cackle scared the cat back into hiding.

Deirdre elbowed his leg and continued to gawk at Mr. Sultenfuss, who was busy licking his chops clean from beneath the end table.

Trevor wrapped his skinny arms around Deirdre. "Thank you for bringing your kitty. I love him."

Deirdre's heart melted like butter. It'd been pretty much *never* since she's experienced the loving innocence of a child. It was the purest thing she'd ever felt. But she just got here. And, really, the love was directed toward the cat, so she forced herself to stay intact. "Aww, you're welcome, sweetie. I'm glad he makes you happy!" She patted his back gently.

****

Deirdre crushed the pizza box from dinner as Rob settled the boys in their beds to relax. She searched every cabinet for a recycling bin, learning the way around the kitchen.

"So, are you going to tell me what happened with Cliff or what?" he asked when he reentered.

Deirdre spun around and swiped her greasy fingers on a dishtowel. "With Cliff? What do you want to know?"

He pulled a chair away from the table and sat, propping his cast onto the wooden surface. "What happened? I mean, something obviously went down for you to be here."

Deirdre yanked a paper towel from the roll. "Let's just say it didn't work out."

Rob raised a brow. "You're beautiful. Smart. I can't imagine what would've gone wrong."

"Why? What do you know?" Deirdre said, then held up a hand. "Because you obviously know more than you're alluding to."

Rob's heightened brow twitched. "I have my suspicions."

"On?"

"His sexuality."

She swung a fist and punched him square in his good arm.

"It's only a hunch. Geez."

"Fuck you."

"Why are you so angry?" Rob became reserved for a minute, then continued. "'Cause if that's the thing—that he's gay—then that's on him, not you."

Deirdre glared at him and slowly settled into a nearby chair. "Explain."

"My sister is into chicks...doesn't flaunt it or anything, but doesn't deny it either. She is who she is. Anyway, I know not all people are comfortable with how they're born, but they have a choice. Cliff pursued you, knowing he liked dudes, which made your relationship with him a farce. Doomed from the beginning. So, to me, that's on him, not you."

Deirdre considered this, then got up. "I'm going to

unpack. Erin will be here in half an hour for a doctor's appointment. Thanks for the chat. Let's keep it between us."

Dee walked down the hall on tippy-toes, careful not to disturb the kids, then closed the door. She stood in the dark and felt along the wall for a switch. The light cast down on the guest bedroom, which was painted a primary blue and filled with football paraphernalia. "Men and their caves," she said, shaking her head.

Her eyes wandered to a series of plaques that hung above a dozen trophies lined on the bureau and spotted a ceramic statue of a quarterback catching a ball. *Geesh. He must've been some athlete.* She touched a pair of cleats dipped in gold that hung from the mirror and turned to a bookshelf, eyes trailing along a row of spines, mostly sports-related titles, until she came to a photo album. She hesitated and glanced at the closed door before returning all attention to it.

Plastic crinkled as Deirdre opened the album. She studied the four-by-sixesof Rob and Megan throughout their relationship: in front of his fire truck, at the beach, on his motorcycle. Deirdre's fingertips grazed the pictures of the young couple. She closed the book, about to return it to the shelf, when a wallet-sized photo slipped out and fell to the floor. She picked it up and saw Megan dolled up as a bride, clutching a bouquet of Gerbera daisies. Standing near was Rob in a crisp, black tux. *Marriage. That's what happens when you're in an honest relationship.*

There was a soft knock on the bedroom door. Deirdre hurried and put the stuff back. "Come in."

The knob jiggled a bit. Dee could tell it was one of the kids by the flimsy wayit was being handled. She hopped over the garbage bag and helped open it.

"I just wanted to say good night," Trevor said, looking up in a sleepy haze.

Deirdre bent down and hugged him. "Good night, lil' man. Sleep tight, don't let the bed bugs bite."

He smiled and pecked her cheek. "Don't let the buggy bugs bite."

Deirdre's heart did a jittery flip. She picked him up and planted a bunch of kisses on his face. He laughed, shaking his head from side to side, but succumbed to it and buried his cheek on her shoulder. Dee stood in the middle of the doorway, cradling the boy until she mustered up the courage to let him go and then retreated for the night. It was now that she realized he'd been loving on her this whole time, the cat notwithstanding.

She reentered the room feeling as if the real purpose was to be a nurturing figure the boys needed while their mother was in the hospital. Not as a replacement mom, but rather as a "cool aunt" kind of person they could resort to. *Who has time for a boyfriend, anyway?*

Deirdre pulled the cell from her pants pocket and plopped onto the bed. The battery was low, but she dialed anyway.

"Hello?"

"I hate you," Deirdre said.

"I'm sorr—"

"But I forgive you, Cliff."

"You do?" A hint of surprise and gratefulness crept through the connecting line.

"It doesn't mean I'll forget." Deirdre rolled over and rested on her elbows. "But, yes, I forgive you."

"Thank you," Cliff said and let out a breathy sigh. "None of this was your fault."

"Shh. This isn't about whose fault it was. It's about being true to yourself and others—like me and, I hate to say it, your mother."

"What do you mean?"

Mr. Sultenfuss catapulted onto the bed from the dresser, but she ignored him. "Well, you're not gonna burst into your house and be like, 'Hi, I'm gay,' but if you can't keep it a secret anymore or if it comes out some other way, you've got to be prepared, you know. Be ready to talk *and* have a thick skin about it."

There was no response from Cliff.

"Okay, well. Bye, then."

"This is why I love you," he said, finally.

"Thanks. But seriously, think about what I've said." Deirdre ended the call and reached out to stroke the silky ball of fur squirming next to her. "Well, Mr. S, I guess it's official. I'm a cat lady."

Chapter Thirty-One

The gynecologist's office was jam-packed with women of all ages, shapes, and sizes, leaving no room to sit.

"Even the floor is overcrowded," Erin grumbled, worming through the vestibule as Deirdre held the door open. She tried not to step on anyone as she went to reception. "This is crazy. I don't know how many more of these lengthy appointments I can handle. It's so obvious they overbook."

The secretary barely peeled away from the computer screen. "We'll call your name when it's your turn. Have a seat."

"Newsflash—there are no seats!" Erin hammered the pen atop the clipboard and walked away.

At the other end of the room, Deirdre pushed a coat rack into the corner. "Come and sit here," she said and patted the single square shadow on the carpet. "I'll wait in the car until it's your turn. Text me, and I'll come back in."

"You got it. And, thanks again for this," Erin said.

Once Deirdre left, Erin tried to get comfortable. She skimmed a parenting magazine, massaged each leg, checked the hour hand on her wristwatch, but nothing could deter the nerves as she waited for the results of the tumor.

She took out the phone and dialed Jay-Jay. "Are the

kitchen cabinets being delivered today?"

"Not exactly." There were voices scrambling in the background wherever he was. "I canceled the order."

Erin took the mobile and banged it against the carpet repeatedly before returning it to the side of her face. "Please tell me you're joking."

"I thought there was no reason to move forward with a remodel," Jay-Jay quipped.

Erin got up. "You also thought it was a good idea to screw another woman."

A pregnant lady sitting nearby lowered her novel. Erin made brief eye contact with her, then stomped out.

"I don't know how much more I can take," Erin said, pacing the sidewalk. "Everything's fucked."

Jay-Jay talked through static. "Hold up, I'm confused."

"No need to be confused. I'm selling the house. Call them back and reschedule. You broke this, now you'll fix it so that *I* can move on." Erin paused and clutched her stomach. "Oh, my. Ouch."

"Erin, what's the matter?" Jay said, his voice barely audible as the phone slipped.

The sudden pressure in her torso was intense, breathing erratic as she crouched on the pavement. Gasping and sweating, Erin hunched over; the lines in the concrete were beginning to move. Trying to focus, lightheadedness rushed over her as heat emanated from every muscle. "My, my body. I can't." A wave of nausea caused her to throw up and fall over.

The door to the practice swung open, and the doctor rushed to the curb with his staff. They swarmed Erin and eased her onto the lawn. "Don't move," Dr. Ansaldi instructed.

"How'd you—" Erin began.

"Your friend called us," he said, then turned to the nurses. "Let's make a gurney."

Deirdre came running up the block on the phone as two women shook out a white sheet. It puffed like a hot air balloon and floated to the grassy surface.

"What do you feel?" the physician asked, now pumping a bulb attached to Erin's arm.

"Like I'm weightless, and everything's spinning. And, my body…it's on fire."

"Okay, stay still." He turned and addressed his team. "Barbara, call 9-1-1 and get an ambulance. Laura, call the hospital and have them prep an OR. STAT!"

Erin watched the gynecologist address Deirdre, who was now beside him. "Erin is showing signs of distress. We need to investigate further. From what she's explaining of her symptoms, it sounds like—"

"The cyst may have ruptured," Deirdre cut in. "But you won't know for sure until you get Erin on the examination table with the right equipment. Got it. I had to park down the street." Dee yanked keys off her belt loop. "I'll meet you there. Methodist, right?"

"Yes, Methodist Hospital." Dr. Ansaldi studied Deirdre's face for a moment. "Erin's lucky to have you as a friend, huh?"

"It takes a strong woman to know a strong woman. Right, Er?"

Erin mustered the energy to wink before her eyes closed entirely.

****

Deirdre rushed to the main desk of the emergency room. "Harper. Erin Harper," she said, words tight. She placed an elbow on the counter as a woman typed rapidly into a database.

The receptionist's eyes trailed away from the computer and fixed on her. "Are you all right, ma'am?"

"Water. May I have some water?"

The secretary rolled her chair to the cooler. "Why don't you have a seat over by the television, and I'll bring it to you."

"No, that's okay. I really need to see my friend." Deirdre accepted the Dixie cup and chugged the drink.

"She's up in the gynecology wing, fourth floor. Go to Room B."

Deirdre crumpled the empty cup and hurried down the hall. *It shouldn't be like this. Jesus Christ, of all things, she can't lose her uterus.* Sweat formed at Dee's hairline as she headed upstairs.

When the elevator reached the fourth floor, she found the Obstetrics Unit. The entrance was closed. She stared at the door handle, hand trembling.

"Doctor Ansaldi. Paging Doctor Ansaldi. Dial 1-2-2-7."

Deirdre looked up at the loudspeaker. "That's Erin's doctor." She hauled open the door and tore down the corridor.

The curtains of Room B were drawn, but not fully. Deirdre pressed her face against the glass and tried to see beyond the white hangings. Erin had a thin oxygen tube under her nose and an intravenous tube connected to an arm. Two separate bags hung on a metal hook next to the bed. Machines were monitoring heartbeat and blood pressure, yet Erin appeared unaware and drugged. *Ugh, what a nightmare.* Deirdre studied Erin's face. Her skin was pale, eyelids pink.

Just then, a nurse stepped out of the room. "Are you

Erin Harper's sister?"

"No, I'm not. I'm her friend," Deirdre said, meeting the woman halfway. "But, I'm also a medic."

"Yes, yes. Okay, so Dr. Ansaldi confirmed that Erin's cyst did indeed rupture, and it exposed her body to the toxins that were inside it. We flushed them out with saline in an IV. Once the doctor deems Erin stable, he'll operate to rebuild the uterine wall. She'll be here for a few days but is expected to make a full recovery."

Deirdre dawdled with the zipper on her jacket. "Shit, poor Erin."

The nurse put a hand on Deirdre's shoulder. "This is good news. Erin will be up and back to normal in no time."

Deirdre gave the woman a strange look. "Normal? So that means she still has a chance at pregnancy?"

"That's not for me to say. The doctor will be out with a full report shortly."

Deirdre hesitated, then headed to the rows of empty plastic seats. She sat and pulled out her phone to relay the news to Gail when a man doting a stethoscope approached her. "Dr. Ansaldi?"

He nodded. "Upon extensive examination, we concluded that Erin's uterine wall needed total reconstruction; the tumor was rather large, and—"

Deirdre stood and held up her palm. "I know, I know."

Dr. Ansaldi was startled. "You do?"

"Yes. A nurse informed me earlier," she said. "Anyway, what does this mean for Erin and conceiving?"

"I can recommend other options."

"Like?"

"Adoption."

"No way. She'll never go for it. So, she really won't be able to have a baby?"

"I'm afraid not," the doctor said, his eyes straying off. "Erin and I can discuss this further during a postoperative visit but, right now, she's in recovery, so you can go home, and we'll call you when she's awake." He did a quick military-like turn.

Deirdre maneuvered around and blocked him, gritting her teeth. "Having a child was *all* Erin wanted to do. This will absolutely kill her."

"As you may know, your friend has been in and out of my office for years with gynecological problems. The news won't be as shocking as you think. Now, go home and get some rest. If you'll excuse me."

She watched the surgeon make his way out of the conversation and down the hall. "Well, I'm *not* leaving, despite what you think," Dee called out and soldiered to the seat. "So, you better keep me apprised!"

Deirdre dropped again onto the hard plastic. *There's no way in hell she'll live through this while Jay-Jay becomes a father.* She scrolled through her phone for Gail's number and pressed Call.

"Hi, you've reached Gail O'Neil…"

Deirdre inhaled and prepped herself for the deliverance of an even-keeled message when the recording finished.

"Hey, Gail. It's Dee. Listen, please call me when you get the chance. It's about Erin…"

Chapter Thirty-Two

Gail squinted hard to read the numbers on each building as she drove down the bumpy dead-end road. Her car inched toward a large yellow mansion perched on a sprawling lawn. The lush tall shrubbery at the curb created an emerald barricade between the public street and the private property. Gail parked in front and stared up at the swaying brush. There was a single red flower amid the green backdrop. The petals danced in the wind as if greeting her. She took hold of the cell phone, clicked away from the voicemail, and snapped a picture.

"Thank you, Harry," she said, admiring the photo, and then grabbed the luggage off the passenger seat.

A finely pruned path led to the main entrance of the bed-and-breakfast. Gail hesitated, then rang the bell. Antique furniture decorated the porch. A cream-and-gold porcelain lamp with a downward swooping shade sat between stacks of yellowing books on a weather-worn table. Next to that was an old wooden rocker and another table, its legs uneven, covered in a turquoise paint. Gail, in awe, took another photo.

"You must be Gail," a petite, white-haired lady said, appearing behind the glass enclosure. "I'm Zofie. Come inside. It's chilly out there."

Gail stepped into the house and immediately admired the giant crystal chandelier twinkling above them.

"Wow," she said, marveling the décor. "Zofie, this place is—my gosh." Gail swiveled around, looking up. "The high ceiling, grand fixture, the maple crown molding."

She walked in further to one of the plush couches and stroked the velvety arm, noticing the tremendous Italian marble fireplace in the dining room a few feet away.

"May I?" she said, glancing again at the innkeeper.

"My pleasure."

Gail approached the mantel and grazed a finger over the smooth stone. She turned to Zofie, ready to shower the home with more compliments, but the woman was busy with a tea set on a glass server at the far end of the room.

"Tea or coffee?" Zofie asked without looking up.

"Coffee, please."

Zofie fixed a cup of steamy sweet-smelling caffeine. "Here. Let me show you around."

They climbed the staircase, Gail careful with the mug. "It's so peaceful," she said. "Am I the only one here for the night?"

Zofie smiled and pushed up her thick spectacles. "No, no, dear. There's a full house tonight. During the day, it's mostly quiet because everyone's out and about. Usually, it's just myself and Leonard. He stays in the suite in the east wing."

"Oh," Gail said sheepishly. *A man.*

The women strolled down a narrow hallway lit by candles in wall sconces. As they walked, Gail remembered the long hall in her grandmother's house, the stretch seemingly infinite. They passed a bathroom and stopped in front of a semi-opened door.

"This is the west room with the porch you requested," Zofie said. "But, since it's a little cold today, you may want to stay in."

Gail peeked inside, noting the ivory Victorian rotary phone with its curvy handle and round golden dial resting on the wooden nightstand, the white crocheted doily patterned bedspread covering the queen-sized mattress, and the simple writing desk with a hutch in the far corner. She envisioned herself reading and sipping hot drinks there until she spied a portrait of a woman with grayish-colored skin above the workstation. Her expression was sickly; the entire piece a reminder of death.

"It is a bit frigid in here," Gail said and let out a quiver. "Have anything else? I don't mind paying extra."

"There's another room with a lot more heat and space if you'd like." Zofie put up a hand. "Free of charge. Let me show you."

Gail sipped the coffee and hurried behind to another part of the house, her eyes scanning every nook and cranny. It was all visual candy. She sighed with relief.

They passed a yellowing calendar hanging on the wall that dated back to 1912. The fruity scent of something pear-like wafting close by caught Gail's attention. "Your house is filled with artifacts. Even the air is adorned."

Zofie chuckled.

Upon entering the bigger suite, Gail saw a black cast iron fireplace cover with fancy etching, a striking contrast to the gleaming white marble frame. She pictured herself lying curled up with a warm blanket and a good book in front of it. She surveyed the area for scary art but found none. "I'll stay here."

Zofie handed her a chain with two dangling keys. "This one is for the bedroom, and this one is for the front door of the house. You can sleep in, or I can have breakfast ready for you bright and early. It's your choice."

"Oh, it's no bother. Whenever you wake up," Gail said, not exactly sure what the B&B etiquette was.

Zofie laughed. "Whatever time you wish. It's your holiday." Her Polish accent was endearing.

"Let's aim for eight o'clock. I'm sure I'll be starving by then."

"Eight it is. I'll have Leonard bring up your bags."

Zofie bowed out of the room, closing the door. Gail put the keys and the coffee mug on a round café table a few steps from the fireplace and walked to the floor-to-ceiling glass casement near the bed. *The sunrise must be really pretty from here.* Her mind wandered to the two sparrows gliding by the window. All was quiet until a loud clunk came from the other side of the door. She stiffened. *Is that the other person? Leonard?*

Gail tiptoed to the peephole and saw her baggage at the entrance. There was also a slow thud of heavy footsteps, but no feet were visible in the circumference of the looking glass. When the walking stopped, she cracked the door open ever so slightly, the side of her nose pressed to it for a better view. A behemoth of a man with a dark, scruffy beard was standing by the staircase, wearing a red flannel shirt, blue denim jeans, and hiking boots. "It's Paul Bunyan," she whispered and giggled.

The man looked. Gail jumped backward and slammed the door. She slouched against it, her heart thumping. Had he heard her? He totally heard. She slid to the floor. The rapid sound of the man's feet descending the stairs hung in the air.

Gail crawled to the table and stretched up for the cell phone but stopped. *I can't let anyone know about this.* She turned to the unlit fireplace. *How am I going to face this guy at breakfast tomorrow morning? What if he works here? I'll probably have to see him sooner. So much for "solitude," Gail O'Neil.* A twinge in her bladder had her wishing that she'd kept the original room with the private bath. Who cared if the portrait looked like a cancer patient? It could have been taken down.

Gail waited, listening for any other sounds out in the hall. Everything was still except for the whistling of the radiator. She got up and slowly turned the knob, the door creaking open as she poked out. The long corridor was vacant. She pulled the baggage inside and then, like a mouse, scurried to the next room, quickly closing the bathroom door.

Exhaling a heavy breath, Gail walked to the sink. "You idiot," she muttered in the mirror and laughed at her reflection as she washed up. She reached for a towel and gasped. There was a pristine white clawfoot tub; she'd always wanted one of these, especially since they've made their comeback in recent years. Gail opened the vanity and searched for some bubble bath. Among the collection of trial-size toiletries was a tiny bottle of raspberry-scented liquid soap, a favorite.

Turn-of-the-century jazz music suddenly burst through the hall. Gail clutched the container and jerked around, listening to the song as she tiptoed out. She moved curiously toward the staircase and went to the first floor.

At the bottom of the landing, she could see into the living room where Paul Bunyan was sitting in the middle of the couch, his arms stretched out on either side. His eyes were closed as he concentrated on the music. Gail crept back up a step.

"It's beautiful, isn't it?" he said, eyes still shut.

She nodded but realized he couldn't see that. "Uh, yes," she said. "A bit loud, but, yes."

His eyes sprung open. "Oh, sorry. I'll lower it." He stood and pressed out the crinkles of his jeans before extending a hand. "The name's Leonard."

With the grace of a ballerina, Gail sashayed over and eased a palm into his. "Nice to meet you, Leonard. I'm Gail." Her face went flush, but she kept cool. "Is the record playing on a Victrola?" she asked, eyes searching the room for one.

Leonard snorted. "No, it's playing on iTunes."

The heat in Gail's cheeks intensified. "Oh, right."

"But Zofie has two Victrolas in the study. Come, I'll show you."

As he eased by her, a hint of woodsy musk lingered in his wake. They maneuvered around an old red leather chair and up the staircase.

"This place is pretty spectacular," Gail said.

"It's definitely special." Leonard led them to the third floor. He pushed open a vault-like door, revealing hundreds of books. There were no windows, just walls of text from the floor up to the ceiling neatly organized on built-in shelves. "You can take a look around," he said.

Gail entered and caught sight of a sturdy, masculine desk made of oak. She was afraid to touch anything, so her eyes did all the work. Beside the spit-shined table was an elegant wooden cabinet crafted out of similar lumber. Leonard lifted the lid. Gail stared at the innards of musical history, examining the thick golden needle, the intricate detail of the carvings in the wood, and the iconic gold emblem of the dog with his ear to the horn of a different style player.

Leonard took a record from the bottom of the cabinet and placed it on the turntable. Gail stood by as he took hold of the crank on the side of the exterior and got the antique to play. The sound was surprisingly crisp and clear.

Gail relaxed and began swaying to the melody. "This must be what Heaven's like, huh, Harry?"

"The name's Leonard," he said, turning the handle.

Gail's eyes bolted open. "Not you. I'm sorry, not you."

A high-pitched crackling of the record snagged their attention. Leonard shuffled through the assortment for a different one.

Gail's palms started sweating. She switched the little bottle of bubble bath from one hand to the other. "My mind drifted to my husband, Harry. *Late* husband, Harry."

Leonard pulled out another album. "I do that often myself."

Gail raised a brow. "You do?"

"All the time. My wife died on Thanksgiving a few years back. Worst day of my life."

"Harry died in November too. I cringe every year when it's time for the holidays."

Leonard reset the needle and turned the crank. As the music played, he began humming and tapping his foot. "I like this little ditty. It's upbeat." He spun around and snapped his fingers. "My Nell loved to boogie."

Gail looked on as he bopped about and grinned, his

goofy nature loosening up the atmosphere. She moved her hips rhythmically, joining in the dance as the trumpets played a series of high notes.

Leonard unexpectedly took her hand and twirled her. Gail fell dizzily into his arms, laughing a deep belly laugh. He steadied her and pointed to the small bottle in her fist. "What's that?"

"Oh, this? Just some bubble bath." She slipped it into the pocket of her pants.

Leonard stopped the record and put everything away. "I won't keep you. I know you're here to relax."

They descended to the second floor, walking by a bedroom whose door was slightly ajar.

"That's where I stay," Leonard said, aiming a finger at it.

"Why's the door open?"

"There's nothing in there worth taking. Nothing of mine, that is."

"Oh." She tried to steal a glimpse inside as they passed. Zofie was inside folding what looked to be his clothes. *That's peculiar.*

He stopped at the closed door several feet away and bowed. "Your room, madam."

Gail hurried to it, pulled out the key, and did a quick, awkward curtsey. When she lifted her head again, a framed watercolor on the wall behind Leonard snagged her attention. Her eyes narrowed to inspect the painting.

He turned to the art of two black figures standing in gray shadows. "That's the only piece in the home that's dated after the millennium," he said.

"Are those two figures firefighters?" Gail asked, inching closer to the work.

"Yes. They're standing in the rubble of the World

Trade Center."

"Oh." Water welled up in her eyes. "Excuse me."

She wrenched open the door, hurried into the room, and secured the latch. *I have to stop overreacting.* She dusted herself off and stood tall. "I can do this."

****

The turquoise bathrobe slid down Gail's body and onto the tiled floor as she dipped her French pedicure into the bubbly water. It was hot and ready. *Ah, now this is what's in order after today.* She eased the rest of her foot into the antique tub, followed by the other, and adjusted comfortably.

Lavender candles flickered along the countertop and filled the air with their fragrance as Gail's mind shifted from Erin to the previous conversation with Leonard in the study. *He didn't stay on the topic of his wife. I wonder why. Hmm. Were they married long? Does he have kids?* She tried to bring the focus back to the quiet, sweet-smelling bathroom but was having trouble. *He seems like he comes here often. Is he related to Zofie? Wait. Where is Zofie? I haven't seen her.*

Loud talking came from the adjoining room. Gail's gaze jerked in that direction. It was Leonard, and he sounded as if he was on the phone. She leaned over the edge for a better listen but couldn't make out what was being said. Everything then went silent again.

Gail reclined on the makeshift pillow (a folded towel) and resumed meditation when a knock sounded on the door. She jolted upright, water splashing out of the tub, dousing the candles. "Someone's in here!"

"I know, Gail, we share a bathroom," Leonard said, his laughter reverberating through the walls. "Zofie wanted me to tell you that there's nightly tea downstairs by the fireplace, and she'd love for you to join in if you'd like."

Well, he's surely a helpful mainstay. She tucked a couple of wet strands behind her ear. "Uh, I don't know. Maybe. What time?"

"Brewing starts at eight." There was a pause. "Okay, well, enjoy your afternoon. Hope to see you there."

Leonard's thick rubber soles echoed down the distressed stairwell. Gail studied the environment and smiled. *Antiques, tea, lighted fireplaces, friendly people. This has got to be God's sweet spot.*

When the water went cold, Gail pulled at the chain-linked drain plug and grabbed the nearest towel from the rack. Once dry, she eased into a pair of starched khakis and pulled on a black turtleneck. A few strokes of a comb, some dainty pearl clip-on earrings, and finally, her wedding ring. She was ready to go but looked down at her snazzy black Gucci flats. A bit dressy for grabbing some fast food but, then again, there was that tea afterward.

"Eh, the hell with it," Gail said and reached for the door handle.

The clang of pots and pans filched Gail's attention on the way to the first floor. She glimpsed Leonard in the main kitchen working alone, wearing a chef's apron and standing in front of the stove, stirring something that undoubtedly smelled delicious. The nagging in her gut, however, had her wondering why he was cooking—even if he *was* a regular.

From the foyer, Gail spied Leonard for another minute, trying to formulate a sensible conclusion, a small part wanting to just go in and ask. But after going unnoticed, she decided against it and wormed out the door.

In the car, Gail's cell rang witha voicemail notification. "Hey, it's Dee. Listen, please call me when you get the chance. It's about Erin."

Chapter Thirty-Three

Like a light switch flipping on, Erin came to; anything with tips felt cold: fingers, ears, nipples. She decided right then and there that the room was frosty and nowhere near home.

"Knock, knock."

Erin turned to see Gail sidling in, carrying a floral bundle. She promptly brought the covers up to her chin. "What in the world is going on?" Erin's limbs stiffened from the cocktail of cold and nerves, but then it was the zing in her side. And then she remembered lying on the concrete outside of Dr. Ansaldi's, gasped, and ripped off the sheets.

"No!" she squawked, staring down at a taut gauze-like girdle.

Gail hurried over and moved the blanket over Erin's waist. "Here. These are for you."

Erin looked at the flowers. "Um, thanks." She took the bouquet, curious why Gail was acting nonchalant, which, indeed, was an act. "Gail, did the doctor tell you anything while I was under?"

"Well, he'll be monitoring you. No worries,though.You'll be back to normal in no time, except with more trips to his office while you heal."

"Heal from what exactly?"

Gail coughed and pulled a chair up to the bedrail. "I'd rather the doctor tell you when he comes in. Or

Deirdre! She's better at explaining things."

"This sounds like it's pretty serious," Erin said. "Can you do me a favor and get the doctor for me?"

"Uh, yeah, sure. I'll go ask the receptionist if she could page him."

Erin seized the flowers and watched tearfully as Gail went into the hall to the main desk. But when Gail was quick to reenter, Erin tried to hide her glassy red eyes with the arrangement. "Is he coming?" she asked from behind the petals.

"DoctorAnsaldi, please dial one-one-nine-zero. Doctor Ansaldi, one-one-nine-zero."

Erin's glance darted to the overhead intercom and then to Gail. "You're here. I'm all bandaged. And Deirdre knows too. Something is going on. Please, tell me what the hell is going on?"

Gail moved toward the bed. "Erin, sweetie, the tumor did some real damage to your insides. They repaired your uterus, so that's a good thing—*terrific* thing—but…" Gail stopped and scratched her brow.

"But what?"

"You won't be able to have a child."

The bouquet faltered from Erin's grasp and landed on the floor.

"Shit," Gail whispered and sat at the edge of the chair. "I didn't want to be the one to tell you. I wish this were all a crazy nightmare that we get to wake up from."

Erin tore the sheet off and touched the compresses, water streaming hard and hot from her eyes.

Gail stood again and crawled into the bed.

Erin tried to focus through the burn. "So, this is it. I really can't have kids?"

Gail wormed an arm under Erin and brought her in

close. "I'm so sorry, Er."

"Does Jay-Jay know yet?"

"He does," Deirdre said, entering the room. "I had no choice but to include him when we were at Ansaldi's, and things were getting serious. Because he's still your husband, he had to authorize everything. Please don't hate me."

Erin looked at the ceiling and sighed. "Maybe this really is meant to be. I mean, I always thought I could prove that I'm stable—this good person who could provide and make a baby—a family. But the trouble is, I'm the broken one, not him."

"Pish! You're not broken," Gail said firmly, shooing away the notion. "Don't ever say that again."

"Seriously," Deirdre interjected. "You've already provided. *You* were Jay-Jay's family. And *you* have done a helluva lot, including providing him with a roof over his head!"

"And don't you remember nursing him back to health after all the funerals? He wouldn't be here if it weren't for you," Gail chimed.

Erin thought of the weeks following September eleventh and the overwhelming number of Jay-Jay's friends and coworkers who had perished in the attacks, their wakes sprouting up one after another. He drank himself through each of them, all seventy-nine of them, mixing night and day like dark whiskey splashing onto light icy cubes; the detox was just as brutal.

Gail continued. "Jay-Jay didn't want to be alive anymore. But you, *you* reminded him of how important he was to his brothers—that the department needed him more than ever. He told me you were his guardian angel."

Just then, Dr. Ansaldi entered the room. "Sorry, ladies, but I'm going to have to ask you to leave," he said, acknowledging Gail and Deirdre by shaking a bottle of Percocet.

"Will those knock me out?" Erin looked expectantly at the doctor.

"They'll relieve your pain and, yes, possibly provide some slumber," he said.

Chapter Thirty-Four

Gail descended the staircase to find Zofie's parlor brimming with life, the long arms of the enormous crystal chandelier seemingly gathering everyone under its massive beauty. As hard as she might, Gail tried to push things with Erin to the back of her mind and home in on the tea, but all she could think was that, so far, it looked more American than English. Gail wasn't sure why it would've been an English tea in the first place, maybe because it sounded more enchanting.

She entered the crowd, realizing it was mostly men, yet sighted a young couple she hadn't seen before. Zofie was at the server handing out teacups, and Leonard was busy pouring. Gail stood back, watching as he manipulated the smoking kettle with refined proficiency, entering and exiting small talk as if it were his job, this social different from any she'd ever attended.

"Hello," a man said, looming near her. He was handsome, sporting a bushel of salt-and-pepper tresses, his skin free of wrinkles, and he wore a navy-blue collared shirt with the words "USS Hancock" embroidered in gold on the breast.

Gail stuck out a manicured hand. "Hi, I'm Gail."

She felt as self-assured as Leonard, whom she spied, was still working the room.

The man's hand suddenly touched hers. It was callused but kind. "Roger."

"A pleasure, Roger. What brings you to the B&B?"

"I served with Zofie's husband in 'Nam." He flicked the emblem on his shirt. "You?"

"My husband was a fireman for the city. I'm here for a little R&R."

"B&B for R&R," Roger said and cackled uncontrollably at his own wit.

She gave a meek smile. "Well, it was nice to meet you, Roger. I'm going to get some tea before it's all gone."

"Leaving me already?" he said, stepping in Gail's path. "You shan't go alone." He tried to slip his hand into hers, but she retracted. He escorted her with a hand planted on her shoulder instead, which she wanted to shake off yet didn't. They passed a gentleman with burn marks on his face. Roger then motioned toward the server where the kettle now rested. He grabbed two mugs and scanned the rack for some sugar.

"Looking for this?" Leonard said, holding a fancy little bowl.

Gail's cheeks turned a shade of crimson as he handed it to Roger. Leonard nodded in her direction and then watched Roger pluck cubes with the tiny set of tongs, placing them into the cups. "When you're both ready, find a seat. We're going to begin," he said.

She watched Leonard vanish up the staircase two steps at a time. "Begin?" Gail said to Roger. "Begin what?"

"You'll see," he said, handing her the tea.

She accepted it and turned to the people dispersed about the room. Zofie was on the sofa, chatting quietly with a kid in camouflage. Gail saw there was space on the couch for one more. "Okay, thanks for making my brew," she said and scurried toward the vacant cushion.

"Ah, Gail," Zofie said, the Polish vernacular a soothing Hallmark greeting. She raised a hand to Gail, who took it in hers and gave a soft squeeze. "Come. Sit. Meet Jed."

Jed saluted and then interlocked his fingers, making one big fist that hung between his seated legs as his arms settled on each knee.

"Jed served in Iraq," Zofie said. "With the Marine Corps."

"Thank you for your service," Gail said, tipping her head.

"Eh, thanks," he said, his voice not as patriotic as his slacks.

Across the room, Leonard grabbed an ottoman and pushed it to the front of the fireplace, a bulky guitar made of a light wood—maybe maple—in one hand and a guitar pick sticking out of his mouth. He slung the strap of the instrument around his neck and plopped down on the footstool. He spat the pick into his hand and started tuning the strings as the crowd realized he was there and, in unison, did a collective hush.

Leonard let out a vibrant strum of all six strings, a crisp, clean sound. "Thank you all for joining us tonight," he said, addressing the room. "Please take a seat anywhere—chairs, sofa, floor. We don't bite." He released a rollicking laugh.

Gail's heart shimmied. "He plays guitar?" she asked, turning to Zofie.

Zofie tapped Gail's thigh in an "easy girl" gesture that made Gail feel like a groupie, but she didn't care. This was all too interesting to let insecurities get in the way.

"I'd like to welcome Jed home from his second tour in the Middle East," Leonard said, focusing on the soldier on the couch.

Gail glanced at him. *Second? Geez. No wonder he sounded so glum.*

Leonard started working a familiar melody on the guitar.

"American Pie," someone called out.

Gail started to bob to the beat as the young couple she spied earlier scooted themselves closer. She couldn't help but think how "Kumbaya" they looked, all cheerful as they held hands and exchanged long stares. They were married, Gail noticed, as the glint of a diamond ring attached to a solid white-gold band sparkled on the girl's finger.

After the song, Leonard lowered the guitar and started talking confessional style to no one in particular. "On this night—it was eight years ago, but I remember it like it was yesterday—the world lost a child—a sweet, innocent kid, I was told later by his family." He stopped and scratched his collar. "When our rig pulled up, the house was raging with fire. I mean, it was roaring out of every window."

The tiny flames engulfing the logs in Zofie's fireplace flickered behind him. "At first, he escaped the wreckage, but he decided to run back in. He thought his grandmother was trapped inside."

Gail heard a gasp. The Kumbaya couple's godliness turned to fear, and they groped each other with every word Leonard spoke. "Nobody knew he had gone back in until his little sister said something a few minutes later. By then it was too late. When we found him, he was already gone." Leonard paused and tucked the guitar pick between the strings before he set the instrument aside. "I share this with you because the boy died a hero. He risked his life in pursuit of saving another."

Gail fished for a tissue in her handbag.

"Let us pray," Kumbaya girl said, breaking the stillness. She took her husband's hand and looked to Gail, holding up the other. Gail instantly felt awkward, the kind of awkward she'd experienced in church when it was time for those "peace be with you" handshakes. Nevertheless, she touched the girl's palm and then reached over to hold Zofie's with the other. It was a chain reaction, and soon the occupants of the bed-and-breakfast—Catholic or not—were linked together, heads hung in prayer.

"Thank you for that," Leonard said, acknowledging the woman after several solemn minutes, and seized the guitar again.

"I cheated death," the newly returned soldier said, his southern drawl somber.

All heads craned to listen, except for Gail's. She was fidgeting with the purse handle, afraid to cast a stare onto him since he was sitting on the same couch just to the left of Zofie.

Leonard focused on the man. "Go on."

"I should have died, but I didn't."

The urge to look overcame her. Gail tilted her head slowly toward him. Jed's pupils were moving back and forth in a swift rhythm, scanning the floorboards as if the reasons why God had spared him were lurking under them. "Chow was on. Everybody was storming into the tent—you know, a temporary mess hall where we were stationed, just outside Tikrit. Anyway, my shift was ending—I was manning the gate." He stopped and grabbed at the fuzz of his high n' tight. His eyes squeezed shut, and he sucked in both lips, biting hard on them as he rocked frantically.

"It's okay, brother," Leonard said. "Take your time."

The soldier arched upright as if just given an order to sit straight or drop and give someone twenty and drew in a deep, long breath. "I told Ramirez to go, to eat his lunch before relieving me." He started tapping a heel in quick, steady beats. "The place was mobbed. It always was. He woulda never ate if he didn't get it then. Our shifts were long—fourteen hours, mostly on foot." Jed rubbed his palms on his knees. "There was an explosion. I heard it—felt the heat—and dove onto the ground behind a few sandbags. Smoke and rocks rained down, the entire base covered in debris. That's when I saw a hand. No arm, no. It wasn't attached to a person, just a plan ole' fucking hand. Right there, on the ground a few inches away from me. I knew then that everyone in the tent was wiped out." Tears overwhelmed his eyes, but he didn't move. "I was scared. I was scared to be alive because I knew then that I was the only one who didn't blow up." He smeared the water on his face with the backs of his hands. "I looked at my rifle and waited. I listened for the insurgents, waiting for them to raid camp after the bomb. I waited for a long time. Maybe five hours. Probably more. Enough time for flies to fester on the hand. But no one came. I must've been in shock 'cause I had forgotten about my radio. I reached for it and started screaming away until a unit rolled up in their Humvees. They took me away. After they searched the area, they said multiple bombs went off, you know, synchronized at the same time, and I was the only survivor." Jed got up and shook the kinks out of his fatigues. "Can I play a tune?"

Leonard glanced up, eyes red. "Uh, yeah, of course. Jam away, my friend."

Gail watched Leonard stand and hand over the guitar, but not before giving the combatant a firm embrace. *He gets it. He understands them like Harry did.* She kept focusing on Leonard, who was lingering near the man while he plucked the guitar's strings. Then, when Leonard slipped out of the room, she decided to follow.

"Where are you going?" Roger said, stepping in front of her.

Gail startled backward. "What is it with you?"

The guy stammered to respond, which caused Gail to feel sudden remorse. "My apologies. I was going to the ladies' room. Excuse me." She quickly diverted in the opposite direction and into her room.

This place is definitely unique. Gail sat down at the vanity.

A small knock sounded on the door. Gail held her breath and stared at the slim space between the floor and the bottom of the jamb. *If it's that creeper Roger, I'm outta here.*

"Gail, you in there?"

She tried not to exhale too loudly, hoping he'd go away.

"Gail? It's me, Leonard."

She practically hopped up to undo the lock but stepped back and regained herself.

"Is everything all right?" Leonard said, his face wearing an earnest look as she opened the door. "I saw you run away."

"Oh, yeah. I'm just tired."

Leonard's eyes trailed to his boots, and he shoved his hands in his pockets. "Our gatherings aren't for everyone."

"Oh, no, it's not that." Gail wanted to mention Roger but wasn't sure if the men were friends.

"Well, maybe you'll give the next one a shot, then?" Leonard said, leaning his heft on the balls of his feet.

Of course. "It's a possibility," Gail said, fending desperation, and took hold of the knob. "Thanks so much for your hospitality. Have a good night." She backed into the room and carefully shut the door.

Chapter Thirty-Five

The scent of bacon was so strong, so delicious, Deirdre could practically taste the salty goodness. She rolled over and stretched, getting out the sleepy kinks before throwing on a robe.

"Deeda!" Kenny shouted from his highchair as she walked in.

Rob turned away from the frying pan and waved the spatula. "Morning, Dee. Coffee?"

"Good morning, everyone," she said and kissed Kenny's chubby little cheeks. "Coffee would be great. And so would some of that yummy bacon."

"Coming right up." Rob pressed on the meat, the crackling getting louder.

Trevor pushed his chair away from the table and hopped out of his seat. Without saying a word, he dashed to Deirdre and hugged her. She gave him a noogie on top of his head and picked him up. "School today, buddy?"

"Nope," he said, dimples deepening.

"And why not?" Her face contorted into a confused look.

"It's Parent-Teacher Conferences, so the school gave the kids a day off, remember?" Rob said.

"Ah, yes. Well, that explains it." Deirdre winked at Trevor and put him into his booster chair before occupying the vacant seat between him and Kenny. "Do I have a surprise for you guys! The three of us will be together when Daddy goes to talk to your teacher, and I have just the thing for us to do."

Trevor started bouncing anxiously. "Oh, what? What?"

"You and Kenny are going to help me wash my motorcycle before I head to work."

Trevor's mouth fell open. "No way."

Rob's head swiveled. "Are you sure you want to do that?"

She laughed and answered them both. "Yep."

Trevor's arms flailed in the air. "Yahoo!"

"Yahoooo!" Kenny yelled, pounding on the highchair tray with his spoon.

****

Deirdre dragged the garden hose over as Trevor and Kenny kneeled on the ground.

"Ready," she announced, pointing the nozzle into the pail. "Aim."

The boys' knuckles grew white as they gripped the sides of the bucket. "Fire!"

Water shot from the hose in a forceful stream and hit the bottom of the container, squirting the boys as it filled. They laughed as they jerked their heads away and then started splashing each other.

"Easy, guys. We need the water for the motorcycle, too," Deirdre said, chuckling.

When the water touched the brim, she shut the current and grabbed some soap. Trevor ran to the squishy sponges on his dad's shelf and threw one to Deirdre.

"Like this," she said, squeezing detergent into the pail and then dipping the sponge. She lathered it up and handed it to Kenny as Trevor did his own.

Deirdre watched the boys run back and forth, getting

sopping wet as they cleaned the bike. "If your parents were here, they would crack up."

"I'm going to draw Mommy a picture after this to show her," Trevor yelled from behind the spokes of the front wheel.

"Good idea," Deirdre said, then took the hose and rinsed off the bubbles, turning the nozzle to the boys, playfully soaking them some more.

****

"Cancer sucks," Megan groaned.

Deirdre whirled around. Megan's head juddered and flopped near the edge of the bed. She threw up into a bedpan on the floor, her face pressed against the side of the mattress. Deirdre tugged a bunch of napkins free from the nearby dispenser and rushed to clean up. "How do I have anything left in me?" Megan said and dry heaved.

Deirdre placed the pan under Megan's chin so that she didn't have to move much and rubbed her back. Meg's spine was more prominent than ever. After several episodes of violent purging, Deirdre adjusted the IV so the fluids replenished at a faster rate.

"How are Rob and the boys doing?" Megan asked, her voice a faint croak.

"The boys are at your mom's now. Rob will be here soon. Today was Parent-Teacher Conferences, so he'll have Trevor's report card for you." Deirdre remembered the picture Trevor had made earlier, the one of them washing the Harley. "Be right back."

She jogged across the hall to the lockers to get it and returned. Megan didn't have the ability to hold the artwork, but Deirdre gripped the colorful Crayola scribbling in her hand. Together, they traced the outline of the markings.

"Thank you," Megan breathed, her eyelids falling shut.

Rob entered the hospital room and quickly covered his nose.

"She's been nauseous all afternoon," Deirdre said and grabbed a small dry towel from the rack.

He darted toward Megan's bed, where she lay gaunt. "Honey, it's me." His fingers grazed her forehead.

Megan didn't move, her breathing shallow.

"Her skin is unusually hot," Rob said, concerned.

"It's the chemo. It's more aggressive." Deirdre exited the bathroom with the washcloth now sopping and gave it to Rob, then took the thermometer from the holder on the wall. She eased it into Megan's ear canal until it beeped. "102.7. Not terrible. It's a little lower than before."

Rob placed the cool rag on Megan's head. One eye slowly opened. Rob smiled. "I've got Trevor's report card," he said, pulling it from his coat. "Spoke to Miss Beel, and he's doing real good. You'd be proud."

Megan's mouth formed a tight grin.

Deirdre held a straw up to her lips. "Drink."

Megan struggled to suck on the narrow tube. As the water crept up the straw, Deirdre craned around. "Show her Trevor's grades. It will be the real pick-me-up of the day." Dee glanced again at Megan and winked. Meg blinked in acknowledgment when a loud knock echoed throughout the room.

"Hello," Dr. Kelleher said, entering, and nodded at Rob. He approached Megan's bedside. "Today's a rough one. It's to be expected. What I need from you is plenty of rest." He pressed the back of his hand to her temple and unraveled his stethoscope.

Megan flinched when the metal instrument made contact with her skin.

"Keep those cold compresses and fluids coming," Dr. Kelleher said to Deirdre. "And make sure there aren't any more visitors for the rest of the day. I'm putting a sign on the door restricting entry." He turned to Rob. "Mr. Dunham, please, don't be alarmed. Your wife's body has to adjust to the new treatment."

Deirdre dimmed the lights and motioned for Rob to step outside. "Why don't you go have some dinner with the boys? I'll be here until tomorrow morning. I'll keep you updated."

****

After a long, arduous shift, Deirdre was too exhausted to change, so she rode Fiona home in dirty scrubs.

"Hello, anyone here?" Dee yelled, stepping into the foyer of Megan's house, but everything stayed eerily quiet.

She went into the kitchen and hung the helmet on the spoke of a chair, then headed to the guest room, pulling off the work shirt and crumpling it. When she entered the bedroom, she yelped, quickly raising both arms over her lacey bra that was a wee bit small.

"Um." Rob turned his face.

"What the hell are you doing in here?"

"Sorry," he said, standing angled at the bookshelf. "After seeing Megan that way earlier, I needed to be reminded of her healthier days." He shut the photo album and tucked it under his arm.

"I'm sorry, too." She bent down for the crumpled blouse. "I didn't mean to sound like a bitch. It's just that when I entered the house, I yelled hello and nobody answered. I thought you were out with the boys."

"Eh, at least you're comfortable here."

They both glanced at her chest and laughed. He went to leave, but Deirdre stopped him. "She's going to get better. Remember, it's the side effects of chemotherapy right now. They're vicious."

Rob's eyes strayed away from her gaze. "She's stage four, Dee. How much 'better' is it really going to get?"

His question wasn't in search of an answer, and Deirdre knew it. She also understood that people with the disease can experience days of heightened energy where they can function doing ordinary tasks. But she didn't want to school him. She decided it would be best for him to witness those miraculous moments on his own. And, when he did, that's when she'd ask him to go to the local Harley dealership so that they could buy Megan a bike of her own; thethought of unveiling a motorcycle to her sister-friend sent tingles all over.

Deirdre hugged Rob. "Just so you know, I'm not only Megan's ally…I'm also yours."

Chapter Thirty-Six

Megan sat upright when Gail walked in looking tired, despite sporting a smile. "Wow, how are you?" Meg asked. "I haven't seen you in quite a bit."

"You're always on my mind," Gail said. "Have you talked to Erin?"

Megan eyed her. "Come to think of it, no. Have you?"

Gail put her keys on the tray table and wheeled it over to the bed. "Yes, and no. Well, no, not today, but I know she's home. Deirdre helped her. Otherwise, I've been at the B&B. Anyway, look, I know chemo sucks, but please try to eat something. Nutrition is critical, and I need you to work with me here like Harry didn't." Gail gave Megan the side-eye, and they chuckled together.

Megan looked over the spread: fruit, broth, a scrambled egg, and water. "It's crazy, but I feel somewhat rejuvenated after days of feeling like utter shit." Meg picked up the peach and gripped it like a baseball. "Gosh, I hope I can taste this," she said, admiring the fuzzy orangey skin. Her teeth sank into it, the juice trickling out. She closed her eyes. "Mm, I can, I can."

Gail reached for the TV's remote and scrolled through the music channels for something upbeat. Jack Johnson's "Better Together" was playing on the alternative station.

"Ah, yes, keep this on," Megan said, waving the peach and then dropping it onto the tray.

Gail raised the volume and set down the controller. The struggle to keep both arms up challenged Megan as Gail cha-cha'd over. Their hands met, and they started to sway.

"This song reminds me of my honeymoon," Megan said and shut her eyes. She moved with ease like the azure blue waves of Horseshoe Beach, remembering the leaps with Rob over the foamy Bermuda surf.

When the tune ended, Megan's focus returned to the current milieu of the hospital room, but she didn't want to feed into it. Instead, she inspected all the decorative flower arrangements. "Help me," Meg said and pulled away from Gail.

With all her might, Megan slid a leg off the side of the bed. It dangled in the air as Gail carefully pulled her toward the edge. When Meg slipped off the sheets, the pads of all ten toes touched the cold flooring. She shifted to stabilize herself, using both Gail and the bedrail, quickly fixing on some bright yellow sunflowers. She motioned to the humongous floral centerpiece on the shelf near the heater several feet away, working one foot, placing it a few inches ahead of the other. "You can let go," Megan said.

"You sure?"

"Mm, hm."

Gail slowly released her grasp.

Like a baby teetering to walk, Megan balanced herself and hobbled left, right, left, right, until she reached the radiator. She quickly leaned against it to take a couple of heavy breaths, then snagged the note from the little plastic holder poking out of the vase. "Megan, we wish you nothing but the speediest of recoveries. With love, The Firehouse," she read aloud.

"Those guys really are something else," Gail said.

"The best." Megan placed the message beside the container and plucked a sunflower. She snapped the stem in half and fixed the pretty petals along the ridge of her ear. She touched where long chestnut hair hung for most of her life. "I miss it, but that's okay. It's not going to destroy my chi."

Gail walked to her. "Thatta girl." She stayed beside Meg, who continued removing nearby plants, one by one, from their holders and strategically situated them in new homes.

"Let's put them *all* around the room," Megan suggested and handed Gail some pink carnations. Together, they scattered pieces of plants in random places.

When they were done, Megan clutched two remaining flowers—red roses—and wobbled to the bed. With Gail's help, she lowered the rail and hoisted it onto the springy cushion.

Gail sat too and fiddled with the music stations when she stumbled upon Alanis Morissette's "Ironic."

"Oh, this!" Megan said, dismembering the roses and sprinkling their red parts atop the white bedding surrounding her. "Leave it on." Meg reclined on the surface like an angel in the snow and listened as the singer sang about situations that weren't ironic, which made the song ironic. "Is my getting cancer *twice* ironic?" Megan asked Gail, pausing to think about it. She then belted, "It's like being thirty-four and having cancer at stage four!" She cackled, but mostly to herself. "Oh Lordy, how do you deal with me? I'm so freaking corny."

"Come here and give me a hug," Gail said, grinning, and moved in for an embrace when someone entered the room.

"It sure is festive in here," Dr. Kelleher said, motioning to the flora.

"If I'm going to be staying a while, I might as well settle in." Megan extended an arm over the metal bar.

"About that." The doctor attached the portable pump and checked her blood pressure. "Your vitals are stable, and you'll be heading home sooner than later," he said.

"Really? How soon?" Meg's voice perked and clutched Gail.

"By Monday morning, max. Your next visit will be in a week, so you—"

"Can rest and regain healthy cells. I know the drill." Megan saw Gail grab her purse. "Going back to the bed-and-breakfast?"

"I should. I paid for the entire weekend."

Megan wagged a finger at her. "That's a great thing, Gail. Do *you* for once!"

"I'm trying," Gail said and curled a hand around Megan's pointer. "Hey, listen. I'd like to plan a get-together when you're home this week. Maybe a girls' night at my place…nothing strenuous." She glanced at the doctor in acknowledgment.

"Yes! Maybe a Friendsgiving!" Megan sank a bit. "Or is that cheesy?"

Gail laughed. "That's cute, but I was thinking more along the lines of a potluck dessert-type thing not attached to any particular holiday."

"Oh, like a festive cookie exchange?"

"Cha-ching!" Gail shot up a thumb. "I'll call you

after I've figured out the deets."

When Gail left, Megan turned to the doctor as he puttered with the heart monitor. "I was wondering," Meg said, "can I go on the computer that's in the hall?" Her thoughts were on cookie recipes when, out of the blue, they shifted.

"Of course," he said, "I'll have the nurse bring in a wheelchair."

"No. I want to walk." Megan pushed down on the aluminum partition and, with confidence, swung a leg over the side of the mattress.

Dr. Kelleher, looking a little alarmed, eased around the foot of the bed and held her hand. He smiled nervously but helped her stand. Together, they moved across the floor toward the computer.

"Do you like motorcycles, Doc?" Meg asked as he guided her onto the seat in front of the screen.

He let out a small laugh and jiggled the mouse so that it turned on. "They're nice."

"Nice? Nah, more like awesome. They're the ultimate symbol of freedom." She placed her hands on the keyboard, feeling the smooth keys on the undersides of her fingers. It took some effort, but she began typing, no longer interested in conversing with the oncologist. "Thanks, Doc. See you later."

He patted her shoulder and went on his way.

Megan logged on to a popular virtual marketplace and surfed around the site perusing motorcycles for sale. As part of a lifelong list of dreams, owning a bike ranked in the top ten. "That's it," she said. "It's time to create an actual bucket list."

She signed on to her Gmail account. "You are cordially invited to," Megan read, then paused. "Invited to what?" She clicked on the email:

Dear Mrs. Dunham,

On behalf of the Department of Education, we would like to congratulate you on your Teacher of the Year nomination.

Megan stopped. "Teacher of the Year? Is this a joke? I'm on medical leave." She kept reading:

Because of the notable work you've done connecting the City of New York's youth with the community through various efforts, including, but not limited to, Project Clean Streets, it is our distinct pleasure to award you at our annual Teacher of the Year dinner.

"Who told the board about that?" Meg's mind wandered to when her students asked about the homeless man for whom she bought coffee every morning—the guy who occupied the curb outside of a bagel shop with a crumpled cardboard sign. Their curiosity about helping the needy launched an entire project in conjunction with the local soup kitchen, which spawned "Carolers for a Cause," another venture where the class sang to families in shelters and the elderly in nursing homes throughout the city.

Your principal, Mrs. Baxter, who has nominated you, has been notified as well and will be in attendance once the date is finalized. We hope to see you there.

"Shelly Baxter?"

Megan sat up and created a new email: *Dear Mrs. Baxter,*

~~*Dear Mrs. Baxter,*~~

"A phone call is better." She dipped into the pocket of her robe. "Shit. It's back in the room." *Okay, it'll have to wait until later.* She cracked her knuckles and turned to the computer once more, starting another message with "AD, Achieved" in the subject heading, which stands for "After Death, Achieved," which is a fancy way of saying bucket list without the gut-punch of, *Hello, I'm dying here,* effects.

1. Buy a gown from Oscar de la Renta—*something sparkly and expensive*

2. Go someplace fancy in said gown—*Maybe that awards dinner or this year's firehouse dinner dance, whichever comes first. If all else fails, wear at own funeral*

3. Buy a motorcycle—*again, something sparkly and expensive*

4. Sip wine in the gypsum at White Sands, New Mexico—*a must*

5. Teach an online class—*in something practical yet fun to keep my mind from turning to mush.*

Megan hit the Send button and was done with it. *Better to keep it short and realistic than lengthy and unreasonable, considering the condition I'm in.* She returned to her search for the perfect Oscar de la Renta number. A coral dress featured first in the search results. It was a stunning color on olive skin, so she clicked on the photo to enlarge it. The gown was strapless and had a corset-style bodice. "Not particularly flattering on a woman with no breasts," she muttered and moved on to a long-sleeved black velvet creation with a plunging neckline. "This may actually work." Meg studied the dress's drastic V-shaped front that showed some skin.

This'll be sexy for someone with a flat chest. She checked the price. "What? Only six-hundred and fifty dollars?" She moved the cursor to the "buy it now" option. "Sold."

Megan printed both the receipt and bucket list. She folded them loosely so that they bent only a little when shifting off the chair. Without assistance, she maneuvered to the room and limped to the corkboard that was parallel to where she slept. She uncreased the papers and tacked them to the bulletin board. A stray butterfly shimmied in her belly.

"I did this," she squealed, gazing around at the flowers and admiring the beautified space. *I think Rob will appreciate it, too.* She clutched the rosary beads and thanked God for the positivity radiating inside her. *See, Meg, you can still be happy.*

Chapter Thirty-Seven

Deirdre dropped the dinner dishes into the sink and took Megan's car keys. "Let's go see your mom."

"Yay!" The boys cheered, jumping up and down around her.

She bundled them in jackets, mittens, and hats, seeing how dark the gray November sky was.

"Wait." Trevor ripped off his gloves. "I have to get something from my bookbag." He swished loudly to his bedroom and returned a minute later with a piece of folded pink construction paper. "It's a card for Mommy," he said and showed Deirdre. "It's pink for Rest Cancer."

Her heart fluttered at his innocence. "You're right. Pink is the color for Mommy's cancer." She got up and walked ahead of them to the front door, staving off tears. "Chop-chop, men, let's go." Dee inserted the key into the deadbolt. "We don't want to be stuck in too much traffic."

The children raced out of the house, screaming at each other all the way to the car, something about who was going to sit on their mother's bed first when they got to the hospital.

During the drive, Deirdre spied their little faces in the rearview. Kenny had dozed in his car seat while Trevor counted Mack trucks out the window, the homemade card secure in his grasp. Her insides ached at the thought of them being motherless at an age not yet ripe enough to understand. She circled into the parking garage and found a spot close enough where the boys—mainly Kenny—could walk on their own without having to bring along the stroller.

On the way into the facility, Trevor and Kenny seized each of Deirdre's hands and followed her eagerly up to their mom.

"Why hello, young sirs," Megan announced, bedecked in petals of differing colors.

"Wow," Trevor muttered.

"You look like a goddess," Deirdre said, entering the room. "A healthy goddess."

"Hardly, but thanks." Megan chuckled and bent down to hug her little royals. They embraced her wilting body and tried to touch the sunflower. Meg giggled as they nestled their heads into the deep crooks of her arms. "Guess who's coming home in a couple of days?"

"Yay! I have a present for you," Trevor said, pulling away. "It's pink for Rest Cancer." His high-pitched, chipmunk-like voice hung in the air as he presented the card.

Megan took him up and squeezed until he begged for release. When she let go, he saw she was upset. "Don't cry, Mommy. Be happy again like when you were when I got here."

She wiped her cheeks with a pajama sleeve and pointed to the corkboard. "Now it'll be complete," she said and stood. Deirdre went to assist her. "No, Dee, I got it." Meg inched across the room and fastened the card to the center of the bulletin board.

Trevor jogged over and hugged Megan's leg, then dashed to the bed and hurdled onto it. Kenny tried to do the same, but he was too small for the leap. Deirdre went to help, flipping him onto the blanket in one quick movement.

Trevor raised his eyebrows. "Whoa, you're like a ninja."

"You haven't seen nothing yet." Deirdre hopped onto the bed and gave him a noogie. Kenny pounced on her back and suddenly they were all wrestling on the sheets.

Megan sat on the chair by the radiator, thumbing the rosary and watching as they goofed around. "You're so good with them. Do you ever envision yourself as a mother?"

Deirdre sat up, huffing and puffing. "I love kids and all," she said between breaths, "but I don't put the carriage before the horse, you know what I mean?"

Megan nodded. "Too many women are caught up in the storybook life of marriage and children, but what they don't comprehend is all the work—the reality—that goes into it."

Deirdre thought of Erin and Jay-Jay and how Megan knew none of what was happening with them. She wanted to tell her—*had* to tell her—but with Megan's high spirits, today was probably not the day to share.

"What?" Megan said, concerned.

Damn it. I have the worst poker face. Deirdre slipped out of the bed as the boys played with the buttons on the mechanical mattress. "Did anyone fill you in on Erin and Jay-Jay?" She walked to the radiator and leaned against it.

"Fill me in? No. I mean, Gail was here, asked me if I had spoken to her, but otherwise, hadn't mentioned anything else. What's wrong with Erin and Jay-Jay?"

Deirdre scratched vigorously at her palms. "Things

are complicated for them right now." The air was awkward and still. She started to tell the lengthy story, keenly aware that Megan kept studying the doorway.

"No matter how decorative it is in here or how much 'progress' I'm making, there's no avoiding the feeling of being trapped. I used to multitask—always running, go, go, go—my job to be the helper and the fixer, but now my body is a prison of its own," Megan said.

Deirdre went to remind her that she'll be discharged in a few short days but felt that shutting up now was best. She stared at the floor, feeling like the worst person on the planet.

Megan retrieved her cell phone and started dialing. "Hey, Erin, it's me."

Deirdre quietly went and took the boys off the bed. "Let's get candy from the machine in the hall," she whispered, escorting them out.

A few feet away from Megan's door was the lounge area equipped with a vending machine. While the boys were busy discussing which snack they wanted, Deirdre lingered back in case Megan needed her. She heard sniffling and a lot of, "It'll be okay," which made her heart sink into the bowels of her stomach.

Deirdre waited until Megan ended the call to bring both boys into the room with their treats. They walked to the table as Megan clutched the phone, visibly trembling. Deirdre settled them on the adjacent chairs when Megan lifted herself from the plastic seat.

"Let me help you," Deirdre said.

"I got it." Megan ignored Dee's hand and wobbled to the bed. "I plan on staying off my feet for the rest of the day. It's not like I have a choice, anyway, 'til Monday."

With the shades drawn, Deirdre tucked the comforter snug around Megan. "Please know that when Erin was released, I had arranged to be there to help her get home. Everything was status-quo."

"You're learning," Megan said. "We fire wives are always rescuing ourselves or each other. It's how we have to live."

Deirdre felt the pain in her voice as well as the heroism.

Chapter Thirty-Eight

One light was lit in the entire mansion. At least that's what Gail saw from the street. She parked and moseyed up the path, coaching herself before going inside. *Be yourself. These are good people. You came to relax. Try not to think about the girls right now. Like Megan said, I have to 'do me.'*

She took a deep breath and entered the foyer, the scream of a kettle competing with a radio of roaring trumpets. "Hello?" she shouted.

Zofie shuffled in and brought down the music. "Welcome back. How was your dinner?"

The air was sweeter smelling than ever and was as inviting as the innkeeper. "Eh, simple. I had pizza," Gail said, undoing the buttons of her pea coat, preferring not to talk about Megan, the hospital, or how she had skipped eating altogether.

Zofie took the jacket. Gail sat on the couch closest to the lit fireplace. "Your teas are rather different," Gail said, observing as Zofie set three saucers on the coffee table and placed teacups on top of them. The woman opened a case of imported teas and gestured for Gail to choose one. "These evenings are actually therapy sessions for the guests. I'm not sure if you are aware that most of my clientele are veterans."

Gail checked the selection and pointed to a caffeine-infused vanilla blend, which Zofie put in a cup. "Yes, I read about your targeted audience online before I originally booked. I'm a widow of a fireman. It's what brought me here."

"Splendid." Zofie scurried to the kitchen and promptly reentered, balancing a steaming kettle with a pair of potholders. "But, tonight is rare—not like last—this one is only us."

Gail watched as the boiling water rushed into the porcelain, causing the teabag to spiral aggressively. "How nice—just us women!"

"Not quite," Roger said, sauntering in with china plates and silverware.

The corners of Gail's mouth did a funny dip. When an extra set of footsteps sounded behind him, though, she regained hope.

Leonard strolled into the room carrying a glass cake holder with a freshly baked Bundt underneath. Gail reddened as he moved closer.

"Oh, hello," she said, giving a little wave.

Leonard lifted the cover, the scent of chocolate wafting.

"Smells delicious."

He set the cake down and cut a slice.

Gail took hold of the plate that was offered. "It looks like it came straight from Martha Stewart's oven."

"Martha's got nothing on me." He let out a boisterous laugh.

Zofie appeared from behind Leonard and smiled. "Take a bite. It tastes even better than it looks."

Gail sank the fork into the spongy texture and sampled the goods. "Wow," she said, pointing the utensil at the dessert. "This fudge icing is heavenly."

Leonard grinned and, with his thumb, wiped off the

smudge of chocolate on her upper lip. She batted her lashes, about to explode with embarrassment.

"So, what brings you to the bed-and-breakfast?" Zofie said, sitting in a tall armchair across from them.

"Obviously, Leonard's chocolate cake," Gail said, her face still warm.

They all burst into laughter.

"But on a more serious note, um, well…" Everyone settled to listen. "I was looking for a getaway that didn't require much traveling. Someplace close yet gives you a sense of being removed from the everyday stuff and—"

"She came to the B&B for a little R&R," Roger interjected, wiggling his eyebrows at her.

"From *sickness*. Lately, I've been surrounded by too many good people who are gravely *ill*."

Roger's smile faded. "Oh, sorry."

There was an awkward silence. Gail didn't know if this was a cue to continue like a therapy session or rip Roger a new one. She glanced at the sliver of cake resting on the plate and stuffed a bite into her mouth.

Leonard cut another piece and went to hand it to Roger. "Nope. Can't stay," Roger said, pushing it away. He then turned to Gail. "Don't be too disappointed, my sweet. I'll be back later."

Gail smirked as he walked out. "Someone's overly confident, no?"

Leonard shrugged and took hold of a fork. "Eh, he's just trying his hand at a beautiful woman," he said and poked into the dessert.

Gail's cheeks went from warm to flaming hot.

"Back to our original conversation," Zofie said, shooing a hand in the air as if warding away the discomfiture.

"Well," Leonard said, "I first came here to help Zofie cook, but because this house has so much history, I couldn't stay away." He took a quick bite and swallowed.

Gail's interest was piqued. "History?"

Zofie set down the teacup and turned to a wooden chest beside the couch. She lifted the lid and sorted through some papers, handing Gail an aged black-and-white photograph of a man dressed in a dark suit, his mustache white. Gail examined the picture.

"This house," Zofie said, digging deeper in the trunk, "was built for the Badeau family in the 1800s, right before the Civil War. Adam Badeau was a brevet lieutenant colonel to Ulysses S. Grant during the battle." Zofie unfurled a yellowing map that outlined the neighborhood at the turn of the century and pointed to different rectangles, some longer than others, drawn across the page. "These are divided plots of land. The last name of the owner is written on each. See here? This rectangle is where we are right now."

Gail's eyes narrowed and read the name "C. Badeau" written in cursive in faded black ink. "Who is C.Badeau?"

"A relative of Adam's. A historian who visited the B&B several years ago came specifically to do some research on the family. He was the one who told me that Adam's grandparents occupied this house. He had a lot more knowledge than I did about this home. He also said that Adam stayed here often because of the proximity to New York City."

"Rumor has it he entertained Broadway actors at the bar in the basement," Leonard said and sipped from the scotch he was holding.

"Oh wow. Can I see it? Can I see the bar?" Gail asked.

"Sure. But it isn't restored, so don't expect anything fancy."

They stood and made their way down a pair of steep cement steps. Zofie pulled a chain overhead, a bare bulb casting light on them. Gail walked to the dusty wooden bar where old bottles of beer lined the shelf behind it. She noted the antique rotary dial attached to the ledge. Next to that was a record player that appeared to be from the early 1930s.

"I found 78s in here," Zofie said, motioning to a crate on the floor.

Leonard hoisted it onto the bar sending dust particles everywhere. He and Gail looked at one another and rolled up their sleeves.

Gail began a search and jumped up, holding a dust-covered disk. "An original Louis Armstrong!"

Leonard pulled it from her and wiped away the dirt with his shirt. "Let's see if we can get this puppy to play."

Gail scanned the room for some tools, seizing the opportunity to help restore the machine. "My Harry loved do-it-yourself projects and a good gypsy garage-salefind. He'd be so proud."

Leonard peered at her.

"Over here," Zofie called, standing beside a metal toolbox. Gail rushed over and took it in her grasp, but it didn't budge. She gave it a firm shake, the tools rattling inside.

"Step aside, ladies." Leonard heaved the box to the record player.

Gail kneeled in front of it and opened the lid. Inside

were a few rusty keys resting on top of a mound of other metal things. Gail held out the brown ring to Zofie, who fixed her glasses and leaned in for a better look. "Most of the doorknobs are original in the house, so these may be the keys to unlock them. "I'll go have a look." Zofie took the keyring, her slippers doing their shuffle across the concrete floor, and she disappeared up the stairs.

"So"—Gail plopped onto one of the barstools, a dust cloud forming in the air. She rubbed both palms against her knees, then crossed a leg.—"Tell me about yourself."

Leonard glanced away from the player. "What do you want to know?"

Gail's nose started to twitch. "Uh, uh."

"Oh, boy. That many questions?"

"Achoo!"

Gail's sneeze echoed throughout the basement.

Leonard laughed and took a handkerchief from his pocket. "I thought you were reviewing a long mental list of must-knows."

Gail chuckled and cleaned her nose on his cloth, then realized how unsanitary that was. She held out the material with two fingers. "Ew, I can't believe you just gave this to me, and I just used it."

He sighed and snatched it. "Haven't you heard of going green?"

"Please tell me you're kidding."

He shoved it in his pocket. "Nothing gross. I wash these things every day."

She shook her head. "So, why do you come here so much? Don't you have a family?"

"Of course, I have family," Leonard snapped.

"I'm sorry, I didn't mean for that to sound insensitive." Gail shifted on the seat, sending more dust into the atmosphere, and belted out another sneeze.

He tossed her the handkerchief. "Keep it."

Gail laughed and blew her nose with it.

"My daughter, Lauren, is twenty-one, and my son, Vincent, is nineteen. They're both away at college, which leaves me with what you women call an 'empty nest.' When the walls feel like they're caving in on me, I come here for a change of scenery."

"To see Zofie?"

"Not quite," he said, brow creasing.

"Are you retired?"

"Yep. For almost a year now from the fire department."

"Which house?"

"Rescue 2 in Brooklyn."

Gail stopped lining the tools on the bar like little soldiers. "My husband was in Rescue 4 in Queens for most of his career, but he retired from Rescue 2."

Leonard halted.

"His name was Harry. Harry O'Neil," she said, voice low.

"O'Neil was your husband?" Leonard's eyes widened. "No shit? What a good fireman. We worked together a bunch of times. I was at his memorial."

If it hadn't been her love's funeral, Gail probably would have noticed Leonard. How could you miss someone so big? But, maybe not. She adored Harry too much to have strayed.

"Everything that happened right after Harry's death is a giant blur," she said, rearranging screws from small to large. "Need a screwdriver or something?"

"We don't have any orange juice." Leonard laughed, then apologized for his failed attempt at trying to lighten the mood.

Gail smiled, semi-amused by his humor but mostly excited about the idea that just sprouted. She got up and dragged the old stool to the shelf above the counter, then climbed up to check out the different liquors.

Leonard, who was more interested in repairing the music machine, continued removing the turntable. "Be right back. I gotta get a sponge and a cup of soap and water." He skipped up the steps two at a time.

While he was gone, Gail pored over the alcohol. There was a bottle of Johnnie Walker Black dating back to 1909. She undid the top and took in a whiff, immediately gagging at the potent smell. *Leonard would appreciate this one*. Gail recapped it and put it next to a bottle of Absinthe from 1910, remembering that Absinthe was once banned in the United States. She untwisted the cap of that one and snuck a sip. Her mouth pursed from the bitterness. *And now I know why*. She promptly screwed on the top and returned it to the ledge.

"It's funny," Leonard said, descending the stairs. "I've never spent more than two minutes down here. This is great."

"You're welcome," Gail teased.

"Don't flatter yourself, kid. I'm too busy to pussyfoot around a basement on a leisurely scavenger hunt."

"Are you the maintenance man?"

Leonard stopped by the toolbox and examined various heads of screwdrivers. "Yeah, I guess you could call me that," he said and paused. "And, like I was saying earlier, I do the cooking, so you can give me that title too if you want."

"Is that your inner firefighter rearing its head in the

kitchen?" Gail reached for another antique container.

"No. More like my inner chef making his appearance."

Gail hopped off the stool and put the alcohol on the counter between them. Leonard retrieved a cheap dollar store pair of reading glasses from his shirt collar and moved closer to the label. "No way."

"Way." Gail smiled.

Leonard unscrewed the cap of the vintage Johnnie Walker Black, but she stopped him. "Wait until we fix the record player, then we'll celebrate."

He kept a firm grasp on the glass neck and looked at her. "Oh, that machine will be up and running tonight." He grinned and let go of the bottle. "Guaranteed."

She set the whiskey aside and took up a cloth. As she lightly wiped the top of the turntable, Leonard investigated the body of the player. They worked in silence until Zofie returned.

"Only one of the keys worked," Zofie said, "so I removed it from the batch. Feel free to find where the others belong." She put the ring on a hook behind the counter and bid them a good night.

Gail gazed at the keys. "Could you believe she just gave us permission to basically explore the entire house?"

Leonard didn't answer, his head buried somewhere in the center of the musical contraption.

"Oh yeah, that's right. You don't do scavenger hunts," Gail said and looked away.

"Got it!"

Gail glimpsed in his direction but only saw parts still scattered about. "Got what?"

"The little sonofabitchin' piece that was out of

place." He heaved himself to a standing position and dusted off his clothes. "Go choose a record."

Gail selected Billie Holiday's "Easy Living." It was a newer, cleaner disc compared to the rest.

Leonard took the vinyl and placed it gingerly on the turntable. He put the needle atop of it and wound the crank. The sweet inflection of Billie's vocals came to life through the equipment. Leonard raised his arms in victory.

Gail uncapped the Johnnie Walker and handed him his prize. "Enjoy." Pride was pasted on her face when presenting him with the liquor.

Leonard saluted and ingested some of the aged alcohol, then took her hand. He twirled her around and led them across the room in a fox trot-like shuffle. "Have dinner with me," he said as they danced nose-to-nose. "Tomorrow night. In my kitchenette."

The blood rushed to Gail's face. She glanced down at their moving feet. "Oh, I don't know."

Several hard clunks echoed down the staircase. Both Leonard's and Gail's heads swiveled toward the noise. "Huh. I must be interrupting something," Roger said, half bemused but mostly disgruntled.

"Actually," Gail started, firing a venomous look at him.

Leonard put a finger over her lips. "Actually, this time you are," Leonard said, addressing him. "But we'll all reconvene at breakfast in the morning. We'll be serving at eight."

"Yes, right. Sure thing," Roger said and tried to casually retreat up the stairs backward.

Gail eyed Leonard as Roger left. "Wow, you're good."

"Not really," he said and lifted her chin with his finger. "It's all about the timing. Now, about dinner. It's just two adults eating a meal together. No harm in that."

Gail hesitated, studying his dark eyes staring back at her. "Okay. If you insist."

"I do," he said and dipped her over his knee.

Chapter Thirty-Nine

The faint cry of babies rattled Erin's groggy head, the ceiling lights blinding. She slowly blinked and looked from one side to the other, realizing this was a different type of hospital room. Everything started spinning. She narrowed her eyes and tried focusing on the IV dangling above, zeroing in on an inanimate object, a trick she'd learned when experiencing wooziness after a night of drinking.

When the dizzy spell subsided, Erin scanned her surroundings for family or friends, but no one was around except a plump African-American nurse at the service desk a few beds away.

"Excuse me," Erin croaked. "Where am I?"

The woman looked up from a newspaper. "You're in Heaven's recovery room, sugar."

"Heaven? Recovery? Recovery from what?" she said and ripped off the sheet.

Erin glanced down to see herself covered in bandages. Hyperventilating at the thought of her insides having fallen apart and then being re-stitched, the worst thought popped into her mind. *I died? Oh my God, I must've died!* The room started swirling, and her head dropped onto the pillow.

"Ma'am, are you all right?" the nurse said, approaching the bed.

Erin felt her wrist being squeezed. "I, I don't know.

Maybe?" She panted and strained to look up at the woman's chest for a nametag.

"Trina," the nurse said, using a tone that was a bit more soothing, and tucked Erin's arm under the blanket. "My name's Trina."

"Well, Trina, you said Heaven, so I'm dead, right? Or, if I *am* alive, things are still fucked. Excuse my Fr— French…but really, we wanted children…I'm sorry, I should be more clear. *We*—as in *me*—not him. He got his. Screw him."

The nurse's face softened. "Sweetie, you need some rest. And in Heaven, rest is abundant."

"So, I am dead," Erin said and tried to sit up, but the tenderness in her pelvis forced her down. *Geez, I thought you were supposed to be happy and ailment-free in Heaven. This one sucks.*

Erin looked around for other signs of the afterlife, but there was a suitcase propped on a chair in the corner. "Is that thing mine?"

"Yes, ma'am." Trina's smile was warm.

"Trina, can you grab my cell phone from in there?"

Trina glanced at Erin's luggage. She hesitated, then went to it and found the device. "Here you go."

Erin took the phone and tapped at the screen. "Great. That's dead too." She tossed her head back onto the pillow.

The nurse seemed to ignore the death stuff and instead kept digging through Erin's things. *What is she doing?*

"Trina? Did you find a charger or something?"

Trina didn't answer.

"Trriiinnnnaaa!" Erin sang in despair.

Trina vanished into a cloudy poof.

Erin's eyes sprung open, her heart operating like an overwound clock. She studied the area and realized she was in the same stale room as earlier. No Trina. No Heaven. No wailing babies. *It was just a dream. Crazy Percocet.* She shook it away and went to settle into a comfy position again when another thought jolted her. *That's the problem. The infants were fictitious fragments of a dreamlike state.*

"But they don't have to be!" she announced to the room filled with absolutely no one.

Erin turned in bed to see herself in the window encased by the night sky. And, although newborns hardly ever sleep on day/night schedules, the unit where they stay must be quieter in the evening hours, at least for the mothers' sake. Or at least, this was Erin's rationale, pulling off the covers that draped her.

Erin steadied herself upright and gripped the pole where the intravenous hung. "Nobody will know," she huffed and began walking.

Erin eased passed the nurses' station going unnoticed by the singleton lingering over a jammed printer. She continued to the mother-baby unit and watched through the transparent partition the rows of cribs filled with new life. A smile crept across her face at the subtle movements of one sleeping cherub. The index card attached to the bassinet identified the baby by gender and the mother's first and last name: Male, Abby Wren. Erin chuckled. "You do look like a little tan wren."

Her sights moved on to read other cards and faces when the surname Harper, *her* last name, next to the word *Female*. Erin's eyes darted to the child inside the hard cradle. "No," she choked, instinctively covering her mouth upon seeing caramel skin and the other features of the infant's tiny body. *She looks just like him.* Erin immediately scanned the identification for Lucinda's name but found it was scribbled over with the letters DOA and Jelani's name written above it. *DOA? As in, dead on arrival?* Erin's confusion was instant, the tears impossible to contain.

"It's difficult for new mothers at first," a nurse said softly and adjusted Erin's hospital gown. "Would you like to meet with a lactation specialist?"

Erin stiffened, suddenly realizing she'd have to play along as one of these babies' mothers, otherwise, she'd be in deep shit.

"Yes, please," Erin replied, the sobs growing heavier.

The nurse handed Erin a tissue and left the room. She wiped her nose and then turned back to the bassinet. "I'm not mad at you, munchkin. It's not your fault. You'll be okay. We'll both eventually be okay. Angels will guide us."

She turned away, ducking out before the nurse returned with a specialist, or worse, a breast pump.

Chapter Forty

Gail sang a tune pumping like a pulse in her head as she readied herself for supper in Leonard's suite. The closet door slid open with ease revealing the selection of clothes she'd brought. Gail hummed away and began sifting through the wardrobe. That's when the internal record that was playing scratched to a halt. "Nothing here is good enough for a dinner date!" She tugged at the shirts on the hangers. Then it dawned on her. "Wait. This is a *date?*" She gulped. *Maybe I should cancel. No, no, I can't do that—he knows I'm still here.* She strained to read the hands on the clock. *There're about two hours to shop for an outfit if I hurry with hair and makeup, like, right now.*

At the dressing table, she coiled her hair in foam rollers. "What have I gotten myself into?" she muttered, staring in the mirror, and started ransacking the cosmetics case for some color.

With curlers and all, Gail tossed the pea coat over her sweats, grabbed the wallet and keys, and raced out before anyone could see.

Wind chimes sounded in the local secondhand shop. A lady wearing a creamy full-length cable knit dress with sleek, black hair pulled into a chignon turned away from a mannequin accessorized with baubles. "Welcome to Two Timer," the woman said, smiling. "Are you here for anything in particular?"

"I'd love to see anything you may have from the 1920s era. Maybe a dress," Gail said, scanning beyond the salesgirl. "Size ten."

The clerk grabbed the black-rimmed glasses dangling from her neck and tapped her chin with the earpiece. "Hmm, right this way." She went to the back of the store to a section filled with colorful garments and started separating pieces that were sandwiched together on a rack. "The 1920s were based on a simple, straight silhouette," she said, pulling a cotton lilac number free from the bunch, and raising it.

Gail took hold of it and examined it. "It's pretty, but it's awfully boxy, no?"

"It is quite unshapely. You'll find that's common with most pieces from that decade. What about something from the '30s? Dresses were a bit more form-fitting with belts to accentuate the waistline."

The corners of Gail's mouth turned up. "Yes, please, show me those."

"Sweetie, tell me your size again." The woman placed the specs on the bridge of her nose.

"Ten."

"Ten, ten, ten," she chanted softly, reading the garment tags. "Ah, ha." She wrenched a hanger from the pole and held out an olive dress.

Gail frowned. She didn't do green but then inched in for a better look. The garb was elegant yet simple: a small but sharp collar, short cuffed sleeves that fell just below the shoulder, and chocolate-colored buttons shaped like diamonds lining the middle that trailed down to a smooth leather belt of the same brown shade. Gail admired the pleating under the bust and inspected the length of the skirt. "Hmm, it appears a tad long. May I try it on?"

The lady led the way to a tiny dressing room partitioned by thick, red drapes.

Gail entered, hurried out of her loungewear, and stepped into the soft fabric dress. The material was form-fitting, hugging all the right places. She latched the buttons and fastened the belt before facing the mirror. *I'm having a meal with another man, Harry. Please don't be mad.*

"Sooo," the clerk chirped, "how is it?"

"It's a fit." Gail pulled the curtain to show her.

"It's *definitely* a fit. Like it was made for you," she said, eyeing Gail's curves. "Take your hair down. Let's get the full effect."

Gail freed her locks from the rollers and gave a little shake. Her hairdo was a replica of the wavy shoulder-length style dated back to the creation of the dress.

"Unbelievable," the saleswoman said. "Whoever you're with when you wear this will swoon when he takes notice of you."

Gail grinned shyly, the compliment like a seal of approval, and retreated to the fitting room where she broke into a happy dance until...

"Shoes!" she cried and parted the drapes once more.

"I don't have much of a selection," the lady said, scratching her head. "What's your shoe size? And what color? Brown, right?"

"I'm a size eight. Please say you have something brown in a size eight."

The woman hurried to the front of the store, where there was one small wooden shelf under the window. Two pairs of black boots and one gold sandal rested on the surface. "I could have sworn we had a plain brown heel." She rummaged through some dusty shoeboxes beneath a bench, tearing lids off and throwing them to the side. "Got 'em!" A pair of chocolate-colored strapped high-heeled shoes were held high in the air like a sports trophy.

"What size are they?" Gail asked, crossing some fingers.

"Ugh. They're a seven." The woman pouted and chucked them back into the box. Gail was desperate. She snatched the shoes and dropped them on the floor. "Pray they fit."

The lady gripped Gail's elbow to help her balance. The heels weren't gorgeous, but they matched and were dressy.

"Well?" the woman asked, continuing to hold Gail steady.

"They're kind of tight, but I'll be sitting for most of the evening. I'll take them!"

Gail strutted out of the boutique, resembling a print model from a 1930s catalog. She did, however, incorporate a twenty-first-century twist by popping the dress's collar and, on the advice of the saleslady, left the top three buttons undone to expose some cleavage.

Feeling more like Mae West than a lonely widow, Gail unlocked the doors to the car and lobbed the shopping bags onto the back seat, ready for a first official date since…well, decades. "It might as well have been in the '30s." She laughed then started the engine, tapping the gas pedal with the snug vintage shoe, and headed back to the bed-and-breakfast.

The warm air filled the main foyer with hints of deliciously salted eats. Gail peered around the staircase in search of Zofie, but she was nowhere in sight; the lights were off at the back of the house.

Gail followed the scent to the second floor, where music accompanied the sound of something sizzling on a stove. She knocked on Leonard's half-opened door, but it went unanswered. She heightened the collar on the dress and adjusted the belt, the picture of the two firemen in the rubble a dark shadow in the dimly lit hall.

"Hello-o," Gail caroled and pushed open the wooden barrier that separated her from the fancy suite. Leonard stepped into the bedroom from the kitchenette, removing his apron. Beneath the cooking attire was a neatly pressed polo shirt and crisp denim. Gail instantly noticed the navy-blue stitched emblem of a jockey riding a horse. It stood out on top of the bright emerald fabric, a flattering color for someone with dark features, like Leonard. His black-polished loafers, which differed from the usual hiking boots, were also of note.

"Looking sharp," she said and patted his chest.

"You're looking quite snazzy yourself. Think our stylists planned this?" He pointed at their green clothes, exploding into laughter.

"Eh, you know what they say about great minds." Gail maintained eye contact slightly longer than someone other than Harry.

Leonard took Gail's hand and escorted her up to the second half of the suite. At once, the surroundings mesmerized her: the perfectly preserved and fully functioning Progress stove with oven attachment from the mid-1900s painted in that eye-catching turquoise color that appeared around the mansion seemingly out of nowhere. There was also a restored white fridge with an exposed silver handle that curled upward and an old slop sink that was sparkling clean and framed with wooden shelves displaying a variety of fancy china. At the heart of the room was a petite café table covered in white linen set for two. "This is magnificent," she said, grazing the silky tablecloth and spied the old dial radio from where music was coming from.

"Please, sit." Leonard pulled out the chair and bowed his head.

Gail eased onto the seat, taking notice of his strength when he pushed her closer to the table. She slipped a material napkin onto her lap as he tended to the food on the stovetop. Quietly, she watched him work, studying the broadness of his back, of how his muscles fanned up and out like a boa constrictor's right before it was about to strike. She wanted to touch him, imagining standing behind him and massaging his bulging skin, planting light kisses down his clothed spine.

Leonard turned around, holding a ladle. "Is that a yes or a no?"

Gail squeezed her eyes shut, shooing away the fantasy. "Um, yes?"

He let out a hardy laugh, patting his torso with his other hand. "You have no idea what I just said, do you?"

"You asked if I wanted wine, and the answer was yes," she quipped.

He raised an eyebrow, ostensibly entertained by the wittiness, then set down the utensil and poured a glass of Merlot. "I inquired about a gravy drizzle on your duchess potatoes," he said, his lips curling seductively.

Gail's insides tingled when his gentle breath tickled her ear, but the real stimulation stemmed from the words *drizzle* and *duchess* he was using to reference their meal; the only person to discover that the way to a woman's heart (*this* woman's heart) was through a well-planned menu had been Harry. Until now. Which freaked her out a smidge. But in a good way.

She avoided looking at him and hummed a yes into the goblet before indulging.

"So, tell me about Harry," Leonard said, setting down a dinner plate in front of her.

Gail glanced at the filet of beef smothered in a brown Marsala sauce and picked up a fork. "He was definitely a meat-and-potatoes kinda guy," she said, smiling, and plucked at the fluffy cloud-like potatoes that resembled miniature cupcakes.

She tasted them, the creamy texture indulgent in its own right. "Butter should be one of the seven deadly sins." She closed her eyes and savored the flavor.

"It's most definitely gluttonous." He settled in the seat across from her.

As Gail cut into the beef, she thought of what to share about her late husband. "Well, as you obviously know, Harry was a fireman." A forkful of meat went into her mouth. "Mm, this is so good. Did you learn to make this at your firehouse?"

"Ha!" Leonard rubbed his lips with a napkin. "I taught those clowns how to cook."

Gail tee-heed and ate some more.

"I graduated culinary school a couple of years before entering the Fire Academy," he said. "I was a sous chef at a five-star restaurant in Manhattan waiting for a promotion to head chef when the owner filed bankruptcy out of nowhere."

"Well, gosh. That must have been a real bummer."

"It was." He shook his head. "But then my mother told me about the firefighter's exam, so I took it on a whim. I always thought firefighting was cool—what boy doesn't, right? So I waited to see what would come of that."

"Makes sense." Gail poked at a green bean. "You were out of a job anyway, so why not explore your options, right?"

"Yep. It was the best opportunity to come my way. Not only did I love fighting fires, but I was still able to be in the kitchen pursuing my passion for food. I ended up writing a cookbook and was even on television because of it."

"Shut up! You? On television?" Gail snorted and took a swig of wine.

"Yes, me on television. Why? You can't picture me on the boob-tube?"

Gail laughed harder, tears forming at the corners of her eyes. "I'm sorry." She snagged the napkin and dabbed her lashes. "I haven't laughed this hard in years."

"Hey, I happened to rock every show I was on. Even beat Bobby Flay, thank you very much."

"No, no, I'm not really laughing *at* you. It's just that you, your mannerisms, your whole spiel is just so darn funny." She burst into hysterics again.

Leonard rested his hands on the table and stood. Gail grew silent, eyes following him as he walked to the fridge. "I hope I didn't insult you."

"Insult me? Nah, I'm a big boy." He grabbed a beer and an orange and strolled to the counter, where he cut it in half and then into smaller slices. She looked on as he put a piece of the fruit on the rim of his drink, thinking how it'd been a while since she'd been in the presence of a man—alone—and hadn't realized how invigorating it was; toying with the idea of dating and actually being on a date were two very different things. Excitement, nervousness, fear, fun—they all twisted up into one big ball of anticipation for what was ahead. Not that she was sure of what was to come, but it was the thrill of not knowing that made her feel something. Maybe young again. Or maybe just alive again.

Gail crossed one leg over the other, keeping an eye on Leonard as he returned to the table with the beer. She moved in close to read the label.

"It's a Blue Moon. Can't drink one without a citrus garnish," he said.

Gail looked on as he drank. "A nice retired fireman who likes restoring things and has a proclivity for preparing fancy meals? It definitely won't get any better than this."

Leonard gazed in her direction, their eyes connecting. "We are two very lucky people."

The fever she was experiencing caused her to turn away.

"Hey, do you like mangoes?" Leonard asked, whisking away the bare dinner plates.

"I've only tried mango sorbet. Does that count?"

Leonard pulled a small porcelain bowl from the refrigerator and put it where Gail's supper had been. He took a dessert spoon and sat again. "It's crème brûlée," he said, cracking the hardened sugary shell with a careful jerk of the utensil. "Under the vanilla custard are bits of fresh mango sprinkled with rum." He scooped up the white and orange mixture and held it out to Gail.

The silverware glistened as it moved. Gail parted both lips, allowing it to enter. The creamy filling was an explosion of flavor. Leonard slowly pulled his hand away. She kept her jaw loose, chewing the soft fruit, sights fixed on his, and swallowed. She readied her mouth for more. Leonard grinned and carefully dipped his serving tool into the dessert, seemingly eager to please. As the spoon came close, she licked at it and took it in a little faster this time then swallowed, eye contact strong.

By the fourth bite, Leonard dropped the tableware and rushed to her. His kiss was firm, filled with pent-up tension, urgent for release. Gail pulled away, breath heavy, and then pulled him closer. After a few intense kisses, she stopped. "I, I must go."

Leonard got up, smoothing his slacks. "Everything all right?"

"I don't know. I mean, yes, this is great, but I, I don't know." She snagged her purse.

"Can I walk you back to your room?"

Gail peered up, doe-eyed, and nodded. Leonard kissed the tip of her nose and led the way.

Outside the suite, Gail spied the painting of Ground Zero. The muscles tightened in her throat.

"Thank you for a lovely evening," Leonard said, his eyes focused on hers.

A grin snuck away from Gail's control, as did a tear. "I should go," she said and gave his fingers a little squeeze. "Dinner was delicious. Thank you."

She let go and entered the room without looking back. When the door clicked into the jamb, she dropped onto the velvet chair. *I just kissed another man, and I liked it.* Her sobs were soft until the thought of cheating on Harry seeped in, the weight of it settling on her chest like a boulder. It didn't matter that he was dead.

Gail rose and hurried to the open closet, ripping clothes off hangers and stuffing them into the suitcase. "It's best I leave. Pretend this never happened," she said aloud. "It's all just a big mistake." She walked to the dresser to gather the cosmetics and spied herself in the mirror; the green fitted dress, snug and pretty. She paused, almost breathless at the sight, and thought of the music, the food, but, mostly, the inspiration behind it all: Leonard. *Okay, okay. I'll stay the night. But I leave in the morning, right after breakfast.*

Chapter Forty-One

Erin's foot grazed the pavement.

"Let me help," Deirdre said and rushed around the minivan.

Erin hesitated before stepping out. "Thank you for taking me home." She grabbed onto Deirdre's arm and eased to the ground.

Under a thick shawl and the down of a winter coat, Erin limped up the length of the path, passing the neighbors, who started shouting inquiries from their front lawn. She left the requests for information in her wake—the stitched lady parts, torn leggings, and deteriorating happiness weren't exactly what she wanted people to talk about, especially here.

Deirdre unlocked the door. "You go inside, and I'll grab the mail."

In the foyer, Erin dropped the jacket and agonized up every step. "Have I said lately how much I hate this house?" she groaned. Once at the top of the landing, however, Erin saw the dismal living room had been freshly painted a pale yellow, her absolute favorite color. "Who did this?"

"I did," Jay-Jay said, appearing from the kitchen in paint-stained work clothes. "Do you like it?"

Erin took in a jagged breath. "Why are you here?"

He took two steps forward but stopped. "I want to make things right."

Erin inspected the rest of the room. The classic blue gingham-print couch she'd had eyes on from Pottery Barn was sitting Buddha-like in the center. Behind it was a wooden serving table whose distressed surface was organized with vintage knick-knacks she'd ogled over at the consignment store in their former Manhattan neighborhood. The house was also cleaner than she'd left it. Almost like he'd hired someone to do the cleaning *and* the interior design. *Huh. Imagine if this happened without the infidelity!*

She stood straight again and went to the sofa. Draped over an arm was the blue blanket her grandmother had crocheted when she was born; Grandma, a feminist, had been against the pink movement. Erin turned and, in slow, careful increments, settled herself onto a cushion.

"Man, don't you wish you could unpoke a vagina?" Erin chuckled. "'Cause you almost had me for a second."

Deirdre scooted in with the mail and Erin's luggage. "Oh wow. It really is incredible. You're the guy for my next apartment—whenever *that* is," Deirdre said and then turned to Erin. "I'll get you something to drink. Want a Percocet for the pain?"

Erin patted the bandages. "Thanks. Yes, please. It's become itchy *and* achy."

"Probably from moving around," Deirdre said, already in the next room hunting for a glass, and returned with water and the pill.

"Probably from dealing with a cheater," Erin said, taking the medication. She laughed, then ingested it at a runner's pace. "So, guys, I need you to keep a secret, k?" she continued sarcastically, handing over the cup.

Deirdre looked at Erin, then at Jay-Jay.

"Your secret is safe with me," Jay-Jay said and took a seat next to Erin.

"Cute, but I doubt that." Erin let herself relax, her wavy hair coiling around a few fingers as she got lost in thought, images of being a little girl sprinting across the living room to a homemade fort where all the dolls were tucked inside. It didn't matter that her parents were arguing in the next room; she was accustomed to it. Erin's younger self bent down and disappeared beyond the crook of flannel blankets to where she felt safe with toys, a flashlight, and some books.

Jay-Jay's hand waved in front of Erin's eyes. "You okay, Er?"

Erin flinched. "Yeah. I guess the Percocet kicked in already." She studied Jay-Jay's face—his curly lashes and smooth complexion—and thought of how she never really stopped to appreciate the things they had since marrying but instead dwelled on what they couldn't do. "The living room looks beautiful, by the way." Her mouth was a drunken grin.

"I'm glad you like it, but what's your secret?"

"I went to the maternity ward the other night during my stay at the hospital."

"And?" Jay-Jay began rubbing his knees.

"I cried," Erin said and shrugged. "No one was there except me, and, and so I eyed those see-through bassinets, one with a frail chicken-like baby inside of it, and I cried."

Deirdre sat and petted Erin's head. "It's okay."

"It's not, actually. The baby's identification card said, 'DOA.'"

"As in Dead on Arrival?" Deirdre asked and paused.

"You tell me. You're the medic."

Deirdre looked at Jay-Jay, then again at Erin. "Yes, that's what it means."

"Lucinda died in that building fire Rob responded to the other night," Jay-Jay said, his hands white-knuckled around his knees.

"Oh, I didn't know," Erin said, sulking a bit.

"That's probably because you were preoccupied," Jay-Jay replied. "And rightfully so. You had your own life going on."

Erin considered it, recounting the infant in the cradle. "I feel just as broken as that baby."

Chapter Forty-Two

The loud pop of a carburetor backfiring out on the street woke Gail. Daylight seeped through the windows. Stunned for a split second, she hopped up and scanned the room for the clock. It read 8:00.

She gulped. *Do I really want to go to breakfast? How could she face Leonard after the way they parted?* A deep belly grumble answered that question. She went to the suitcase and swung open the flap, revealing a pile of wrinkled casual wear. *Ugh, there's no iron here. What am I going to do?*

She crawled back to bed and stayed there, thoughtless and hungry, for a while. When her body got as numb as her brain, she pulled off the mattress and rifled through some clothes, pulling out a fuchsia sweater. "What was I thinking when I packed?"

Finally, black yoga pants with minimal creases surfaced. *The styles don't match, but whatever.*

After some makeup and finger combing, Gail put on ballerina flats and peeked out the door. The scent of eggs filled the hall, accompanied by the creak of footsteps downstairs. Gail straightened. *You can do this.*

She exited the room and made the descent with steady movements.

"Good morning," Zofie said, holding a smoking kettle with an oven mitt. "Would you like some tea?"

"Yes, thank you." Gail smiled while approaching

the big oak dining table and pulled at a heavy chair, careful not to bang it against the tabletop as Zofie poured boiling water into a cup. Her heart paused upon noticing that the table was set for only one person amid a feast of fresh fruit, bagels, cheeses, and a basket of muffins. "Won't you be joining me?" she asked, glancing at the empty seats.

"I've eaten already, dear, but if you'd like some company, I'd be happy to sit with you."

Gail tried to ignore the unexpected pang of disappointment from Leonard's absence and tapped at the chair beside her. "Please."

Zofie put the teapot at the center of the spread and lifted the sterling cover from the plate in front of Gail. Smoke slithered up from the scrambled eggs, bacon, sausage links, and stack of golden pancakes. "Enjoy."

Gail marveled at the food. "Surely you are expecting Leonard too with this elaborate breakfast," she said, hoping not to sound too curious about his whereabouts.

"Leonard had to leave early this morning to help his son." Zofie sat.

Gail picked up the cup of tea and blew on it before sipping. *Maybe his son is a troublesome kid.* She envisioned Leonard pleading with a bailiff as his boy stood behind him, wearing a smug expression. She shuddered at the thought of having to deal with a scourge.

"They left about an hour ago. I'm sure you heard them. That old car is nothing but a nuisance, yet his son refuses to part with it." Zofie chuckled. "I think they woke the entire neighborhood."

Gail laughed probably a little louder than necessary, but the weight that was lifted made her feel a lot better about dining without him. Then she remembered that pest, Roger. "What about the other guy?"

"Roger's out jogging. He doesn't normally eat with us in the morning," Zofie replied. "So, did you enjoy your stay?"

Gail let out an internal sigh and thought of her time thus far: the history, the music, and, of course, Leonard.

"I did," she said and started to eat, quietly contemplating if she'd return.

****

On the ride home, Gail did her usual drive-by Harry's firehouse and noticed a celebration happening in the parking lot. Black and white balloons were tied to the fence, and people of all ages were walking around carrying hot dogs and soda cans. She slowed to a stop at the traffic light where a group of men in wheelchairs rolled toward a brightly polished antique fire engine. There were people on crutches and prosthetics gathering near a clown juggling several bowling pins.

"Oh, the Wounded Warrior Project!" Gail continued to watch, thinking of Leonard and how he had talked with the veteran the other night at the B&B.

When the traffic signal turned green, the driver behind Gail honked aggressively on the horn. She jumped, startled by the noise, and stomped on the gas pedal. The tires screeched, lurching the car forward. The front end of Gail's vehicle smashed into the bumper of an SUV, causing an airbag in the steering wheel to detonate. Hot air and powder pummeled her cheeks, but the pressure from the safety device zeroed in on her nose. Gail cupped her bloody septum as men gathered by the car and opened the door.

"You all right, ma'am?" a uniformed serviceman

284

asked, pulling her from the driver's seat.

She lowered her hands and peered up at him.

"Mrs. O'Neil!"

The fireman turned to the others. "Get some ice. We need some ice. It's Harry's wife."

"I'm fine, Victor," Gail said, recognizing him, and eased onto a chair that one of the soldiers dragged over. "Just tell me if it's broken?"

Victor angled her chin and examined the area, including the skin under her eyes. "No shiners forming yet." He touched the bridge of her nose. "Does that hurt?"

"No," she said.

He touched the cartilage, but she didn't react. "It's just red from the impact." He removed a small package of tissues from his pocket and dabbed at her nostrils. "The blood is starting to subside already."

Gail exhaled through her mouth and smiled. "How's the other driver?"

They looked to the street where a woman wearing a tan furry coat was flailing her arms and screaming something in another language. The lady craned around and pointed at Gail with her cell phone. "And you! I am going to sue you."

Victor got to his feet. "Nobody is getting sued because you, ma'am, were texting when the light changed."

The rambunctious woman glared at the phone, then slipped it into the sleeve of her coat. Gail watched Victor resume his seat on the curb.

"Don't worry," he said.

While they waited for a tow truck to haul the cars off the road, a man wearing a military jacket and a prosthetic leg joined them, offering her a hotdog and a soda.

"My gosh, I should be serving you," Gail said, hiding her embarrassment with the tissue in her hand.

"Nonsense." The soldier squatted and waited until she was ready to take the food. "Your husband was a great man. He did a lot for us."

As Gail chewed, her nose throbbed, but she ignored the pain. "Thank you. And thank you for your service to our country," she said between bites. "Harry always admired the bravery of our troops."

The combatant crossed his mechanical leg over a fleshy uninjured one. Gail couldn't help but look.

"How do you do it? How do you manage?" she said, the words practically falling from her mouth.

"What? This?" The soldier wiggled his metal foot.

Gail's cheeks grew hot. "I'm sorry. You don't have to answer that."

"It's okay. I'd say, one day at a time."

"It must be hard, though, no?"

The guy shrugged. "It's the only thing you can do. But it does get better, as long as you're aware that you'll never be the same."

"Huh." Gail stared at the young man, taken by his wisdom when a roar of cheers from inside the gated area caused her to turn. The jester tossing bowling pins was now riding a unicycle while balancing an umbrella on his forehead.

"Nothing's more frightening than a circus clown," the soldier said, pretending to shiver.

Gail laughed.

A tow truck pulled up in front of them, its motor an obnoxious rumble. The driver switched gears to park and jumped out.

"Well, it was a pleasure meeting you—" Gail said, extending a hand.

"Daniel," he said, putting his hand in hers.

The tow truck operator approached them, holding a clipboard. Gail stood and retrieved an insurance card. He took the card and the pen from behind his ear and began walking toward the wreck as he wrote.

Gail gave Daniel a salute and headed to her damaged car.

****

The echoing thud of the duffel bag falling onto the marble floor reminded Gail once again of isolation. She stepped over mail scattered about the entrance and stared at Harry's picture propped on the server. "*…it does get better, as long as you're aware that you'll never be the same.*"

Gail took out her cell phone and dialed the bed-and-breakfast. "Hello, Zofie. It's me, Gail. I'd like to know if you have any availability—say—next weekend?"

Chapter Forty-Three

"A package has arrived for a Mrs. Dunham," Rob said as he walked into the hospital room.

Megan turned in the bed to face him.

Rob held out a big brown box with his unbroken arm and put it on her lap.

"Thanks, babe," she said, examining the parcel's label. "Did you get a hold of Jay-Jay?"

Rob unzipped his jacket and sat. "Yes. He surprised Erin with some impressive renovations."

"He needs to make good on more than that house." Megan shook the box and tried to tear off the tape. "Can you help me with this?"

Rob flipped up his switchblade and pierced the packaging.

Megan separated the cardboard flaps and layers of tissue. "Sheer perfection!"

"Is there a puppy in there or something?" Rob joked and sat back in the chair.

She carefully revealed her new possession. He let out a whistle as his eyes elevated up and down the black dress. "That's some outfit." He focused on the plunging neckline. "Where're you going?"

"I was elected Teacher of the Year by Mrs. Baxter," Meg said from behind the gown. "But that's not happening until sometime in the new year." She peered around the garment. "So, I was hoping you'd take me somewhere."

He felt his nerves get a bit schoolboy. "Game on."

Megan returned the evening wear into the paper bedding and rested on the pillow.

He leaned in and brushed his lips against hers. "Congratulations, Teach."

****

The firehouse kitchen was bustling when Rob walked in.

"What's up, guys?" he said, snagging a piece of raw broccoli from a cutting board and popped it into his mouth.

"Hey, it's the gimp," a guy shouted from behind the tiny wall connected to the dining room.

"Yeah, yeah," Rob said, waving his cast, and joined the man at the table. "You know you miss me, Jerry."

"Like a hemorrhoid."

"Now, now, ladies," another fireman said, putting a platter of uncooked vegetables and French dip in front of them.

"So, when's our dinner dance?" Rob asked, another broccoli bobbing between his lips.

Jerry ripped the flyer from the bulletin board and handed it to him. "Next week."

Rob grabbed the paper in disbelief. "Fuck. How did I not know this? Everything must be all booked by now."

"It's not a big deal. We can pencil you into the seating arrangement. Are you bringing the missus?"

Rob nodded, still examining the information:

Annual Company Dance
Saturday, November 15
W Hotel

541 Lexington Avenue, New York, NY
Cocktails at 7:00 p.m.with dinner n'dancing to follow
*A block of rooms is reserved for this event,
say FDNY when booking

Using the GPS feature of his cell, Rob tried to figure out if Central Park was anywhere near Lexington Avenue. A long time ago, Megan had joked that she was probably the only New Yorker who hadn't taken a horse-drawn carriage ride around the city, and now he wanted to change that.

"Hey, Jer," he said, looking away from his phone. "What restaurant do you recommend in Manhattan? Like Uptown-ish."

"Le Bernardin," Jerry said without turning away from reading the headlines. "It's a classic."

Rob did an internet search on the establishment and discovered it had been rated number one on Zagat's list of 100 Best Restaurants of New York City. He glanced at his coworker. "Man, I knew you were a foodie, but damn."

Jerry licked a finger and gripped a feathery page of the newspaper. "If you can't get a reservation, let me know, and I'll get one for you."

Rob held out his phone. "I need it for next week. Five o'clock. Same day as the dance."

Jerry glanced up, one brow furrowed.

"Please? I want to surprise Megan."

Jerry knew Rob's situation. They all did. He got up from his seat and grabbed Rob's cell.

Rob watched him leave the room as he said hello to someone on the other end of the line and suddenly his palms were clammy. He rubbed them on his jeans as he stared at the dinner dance flyer. *If this works out, we'll be set: early dinner at Le Bernardin, carriage ride through the park, then dancing, and an overnighter at the hotel.*

Jerry reentered the room and tossed the phone to him. "You're in."

Chapter Forty-Four

"On the count of three. Ready?" Deirdre said, securing her arms around Megan's ribcage.

Megan initiated the count and anticipated the lift-off, hoping her bones wouldn't hurt too much.

Deirdre hoisted her into the wheelchair, her face reconfiguring into an expression of horror and surprise.

"I know, I know," Megan said. "I've got to try to eat more. Don't worry, I will once I'm home, and especially at Gail's cookie party."

Deirdre settled her into the leather seat and released the brake. "Yes, that'll definitely do the trick. Know what you're baking yet?"

Megan winced from the jostling. "No, but I'm sure the boys will want to help, so probably something on the simple side like oatmeal chocolate chips." When she laughed, she latched onto the chair handles.

"Honestly, what's your pain level from one to ten, ten being the worst?" Deirdre asked, sounding concerned.

"A four if I'm still. Five when you move me," Megan said, hoping Deirdre wouldn't notice the bogusness of her response because she was almost out, and nothing was going to stop her from getting home.

"So," Deirdre said and maneuvered the wheelchair. "Are you excited to see Erin? Jay-Jay redid their living room."

"Yes, I feel as if I haven't seen her in forever. I'm so glad Jay had enough sense to do that, especially now." Megan fixed her cancer cap. "Okay, I'm ready."

Their images reflected off the linoleum as they wheeled out of the room to the computer area, where a technician was working under the desk. He slid out and stood when they got close.

"You're all set, ladies," he said, removing the rolling business chair from the workstation so that Megan could remain in her seat.

Megan watched Deirdre type in Erin's phone number and establish a connection on the computer. Like a rod of lightning striking, Erin's white face burst onto the screen.

Deirdre waved. "Hey, Erin, can you hear us? Just checking to see that the technology is working."

"Hi. Yes, I'm here," Erin replied.

Deirdre moved out of the way, and Megan scooted herself forward. She gasped at the sight of Erin who, not coincidentally, drew a loud breath in return.

"Hi," Megan whispered, her lip twitching. She held up a hand to the monitor.

Erin placed her palm on the screen over Megan's. "Hey."

They stared at one another as if possessed when suddenly Erin pulled her hand away and slouched back in her chair. "Sorry, I can't sit up like that for too long."

"It's okay. So, are you starting to feel like yourself, at least a little?" Megan asked, then let out a raspy cough.

"Meh. Maybe in another day or so, but we'll see." Erin glanced up. "And you? You don't sound too good."

Megan looked over both shoulders, then got closer to the screen. "I was doing better, enough for them to send me home, yet today I feel like crapola. I'm not telling them,though, because it's all a crapshoot—one day I'm good, one day I'm not. I gotta get out of here for a little while," Megan said, her whisper abrasive.

Erin tapped on her thermos. "I hear ya. Speaking of crap, I've been constipated since yesterday. The doctor says I have to keep hydrated." She took a sip and made a face. "I hate water. Isn't life the mother of all bitches?"

Megan repositioned herself in the chair, the sores developing on her butt a painful reminder of her life with less mobility. "Yeah, it is. And then you die." Megan tried to laugh but started battling another vicious bout of phlegm.

"Sweet Lord above, look at us," Erin said and rolled her eyes. "Your boobs are gone. My vagina's been excavated. Who'd we piss off in Heaven?"

The women looked at one another and simpered.

Erin slouched closer to the monitor. "Did Deirdre tell you that I saw Jay-Jay's baby in the hospital?"

"No, I hadn't heard anything. Are you okay?"

Erin flashed Megan a faux smile she recognized. "I want to be."

Megan's forehead wrinkled. "You know you don't have to do anything you don't want to do. HashtagTeamErinForever."

"I'm scared, Meg," Erin whispered.

Megan leaned forward and lowered her voice too. "Why are you scared?"

"Lucinda died," Erin said. "That poor child doesn't have a mother."

One of Megan's eyebrows arched. "What? How?"

"I don't know the particulars, but she was in that house fire. The one with Rob." Erin settled back in her chair again. "And Jay-Jay has been doing all sorts of kind things for me. Half of me wants to believe he truly is sorry, and the other half wonders if he's doing all that because Lucinda is dead." Erin stopped talking and rubbed her forehead. "Anyway, word on the street is that Gail is getting all the fire wives together for a dessert exchange thingy. You going?"

"Yep, I wouldn't miss it for the world."

"Yeah, I'll be there too. Oh, and the firehouse is having the company dance next week."

"It's next week?" Megan said, a wind of disappointment sweeping in. "That, I didn't know…"

She thought of the new dress, of how she'd asked Rob to take her some place, any place to enjoy herself, the purchase, and him, of course, so why hadn't he mentioned it? She lowered her head.

"Yikes. I didn't mean to upset you," Erin said. "Don't worry. Obviously, I'm not going either. A girl's night in someone's house is just about all we can handle at the moment."

Megan hadn't told her about the bucket list and didn't have the willpower to get into it.

Deirdre walked over, holding a chart. "Sorry to interrupt, ladies, but it's time to check vitals," she said, tapping at the manila folder.

Megan straightened. "I have to go. Talk to you later?"

"Sure. I'll text you. Bye, girls." Erin ended the call.

Deirdre released the foot brake and pushed Megan to her room. Once inside, Deirdre kneeled and made direct eye contact with her. "I couldn't help but hear what you and Erin were talking about when I came to get you. Just so you know, Rob is planning something special for next week. I'm not sure what it is, but I'd be willing to bet you a hundred bucks that it's going to be great."

Megan saw the sincerity on her face. "Did you hear him talking about it or something?"

"Yeah." She used the arm of the wheelchair to get up. "Something like that."

After getting situated in bed, Megan reached over the metal bar and slipped a hand into the postal box to feel the fabric of the gown between her fingers. *Please, God, let her be right.*

Chapter Forty-Five

Deirdre busted into the house. "You have to say something. She needs to know!"

Rob eyed her as she slung her motorcycle helmet over the spindle of his chair and peered at his open laptop. He tilted his head. "What are you talking about?"

"This." Deirdre pointed at the confirmation email from the W Hotel. "Whatever plans you've made, tell her."

"What? Why?"

"Because she's homesick, depressed with her body and, with all the shit she's been through—*is* going through—a pick-me-up would be *really* good for her right now."

"Roger that," he replied and stabbed at a button on the keyboard. In the distance, the reverberation of the printer's gears jerked into motion.

"Let me know if you need anything." She undid the side zippers on her riding pants. "I mean, besides babysitting."

What the? Rob caught himself staring while she kicked off her shoes and wormed the outerwear down her legs as she walked toward the guest bedroom. He shook his head and distracted himself from anything sexual by going to the printer.

He heard her body drop onto the mattress. "I need a vacation," she said, her voice muffled.

"Same," Rob said and stepped into the room. "Hey. There is one thing…"

Deirdre lifted her head. "What's that?"

"I want to buy a motorcycle for Megan."

Deirdre popped to a standing position. "Man, I was thinking the same thing a few days ago!"

They stared at one another, his mind already on a joyride to the dealership. Deirdre moved in for a high-five, but his hand was still bandaged. He laughed as she gave him a quick, awkward pat on the chest instead.

He swirled his car keys with his other more operable limb. "Let's do this."

The glare from the sun's rays poked at Rob's eyes as he drove out of the neighborhood. He flipped down the visor, squinting hard against the light, and then gunned it. As the four-door sedan raced along the deserted road, Deirdre touched the dial on the dash.

"Nobody messes with my radio," Rob said, swatting her hand.

She biffed his forehead and rolled the window down.

Rob looked on as she closed her eyes and inhaled the cool air, enjoying the simple pleasures of a brisk autumn day; the sun illuminated her peachy skin. He missed the days when Megan was healthy. Just then, Deirdre shimmied back in the passenger seat, causing Rob's vision to dart to the street again.

"Erin mentioned the dance to Megan," she said, leaning on the headrest. "I don't think she meant anything by it, you know, with everything going on, but it upset Meg anyway. That's why you have to tell her something about your plans."

"I'm going to," he said, remaining focused on the

road.

The car radio suddenly seemed louder without all the talking.

"You're a good guy." Deirdre patted his arm. "And Megan's a lucky gal."

As the motorcycle shop became visible on the horizon, Deirdre uncrossed her legs and perked up. "I always get butterflies when I come here," she said, her voice giddy like a nine-year-old on the first day of summer.

Rob maneuvered the car into a vacant spot in the lot and shut the engine. "I'm glad we're doing this."

"Me too," Deirdre said and hopped out of the vehicle. "She's going to be so surprised."

Inside the showroom, Deirdre ogled the shiny new bikes that lined the store in neat rows. Her fingers traced the smooth edges of a gas tank of a brand-new Harley Superlow painted in a brilliant pearl-like shimmer. "The color of this one reminds me of Megan's rosary beads."

Rob touched the black leather seat. "You're right." He backed away for a full view. "It's almost identical to it."

"The Superlow is a perfect motorcycle for the Mrs.," a salesman shouted from across the floor. He was incredibly short, wearing a gray suit that made him resemble an overweight stockbroker rather than a Harley Davidson dealer.

Deirdre and Rob exchanged glances as the guy waddled toward them.

"Have a seat, my dear," the boisterous man said, panting as he approached them and placed a hand on Deirdre's back.

She flinched. "I already ride." She gripped the

throttle and swung a boot around the backend. She sat tall and positioned the machinery upright, flipping the kickstand without so much as batting a lash. "We're here for *his* wife, my friend."

The man nodded and extended his palm in Rob's direction. "I'm Merv."

Rob accepted the handshake.

Deirdre stood and sat again, rocking the bike back and forth.

"Is your friend—*his* wife—your size?" Merv said to Deirdre and rubbed at the five o'clock shadow sprouting from his chin.

"She's shorter than me by a couple of inches." Deirdre moved the handlebars side to side.

"Why don't you take off your boots to get the full effect from her perspective?"

Deirdre stopped shifting the bike and glanced at him. "Good idea."

She flicked the stand downright and kicked off her shoes. The motorcycle was harder to manipulate with her legs stretched further around the body of the machine, which gave her more resistance.

Both Rob and Merv watched her struggle.

"The Superlow is over five hundred pounds of metal. Are you sure your friend can handle that?" Merv said.

"This is the lightest you have on the market, correct?" Rob said.

The salesman nodded. "Unless you want to check out some dirt bikes."

Deirdre held up a hand. "No thanks."

Rob walked closer to the motorcycle. "It's a two-seater, so Megan will have to be the passenger."

Deirdre's face brightened. "You mean you're going to ride?"

Rob worked his fingers through his hair and smiled. "Looks that way."

She hopped off and smacked the seat. "Straddle that bitch."

The sales clerk laughed, thinking the woman was joking but stopped when Rob climbed onto the motorcycle, careful not to hit his cast.

"It comes off tomorrow," Rob said sheepishly.

Deirdre's brows rose. "Really?"

"Yes, ma'am. Then I get a soft cast—more manageable. The doctor told me yesterday." He turned to Merv. "Write up the paperwork. This puppy is sold."

"Yes!" Deirdre threw up a palm and motioned for a high-five, this time directing it at the correct hand.

Merv led them to a cubicle at the back of the dealership. "I'll need your driver's license," he said, looking over his shoulder.

After a brief exchange of personal information and a credit check, Rob and Deirdre followed the man to the garage, where the bike was prepped and ready to go. Merv handed Rob the keys, who tossed them to Deirdre. "No wheelies," he said, voice menacing, and headed to his car.

Chapter Forty-Six

Erin started to walk without slouching. She took a few steps to the window and saw Jay-Jay's pickup double-parked in front. *Huh. That's odd.* She strained for a better look.

"Someone is feeling better," Jay-Jay said from the landing.

"You scared the bejesus out of me. Aren't you supposed to be at work?"

"I do have work, but later. Come with me." He pointed to the back bedroom. "I, uh, have something to show you."

Suspicious, she resumed sights outside. On the street, his truck was filled with the usual tools, but there was also a giant cardboard box. She squinted yet couldn't make out what it was. "Okay, let's go," she said. "But I'd appreciate it if you called before popping in, you know."

At the opposite end of the house, Jay-Jay pulled open the curtains.

Erin stepped to the casement. There, up in the tree situated in the middle of the yard, was a brand-new treehouse. Without hesitation, she grabbed the binoculars from the dresser and angled them at the structure. "Shut up." An arched door led inside of it like those found in cottages. Just off to the right was a small, round porthole. "Is that a?" She adjusted the lens. "It is!"

A large spotting scope was poking out from the enclosure. Erin lowered the binoculars. "So, this is a research lab for my birding?"

"That was my intention, but really, it could be whatever you want it to be."

She looked at it again and then at him. "But, why?"

Jay-Jay pressed a finger over her lips. "You, my dear, have always deserved this." He kept his gaze on her.

After a moment, she pulled away. "I-I—thank you. It's a nice gesture." She looked at him, then led the way to the front door.

"Enjoy the peace and quiet out there," Jay said and kissed her cheek.

She hid a smile with her hand. "Thanks. See ya."

Erin closed the door and leaned against it. *He needs to stop doing this.* She pushed off and went back to the window. *Really? Another pigeon?* Her eyes narrowed for a better look at the bird already perched on a branch near the treehouse and noticed its feathers appeared lighter color than that of a pigeon. The binoculars dangling from her neck assured the lightness of color seen with the naked eye. *Holy shit, a turtledove!* Erin snatched a journal from the sea of literature, then grabbed a pencil and secured it behind her ear.

Out in the yard, she stuffed the notebook into the inner pocket of the vest and stepped onto the perfunctory ladder attached to the tree's trunk. All focus was now on the four remaining planks. Cautious not to tear any internal stitches, she began the ascent and then attempted to ease inside but stumbled forward, doing a sort of commando roll into the miniature conservatory. "Holy hell," she said, flopping onto her backside.

Erin studied the ceiling, catching her breath. She sat up and explored the rest of the little house. Everything was made of wood, save for the spotting scope. She reached out and touched the smooth leg of a tiny desk standing flush against one wall. On the other three was a series of long nails sticking out of them. "Look at that. He even designed makeshift supply hooks."

She got to a standing position and walked to the scope feeling conflicted: like the luckiest bird that acquired the most exquisite yet emptiest of nests.

Chapter Forty-Seven

"Whose big idea was it to have this dessert thingy?" Gail said, swatting flour particles as she single-handedly poured some into the mixer.

"Yours." Erin laughed and pressed a snowflake-shaped cookie mold into a thin blonde blanket of smoothed dough.

"Dessert swaps are fun. The ladies will have a blast," Megan said, her whisk rapping against a bowl of raw egg. "You're doing a good thing. I couldn't wait until you started up your socials again and, finally, I'm well enough for it…at least 'til tomorrow when I get a check-up for the next round."

Gail put down the bag of flour. "Already? Why so soon?"

"I think Dr. Kelleher was onto my faking the whole thing about feeling a hundred percent better. Who knows? Who cares? Enough about cancer." She started to stir again but then stopped. "Are we playing any games when they get here?"

"This isn't a children's birthday party." Gail snorted.

Meg combined her ingredients with Gail's and wiped the drippy yolk from her fingers onto her smock. "True, but still. We've got to do something."

"We can introduce ourselves," Deirdre chimed.

"Snore!" Erin said.

Meg saw Deirdre's cheeks flush. She knew Erin had forgotten that Dee was new to this. "I think that's a great idea, but after that, we should do something a tad more fun."

"Like what? Beer pong? We're grown—not in college anymore!" Erin replied.

"Okay, okay. No party poopers," Gail retorted. "Maybe we can put a strong holiday drink in those little pong cups instead of filling them with beer. What do you think?"

"Oh, there are these cinnamon roll shots I saw on a food app. They'd be perfect," Megan said, ripping off her apron, and wheeled to Gail's liquor cabinet.

"Food app?" Gail's brow furrowed.

"You know, the apps you download onto your phone?" Deirdre asked.

"They have one for cocktails? Oh, for Christ's sake." Gail's eyes rolled skyward.

"Don't knock it till you try it," Meg called from over her shoulder. "It's quicker than hunting through a cookbook."

"I'm sure. It's just incredible how a phone can control your life. My son has his entire house programmed to it: the HVAC system, his appliances, he even has security cameras at his front door so he can watch the delivery men. Imagine that!"

Megan glanced at Erin, but she was busy pulling a batch of snickerdoodles from the oven. *He should have taught his mom—a woman who lives alone in a big house—how to do those things.* She bit her lip and returned to the shelved alcohol.

A beeping noise sounded from Megan's pocket. She pulled out the cell and held it over her head like a bullhorn. "Speaking of gadgets, the alarm on my phone is going off. We have exactly one hour to finish baking *and* get this kitchen party-ready."

"Well, then. This'll be the last of 'em," Gail said, globs of batter pouring haphazardly into a muffin pan when her phone went off. "My turn." She chuckled and with a clean pinky, pressed the home screen.

—What time does the dessert exchange start?—the voice text message read aloud.

Gail responded verbally with a simple:—6 p.m.—

—You want us that early? Lol…—

Gail made a fist and waved it at the phone.

"Who is that?" Megan asked, wheeling over.

"Fucking Shelly." Gail huffed and snuck a glance at Deirdre, who was across the room, distracted with a pie crust. "She complains about, literally, everything. At last year's firehouse Christmas party, Shelly bitched and moaned about her son's girlfriend," Gail whispered. "Her complaints were about *Deirdre!*" Gail paused, a wry smile stretching across her face. Megan gasped. They knew something that Shelly—the straight-laced, churchy girl, I-have-everything-under-control-because-I'm-the-boss-Shelly didn't: Her precocious son, Cliff, was gay. And their best friend was his ex-girlfriend.

"Maybe we shouldn't have invited her," Megan said.

Gail rolled her eyes. "You know we'd never hear the end of it from Shell-Hell at this year's Christmas party if we didn't," she muttered. "Ho, ho, ho, this night is gonna be a doozy." Her hands squeezed the phone as she yelled/texted.

—6 P.M.—SHARP!—

"Who's ruffling your feathers over there, girl?"

Deirdre scooted onto a stool by Gail.

"Uh, it's just one of the fire wives pestering about minor details, that's all." Gail crammed the mobile into her pocket.

"Excuse me for a second." Gail slid off her seat and tugged lightly on Megan's sleeve, motioning for her to follow. "Ladies, can you keep an eye on those blueberry muffins? Oh, and the Russian tea cakes? We'll be back in a minute," she said, circling a finger at Deirdre, Erin, and the oven.

"Where are you two going?" Deirdre asked.

"I want to show Meg some of the holiday glasses we could use for her fancy beverages," Gail said and winked at her.

Deirdre winked back.

"I don't like the sounds of this," Meg said, entering the butler's pantry. "What are we going to do?"

Gail stowed behind one of the shelves. "I have no freaking idea, but we both know this could get ugly."

"Shit," Megan said, squirming in her chair.

Gail tapped her nails frantically atop a cereal box. Meg silenced her. "Maybe Deirdre should know beforehand—give her time for a strategy of her own."

"Yeah, and what if it's an *exit* strategy? We don't want her to leave!" Gail massaged her temples.

"True. But I'd rather her know now than have her pissed at us afterward." Megan wheeled backward. "She should have her shock-and-awe moment with us, not in front of her ex's mother and a bunch of strangers. That's just cruel."

"So, you'll be the one to tell her. Thank you so much." Gail squatted in front of Megan and engaged her in a hug.

"But, I didn't say that." Meg's words were muffled by Gail's wool cardigan.

"Don't be silly. It's best coming from you—you're the one closest to her." Gail stood and took hold of Megan's handlebars. "Deirdre, darling, Megan has something to tell you," Gail announced as they reentered the kitchen.

Deirdre took off the oven mitts. "What's up?"

"Oh, never mind. Dee, can you help me with the cinnamon shots?" Meg grabbed the wheels of her chair.

Gail flashed Megan the side-eye. "What are you doing?"

Megan ignored it and wheeled to Deirdre.

"Let me use the bathroom, and then I'll help. Be back in a jiffy." Deirdre headed down the hall.

Gail grumbled and scuttled to Erin, who was plucking tea cakes from the pan. "They're a bit browned on the bottoms," Erin said.

Gail pushed the pan to the side. "I need you," she breathed. "Cliff's mother is coming tonight. Deirdre doesn't have a clue. What do we do?"

"Oh, that's easy. Just get her drunk." Erin was matter-of-fact.

"Ah, I should've thought of that." Gail slumped back against the counter. "Deirdre's easy to liquor up. I can start now."

"Not her," Erin said, inching toward Gail, a hint of mischief in her stare. "Shelly."

Gail let out a cackle, which Erin covered quickly with her hand. "Ssh!"

"I'll be the bartender tonight," Erin continued and retracted her fingers. "Megan will be in charge of the cookie table."

Megan frowned. "Why?"

"Because we have to tame Shelly." Erin beamed as she rubbed her hands together.

"Just be careful, she's my principal!" Meg whisper-yelled. "Oh, and I'm still making my shots 'cause I already planned it."

Gail chirped up. "And what's my job in all this?"

"Your job is to do what you do best—host! Greet the guests, make everybody feel comfortable, you know, shit like that," Erin replied.

Megan shook her head and went back to the liquor cabinet.

****

"I'm going to gain ten pounds if I keep this up," Megan overheard a woman say as she gleaned the spread of sugary goodies on the kitchen table.

"Would you like one of these instead?" Erin asked, holding up a sparkling crystal goblet from her drink station.

"It's one of those lesser calorie concoctions," Deirdre added, rotating between the two.

"Oh, I would," a voice sang from behind them.

"Sure!" Deirdre said and spun around. Her cheery expression dissolved when Cliff's mother stood before her. "Mrs. Baxter?"

Shelly's eyes worked over Deirdre like someone spying her latest loser. "Deirdre. What are you doing here? You're not a fire wife *or* girlfriend, for that matter." Her snarky chuckle was loud enough for everyone to hear.

"Actually," Deirdre said, moving in.

"Game time!" Gail called, waving a blue Pictionary box over her head.

The herd of onlookers trailed back slowly into the living room, but Megan could see that Deirdre's eyes remained on Shelly. Megan lingered nearby, just in case she had to intervene.

"Oh, Deirdre, my love, your team will be over there," Erin said, passing Megan and approaching Deirdre. Erin gripped her shoulders and steered her to one of the couches far from where Shelly was.

"Thank you," Deirdre mumbled.

"And you," Erin said, crossing the room again and heading in Shelly's direction. "Your team will be right over there."

Megan watched as Erin escorted Mrs. Baxter to the sofa diagonally from Deirdre.

"Now," Erin said and clasped her hands together. "Both Deirdre and Shelly are the team captains."

Megan's eyes widened. *What the hell is she doing?*

Gail scooted closer, but Erin continued. "First, Deirdre picks, and then Shelly, and so on, until no one remains. Understood?"

Deirdre pulled up the sleeves of her sweater. "10-4," she replied and gave a firm nod in Shelly's direction.

Megan wheeled closer to Deirdre and held out a cinnamon shot. "Here. Looks like you'll need this."

"Thanks, Meg." Deirdre accepted the glass. She slurped the alcohol and, once done, placed it on the coffee table next to them. "Stay here, Meg. You're on my team."

"Gail," Shelly stated proudly. "Come. You're with me!"

"Oh, no. I can't," Gail said.

Megan stared at Gail, and they smiled at one another. *Thatta girl. Stay out of it.* She then busied herself with her purse, feeling around for the pen.

"I'm the hostess. Have to oversee operations. Can't play," Gail continued and opened the cardboard box of the game, sorting the pads and pencils.

Deirdre leaned into Megan, looking in Shelly's direction. "You realize that whatever I draw now is going to be penis-shaped."

When Megan laughed, a puffy white cloud filled the space between them.

"What the?" Deirdre backed away.

"It's medicinal," Megan said. "Kelleher insisted."

"Can I get a hit of that?" a wife named Trish asked. "I've never smoked it in oil form before."

All the women turned to them. Megan's sickly tone became rosy as she held up the vape, feeling like the Statue of Liberty with her torch smoldering in a sea of quiet.

"Not before me," Gail said, breaking the silence, and strutted over.

"Gail? You smoke?" asked Shelly in a tone of disgust. "Why?"

"Because why not? All my husband ever wanted in life was to help people and then retire with the two things he couldn't have as a fireman: a beard and a joint."

Gail grabbed Megan's electronic joint and put it to her lips. She drew in a deep dramatic breath.

"Fair enough," Shelly said, reaching for it.

Gail pulled it back. "Miss Prim-N-Proper wants to smoke pot?" A plume of smoke burst from her mouth along with a hard snicker-like cough.

Embarrassment flared up deep within Megan's belly.

Shelly ripped the vape from Gail's hand. "Oh, shut

up. I've smoked *weed* before."

Every eye was on the well-groomed senior whose wicked personality aged her more than the physical features did. Shelly inhaled a little. "Holy moly. I need a prescription of this," she said, her words tight before handing back the pen.

Some of the women sniggered, except Deirdre. "Get cancer and you could."

"It's okay," Meg said, pushing herself closer to Deirdre. "It's actually kind of funny." She faced the ladies and held up the marijuana. "In honor of Harry and all the other firefighters who never got the chance, I'll leave this here for anyone interested." She placed it in the center of the coffee table.

"Game on!" Gail said, propping up an oversized sketch pad on an easel. "Shelly's team will go first."

Shelly snatched a card from the deck and studied it.

"Ready?" Gail asked, picking up the small hourglass.

Shelly took up a Sharpie and uncapped it. "Ready." She started drawing a long sloping letter U.

"A ditch," Trish called out.

"No, no, no." Shelly pressed harder on the paper with the marker and made some random strokes along the edges of the U.

Deirdre moved in closer to Megan's ear. "Why is *she* the one drawing a penis? I'm so confused."

Megan giggled into her hand.

"A dick!" someone yelled, raising her drink in the air.

Everyone burst into hysterics.

"Well?" the lady said. "Is it?"

"Of course it's not." Shelly's face was a banner of

disappointment. "It's nothing phallic at all."

"Could have fooled me," Deirdre said. "Just like your son did."

"Time's up!" Gail shouted, jumping in front of the easel.

"Wait a minute," Shelly said and snapped the marker shut. "What's that supposed to mean, Deirdre?"

Megan grabbed the vaporizer off the table and went to Shelly. "Here, smoke some more." Erin followed with a tray of holiday shots. "And have one of these."

Shelly looked at their offerings. "You don't really think either of those things are going to make what Deirdre said disappear, do you?" She stepped around them and glared at Deirdre.

"Ah, stop being so negative, Shell," Erin said and took the joint from Megan. "Dicks, shmicks, who cares—lighten up. Or, shall I say, light up." She puckered her lips and puffed, turning back to the picture. "What were you trying to draw anyway?"

"The state of Florida," Shelly said. She walked to the easel and used the marker as a pointer. "And these are palm trees." She tapped on the random strokes. "Not pubes!"

The wives erupted into a choral of laughs. Erin's body jolted so hard from the hilarity that she had to sit.

"Well, it goes with the whole retirement thing," Shelly said and shrugged. She returned the Sharpie to the ledge.

"I'm sorry, Meg, but I have to tell her."

Before Megan could register what Deirdre meant, she was already marching through the crowded living room. *Oh no, don't do it, don't do it, don't do it.* Deirdre stopped abruptly in front of Shelly and glanced back at

Megan. Meg shook her head and continued to pray.

As if she'd heard her prayers, Deirdre diverted toward the front door.

"Where are you going?" a voice called, but she ignored it.

"Ladies, continue without us for a minute." Megan rolled out of the room.

Out on the front porch, Meg, Gail, and Erin found Deirdre sitting on one of the wicker rockers.

"Everything okay?" Gail asked.

"Is it true what you said about what firemen want, you know, after retiring?" Deirdre said, deflecting.

"Ha! Jay-Jay talks about beards and blunts all the time," Erin said, dropping onto the rocker next to her. "Wants a stash of fatties at his disposal and a crazy long beard like those guys in ZZ Top."

The girls laughed as Erin scratched her chin.

"It was very big of you to walk away," Gail said, patting Deirdre's arm. "I know it took every ounce inside of you to do that. I just wish she wouldn't ruin your night."

"Eh, she'll find out on her own." Deirdre simpered. "And, believe it or not, I'm having a great time."

"Good!" Gail said. "Then let's get back in there and enjoy what's left of it."

Chapter Forty-Eight

Megan rushed to the bathroom after blood was drawn; the ripple of nausea mixed with cottonmouth from not eating took over. She kneeled in front of the faucet, turned it on, and slurped water as fast as she could. *Ah. That's the ticket.*

She stood again and retrieved the travel toothbrush and paste she'd stowed in the little zipper compartment of her handbag for times like these: cancer check-ups and treatments. *Maybe I'll order a fat, juicy Porterhouse this time.* She smiled, happy that something delectable was on the horizon, a small tradition she and Rob started upon the recurring trips to medics, and began brushing her teeth. That's when a fierce pressure pounced on her chest as if a baseball player had swung a hefty bat as hard as he could into it.

Meg dropped the toothbrush and grabbed onto the sides of the sink. The fight for oxygen grew intense, the room engulfed in a spin. By rote memorization of the emergency call system, Megan lowered herself onto all fours before losing total control and pulling the cord. She lay limp on the cold, white tile of the single stall, wheezing as the automated lights overhead shut off. She tried to wave a hand to get them to turn back on but was unsuccessful. Then footsteps strolled by.

"I think someone rang, but the light's off, and the door isn't unlocked," a voice said, jiggling the handle.

Too weak to speak or move, Megan prayed whoever it was would check the perimeter instead of presuming it was empty. Silence, no movement from the other side. Megan panicked, straining to see between the crack of the doorjamb for feet. Nothing. Her mouth, now drier from grappling to breathe, was numb. Her eyes closed in defeat when, at that moment, an orderly barged in, flickering on the lights. The woman jumped back and dropped her cleaning bucket on the floor. She screamed in Spanish while running out.

A slew of hospital personnel stormed into the space where Megan was semiconscious. They lifted her onto a gurney. As they hurried to a different part of the hospital, a doctor jogged alongside, his stethoscope glued to her chest. Meg was unable to tell him to stop, that the added weight was preventing her from taking in an already dismal amount of oxygen one could manage on their own, until a nurse appeared on the other side and placed an O2 mask over her face.

"Breathe, Megan, breathe," the nurse shouted.

Megan wanted to obey, but her airways were strained. She tried to concentrate on a rhythmic air-intake pattern, imagining shriveled lungs expanding like two tiny red balloons, until the ability to take in a copious amount was possible.

"We need to take a chest X-ray."

She opened her eyes and focused on the doctor.

"And let's do a CT scan as well," he added.

She strained to see the person writing notes. The woman dropped the folder onto the foot of the bed before wheeling Megan into a nearby elevator.

"Do you think I've developed asthma?" Meg asked through the plastic apparatus.

The nurse checked her watch and glanced up at the lit numbers.

I don't think she can hear me. Megan continued to stare up at the woman and tried again. "It can't be more cancer, can it?"

The elevator dinged and the doors parted ways. The nurse grabbed each side of the portable bed and rolled Megan to a room with a large imaging machine. She locked the wheels with her sneaker, patted Megan's shoulder, and left.

Is she deaf? Megan turned and looked over at the digital imaging contraption as well as the rest of the facility. It was as dreary and lifeless as a morgue. There was a big rectangular cut-out in the wall adjacent to her that was filled with blackened glass, which she presumed was the office of the X-ray technician, so she willed the energy to raise her hand and wave. Just then the door opened, and a busty blonde entered.

"Megan Dunham?"

"That's me," Megan said weakly and redirected her wagging fingers toward her.

"I'm Patty, your X-ray tech."

The bubbly woman leaned over and removed the oxygen mask, her gold cross pendant dangling like a pendulum above Megan. A whiff of her strong perfume perforated the air.

"How do you feel without this on? Are you okay breathing on your own?" Patty asked, her voice peppered with an upbeat southern twang.

Megan drew in a breath and forced herself to speak up. "I'm all right, but can we do the regular X-rays before you stuff me into that thing?" She shifted her attention to the sleeping monster across the floor.

"You got it, puddin'."

Good God, she can hear me!

Megan watched as Patty grabbed a weighted vest from the adjacent wall.

"Why'd the doctor order both tests? Don't they show the same results?"

"Not necessarily," Patty said, draping the garb over Megan gingerly. "An X-ray shows the lungs, yes, but a CT is a computerized tomography of the chest cavity. It provides us with the most detailed pictures."

"So, one can show a lot more than the other?"

"Uh-huh. The doctor probably wants a faster look, hence the X-rays. The CT takes a little longer to develop."

Megan closed her eyes and muttered a *Hail Mary* as the technician set up the camera.

"What religion?" Patty said, looking away from the equipment.

Megan opened an eye. "Catholic."

Patty stopped tinkering and walked back to Megan. She held Megan's hands, shut her eyes, and began reciting the *Our Father*. Megan listened for a few seconds and then joined in.

When the prayer was finished, Patty continued. "Please, dear Jesus, have mercy on the soul of this young patient before me. Please guide her in her journey toward you, however long we anticipate it to be, and, please, make the mortal ending as painless as humanly possible for her and all of us. Amen."

Megan's eyes sprung open.

Patty motioned the sign of the cross with a thumb on her forehead, then kissed her own curled fingers and aimed them skyward. When she was done, she gazed down at Megan. "I'm an ordained minister. Sending blessings to Heaven offsets the doom and gloom of this place."

Megan's mouth formed a nervous grin.

"Have you anyone to keep company?" Patty continued, resuming focus on the film in the X-ray machine.

"My husband and best friend are supposed to meet me at Gallaghers Steakhouse for lunch, but here I am."

Chapter Forty-Nine

Deirdre wheeled the motorcycle out of the garage and rested it on the stand, leaving the motor running.

Rob came outside wearing his old helmet. "She's going to love this," he said, fastening the chin guard. He threw a leg over and sat close behind Deirdre, who was zipping her jacket.

"We're good to go?" she asked and revved the engine.

"All good."

They wheeled out of the driveway and exited the neighborhood. The wind howled as they picked up speed and merged onto the highway.

"You okay back there?" Deirdre yelled, her gloved fingers tight on the handlebars.

"Yep." Rob's newly uncasted limb wrapped around her waist.

The modernistic Harley Superlow glided through the Brooklyn-Battery Tunnel and up the Westside Highway toward Gallaghers. When construction slowed all lanes, neighboring drivers gawked at the bike, its glittery paint like a Swarovski crystal in the sun. A few kids at the back of a yellow school bus banged against the glass and waved. Deirdre tapped on the horn. The children only got wilder and cheered, giving her and Rob a bunch of approving window thumps.

"It's like we bought a piece of Hollywood," Rob

said.

Deirdre gave the throttle a firm twist and gunned it when the road opened up again. She turned onto a side street and entered a parking garage.

"Can I help you?" the attendant said, walking to them.

"Wait a minute," Rob said, pulling his phone from its case. "Megan just texted me that she's still at the hospital, and we should meet her there instead."

He and Deirdre locked eyes and helmet straps.

"Uh, sorry, no, thank you," Deirdre said over her shoulder to the attendant and made a U-turn.

When they arrived at the hospital, Deirdre situated the bike in front of the ticket booth. "Take care of this one, José," she said, pulling off her riding gloves, and tossed the keys to a young man in a black puffy jacket with his name sewn on the breast.

"Si, Senorita Deirdre," he said, catching the metal ring.

She led Rob down a narrow hallway and into a graffiti-filled stairwell.

"Don't touch the railing, it may have an STD," she half-joked and hopped up the steps a few at a time.

They entered the hospital and headed to the blood lab. Deirdre draped her upper half around the doorjamb and checked for Megan's chart in the holder, but it wasn't there. "Hey, do you know where Megan Dunham is?" she said, grabbing the shoulder of a staff member passing by with a tray of medical instruments.

The woman glanced up. "Hey, Dee. She was talking to Dr. Kelleher and Patty, the X-ray tech, and they wheeled her off. Try the darkroom."

"Thanks." Deirdre looked at Rob. "Okay then,

follow me."

After a few turns down several hallways, they came to a closed door with a red sign on it: Darkroom. No Admittance.

"Knock, knock," Deirdre said, her lips pressed to the crack of the frame. "It's Deirdre Henricksen. Is Megan Dunham in there?"

The door creaked open. "Come in," Patty said, signaling them inside.

Deirdre and Rob stepped into the darkened room, pictures of human insides glowing bright against the fluorescent white lighting on all four walls. When the door shut, Dr. Kelleher greeted them. Megan, who was in the center of the room, turned the wheelchair and faced them.

"What's all this?" Rob said, rotating slowly, mesmerized by the images.

Megan started to sob.

"No. This can't be," Deirdre whispered, moving toward the pictures.

Alarmed, Rob turned to the doctor.

"The cancer has traveled to Megan's lungs," Dr. Kelleher said and buried his hands into the slits of his lab coat. "Those cloudy shapes you see on the scans are tumors."

Rob stood frozen in disbelief. "But, but, I thought she was getting better. With all the treatments over the months; for almost a year." He looked to the doctor and then at Megan. "I thought you were only coming here for routine blood work."

"Yes, I was, until, out of nowhere, I couldn't breathe and almost fainted, which warranted more tests."

"I'm so sorry," Dr. Kelleher said and stepped out,

pulling Patty with him.

Rob went to Megan and wrapped his arms around her. "What are you thinking?"

"I'll tell you later. It's okay," Meg replied.

"Okay? Okay? Nothing's okay!" He jumped away and spun around, his eyes wild, as he shot up both middle fingers. "Fuck you!" he yelled, pointing at all the images.

Deirdre spied him as he did the very thing she'd done on the hospital's roof. "Come on," she said, finally taking herself away from the X-rays and walking to them.

"They assigned me a room, but it's only for a little while," Megan said. "Let's all talk there."

Rob cleaned his face with his sleeves and then held the handles of the wheelchair. "Let's go."

When they entered Megan's room, Rob kneeled by her and cleared his throat. "You have a place to wear the dress."

Megan raised a finger to his cheek. "I know. And I can't wait."

Deirdre put the brake on the mobile chair, which Rob had forgotten to do, and started tiptoeing backward.

"No, Deirdre, stay," Megan commanded and turned again at her husband. "I'm ready to check out of this place for good."

Rob took her hand from his face and held it.

"They gave me the information for hospice. We can make the arrangements before we leave," she continued.

Deirdre dropped to her knees and wrapped herself around them. "No! No hospice. I'll be your full-time nurse for as long as it takes."

"Don't be foolish. You can't do that. This is your career. You can't just leave it," Meg said.

"I have enough vacation days to cover me for a while. Trust me. I'm not leaving your side. I won't."

Deirdre felt Meg's squeeze on her arm. "I love you more than words. Now, please help me out of this awful chair and come lay in the bed with me for a few minutes. We have to talk."

Rob went to pick her up, but his weak arm got in the way.

Deirdre intervened, scooping her out of his enfeebled grasp, and positioned her in the middle of the mattress. She then walked to the other side and carefully climbed in.

Rob crawled onto the bed, facing Megan.

Megan wormed her body between them. "I want to be cremated," she said. "But, instead of putting all the ashes in an urn, I'd like for you guys to plant a tree in the backyard with the boys. Mix my ashes with the soil so that the tree is special for the kids, you know, so it becomes a place for them to hang out with Mommy. Tell them they can treat it like a private spot to come to for some quiet time or just to talk, or even sit under it and read a book if they want."

Deirdre looked on, every now and then muting her emotions with the pillow, but Rob had a harder time holding back.

"Don't." Megan swiped his dampening cheek. "It's okay. *I'm* okay with this. Let's be ready for when it happens. For us. For our sons." Her hand rubbed Deirdre's hip. "You okay back there?"

Deirdre rested her hand on top of Meg's and managed a muffled, "Mm-hmm."

"Oh, come on. I need you both to be strong. You're my tribe, and my tribe needs to keep it together." Megan eased onto her back. "You know what I'd love more than anything?" She wriggled her fingers between Deirdre's. "You and Rob having picnics under the tree with the boys, keeping the family close-knit with the memory of me strong for them." She gave Dee's arm a good shake.

Rob popped his head up and set it atop a folded hand. "Okay, correct me if I'm wrong, but are you saying that I have to remain friends with her?" he asked, pointing a haggard nail at Deirdre.

Deirdre shot up. "Ew. You can't expect me to stay friends with him. He's got cooties!"

Megan let out a raspy cackle as Rob threw a playful jab at Deirdre's bicep before lying down again.

"Listen. I can't dictate your friendship, but if you two stay buddies, I think that'd be cool. And you know the kids would love it—the cat, the motorcycle—shit, I think you're trapped, Dee," Megan said and laughed some more.

Deirdre closed her eyes and snuggled against Megan. "That's all right. I don't consider hanging out with three cute children entrapment."

Rob's head bolted up. "*Three* cute children?"

Deirdre and Megan looked at each other and snorted.

"Yeah, ha, ha, very funny," he said, dropping onto the bed. "Women. Always making men the butt of their jokes."

Chapter Fifty

Jay-Jay waited at the corner, ducking low in the driver's seat as he spied Erin getting into her car. On the phone earlier, she had thanked him again for the Lady Lair he'd built, saying she couldn't wait to get in there to do some real research but wouldn't be able to focus on any birding studies if she didn't first work on those "very strong curiosities" about babies and motherhood: "I've come to the conclusion that if I don't give cuddling another shot, I'm just not sure when—if ever—those feelings would go away. I can't live with that uncertainty."

Jay-Jay continued watching as Erin secured herself behind the wheel of their sedan and reversed out of the driveway. He cowered some more as she drove past, hoping not to be spotted. When her vehicle was further away, he poked his head above the steering column and unclicked the door latch.

He left the truck parked and retrieved a couple of paint cans and a bucket of painting supplies. He shuffled up the street and into the house where everything was silent and then made a dash for the computer room. He set the stuff on the floor and reached into his pocket for his buzzing cell phone.

"Yes, I'm here. Have them come in through the main entrance," Jay-Jay said and raced toward the front of the house. "Thanks. See you in fifteen."

He shoved the phone into his jeans and started removing everything from the old kitchen cabinets, piling stuff onto the nearby dining room table. He wiped his forehead and worked fast so that the installers would be able to erect the new ones efficiently.

A delivery truck pulled up outside as Jay-Jay cleared the last shelf. A few workers speaking Creole talked loudly up the path and entered the house.

"In there," Jay-Jay said, meeting them at the top of the stairs and directing them to the kitchen.

As they began working, Jay-Jay ran to the office. He opened the windows, set down a drop cloth, and started painting the room a light gray. When he returned to the bucket for a fresh roller, the doorbell chimed. He peered out the window. "You've got to be kidding me. Not now." He dropped the roller in the pail and headed for the door.

"Hello," Gail said, face bright.

"Hi," he said, opening the screen door. "Erin's not here. She said something about going to the hospital to meet with the lead volunteer."

"So, she's volunteering in PEDS again? That's excellent news!" Gail glanced at her wristwatch and looked at him. "Okay, then. I was just popping by before I left for the weekend." She turned halfway and stopped. "I'm sorry, Jay-Jay, where are my manners? How are you doing with everything?"

Jay-Jay slid his fingers into his rear pockets. "Good. I'm good. Keeping busy." He motioned to the house, the sound of hammering and drilling distinct between their sentences.

"I'm glad to see you're safely juggling being a new dad while trying to mend things with your wife."

Jay-Jay stood at the door as Gail started descending the stairs. He wanted to give her a grand tour—the renovations the only thing he really had any control over—so that Erin would finally, at the very least, be happy calling it home. But he stopped himself. Underneath it all, he felt Gail judged him for straying in the first place.

He watched Gail settle into her vehicle. She glanced at him and waved. He flapped his hand, tempted to yell, "Wait!" but Gail was Erin's confidante, not his, and so what he had to say was just that—words. He stuffed his hands deep in his pants pocket again and turned away. *If people are going to know I'm serious about my commitment to Erin, it's because they are seeing it, not hearing about it.* He stared up at the kitchen window and smiled, proud that these house projects were part of the proof.

****

Erin stared through the plexiglass at the sea of babies. Some were wailing inconsolably, while others wore dreamy expressions of pure content.

"Aren't they just precious?" the director said, walking up to Erin.

"Oh, hi, Trudy. I could never thank you enough for giving me a do-over. Everyone's been so nice."

"It's no problem at all. Those ladies in there only get a breather when folks like you donate your time to us. We truly appreciate the help." Trudy pulled open a door. "I'll show you to our lead volunteer, Allen. Follow me."

Erin clutched her tote and hurried into the unit behind the woman.

"Good morning, Allen. This is Erin Harper, the new volunteer I was telling you about," Trudy said, gesturing to Erin.

Erin stepped into the room and acknowledged the gray-haired senior, who looked away from the baby he was rocking in a chair.

"Hello there, Erin." The guy used his chin to point toward an empty rocker next to him. "Come and join me."

Erin nodded, accepting the seat.

"This is Xavier. He's a little over a week old."

"All righty, then. I'll be back in a few," Trudy said, leaving the door slightly ajar in her wake.

"So, what brings you here today, Erin?"

She focused on the large circular pacifier taking up half of Xavier's face. "The babies," she whispered.

"Yes, but what's in it for you?"

The twinkle in Allen's eye reminded her of the Santa Claus she'd visited as a child every year at the mall. Unlike most Santas, the one she saw was caring, took time to hear everyone's wishes, and reminded them to brush their teeth and eat vegetables. This man seemed like that.

"I'm not sure. Originally, I wanted a connection, but I'm not sure that's even allowed with someone else's baby."

"Why in the world not?"

"Well, because it's someone else's baby," Erin said in an *am-I-really-restating-the-obvious* tone.

"That's rubbish. I get attached," Allen said, patting his tiny friend as he spoke. "And I think the parents are even more grateful that I do. It relieves them of the guilt they feel for whatever reason they're feeling it."

Erin eagle-eyed the retiree as he handled Xavier affectionately. He appeared poised yet confident as a cuddler.

"Some mothers have told me outright that my being here gives them a chance to focus on recovering from the birth, mostly those women who've had cesareans."

Erin whipped out a leather journal and flashed it at Allen. "Huh, that's good stuff. Do you mind if I take some notes?"

"Whatever you need to do," he said, tapping the pacifier in the baby's mouth.

She flipped to a blank page and yanked the cover off a pen with her teeth. "Tends to get attached. Is controlled yet self-assured," she muttered while scribbling. "Parents approve."

"Writing a book?"

"No." Heat flamed her cheeks as she dropped the pen and its cap inside the diary and closed it. "This is how I learn."

"Maybe in school, but here you'll learn by doing." Allen stopped bouncing Xavier. He scooted to the edge of the chair, manipulating the baby so that he was upright. "Bend this arm, kind of like a ballerina, so that you'll cup the baby's underside when I pass him to you."

Erin tossed the book into her bag and extended a limb, folding it into an arc. "Like this?"

"Yes. Now, before I give him to you, did you notice anything in particular that I was doing while Xavier was in my grasp?"

"Um, well, you rocked him, of course." Erin's pupils danced about. "And, and—"

"Relax, it's not a test. You're doing great."

Erin rubbed her palms against the tops of her thighs. "I saw you moving him a lot."

"Yes, he really likes it when he's in motion."

Erin wondered how the guy knew that, seeing as how the baby couldn't talk. "Does he cry when you stop or something?"

Xavier started wailing as if on cue.

Allen resumed bouncing him; Erin watched as Xavier's snivel came to a halt. "Like magic," Allen said, chuckling.

She so desperately wanted to jot this all down.

"Okay, your turn." Allen held out the squirming bundle.

The thumping of Erin's heart traveled to her ears. Like a robot, she moved in with a curvilinear arm and used the other to guide the baby into her grasp. Almost immediately, she started a rocking rhythm that hopefully would soothe Xavier from the transition. His tiny spine slithered into the crook, and she pulled him in close.

"I feel his chest—he's breathing so fast," Erin said, overpowered with trepidation.

Allen rested a palm on her knee. "All babies belly-breathe. It's your breathing we need to regulate," he said, smiling. "I call it 'baby yoga for adults.' First, keep Xavier close as you settle onto the rocker, maintaining that cadence you've established when I handed him to you."

Erin worked her backside against the cushioned spindles of the chair.

"Once you feel comfortable, look down at the baby. See how his eyes are closed in that angelic, peaceful way? Close your eyes in that same way."

She tilted her head and gazed at Xavier's soporific features, getting a whiff of his fragrance, one similar to that of clean clothes. Her heart calmed, eyes falling shut.

Allen continued in a tranquil, melodic tone. "The

key to attachment is to exude the safety you seek for the baby from yourself. Once that reaches your surface, there's this inexplicable Zen that occurs—it'll be recognizable to you, and Xavier, who will show it in his reception of your touch. This will set the precedent for you in your future endeavors with children."

Erin listened hard as the man spoke, his words unveiling a truth she should have known but didn't until now.

Chapter Fifty-One

Gail unlocked the hinge of the car's trunk and glared down at the pile of luggage.

"Definitely too much," she said and wrestled to get an overstuffed suitcase out. She gave it a good tug and launched it like a whale lunging itself across the surface of the ocean. It flopped onto the black tar street.

In the distance, there was a faint laugh. Gail looked toward the bed-and-breakfast and lifted the rim of her sunglasses. Zofie was standing on the porch, watching from under a large straw hat.

"Need help?" she offered, waving a gardening glove.

"No thanks, I got it." Gail returned the glasses to her face.

Zofie tapped the brim of her hat and resumed tending to the abscission of her potted plants.

The morning birds sang in the tree above as Gail peered into the trunk at the second piece of super-sized luggage. *No need to embarrass myself further.* She left it there and slammed the hatch, sending the fowl squawking away, and heaved the lone beluga lying in the road to the house.

"There's a pitcher of cold water and some fresh granola on the server. Help yourself," Zofie said, pruning an overgrown geranium. "Your key is there as well."

Gail hurled her things up the cement steps.

"Thanks."

"It's a full house this evening. As always, we'd love your friendly company and conversation," Zofie added.

Although Gail wanted to see Leonard, she was relieved that it wouldn't be alone.

"Oh, and do be prepared. We have some new returns from Afghanistan. Sometimes I think I should be serving wine instead…"

Gail laughed. "Okay, I'll prepare. See you later."

Inside the house, an explosion of dueling instruments hushed Gail's footsteps. She stopped at the center of the foyer, her heart starting to pound along with a bass guitar as she checked the living room for Leonard. There was no sign of him, but in his place, Gail was greeted by that same invitation of pear. She grinned, feeling incredibly lucky to experience another round of this feast for the senses.

On the way to her rented portion of the home, Gail noticed Leonard's door was shut. She paused in front of it and wondered if he was inside but refrained from knocking. She carried on, body hunched low, wrangling the suitcase down the narrow hallway, pausing and panting as she dipped a hand into a bag and pulled out a chain. Slipping the thin, lengthy key into the rusty keyhole with the flick of a wrist, the portal to solitude was unlocked.

Gail stepped over the bag and into the same bedroom as the last time, stretching out her arms, saying hello to the wrought iron fireplace and long, flowing treatments on the tall windows. She removed her jacket, placing it on the back of the lazy boy near the mantel. "Did you miss me?" she muttered, rubbing its velvety wing.

"That all depends," said a voice by the doorway.

Gail jerked back, the rack of tools for the fireplace crashing to the floor.

Leonard's bottom lip twitched. "I am so sorry." He pulled his hands from the center cuff of his sweatshirt and entered the room. "Allow me." He picked up the shovel.

Gail took the poker and jabbed playfully at his jeans. "Don't. Ever. Do. That. Again."

He grabbed the broom. "I believe this is yours."

"Ha, ha." She snatched it from him and put it on the hook. "How'd you know I was here?"

"I didn't. Zofie just informed me." He pointed at the luggage by the foot of the entry. "And that's probably why." He let out his signature laugh, as rowdy as a crowd encircling a flash mob.

Gail never recognized the earful as endearing until now, as his aliveness plucked at her heartstrings. "I don't need help, but thanks for the kind gesture," she said and walked to the suitcase.

"Nonsense." He marched to the bag, sizing it up. "How long are you staying?"

"Oh, I don't know. I reserved two nights, but I was thinking of maybe adding on some more if all goes well." Gail felt the blood rush to her face, realizing what she'd just said.

He gave her a curious look and hurled the baggage onto the mattress. "I'm glad you're here." He cleaned sweat from his brow and returned his hands to the cuff of his shirt.

"Thanks," she said, whisking strands of hair away from her eyes. "Will you be at the tea tonight?"

"Mm-hmm." He checked his watch. "Oh geez, I'm

late. I'm sorry, but I've got to go." He darted out of the room with the alacrity of a stealthy pronghorn.

Gail sat on the edge of the bed. *Go where?* Her confidence slid down her esophagus like a slug. *What if he's already seeing someone—because he very well could be. But then why would he waste his time cooking* me *dinner?* She eyed the monstrosity housing every decent outfit she'd spent the week assembling.

After a few long minutes of trying to tame the anxiety that continued festering, she sprang to her feet, grabbed the car keys, and fled.

"Morning, Gail," the groundskeeper said, raking debris into a neat pile by the gate.

"Hi, Tony," she replied, hurrying up the path.

The sight of Harry's tombstone erased the clutter from her mind. She fanned out the flannel blanket she'd brought and set it over the grass, pushing down on the ballooning material so it flattened beneath her.

"We need to talk," she said, getting closer to the slab. A squall forced the quilt up and around her. She hugged it, finding solace inside. "Thank you. I needed that." Even beyond the grave, she knew her husband was everywhere.

"Harry, I—um—have a confession." She paused and surveyed the tomb. "I think I like someone, Harry, but I don't want you to be mad. It's just that I miss the nearness of another—you know, the physical part. I can't survive solely on attachments from Heaven."

She sobbed into the encasing fabric when she felt a hard tap on her shoulder. She looked up, but no one was there. Spooked from the touch, she fumbled while standing and spied a gold ring glistening in the balding grass. She bent down and studied it before picking it up.

"Hey, Tony," she yelled and charged toward the cemetery gates. The checkered sheath flapped behind her like a superhero's cape. "Has someone reported missing jewelry?" She stopped in front of him, winded from the sprint, but steadied herself and held up the ring.

He removed his weathered baseball cap and narrowed his eyes. "No, not that I'm aware of. Where'd you find it?"

She shook her head. "You're probably not going to believe this, but it fell from somewhere—I don't know, maybe the sky? It struck my shoulder."

Tony's eyes fixed on hers.

"Seriously! I thought it was an acorn or something, but when I got up, there wasn't anything on the ground except this."

He took the gold in his hand and examined its plainness. "From the looks of it, it's a man's ring."

"Try it on," she said, nudging his hand.

He hesitated at first, then wriggled it on.

She gripped his palm. "It's big. But, you're right, it's definitely for a man."

He gave it back to her. "Hey, finder's keeper's," he said and took up the rake.

"Thanks, Tony. Have a good day."

She clutched the jewelry and practically skipped to the car.

Chapter Fifty-Two

Erin observed the nurses as a faint chime dinged in her pocket. She carefully retrieved her cell phone and saw it was a text from Gail:

—I know you're busy with errands, but I need to see you. It's pretty important. Where can I find you?—

"I'm so glad you signed on as a regular," Trudy, the PEDS director, said, whizzing by. "This section of the wing is special."

Erin tucked her cell away and followed Trudy.

"These babies are born to mothers who have drug addictions. Not exactly comforting, but not all the littles are severely affected by it. For example, that infant over there developed jaundice postpartum—that's it—which is completely curable." Trudy pointed to the bassinet Erin previously had her sights on. "See the spotlight over him?"

"I do."

"It's called phototherapy. This treatment will help his system get rid of the excess bilirubin."

Erin studied that cradle and then another where tiny tubes weaved in and out of a baby's body like a roadmap of exterior veins. She didn't ask about that infant's condition, but it was pretty obvious that he wasn't one of the lucky ones. "I can cuddle that lil' guy with jaundice if you want me to."

"Mm, he's in a fragile state right now, so I won't be

able to honor your request."

Erin was still optimistic. "Okay, then how about Xavier? He really has warmed up to me."

"Oh, you haven't heard? Little Xavier went home just this morning!"

Erin's gut panged with a sting of sadness.

"There is, however, a little peanut in ocelot two. She's simply delicious. Want to meet her?"

A girl? Erin re-blossomed. "Yes, please."

Trudy walked to a crib at the end of the nursery. Inside was the baby with caramel skin like Jay-Jay's. She immediately looked for the identification card, but nothing was there. *Relax. Jelani's not the only one in this world with colored skin.* Erin took a breath and looked at the bassinet again. She saw the most seraphic face she'd ever laid eyes on. She watched with elevated anticipation as Trudy dipped her hands in and extracted the child.

"It's like she's glowing," Erin said, beaming as she watched the baby. "What's her name?"

"She doesn't have one yet. Mom was under sedation when she was born, so we're temporarily referring to her as Baby A," Trudy said, angling her elbow in the direction of the rocker.

Erin moved briskly to the chair and sat, shifting herself fully onto it. "Okay, I'm ready."

With Baby A secure in her arms, Erin allowed herself to follow the breathing pattern of the infant so that their bellies moved in sync.

"Allen taught you well," Trudy said, smiling with approval. "I'll leave you two while I make my rounds to the others."

Erin's eyes started getting heavy, the swishing of uniformed polyester becoming another beat to the symphony in Erin's mind.

"Oh goody, I'm glad she's taken a liking to you," a passing nurse said as she walked by.

Erin's eyelids fluttered open; the child still sound asleep on her chest. "Has she given other cuddlers a hard time?"

"Kind of. She wasn't happy with people touching her. We assumed she was uncomfortable being swaddled, then thought it was colic, but by the looks of it, it may be neither of those things. And, lucky for Baby A, we finally have a match," the nurse said, but her grin turned grim. "She's really going to need all of the attention we can provide."

"Why's that?" Erin stroked A's cheek. "I mean, besides the obvious?"

"Her mom died."

The creaking from Erin's rocker came to a halt. "And her father?"

"He comes to visit but is petrified. He has asked us to keep her while he gets counseling."

The tip of Erin's nose met the top of the baby's scalp. She gently made small figure eights as she tried to make sense of the news. "There's got to be a next-of-kin lined up to help the father."

"It's a sticky situation. He's been considering foster care."

The nurse's words hung like icicles in the space between them. Erin wondered how Allen handled these situations; they hadn't discussed any of this in her previous visit.

The woman checked the pager on her belt. "I'll be back in five."

Erin continued caressing the baby when her

imagination raced with visions of herself happily feeding Baby A in a high chair. Out of nowhere, Erin's chest got tight. *Maybe this is it.* She brought the infant up to her face and inhaled her sweet scent. "Maybe this is our chance to defy the odds," she whispered.

Another baby in a darker corner of the room burst into hysteria. Trudy appeared and rushed to it.

Erin's phone chimed again. *Oy. I forgot about Gail.* She shifted Baby A to respond:

—I'm at the hospital…all is well. I'm leaving soon. Meet me in Parking Lot D in a half-hour.—

After the message was sent, she dropped the cell into her bag and rested again, stealing a few more minutes with her new favorite bundle.

****

Erin watched as Gail steered her car alongside hers and shut down the engine. She opened the window and bent forward, hardly able to sustain her joy. "You first. But make it fast. I'm bursting with news."

Gail assented, outwardly skittish.

Erin saw her fidgeting. "What's the matter? Why do you seem so nervous?"

Gail held up a band looped on her thumb.

"Whose is it?" Erin asked.

"Don't know."

"Where'd you get it?"

"It bounced off my shoulder at the cemetery." Gail stared at it.

"Did someone throw it at you?" Erin reached for it.

"No, that's what's so bizarre. I was wrapped up in a blanket talking to Harry when suddenly this thing fell from the sky and hit me."

"Humph." Erin examined the ring, twirling it slowly

around her finger. "Was there a bird's nest in the tree?"

"Nope."

"Well, did you ask him a question?"

Gail nodded. "I asked him if he'd be okay if I dated someone."

Erin smiled and extended her finger horizontally, the band rocking quickly. "He's still a slick bastard," she said, chuckling. "It's totally Harry. Look at how big this thing is. He's totally fine with you moving on. That's why he gave you this. It's for a man. For *you* to give to whomever you think is special enough." She went to return it but retracted. "Don't go giving it to any ole' body. *This* is special. *This* is Harry's approval to move forward but ease into it. No need to rush."

Erin dropped the band into Gail's open palm and decided to hold off on sharing her update.

Gail closed her hand and moved in for a hug. "Thank you, Er. I was hoping that's what it meant."

Erin kissed her temple and let go, silently settling into the driver's seat of her vehicle.

"I saw Jay-Jay earlier," Gail said. "Can't wait to see all the improvements when they're done!"

Erin looked up, confused. *More?* Her lips parted when a car alarm nearby started blaring.

"I'll let you go. Call me later," Gail shouted, shooing away what she'd said, and rolled up her window.

On the way home, Erin contemplated how to mention Baby A to Jay-Jay. She worried if it was too awkward to even bring it up or if he'd even believe that she'd fallen for another person's child. Either way, there was a deep pang in her gut, but she couldn't yet identify why it was there.

Erin parked and went into the house. "Ugh, this

place is an albatross," she said, stepping over tools to get up the steps. She entered the kitchen and flipped on the light. "What the?"

Mounted on the walls was brand-new creamy oak cabinetry, which popped against the blue and white geometric tile work. "Shut. Up," she muttered and rushed to it. "These tiles look hand-painted like those nineteenth-century French Provincial ones." She grazed her fingertips over them, then went to the counter to put her pocketbook down. It was no longer a dull Formica; rather, it was a shiny block of marble with beveled edges. She spun around and took in the rest of her completely upgraded cooking space. It was equipped with a copper farmhouse-style sink and a beautiful matching hood above a sprawling gas range. And, underneath that, was a fancy black and copper side-by-side double oven. Erin walked cautiously to it and opened and closed its doors.

"This entire kitchen is a work of art." Totally mesmerized, she went to the refrigerator and pushed the buttons on the computerized ice dispenser. Cubes fell out of the shoot and dropped to her feet. That's when she noticed the old, cruddy flooring had been replaced with distressed wooden planks.

Erin turned back to the counter for her cell phone when Jay-Jay appeared in the doorway. "This is amazing," she said. "Every single ounce of it."

"I was hoping we'd finally experience a new beginning to something. Something we need, I think, to jumpstart the positivity," Jay-Jay said. "Don't you agree?"

"I do, actually." Tears welled, but she pulled herself together. "I have to tell you something." She hesitated, then pushed herself to continue. "There's a baby girl I met today."

"You met Baby A?" Jay-Jay's voice cracked.

Erin's brow did a serious plunge. "How do you know?" Then she connected it all.

Jay glanced at his feet and shoved his hands in his pants pockets.

"So Baby A *is* yours," she asked rhetorically.

He shifted in his shoes. "Yes, she is."

A small grin formed on her face. She stepped closer to Jay, took his hand, and put it on her torso. "This is where I assumed a baby would grow, but," she moved his hand up to her heart. "I learned that's not always the case."

Jay-Jay's eyes lit up. "Are you saying what I think you're saying?"

Erin squeezed Jay-Jay's fingers. "I am."

Chapter Fifty-Three

Spattering horns tooted something welcoming as Gail reentered the bed-and-breakfast. In her room, she shut the door. Music was replaced with laughter coming from another part of the house not too far from hers. Gail pressed her ear to the wall. The tenor overtones of a young male pulsated through it. A subsequent giggle from a girl whose education hadn't yet seen its college degree pierced the air. *That's definitely the Kumbaya couple.* Gail tried to eavesdrop, see what godly people talked about, but their sentences were short, choppy— barely audible. She gave up and retreated to the fireplace.

"So, when was the last time you were used?" she said, pulling the cast iron blockade from the opening, and went to inspect the insides. The damper was open, so she grabbed a bunch of newspaper from a heap beside the place and situated crumbled bundles under the grate. "There."

She lit a match and tossed it in, then reclined back on her heels. The room quickly filled with smoke at the same time she heard someone in the hallway.

Gail leaped to her feet. "Is someone there?" She heard shuffling but no response, so she flung open the door.

"This was a bad idea," Roger whispered and went to turn away.

Gail eyed Roger suspiciously. "What was a bad

idea?"

"Nothing," he said, "Just, uh, these silly old slacks."

The corners of Gail's mouth perked as Roger swatted hard on his khakis. She bit her lip to fend off impending laughter when she realized he could probably help her.

"Actually," she said and took a step back into the room. She gestured for him to come in. "The fireplace is giving me some trouble."

Roger straightened, a smile spreading on his face. "Is that what the smoke is all about?"

Gail explained the situation as they went inside but then stopped. "Oh, who am I kidding. This is probably going to require an actual repairman."

Roger got to his knees and examined the flue, ignoring her remark. Gail was about to close the door when Leonard walked by. She froze.He continued to his room as if he hadn't seen or smelled a thing.

"From here, it looks as if there may be a clog," Roger said.

She approached for a closer look. Roger grabbed the poker from the rack and jabbed it into the abyss of the chimney. Black soot sprayed down, covering them.

Gail jumped back and wiped her eyes. "Ugh, I knew this required a professional!"

"I'm sorry," Roger said, getting to his feet.

"Don't apologize. Just stop interfering and g, get— get out!"

Roger didn't question her this time and fled the scene.

All that for nothing. And Leonard probably thinks I'm into this guy. Gail turned the latch and marchedpast the ashy mess toward the big Victorian dresser. She grabbed a towel and wiped her face and hands. Looking down, she counted six drawers, three on the left, three on the right, and debated between keeping her things in the luggage or tucking them into the furniture; she'd never been one to use any of it in hotels when she traveled.

Like an old dog refusing training, she left everything the way she'd originally arranged it in the suitcase and, with a pincer grasp, riffled through it for something suitable for tea. "That's it!" she said, eyeing a silky salmon tunic and plucked it from the pile. She held it up and began speaking to it. "I'll invite Shelly here tonight and introduce her to Roger. He's a widower, she's single, it's genius!"

Gail paired the shirt with black Capri leggings, then spread the clothes atop the comforter, careful not to get soot on anything. She removed the cell phone from her pocket when the nearby toilet flushed, followed by the exit of a patron.

"But first, a shower." She placed the phone on the dresser, grabbed her outfit, and raced to the bathroom.

Chapter Fifty-Four

Megan was a dark shadow on the porch, sitting bundled in two quilted robes and a wool hat, warming her hands on a mug filled with freshly brewed coffee. "You two never cease to amaze me," she said, her voice carrying from the wheelchair as Deirdre and Rob hammered away at a wooden ramp in the grass. It had taken most of the day, but the two had successfully transformed the Dunham residence into a place of comfort and functionality for Megan.

"When is our appointment again?" Deirdre said, stopping mid-swing.

Megan squinted at her wrist. "Noon. We have a little over an hour."

"I got this," Rob said and grabbed the hammer. "You ladies go get yourselves pampered and have a good time."

Deirdre patted Rob's back and stood. "I'll prepare lunch first."

She gathered Trevor and Kenny from where they were playing on the lawn and brought them in with Megan. "Mac and cheese for everyone," she announced as they entered the kitchen.

The boys cheered as Megan let out a little clap. "It's so great to be home!" She rolled to a low cabinet for the macaroni and cheese mix.

The kids went to the counter with butter, measuring

cups, and milk.

"Mommy, who's coming over today?" Trevor asked, reaching for a spoon in the utensil drawer.

"A few ladies who know how to do hair and nails—girly things." Megan petted him as he waved the spoon overhead.

"Party!" Kenny said. "Is it your birthday, Mama?"

Deirdre put a pot of water on the stove. "No, no, sweetie. It's not that kind of party."

Kenny's smile drooped into a pout.

"But we can pretend it is!" she said.

Trevor pushed a kitchen chair to the refrigerator and climbed up. "We have ice cream in here. All we need are candles." He took out little Dixie cups filled with vanilla and chocolate flavors.

Megan rolled to a drawer and took out a pack of tiny blue candlesticks and matches.

"No, Mommy, we do it," Kenny said, snatching them from her.

Deirdre winked at the boys and wheeled Megan out of the room. "Don't come in until we say." She disappeared to the kitchen again.

Megan strained to hear what was going on. Deirdre was apparently fiddling with the ice cream and candles.

"Okay, on the count of three," Deirdre called out. "One…two…three…Happy Birthday to you…"

Megan wheeled herself slowly toward her singing sons, who were bouncing excitedly next to Deirdre.

"Make a wish, Mom," Trevor said, holding his treat to her.

She drew in a deep breath, pausing for effect, and then blew out the little flames.

Deirdre and Megan both set the boys up at the table,

allowing them to eat dessert before lunch. "So, what hairstyle are you having the beautician do for tonight?" Deirdre said and put a dollop of ice cream in her mouth.

"Well, with the plunging neckline of the dress, I was thinking of an up-do with a few loose strands here and there." She swooped Deirdre's hair off her nape and twisted it into a bun, freeing some hair from her crown. "Something like this." She tilted her head, studying her friend.

"Oh, very Cinderella-like," Deirdre said. "And what an enchanted evening it'll be."

"Where are you going, Mama?" Trevor said, chocolate ice cream framing his mouth.

"Daddy's firehouse dance, sweetie. Remember?"

"Oh yeah." He dipped his dessertspoon into the bowl of mac and cheese as the stylists walked into the house.

Deirdre leaped to her feet. "Hi! Thank you for coming. You can set up in the bathroom." She led the way, Megan following behind.

"You can sit here." Deirdre closed the toilet cover and then helped Meg out of the wheelchair and onto the seat. "Enjoy," she said and kissed the top of Megan's forehead. "I'll be back in a few to check on you."

Megan focused on the beautician. "Hi, I'm Megan."

"I'm Jennifer," the woman said, smiling. She opened a big case of makeup and started talking about different colors and shades.

Megan acknowledged the lady even though breathing became difficult. She tried to ignore it as Jennifer began applying foundation, but the struggle for air grew painfully obvious.

"Are you okay?" Jennifer said, stepping back.

Megan shook her head as she wheezed. The cosmetologist bolted to the door and opened it. "Hello? Deirdre? I need help here." Minus the sound of an electrical drill coming from outside, the house was still. Jennifer turned to Megan, who pointed to the door. "Okay. Stay here. I'll be right back." She raced out. When she returned, Deirdre was in tow, clutching a nebulizer and albuterol treatment.

Megan looked on as Deirdre filled the vial and plugged the machine into the nearest outlet. She then wrapped the stretchy elastic of the mask around Megan's face. "Steady on the inhale. Yes, yes. And, now, exhale. Just like that. Inhale, exhale, inhale, exhale." Deirdre's voice was smooth and rhythmic as Megan stabilized. "You look beautiful already," she said, grinning.

Megan blinked in reply and motioned to the head of a mannequin on the countertop. The beautician was primping the wig into the sweeping up-do, fastening it with a black, beaded accessory.

"I love the fishnet meshy thing attached to the barrette," Deirdre said. "Is that going to slope here?" She pointed to her temple.

Megan nodded.

"That's gorgeous. Like what women wore back in the day. I can't wait to see it on you."

After a few more minutes, Deirdre removed the plastic covering over Megan's mouth. "Listen, you'll need to take this with you when you go tonight." She coiled the cord of the nebulizer. "Those bronchospasms can happen at any time, which you know."

"Okay," Megan whispered.

"I'll be right in the kitchen if you need me," Deirdre said to Jennifer and walked to the door. "I'll keep this open, though, just in case." She winked at Megan and left.

"Let me know if you need me to stop," Jennifer said, approaching Megan now with the wig. "I just want you to try this on so I can make adjustments before we continue with makeup."

"You're so good at this," Megan said and removed her wool hat. "They forewarned you, I see."

The cosmetologist looked at her, wearing a sympathetic frown. "You're sick."

"Yep. Lung cancer is the latest ailment. You're one of the few who knows. That's how recent the discovery was made. And that's in addition to stage four ovarian cancer, oh, and breast cancer. Let's not forget how it all started." Megan turned her head as Jennifer adhered some bobby pins into the bun and continued. "Yeah, it's only a matter of time now. I'm basically a dead duck. Quack, quack, motherfucker." She giggled, but the woman stayed silent. "Ah, you weren't made aware of *all* the diagnoses. It's okay. Cancer isn't contagious. You won't get it."

Jennifer stopped midway. "I'm not afraid of you. I'm just shocked 'cause you're so young."

"Yeah, well, what can you do?" Megan tilted her head the other way. "I'm really excited about tonight. Thank you for making me feel pretty."

Megan glanced at Jennifer as she lifted the wig up and away from her scalp, noticing tears dampening her face. "Let's put on some music, shall we?" Megan attempted to deflect the awkwardness and pulled the cell phone from her robe. "I've got Pandora—name your station."

Megan turned on some lively dance tunes as

Jennifer started working on her lashes and lids. In the middle of a song, a face-to-face call blared in. For a moment, the screen of Megan's phone went blank, but then half of Erin's face appeared. Since the stylist was busy working a mascara wand over Megan's right eye, she held the cell on the other side and answered.

"Wow, look at you," Erin said.

Megan's glossy lips molded into a hammock of tranquil grace.

"So, you're going to the dance after all?"

"Yes. Followed by a horse-drawn carriage ride."

"Sounds romantic. How are you feeling?"

"Not as good as I look, but it's become the norm. How are you doing?"

There was an unmistakable silence. Erin watched the artist dab a bit of shimmer beneath Megan's eyes to conceal the dark circles. "Um, well, I've come to terms with, you know, my faulty uterus and not being able to have my own kid."

"That's a good start," Megan said.

Erin tried to bite back her smile. "And there's something else."

"Oohh, do tell."

"Um, well, I've been looking after this little angel in the PEDS unit. She's given me this sense of purpose, like I can be a mom, even if it's not biological."

"Oh, gosh. That's fantastic news!"

"It's Jay-Jay's," Erin said and bit her lip.

"Well then, Jay-Jay must be excited, too." Megan looked up as the makeup artist blended more cream under her eye, then sighed. "I can't tell her my lung news now."

Erin straightened and got closer to the screen. "What

news? Tell me. That's not fair."

Megan aimed the phone at the cosmetologist. "Can you?"

"*Me?*" Jennifer glanced at Megan and then at Erin on the phone. "Uh," she said, her voice quaking like the earth in an aftershock. "Megan," she croaked, then abruptly cleared her larynx. "Megan has lung cancer."

Erin lost composure.

Megan turned the phone and looked directly into it. "Don't. It's all right. I've accepted my fate." She adjusted her robe in a no-big-deal fashion. "Listen, I've got to finish up here, but don't worry. All's fine. Just roll with the punches like I am, okay?"

Erin looked horrified. "I, I've been so wrapped up in myself. Oh, my—I'm so sorry I haven't been there for you," she said, her eyes unblinking. "We've always been together—college, the sorority, weddings. I feel like such a shit friend."

"Don't be ridiculous. You just had major surgery," Megan said, dismissing her claim.

"I'm sorry to interrupt, but, Megan, I need your full face back." Jennifer held out a giant poofy brush.

"Go, go. Have fun tonight. But you better call me tomorrow," Erin said, waving. "Oh, and, Meg, you look like a princess."

After the call, Jennifer applied some shimmer and then helped Megan into the wheelchair. Together, they went to the bedroom.

"I've got it from here," Megan said and slipped her an envelope filled with money.

"Thank you so much. Have a great time." She smiled and rubbed Megan's shoulder, then left the room.

Megan wheeled herself to the dress hanging from

the armoire and gave it a gentle tug. It fell onto her lap, and she deftly slipped into it.

As she went to stand, Rob entered. She straightened her posture before the mirror and adjusted the hemline, the black beading twinkling, the material hugging her petite frame. She turned slowly to him. "You like?" She flirtatiously twirled one of the cascading curls dancing about her shoulder.

"Me love." He ran his hand down her waist and pulled her in for a kiss. She smiled as he laced his fingers with hers and led her toward the door. "Hey, boys, come in here," he called out as they walked.

Trevor and Kenny ran in and stopped in their tracks.

"Wow," Kenny gasped.

Trevor grabbed his mom's hand and kissed it. Megan's chest muscles fluttered from affection. She bent down and cupped his face. "I love you so much." She kissed his nose, then turned to Kenny and did the same.

"I like your hat." Kenny poked a finger in the delicate netting.

She laughed and thanked him, using every ounce of energy to straighten her legs. Rob noticed the struggle and held her arm. They walked to the wheelchair, and she sat.

"Okay, boys, you be good for Deirdre. Don't give her any trouble," Rob said, pushing Megan out of the room.

"Don't worry 'bout a thing," Deirdre said, peering out from the kitchen. She swung the towel over her shoulder and whistled at them. "Looking good, you two."

Rob stopped walking and smoothed the creases of his tux, playfully puffing out his chest. "I know, I know," he said and tugged on the lapels.

Deirdre grabbed the towel and hurled it at him. "Yeah, yeah. Have fun, you guys. We'll see you sometime tomorrow."

Chapter Fifty-Five

Erin swallowed hard at the thought of Megan's latest diagnosis as she entered the pediatric unit. She signed in, greeted several nurses at the station, then made her way to Baby A's cradle. She leaned in and touched the infant's face. "Hey, baby girl. You miss me?"

Erin scooped up Baby A, who quickly lay peaceful in the crook near her collarbone, breathing rapid, all belly, and legs splayed like a frog's. Erin eased into a chair in slow, small increments and readjusted herself. The lead nurse walked over and put tiny booties on the child, then fixed the cap on A's head.

"Has anyone come to check on her today?" Erin asked.

The medic gave a sullen frown. "The hospital is working on the next steps with the foster care agency."

Erin's chest tightened as she looked down at the baby. *Why would Jay-Jay do that, especially after yesterday?* "No," she said and forced herself up. "That can't be. I'll be right back." She resettled Baby A in the bassinet and exited the nursery in a confused daze.

Medical staff whizzed by like fiery asteroids. Erin found the vending machine and leaned against it. "My best friend has lung cancer. And I'm in love with a dead woman's baby whose father happens to be my husband," she murmured, glaring at her reflection in the glass.

"Mrs. Harper?"

Erin turned to see a stoic blonde in a perfectly tailored pantsuit. "Yes, that's me."

"My name is Kristine. I'm from Ready Start Adoption Agency. I was told you're Baby A's cuddler. Can you come to my office to discuss the infant? I just have a few brief questions."

"Sure," Erin said, wiping away tears. "But I'll need the address. I don't know where your agency is located."

Kristine grinned. "It's actually down the hall."

Erin stretched her spine. "Oh, I didn't know agencies had offices here."

"We don't," Kristine said. "Correction. We *normally* don't. But because we've had more cases from here lately, and they had the space, they set me up with a work area. I'm still deciding if that's a good or bad thing."

The woman sighed and recovered a thick three-ring binder from her leather briefcase. "Shall we?"

Erin nodded in between sniffles and followed Kristine through the corridor to a room that was dimly lit with no windows.

"Please. Have a seat."

Erin obliged as Kristine sat on the chair behind an old aluminum desk. She watched the lady flip to a color-coated section of the book and click her pen.

"We hear you're doing a great job with this little gal," Kristine said and began scribbling on one of the pages.

"It's all her." Erin reached into her purse for a tissue. "What's going to happen to her now?"

"Arrangements are being made. Being so young, she obviously needs around-the-clock care."

Erin dabbed her eyes, unconsciously smudging

more makeup. "Have you ever had a cuddler adopt a baby?"

Kristine stopped writing and gave a wry smile. "No. Why? Is that something you were interested in?"

"Yes," she whispered, twiddling the Kleenex in her lap, then gazed up at Kristine. "I'm ready to be a mom."

Kristine checked her watch, then clicked the pen closed and stood.

Erin's heart worked overtime. She looked at the woman, her eyes clouded. "Where are you going?"

Just then, Jay-Jay walked into the office.

"Glad you could make it, Mr. Harper," Kristine said and shook his hand. She pulled a plastic chair up beside Erin. "Please, have a seat."

Kristine sat again and flipped to the back of the binder.

"Jelani, what's happening?" Erin's words were quivering.

"An adoption," Kristine replied and pulled out a thick packet. "The process begins with an application. Read it over carefully with your spouse and your lawyer, crossing every *t*, dotting every *i*, and notarizing the required pages." She handed the papers to Erin, then closed the book and tucked it into the belly of her carry case. "Once we receive it completed, I'll be in touch." Kristine pressed her knuckles on the desk and stood. "Congratulations, Mrs. Harper."

Chapter Fifty-Six

"My son is sort of a big deal," Shelly Baxter said, her knuckles white on the teacup. "I mean, a big deal to me. But also to the fire department."

Gail's eyes unconsciously rolled as Roger's pinballed from her to Shelly.

"How so?" Zofie said, comforting Shelly's knee with small pats.

Gail stared at the floating particles in the mug, not exactly sure where Shelly was going with this.

"Well, we all love him," Shelly said, chuckling. "For starters, he's charming and real handsome. As a firefighter, he's a master, a former Marine, so they always rely on his excavating tactics when it comes to search and rescue."

"That's impressive," Zofie said.

Gail saw Leonard nod in the background.

"But earlier today, I found out something about him, something that I"—Shelly's voice was fractured—"I just had no idea."

"Hmm, so it was unexpected?" Zofie asked.

"My son is gay."

Gail sipped her tea in an attempt to hide her face. *Good for Cliff. He's finally owning it.*

Leonard quietly stood and left the room. Shelly stopped talking and turned to Zofie for a conversation derailment. Zofie grinned in her direction. "As many of you know, my husband served in Vietnam," she began. "Before 'don't ask, don't tell.'"

While Zofie talked, Gail inched her way to the far edge of the couch, then snuck away when no one was looking.

"Why'd you walk out?" Gail said, entering the dinette behind Leonard.

"It had nothing to do with Shelly or her son," Leonard said, gathering some clean mugs from the table. "Truth is, I didn't want to get in the way of you and Roger."

"Roger?" Gail caught the volume of her voice and whispered, "Whatever do you mean?"

"Wasn't he in your room the other night?"

Gail leaned on the counter next to him. "Oh my, are you—" She started to laugh uncontrollably.

Leonard peered over his shoulder and grabbed some saucers. "What's so funny?"

Gail gazed at her shoes. "The fireplace was broken. He happened to be in the hall when some smoke entered the room. He came in and tried to fix it, but, of course, he just made it worse." She shook her head. "Actually, he's the reason I brought Shelly here. I thought they'd make a good match. Whatever. Going back to what you were saying. I, I actually haven't dated—anyone—at all."

Leonard arranged cups onto little dishes. "I went on two dates: blind ones," he said, eyebrow arching. "If that tells you anything."

"They were that good, huh?" Gail laughed and then stopped abruptly. "So, you've never dated anyone from here?"

Leonard stopped organizing the dinnerware and

turned to her. "Is that why you think I'm here? To pick up women? Because it's not. It's actually the last thing on my mind when I come here."

Gail put up her hands and sidestepped. "No, no, no."

Leonard took hold of her. "Wait a minute. I think we've got each other all wrong. For me, you showing up here was a complete surprise. There's this thing about you—you're sad, yet full of life, you're hurting, but you laugh and joke and dance anyway. You're a real game-changer. At least for me."

Her insides flamed, but she didn't look away. "You see those things? Is it that obvious?"

Leonard halted for a second, then came to. "No. I mean, I notice, but I don't think other people notice. I think I see it because I feel all those things, too. I guess it just becomes a part of who you are when you're a widow. Like this secret language."

Gail's eyes grew large. "So, you knew the humiliation I was feeling?"

Leonard smiled and kissed her chin. "Let's go back in there before Roger starts to wonder." He flashed a sarcastic glance and weaved his fingers with hers.

Chapter Fifty-Seven

Light music played as Rob and Megan were chauffeured to a quaint table arranged for two at the far end of the Les Salons Bernardin lounge. Recessed lighting and small candles decorating the dining room exuded a hint of glow throughout. The architectural design of the floor-to-ceiling windows allowed the city to be a subtle yet integral part of the ambiance.

Rob positioned Megan's wheelchair for her to comfortably sit by the table, facing the crowd, which was how she preferred.

"I don't understand how people could eat with their backs to everyone," she'd said every time they frequented a restaurant.

Rob would often shrug and say, "I don't mind because I get to focus on you." That line always caused Megan to blush.

Megan focused on the action at the white marble-top bar in the main dining area decorated with colorful drinks in fancy glasses that disappeared as rapidly as they came into view.

Forks clanked against porcelain as the wait staff delivered the first course: an almost raw selection of seafood, including caviar and oysters. Under the bustle of dispersing plates was soft music. Megan struggled to hear it, then suddenly perked up. "Honey, listen."

Rob stopped toying with the meat on a half shell and

tried to concentrate. "It's Phantom," he said and smiled at the concurrence.

Megan sang along to "Music of the Night" from *The Phantom of the Opera*, her favorite Broadway show, as she raised a piece of New York toast covered with tiny pearls of dark caviar. When the male vocalist hit the highest of notes, she closed her eyes and chewed the food in the same tempo as the instrumentation. When they reopened, the waiter was beside them with a pairing to complement the cuisine. Megan nodded in acceptance of the flute. "Mm," she hummed, savoring the marriage of the buttery Osetra with the crisp bubbly liquid. She drained the glass and set it on the table, then rested a hand over Rob's. "I just want to thank you for this. For all of it."

Rob put down his flute. "You are the love of my life. I'd do anything for you. Just know *we* are the original duo. No one can, or will, *ever* replace you. Remember that."

The aggressive yet eloquent harmonies of the opera came to a soft conclusion, and Megan leaned into Rob. "I've passed the point of no return," she said, reciting words from the musical. "Just enjoy me while I'm here beside you."

The arrival of the second course invited a change of conversation, a welcomed reprieve for both of them. They indulged curiously at the dish and the next two that followed.

"This establishment makes eating an epic experience," Megan said, finishing her final course, a hazelnut praline dessert. "I am officially entering a food coma."

Rob laughed as he stood. "I'm going to close our tab

and fetch our coats."

Back on the street, Megan heard galloping hooves clacking against the pavement. She craned her head and saw a stagecoach making its way up 51st, led by a beautiful Clydesdale.

"He's a real stunner," Megan said when the horse stopped in front of her.

"And friendly," the driver said with Scottish enunciation. "His name's Chip."

She lifted her bottom from the mobile chair. The Scot took her hand and placed it on the mare's chocolate-brown fur and guided her fingers along the side of it. "Hi, Chip," she said, rubbing the side of the animal's belly. "Rob, do you see this?"

She turned her head and saw Rob wrestling to get the wheelchair into the carriage.

"Let's switch," the man suggested and hurried to him.

The Scot secured the wheels as Rob went to Megan. "Ready to go?" Rob asked, patting the horse, then helped Megan up and onto the bench of the vehicle.

The stagecoach traveled north up Seventh Avenue to the east side and turned onto 59th Street, heading toward the entrance of Central Park at 60th. Megan and Rob sat close, fingers interlocked as they absorbed the sights of the city. Taxis whizzed by, occasionally pressing on their horns. It didn't deter the animal, but the noise worried Megan. "I feel bad for the horse," she whispered as they trotted up the street.

Rob's thumb stroked the top of her hand. "Try not to think about it."

They entered the park, the lush trails a respite from the quotidian traffic, and were enamored by the vast expanse of trees still adorning their multicolored bounty. "Thank you for this." Megan nuzzled her nose along Rob's chin.

He pressed his cheek against hers. Together they witnessed several waterfowl scurrying in the grass, their honks like laughter as they flapped wildly at each other.

"Sounds like us when we're hot and bothered," Megan joked.

The paths were lined with lanterns that gave off enough light for the horse to navigate back onto the avenue.

"The W Hotel, correct?" the driver called out.

"Yes," Rob and Megan shouted in unison.

The man waved a gloved hand and steered Chip into the brisk of the night when Megan felt tightness in her throat. "Oh no," she whispered, grabbing her neck.

Rob reached for the tote bag containing an inhaler. "We need to get you out of the cold," he said. He handed her the breathing apparatus and inched to the front of the buggy. "Hey, is it possible that we go faster? My wife is having an asthma attack."

The Scot jolted Chip forward. The couple slid backward in the seat as Megan focused on the pump, squeezing it several times into constricted airways.

"You all right?" Rob said, bracing Megan as they came to a halt in front of the hotel.

"Fine," she squeaked and gave a thumbs-up.

"Come on. Let's get warm." Rob ushered her out of the coach, and they walked in through the W's main lobby's revolving door. He set her on a plush couch. "Wait here."

Megan watched him run to retrieve the wheelchair and collect their luggage kept in a storage closet near the concierge.

"We're on the eighth floor," he said, wheeling the suitcases to her and setting them on the ground before settling her to the chair. "It's not exactly a penthouse suite, but who cares, right?"

Megan giggled. "Oh, darling," she said, her articulation a faux British accent, "one mustn't fret one's civil servant status."

They went to the elevator bay, a chime signaling.

"To the royal ball, Jeeves," Megan joked, clapping twice as the doors parted.

****

Bassy music permeated through the speakers; the only bright lights were flashing strobes. Rob gripped the handles of Megan's chair and wheeled her into the main dining hall. She spotted the dozen empty seats, then noticed the entire firehouse on the dance floor. She smiled, bobbing her head to the music, and looked up at Rob.

"Wanna dance?" he shouted.

"Yes!" She flailed her arms as he pushed her toward the crowd and let out a little, "Woot! Woot!" as some of the wives took sight of them.

Everyone gathered near, forming a circle, and cheered at their arrival. Behind Megan, a few guys slapped Rob's back and exchanged burly hugs with him, offering up their extra beers when the deejay abruptly stopped the music. "I was just informed that our special guest has arrived. Please take your seats."

People started scrambling back to their tables. Just as Rob pushed Megan toward their seats, a spotlight beamed down on them. The room quickly grew silent.

"Mrs. Dunham, if I may," the captain of Rob's

firehouse said and took her hand. Rob stepped back, amused, as his boss kneeled on one knee. "It is with distinct pleasure to welcome you, our guest of honor, to this lovely evening of dining, dancing, and shenanigans."

Megan laughed as the captain kissed her hand. He then took a bouquet of pink roses from the deejay and presented them to her.

"Thank you," Megan said, cheeks flushing.

"That's not all." He stood and grabbed her next gift. "It's not your average fire department shirt," the captain said and held up a navy-blue T-shirt with the firehouse logo on it. "As you can see, this one is in celebration of life—your life." He showed off the dark material that adorned a pink ribbon on the front. In the center of the loop were the numbers of the engine and rescue companies. He flipped the shirt, revealing pink FDNY lettering on the back. "Because you're our hero. A true survivor."

Everyone stood and clapped as the captain draped the T-shirt over Megan's torso. A few other firemen walked about the dining room carrying boxes, gifting each firefighter and their spouse with one.

When the cheering settled, the music resumed, and Rob wheeled Meg off the dance floor. "Please take me outside," she turned and said to him. "I'm no survivor."

Rob diverted them into the hall. She coughed, which led to a fight for air. He took the inhaler from a bag and put it to her lips. "Yes, you are. Right now, you're living, and living is surviving. Don't you dare discredit yourself of that."

The two engaged in a stare-down as Megan's breathing regulated. Rob looked at her admiringly while they concentrated on the music, the walls vibrating around them.

Megan continued to listen. "They're playing our jam." She started bopping along with the '90s tune, her mind returning to the night she met Rob: summer 2005. Keg party. He was sober;she a belligerent dancing mess surrounded by Erin and some sorority sisters. This particular song came on the radio, a "Flashback Friday Favorite," and somebody blasted it, sending Megan's "beer balls" into high gear. She grabbed the closest guy—Rob—and gyrated against him while singing. He stood there, embarrassed, knowing none of the people cheering, but by the end of the spectacle, he asked her out on a date, anyway. She agreed, gave him her number, and didn't remember him when he called the next day. But because he was so easygoing on the phone, she decided she'd go out with him, like setting herself up on a blind date. She joined him at his firehouse, where he was volunteering between semesters, and, from there, they went to dinner. They've been having dinner together ever since.

"Come on, let's go dance," he said, breaking her trance.

"Not before I get my drink on," she said and laughed. "Vodka and tonic, here I come."

"Oh boy." Rob rolled his eyes and pushed her to the bar at the far side of the ballroom, the crowd a sea of fire department T-shirts.

"It's mostly cubes," she said when Rob handed her a small glass.

The drink was cold yet warmed her insides. She chugged it like a shot of tequila and asked for another. Rob raised a brow but respected her request.

Megan took the second round and graciously sipped. "The ice is going straight to my head," she joked but felt something else altogether. She returned the booze to him and winced. Her innards ached; something more than a mere signal from body to brain saying she was no longer a college student. "No, not tonight," Meg whispered as if channeling the disease could stop the pain.

"What's the matter, sweetie?"

"Nothing. Nothing at all." She was lying, and they both knew it, but Megan pushed the brakes forward, leaving no room for discussion. "I want to dance out of this confinement." She shimmied to the edge of the seat and reached for Rob.

"Are you sure you want to do this?" he said, taking her into his arms.

"I need to be up and close to you."

The surprising urgency prompted him to hold her with all he had. He moved leisurely across the shiny hardwood as Sia's"Breathe Me" played over the speakers, stroking her back as she rested against him. "Do you need to go to the hospital?"

"No. Just dance. This is perfect."

Meg closed her eyes, inhalation shallow, and didn't negotiate with the constriction. Instead, she focused on her heart, the once-hurried rabbit that had slowed to the steady pace of a tortoise but was now regressing to a snail whose movements were barely noticeable. Her scalp twinged then went numb, the prickling working its way down.

****

Rob hummed along to the melody of the song as Megan became limp. "Meg?" His voice was tight. "Meg, please." He clenched her body, eyelids firmly shut, and gave a little shake as he swayed. Her head slumped clumsily off his shoulder. He dropped to the ground, cradling her. "Please. No."

People backed away and then swarmed in like bees to a hive. Someone yelled to the deejay to shut the music while another shouted into a cell phone at a 9-1-1 operator. Others talked to Rob, but he didn't seem to hear them. All he did was stare at Megan lying unconscious in his lap, the speed of time weaving in and out of motion.

Someone placed two fingers on her wrist, but Rob was sure there wasn't a pulse.

"You knew," he said and pressed his face to hers. "I just wish I had." His body jerked in between sobs as he rocked her. "I wish I knew. God, why didn't I know?"

The captain kneeled beside Rob. "The EMTs are here."

Rob looked up at a set of paramedics, a stretcher at their side. He loosened his grip as they carefully unraveled her from him. He sat unwavering as they worked chest compressions and attached Megan to portable machines. As they raised the gurney, the captain lifted Rob.

"She's dead," Rob said, focused somewhere over his boss's shoulder. "My wife's gone."

Chapter Fifty-Eight

Deirdre startled awake from an intense squeezing sensation around her clavicle. *What the hell?* She joggled upright, gasping and tugging the rosary wrapped tightly about her neck. *Oh my God, the kids.* She swatted at the dark in the nightstand's direction. "Where the eff is the baby monitor?" she said and accidentally smacked it, losing it somewhere behind the furniture.

She hopped up and rushed to the boys' room, but they were sound asleep. Back in the bedroom, she flicked on the light, scanning the dresser for her phone.

"Come on, pick up," she said, calling Megan's cell, but only heard her recorded voice recite instructions for leaving a message. She hung up and dialed Rob. It rang a few times, and then there was a person sniffling on the other line. "Hey, Rob?" The sniffs became deep, uncontrollable sobs. "Rob, talk to me. Is Megan okay? Tell me she's okay."

"No. She's not."

Deirdre heard a click, and the call ended. The cross grew hot at the base of her throat. She slowly sank to the floor of the guest bedroom, feeling it was no longer Megan's and that she was no longer a guest. "The boys. Who's telling the boys?" A scary type of confusion set in, not sure who or what anyone was anymore.

She took a breath and dialed Erin's cell but no answer. *I can't leave this on a voicemail.* She jumped to her feet and ransacked the desk for an address book. "Gotcha!"

She thumbed the yellowing alphabetical pages of a spiral-bound journal. "Erin, Erin, Erin. Come on, where are you?" Erin's name wasn't under *E*. "Shit, what the hell's her last name? Harper!" She licked her finger and ruffled through more pages. "Come on, come on, come on, you've got to have a house number."

In blue erasable ink, *Harper, Erin* was neatly written under the letter *H*. Deirdre leafed past it, then riffled the papers back to *H* again. She studied the information and pressed the series of numbers in the inscription.

"Hello?"

Deirdre paced the small area between the bed and the furniture, trying to listen beyond Erin's voice for any disturbances; she couldn't tell a woman potentially surrounded by others that her friend was dead. *But what if she already knows?*

"Hello?" Erin repeated.

There was a stillness that trailed behind her words, no indication of sadness or any other emotion. "Erin, it's Deirdre."

"Deirdre, hey. Everything okay?"

She now knew Erin hadn't a clue. "I have to tell you something. It's about Meg." Deirdre squeezed her eyes shut. "She's, she's…"

"What? Oh, my God! No. No! Please don't say what I think it is."

"I'm sorry. I'm so, so sorry," Deirdre whispered and dropped her head, listening as Erin screamed and cried into the phone. When Erin finally settled a bit, Deirdre continued. "Based on the time I spoke with Rob, I suspect something went on at the dinner dance."

"I'll call Jay-Jay. He's working at the firehouse tonight. He's got to know what's going on," Erin said and hung up.

Chapter Fifty-Nine

Erin threw open the weighted door of the house and fled to the car, her bathrobe flapping in the wind. She wrestled with the seatbelt in between gulps for air and overwatered eyes. Her fuzzy slipper pounced the gas pedal after the engine sputtered on, then skidded out of the driveway and into the night.

She pulled up to the Queen Anne. It was well lit, life happening inside. She dialed Gail but was redirected to her voice mailbox. Erin dropped the phone into the center console and exited the vehicle. The front lawn was bustling with chirping crickets nestled in nearby patches of grass. She climbed the stairs and tried to peer in the porch window, but the lacy treatments weren't as translucent as they appeared. Through strained eyes, she barely made out any of the people—possibly all men— sitting by a glowing fireplace in what resembled a communal area.

Erin took in a big breath and gripped the door handle, stepping inside. Her furry slipper, however, caught a curled corner of the welcome mat, and she stumbled into the foyer. Everyone's head jerked in the direction of the noise as Erin grabbed onto a nearby coat rack, trying desperately to regain balance, but ended up dancing ridiculously to her fate.

"May I help you?" Zofie said and stood.

Erin pushed off the pole of jackets and rolled slowly

to a sitting position. "Is Gail here?"

Gail leaped to her feet. "Erin? Erin, is that you?"

Erin looked up and saw her friend across the room. She also spied the twenty-some-odd other people gathered together, their eyelids flitting like bat wings in between stares. She immediately felt like a fool and yanked at her bathrobe, tying the belt tight to cover some extremely unflattering nightwear.

"Are you okay?" Gail helped her up.

"I'm so sorry if I interrupted something." Erin clutched Gail's forearm and planted her slippered feet onto the ground.

"Don't be silly. We're having tea. Want some?"

Erin nodded but started weeping immediately.

A man got up and retrieved a chair from the dining table. "Here, sweetie, have a real seat," he said and helped her into it. "I'm Leonard, Gail's friend. You may not want to share what's on your mind, but that's what we've been doing all night, so feel free to let 'er rip."

Someone chuckled lowly, causing Erin and Leonard to exchange small, unexpected smiles, which set off another episode of crying. "It's Megan."

Gail's body became rigid.

"We...we...we." Erin hyperventilated.

"Ssh, relax," Leonard said and pushed her hair away from her eyes.

Gail stared, stiff as stone. "Did we lose her?"

Erin bobbed her head.

"Excuse me," Gail said and wormed by them. The front door opened and then shut again.

Zofie pulled a hefty wooden chair beside Erin and offered her chamomile.

Erin accepted the teacup, and Zofie positioned

herself in the adjacent seat.

Leonard got up and headed to the main entrance. "I'll be back."

"So, tell us about Megan," Zofie said, the crowd gathering closer to the women.

"She was my best friend." Erin glared into the cup.

Kumbaya Girl scooted to Erin's feet. "Was she Gail's daughter?"

"Something like that. There are four of us. We've been through it all: births, deaths, you name it. We all coupled up with the same type of guy and wanted the same kind of things: kids, a comfortable bank account, *health*…we didn't all have the same fate, though." Erin pounded a fist on the wing of the chair and sobbed.

There was a collective hush. Only the pops and crackles from the fire in its place, its orange flames radiating the room with warm hugs.

"She was supposed to be the godmother of the baby."

"Baby?" Gail said, reentering the parlor.

"That was my news the other day. Jay-Jay and I decided to adopt the baby."

Gail draped her arms around Erin and gave her a firm squeeze. "I'm sad and happy and everything in between."

"Me too," Erin said, clutching Gail. "Me too."

Chapter Sixty

Vibrant sketches of stick figures done in primary-colored crayons decorated an easel beside the urn. An acetous taste filled Deirdre's mouth as she observed the smiling faces drawn by Megan's boys. The thought of death being an incomprehensible concept to young children wallowed deep in her esophagus. Her fingertips traced the beveled edges of Meg's container as the overhead lights in the viewing room buzzed like the ones in an OR. She studied the details of the metal urn. *Smooth as bone yet still not bone. I can't believe we're ultimately reduced to this.* She took a small step back and fixed the crooked rosary atop the urn, careful not to knock anything off the Harley Superlow, then motioned the sign of the cross before kissing the beads adorning her own body.

"I won't let you down," she said, kneeling on the cushioned pew before the lectern. A strong hand gripped Deirdre's shoulder. It was Rob, accoutered like the widower he had become, suited in black. "You look like shit," Deirdre said, turning to him.

"So do you."

She leaned against his leg, pressing her cheek into his hip, and sobbed. Tears fell down his cheeks as he massaged her back.

****

As Gail entered the funeral home, a distressed

379

screech echoed in the lobby. She paused, lifted the large black sunglasses, and dabbed away the sadness. After several seconds, she continued to the private room where Deirdre and Rob were hunched over Megan's remains. She turned her attention to the guestbook on the podium and reached for the pen. The first page was blank.

"May I help you?" the funeral director said and walked to her.

"I was just wondering if I'd arrived before Megan's parents and other relatives."

"Her husband's here, but the rest are stuck in traffic." He stretched an arm and checked his watch. "But that was half an hour ago, so they should be here soon."

The sound of the glass door separating from the jamb prompted Gail and the man to turn.

"Gail, I need you," Jay-Jay said, poking his head inside.

"Coming."

He dipped out again. Gail turned to the director, a heavy sigh exhaled while she adjusted the lengthy brim of her black, silk-crowned swinger hat. "Today is going to be quite an emotional one."

At the car, Gail saw Erin's head tucked between her knees. The closed passenger window separating them stymied the sounds of gurgling. Gail opened the door, the smell of vomit nearly knocking her over. She took a step back from the vehicle to catch a whiff of fresh air and then leaned in to rub Erin's back.

Erin glanced up. "I don't think I can do this." She heaved and hurled into the wastebasket at her ankles.

"Death is like a laxative for Erin. She wasn't able to move from the toilet all morning," Jay-Jay said, stroking

Erin's arm. "And now...here."

Gail searched inside her purse. "I have Tums." She shook the tablets free from the bottle and forced them into Erin's clammy palm.

"Wow, you carry a whole bottle?" Jay-Jay asked.

"Life is like a laxative for me." Gail rattled the container and tossed it in her bag.

Cars trickled into the lot and parked. Gail watched people exit them and walk in groups toward the funeral home.

Erin chewed the medicine and slurped water from a thermos. "Okay, it's now or never."

Gail grabbed one arm as Jay-Jay reached for the other. She made eye contact with him as Erin stepped out of the car and flashed him a sympathetic grin.

****

Erin reached the viewing room, catching sight of a few sorority sisters and some medical staff in their easily identifiable clothing and teenagers—several of Megan's former students—standing single-file, talking softly among each other. Erin wriggled by them. Some gave knowing, supportive looks, while others stared at the quiet, mysterious woman making her way to the front. She didn't say anything to Deirdre and Rob when she hugged them; she didn't have to.

As Erin mustered the courage to face the urn that was propped up on a gorgeous Harley, a nauseous feeling consumed her. She choked it back and slowly approached the display.

"God, no, no, no," she mumbled, eyeing her best friend's name embossed on metal, and wept into a tissue. Jay-Jay touched her shoulder. She pivoted and clung to him. "Why? Why, God?"

"Come with me," he said, escorting her to a row of empty chairs at the far end of the room.

****

There were whispers in between loud sniffling as the last of the line of people prayed before Megan's ashes. That's when Shelly Baxter stepped in, carrying a thin, large box. Several watched as she walked to the head of the room. She removed a skinny easel from the box and then propped a shiny wooden plaque onto it.

The funeral director situated a microphone on a stand beside it and tapped her elbow. "Whenever you're ready," he said.

"Oh no, not me," she said and pointed toward Rob.

Rob, who had been stolid since the procession began, nodded in their direction and finished greeting mourners, repeating that the boys were home with a babysitter. He stepped up to the front of the small setup, the buzzing of the crowd coming to a halt.

"Some of you may know that Megan was nominated Teacher of the Year, an accomplishment she wouldn't get to celebrate." The rumble of his larynx echoed in the amplifier. "Anyway, Megan loved poetry. It got away from her after college, but occasionally she read it when the kids were asleep. This one captures her journey, of how she achieved so much yet was still so far from getting to where she wanted to be."

He pulled a folded card from inside his jacket. There was a long, arduous pause as he stared blankly at the note, the words quavering in his grasp. His head jerked up, anxious as he studied the room. He attempted to steady himself, but his body twitched when he went to speak, and nothing came out. His eyes met Gail's and started to water.

****

Gail got up and approached Rob. "Do you want me to read it?" she said, her mouth close to his ear.

"Ye-yes."

Gail eased the speech from his clamped fingers and stepped up to the microphone. "Megan would recite some poems to me, but I didn't understand them half the time," Gail said, reading from the paper. A glimmer of a grin dressed her face. "Emily Dickinson was her favorite poet. I found this taped to the inside of her journal:

"While we were fearing it, it came—
But came with less of fear
Because that fearing it so long
Had almost made it fair—

There is a Fitting—a Dismay—
A Fitting—a Despair—
'Tis harder knowing it is Due
Than knowing it is Here.

They Trying on the Utmost
The Morning it is new
Is Terribler than wearing it
A whole existence through."

Gail stopped to face the grievers and noticed that Rob had found a seat beside Deirdre. His fingers were interlocked with hers, crumpled tissues poking through the crevices. Gail turned away and spotted a truckload of on-duty firefighters in bunker gear at the back of the room. She instantly recognized a few, some who had attended Harry's wake. Her lids pressed shut. "You will be deeply missed," she said, her voice a quick swoosh like a fast secret between friends, and returned the microphone to the stand.

Gail sandwiched through the masses that had stockpiled seemingly out of nowhere and navigated to a deserted part of the hallway. She leaned on the water fountain and hung over it, the drain swallowing her tears.

"That took real guts," a man said, slithering into the space between the fountain and the wall.

Gail looked up and saw Leonard in a fresh black shirt and trousers. He took her arms and propped them on his waist, forcing a hug. Gail put a cheek in the crook of his pectoral muscles and listened as his heart played a two-step that quickened when his chest puffed and slowed on deflation. *Life.*

"Been here long?" she said.

"Eh." His chin rested on the top of her silky hat. "Got here as the eulogy started. Long enough to see you rescue Rob." He rubbed the base of her lower back. "He'll be forever grateful you did that."

Gail gave his belly a little squeeze. "Stay with me?"

"For as long as you need, love. For as long as you need." The vibration of his vocals tickled her ear.

After visiting hours, Gail and Leonard followed the herd into the parking lot. Leonard led the way to his car and helped her inside. On the main road, he flicked on his headlights and blended in with the caravan, driving to the memorial ceremony at the lake near Megan's old church. Gail glanced at him as he stared out the windshield in deep concentration. "Being sprinkled into nature is the way to go," she said and resumed silence.

When the car's tires touched gravel, she sat up straight. Leonard parked between two painted partitions and shut the engine. He stepped out, walked to the opposite side, and opened the door for her.

"Hold on to me. These pebbles will twist an ankle in seconds," he said, squatting near the seat.

Gail's arm intertwined with his, a twisted pretzel that balanced her out and through the lot. They strolled behind the procession, Gail's ears attuned to the crunching leaves underfoot as they worked their soles over late autumn sediment.

"Death is hardest on the living," Leonard said, his fingers jingling coins in his pocket.

"You got that right. I couldn't keep it together for a while after Harry."

A forceful bluster of air sent Gail's hat flying. Leonard uncoiled his arm and chased after the thing, catching it about five feet away. Gail wobbled her sinking heels to him, her body falling onto his. He returned the accessory strategically to its place and gripped her middle, sending an electric-like surge through her heart that she hadn't felt in ages.

"You're really something special," he said, presumably forgetting his surroundings. "Think we can try eating together again sometime?"

"I think we can manage that." Her delighted expression peeped out from under the brim of the hat. "What's funny is that both Harry and Megan would have wanted us to."

"Oh yeah? How do you know?"

Gail was tempted to show Leonard the gold ring buried deep in her purse but decided to hold off. "I just know," she said, wearing an impish smile.

A word about the author…

Dawn Turzio, award-winning writer and former Howard Stern intern, is armed with interesting insider background to all things FDNY, NYPD, USMC, the Navy, and the Army. Dawn's essay, "A Year After Hurricane Sandy, A First Responder's Wife Reflects," was selected as the feature story for national firefighter magazine *New York Firefighters Now*, where her family was photographed for the issue's cover. Her work has also gained exposure from the television show *Inside Edition*, which contacted her for an episode about women's dating preferences based on an article she'd written titled, "Why Are Women Attracted to Men in Uniform?" published by YourTango.com.

Dawn's work has been featured in *Chicken Soup for the Soul*, *The New York Times*, *The Huffington Post*, *New York Magazine*, *Salon*, *MSN Lifestyle*, *Yahoo!News*, *Parents Magazine*, *Brain*, *Child Magazine*, *TheGood Men Project*, *Entropy Magazine*, *Hello Giggles*, *New York Press*, *New York Firefighters Now*, *WittyBitches.com*, *Skinny Dip City*, *Cupid's Pulse*, *TheWrite Life*, and *The Staten Island Advance*. She spearheaded a feature column *Fire Wives*, which detailed theimplications of "uniformed living" in *Jersey Firefighters Now Magazine*.

The first woman to graduate from the television and film studies program at St. John's University, Staten Island campus, Dawn has worked in production for E! Entertainment Television on *The Howard Stern Show*, *AJ Afterhours*, and *E!News Daily*, which has been recognized by *The New York Times*.

For more, visit www.dawnturzio.com

CPSIA information can be obtained
at www.ICGtesting.com
Printed in the USA
BVHW031738231022
650096BV00013B/346